EAST ATLANTA

DAUGHTERS OF THE WILD

Also by Natalka Burian

Welcome to the Slipstream
A Woman's Drink: Bold Recipes for Bold Women

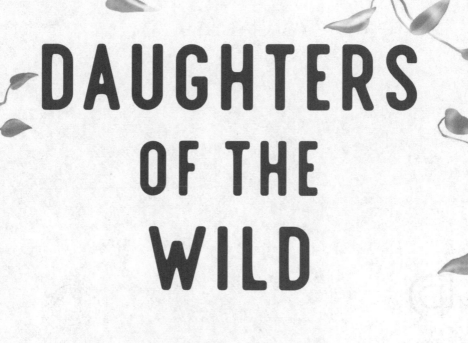

DAUGHTERS OF THE WILD

NATALKA BURIAN

PARK
ROW
BOOKS

PARK™
ROW
BOOKS™

Recycling programs
for this product may
not exist in your area.

ISBN-13: 978-0-7783-1001-3

Daughters of the Wild

This edition published by arrangement with Harlequin Books S.A.

Park Row Books
22 Adelaide St. West, 40th Floor
Toronto, Ontario M5H 4E3, Canada
ParkRowBooks.com
BookClubbish.com

Printed in U.S.A.

For Jay

DAUGHTERS OF THE WILD

WEST VIRGINIA, 1898

It was the middle of the night, but the sky screamed with light, knocking Helen Joseph awake. She rolled out of her blanket, almost crushing her dreaming baby sisters beside her on the floor. The cabin was filled with sleep; no one else had noticed that strange, streaky flash. Helen thought maybe she was still sleeping, but flowed along, anyway, following her legs out the door, following the thin, bright trail that lingered against the dark, stretching all the way to the place where it careened down.

Something had landed; she knew it. But she wasn't sure if it had landed in her dream or on their farm. She walked up the mountain slope toward that twinkling plummet, surprised to feel that the ground was hot under her bare feet. The earth grew warmer and warmer as she drew closer, until she had to skip from step to step. The soil beneath her calloused feet rippled, alive as a serpent, shoving her off balance. Helen landed heavily against the thorny trunk of a cottonwood tree as the earth lurched under the impact of whatever star had just fallen. The lingering wash of light intensified. The brightness made her teeth hurt. She closed her eyes so tightly that her cheeks pinched, and waited for the rumbling to stop. It didn't stop, not for a long while. With her eyes closed and her body stomach-down in the forest brush, it was like wrangling a semiwild dog, praying you didn't lose the hot, moving creature to the open spaces beyond.

Helen felt this same kind of desperate holding, a blade of sharp regret waiting to slice through her if she let go and lost it. Eventually, like a settling animal, the earth quieted and cooled. Helen opened her eyes and stood up, straightening her forest-stained nightgown. The sky had grayed with daylight, so Helen didn't have to squint her way through the wood looking for the fallen thing. She heard a sound humming through the quiet bodies of the trees and tracked it to its source, winding her way around churned-up stones and seasons-ago debris.

A hole in the ground—small, the size of a child's closed fist—glowed jewel green and sang out at her. Not words. Just a feeling. Helen knew she was supposed to protect it with soil, and to care for it. The thing's demands coiled around her feet and hands, gently pulling her forward.

Helen's hands were planting-skilled, so she covered over the opening like she would any seed. Unlike any other seed, though, this one began to grow right away. A bright vine swirled and opened out around her in the space of two stunned breaths, in and out. The plant looped around her wrist, holding her where she still crouched in the dirt. The tie was not sinister. It was a connection. Helen wasn't afraid or worried—she felt chosen, happy. Happier than she'd ever been. The vine pulsed out at her, a drumbeat of feeling, and she bent toward its caress as though receiving an answer.

As she dipped closer, a link between her and that gleaming astral coal snapped into place. She felt it, sudden and secure, in the space behind her belly button, like a lid on a pot. And just like that, Helen Joseph knew exactly what to do to keep this glowing creature alive.

1

WEST VIRGINIA, 1998

The garden was quiet, submerged in the kind of heavy, consuming sleep a child needed. Long summer days provoked this kind of thorough repair, from the land itself and the people who tended it. Cello loved these summer sleeps for their forgiving softness, and the nourishing visions they brought him in the night. When Joanie shook him awake in the dark, a finger pressed against her mouth, he almost turned back into his soothing, murky dream. Almost—Cello could never say no to Joanie. He flung himself back into consciousness, back into the trailer with Joanie and his other foster siblings. She gathered her hooded sweatshirt close across her chest and pointed for him to follow her outside. He pulled on his boots and gently closed the trailer door.

Joanie was already huddled over a cigarette, shivering, even though the night was hot. Since the baby had been born, she seemed permanently chilled. Cello reached out to her, but instead of taking his hand like he hoped she would, she passed him the burning Grand Prix.

"I found someone," she said. The shoulder of her sweatshirt slipped down, exposing a too-sharp clavicle.

"What do you mean?" Cello tried not to look at the crescent of skin, and instead looked away, to where North River Mountain blotted out the clear night sky with its dark hunch.

"A buyer." Joanie reached out for the cigarette and Cello passed it back without dragging from it.

"What? What do you mean a buyer?" he asked, wishing he sounded more confident, less confused. It was an unexpected proclamation. He and Joanie had nothing of their own to sell.

"Franklin Lees. He came to my wedding—that's where I met him. He's been trying to one-up Mother Joseph for years. Wants a crate of cuttings. From the Vine." A slight tremor began in Joanie's hands, and Cello saw the lit cigarette end wobble.

"No. Absolutely not," he said, stepping toward her. He crossed his arms tightly, careful not to touch her. Of all the things at the garden that could be bought or sold, the Vine of Heaven was the only immutable constant. It had been there before them and would go on after them. Cello worked with it every day, but it was still a source of mystery—like cutting keys to doors he would never open. He knew that secretly removing the Vine from the garden was as impossible as removing his eyes from their sockets—it was the rule every member of their foster family understood. Letta would always know. Anytime it was pulled from the earth, she said she could feel it in her body. She had to lie down in the dark anytime a plot was cleared.

"The Vine belongs to *me*, too. I work hard enough for it. If I want to sell it, I should be able to sell it." With a vicious tap, she sent a drift of glowing flecks from her Grand Prix onto the ground. "He'll give me a car, Cello, and enough cash to really get away. Us, I mean. We can't stay here anymore." Cello didn't ask if the "us" Joanie meant included the baby, or him, or all three of them. He saw the determination in the tensed muscles of her face and throat.

She had been closed off since the birth, like the separation of that little body from her own had torn her partially away from this world. But he also knew that Joanie was desperate enough to undertake the transaction without him, and that she would fail without his help. If she failed, and Mother Joseph found out, Joanie would be destroyed. Cello nodded into the dark, like a hypnotized man.

"Wait until tomorrow night, when it's dark," Joanie said, and Cello shuddered where he stood, trapped by Joanie's grim resolve. "And make sure you wrap what you cut really tight. Like you're smothering it. I'll take care of everything else."

"Alright, Joanie. Alright," he answered, knowing it was what he would always say to her.

When Cello went back to bed, he dreamed of the earth splitting open. He dreamed of a crack running through the garden, upending the trailers and all of the old car carcasses in a rusty wave. The children screamed and scattered, and Joanie was swallowed up by that blank, dark seam, falling farther and farther into the center of the earth. Cello peered down into the crack, at the toes of his boots nearly dripping over the edge. Before he could jump in or run, his eyes flickered back open into their small, ordered world. The thin wail of Joanie's baby woke him over the other sleeping bodies, and Cello jumped up to soothe him so the other kids could rest a little longer.

The baby slept in a crate in the trailer's kitchen, and Cello had to step over Emil sleeping on a pallet of old blankets to reach him. The baby had a name, of course, but Cello hated to use it, hated that the baby bore the name of his biological father. Every time Cello held him, he was stunned in stupid love by the baby's light, warm weight.

He took the child outside into the dewy night, and stared down into his blinking little face. The baby knew Cello loved him, as much as babies could know anything. If Joanie fled without him and took the baby, Cello didn't think he would recover.

But he didn't know if he could endure a life away from the garden, either. His heart was buried as deep in the earth as the sacred Vine of Heaven that twisted and bloomed around them.

Mother Joseph had chosen each child and brought them to Letta and Sil and the garden's fecund swirl. None of them really belonged there, but there they were, inexplicably held. Each child had come to the garden with a hastily signed, official document. Mother Joseph made sure this at least was done according to the law. Including Cello and Joanie, there were six of them. The youngest was Emil, who was five, followed by Miracle who was eight. Sabina and Marcela were older, thirteen and sixteen. Cello had always envied them a little for being real sisters.

The rest of them weren't blood-related. They mostly looked alike, except for Cello. The kids had the same burned-tanned skin, and their hair and eyes were all shades of dark. Cello guessed that it was the way they lived—mostly outdoors, always out under the sun. Letta liked that they all looked the same. It was easier to pass them off as a family if anyone came to the farm.

Even Joanie looked that way: dark and darker. He was lighter than the others, even after years of working outside, and his hair was long and straight and blond. He hated how greasy he looked compared to the rest of them, how he looked like a stranger.

When the kids were old enough to ask, the questions came. They were a painful surprise each time. *How did I get here? Will we always stay?* There had never been any parents at the garden, only Sil and Letta. Parents had meant nothing—none of them had seen what it looked like for a mother to love a child until Joanie came home pregnant. When the tenderness began to show, when it started to lift from Joanie's body like a haze of pollen, it had been Miracle's turn to ask.

"There's really a baby in her?" She combed her short, dark hair away from her face as she leaned in over Joanie's belly.

"Of course, dipshit," Marcela said.

"And it really comes out? Like an animal?" Miracle drew in her breath, astonished.

"Yeah," Sabina said, her voice soft as she concentrated on rinsing out a round of washing in the sink. It was winter—February—when Joanie was nearly six months along. There wasn't much to be done outside, so the six of them huddled in the kids' trailer. Emil was asleep—still taking naps, he was so little.

"That's how I came out?" Miracle asked. "Really?"

"Of course," Cello told her.

"But Letta didn't—"

"Oh, God, no!" Marcela called from her seat on the floor, scraping the peeling polish from her toenails.

"Then who?" Miracle had looked right at Cello then, her small mouth twisted, suppressing an enormous feeling.

"Who knows?" Marcela said, tying back her furiously curly hair. "You just showed up one day. Mother Joseph said she came by a new little one, and did Letta want to keep you."

"Course Letta didn't say no," Sabina said, her smile a warm flare shot out specifically for Miracle. "You were the prettiest baby. And Sil was so happy. We had a drought then, and the day you came, it rained."

"We saw Marcela and Sabina's real mama," Joanie said, looking up from her small globe of a belly.

"Who was she?" Miracle whispered.

Joanie looked over at Cello, unspooling the memory between them like two ends of a skipping rope. Mother Joseph's truck had driven up to the trailers and the driver ejected a woman with a push from the cab. She was covered in lesions, a small, gaunt body wearing two different shoes. She'd dropped the children by the door like some macabre stork, and was swallowed back into the truck in the span of a minute. The two little girls hadn't looked back once at the person who abandoned them. Marcela gripped her toddler sister against her side tightly and wailed when Letta first pulled them apart. Blood dribbled down Sabina's soft little arms where Marcela's uncut fingernails had held her close.

"She was nobody," Marcela said as she lifted herself from the floor and moved to her sister's side. She dipped her hands into the sink and began to wring out the wet clothes that pooled there.

"You remember her? Did you ever see her again?" Miracle asked.

Sabina shook her head.

"It's a good thing we didn't, because I would've strangled her if I had." Marcela violently unfurled a small, green T-shirt— Emil's favorite—as she said it.

"What about Cello and Joanie?" Miracle asked, looking over to where they sat, Joanie on her cot, Cello on a plastic crate.

"We don't have the same parents," Cello said, knowing that wasn't what Miracle had meant, but unwilling to tell her more.

"Well, Joanie's baby's gonna have a mom," Sabina said, turning to nod at Miracle. "And that's nice."

"Yeah, if nobody tells Mother Joseph about it," Marcela mumbled.

"Of course nobody's gonna tell her," Joanie said, propping herself up against the trailer's thin wall. She shot Marcela a sharp look, as though pinning the conversation closed.

Cello wondered now, with the child in his arms, if someone *had* told on Joanie. It would explain her panic, and her urgency. If Mother Joseph had found out about the baby, of course Joanie would be desperate. He swore—on his own two hands—that he would do anything to keep Joanie and the baby safe. He felt the soft waves of the baby's tiny snores even out, and because it was still nearly dark, Cello carefully set the baby down beside Joanie, and left to do what she had asked.

Cello would never have believed he could be coldly deceitful, that he could betray the only family he'd ever had so swiftly or so easily. But it *was* easy, because Sil and Letta didn't suspect him. It was Joanie who they watched carefully—she was un-predictable. They watched Marcela, too, because she was self-ish. Nobody watched compliant, steady Cello.

The chill of the almost-morning raised gooseflesh along Cel-lo's arms and on the back of his neck. Sil and Letta would still be sleeping. Cello decided to cut from the very first plot that had ever been planted at the garden, because Sil checked it the least. Cello secretly hoped the cuttings would languish away from their parent plant. That way, Franklin Lees wouldn't get what he wanted, but Joanie would, and his loyalty to the garden wouldn't be too corroded. He still felt a tingle of nausea as he approached the old grove, dripping with green and fragrance.

The black walnut trees that stood nearby smelled ancient; Cello could almost feel the human lifetimes they'd passed crammed close together. He steadied himself on one of them, laying his palm on the bark the same way he'd settle an animal. Cello shuddered under another wave of guilt—how could any living creature trust him now? He wondered how permanently this transgression would change him.

The oldest plants in the clearing grew to Cello's eye height. The sturdy central stalks were crisscrossed with yarn-fine shoots, and their blue floral crowns seemed to nod as Cello drew close. They harvested from the base of the Vine, removing only its crawling, twisting ivy-like appendages. The plants did well in the shade, and did best in this particular grove. Letta said it was because her ancestor had found the very first Vine rippling up through the forest floor in this exact spot. The Vine still leaned on and swelled against the trees, but had matured over many decades to stand on its own. Cello looked closely at the near-est plant, not sure where to make the cut. Any abrasion in the stalk would ruin it—since that was where the sap pulsed most aggressively.

Cello wondered if Franklin Lees would even know what to do with it, how to plant it, how to tend it. He took an X-Acto knife out of his back pocket and sliced off three of the young-est shoots, still spiraling loose, not yet fully tethered to any-thing. He untangled them, and, as gently as he'd held Joanie's baby that morning, he wrapped them in an old T-shirt on the ground. Joanie had said to smother it, but Cello couldn't bear to think of the Vine slowly suffocating in the summer heat, rolled up in the bone-dry fabric. He settled a few handfuls of damp earth between each fold, and carried the bundle out of the grove. He hid the soft parcel behind the deflated tire of a decaying Oldsmobile, more fossil than machine now, that Sil had parked out back years ago.

Cello snuck back into the trailer and checked on the baby to make sure he was still asleep before easing himself down onto his own cot, turning his back to the rest of his dreaming family. He wasn't sure how much time was left before Letta came in to wake them, but he forced his limbs to quiet and his breath to even so that Letta wouldn't be able to see the way the disgrace gripped his body. His pulse slowed as he thought of Joanie, of her relief. Imagining Joanie at peace brought him the same com-fort as a cool washcloth to the back of the neck.

2

"Morning, children!" Letta crashed open the kids' trailer door. It didn't lock, and never fully closed, so whenever the wind was up, a constant whistling through the gap between the metal door and the frame serenaded them. Cello had always wondered if the trailer came that way, or if it had been mutilated by Letta's brusque entrances and exits.

"Breakfast time!" she trumpeted. Letta pulled covers—and kids—off bunks. Cello could still smell the dew on the air. It was earlier than they usually woke up. His throat burned with nerves; could Letta already know what he'd done?

"Come on, come on." She adjusted her rose sateen robe over a jutting sternum. "Miracle—out!" She banged her ring-coated fingers against the wall beside the little girl's head. Miracle scooted out from under the blanket so that just a tiny strip of her forehead showed. They all knew she'd be punished for wetting the bed. Instead of inspecting Miracle's bedding, though, Letta sidled up next to Joanie's cot. She lay on her side, the baby beside her in the sheets.

"Come here, handsome," Letta cooed at the baby, slipping Joanie's hand from the baby's belly. "Come with Mama Letta." She bent over, plucked the baby away and swaggered back to the flapping, open door. "Come on, the rest of you," she called over her shoulder. Sometimes Cello believed Letta was completely rotted away inside, but her tenderness for the most helpless things—for Joanie's baby, specifically—it was real.

The kids fell out of their beds and wandered after Letta into the humid morning. Cello didn't say a word, even to Joanie. He just pulled Miracle from her bunk and peeled the damp, stinking sheets from her mattress.

"Get dressed, Miracle," Joanie said, her voice as harsh as Letta's.

Miracle pattered to the corner where they kept all of their clothes in two piles: one clean, the other dirty. No one had their own things—they all shared and somehow it worked out. Only Joanie had clothes that were her own, mostly because she was the oldest, and because she had already been married.

When Joanie's husband died, it was sudden and complicated. She had lived away from the garden for a little while with her new husband, but came back with the baby in her belly once he was gone. Letta had set up the marriage, of course. Joanie never would have picked Josiah Joseph—sixteen-year-old Joanie wouldn't have picked anyone.

Cello watched her put new sheets on Miracle's bed, the way her body stretched and moved. He could see the old marks on her back from her time at the Josephs' between the straps of her camisole. The evidence of that harm eased his guilt a little—his betrayal was a fair price to keep her away from Mother Joseph, to keep her safe.

Cello followed Miracle outside where the others were already eating in the grass, a row of faces spooning cereal into their mouths. The dense constellation of freckles across Emil's nose and cheeks was indistinguishable from beneath a layer of the garden's grime.

"Y'all are filthy," Cello said, shaking his head.

"Cello, why don't you take the kids for a swim while Joanie and I have some girl talk." Letta bounced Joanie's baby in the shade of an old beech tree. "You kids listen to Cello. Don't want any running off." Letta didn't look at the others as she said it— only at him. "Lots to do today."

"Yes, Letta," Sabina and Miracle chorused.

Letta carried the baby back into her and Sil's trailer. When Cello and the others left for the creek, Joanie still hadn't come out of the kids' trailer.

The water that morning was muddy, and Cello guessed it must have rained sometime overnight. Usually he wouldn't miss a thing like that, the sound of rain pouring over the trailer, pouring over the ground. Cello liked to know everything that happened to the soil, and he was surprised that he hadn't noticed something as significant as a rainfall. Maybe Joanie's plans had dulled him. Maybe secretly slicing away the shoots of the Vine had changed something, melted away at his connection to the garden.

"Hey, Cello!" Miracle splashed at him from the shallows of the creek.

"Careful, don't fall," he called back. "Try to keep the mud *off* you."

The kids were noisy, unfolding into regular children away from Letta's gaze. Emil chased Sabina through the shallows with a handful of mud, and she squealed away, ducking behind Miracle.

"Are you in trouble, Cello?" Marcela flounced over to where he slouched on the bank. "You look like you're in trouble."

Cello was quiet, squinting against the strengthening sun.

"You did something you weren't supposed to, I can tell."

"Shut your mouth, Marcela. You'll get in trouble yourself if you go around accusing people."

"Well, did you?" she asked. Her dark eyes narrowed as she examined him. She was trying to read something there, Cello thought. Something she had no business reading.

"Course not," he said as he rearranged his feet in the sticking mud.

Marcela looked almost disappointed.

The little kids were naked, but Marcela and Sabina were too old for that. They swam in their clothes, the way Letta had shown them. Still, Cello could see their bodies, no longer the bodies of children, beneath the sodden cloth. He knew just by growing, the girls were in danger; women always had to do terrible things at the garden.

He turned away, thinking it would propel Marcela back to the water. Instead, she moved closer.

"What was it?" She was quiet, like she knew the other kids shouldn't hear her ask.

"Enough," Cello said, careful to keep his voice even. "It's none of your business. Swim or go back. I have to watch the little kids."

Marcela just shook her head, drops of creek water from her hair splattering Cello's shoulder. She stared down at Cello's slouched figure. "You look so guilty." Her voice was grating, unpleasant, like she was trying not to cry. "Whatever you did better not get me or Sabina in trouble."

"It's nothing like that," Cello muttered.

"Nothing like that, but it is something. If you did something dumb, leave the rest of us out of it." Marcela was louder now, her voice raspy and furious. Marcela walked off toward the creek, her hair a dark spill of ink against her mottled-gray-T-shirt-covered back.

Joanie had asked this favor of him; it was his decision alone to help her, and the consequences were his, too. He looked out to where the rest of the kids splashed.

"Time to get out!" he called, heading down to the stone-studded shore.

★ ★ ★

They walked back to the trailers and the kids dried off in the sun. Cello hadn't swum, since he was just going to get dirty again.

That morning, the garden would need every pair of hands. They had planted too much. Letta was always greedy, always pushing. There was already more work than they could do, but still she wanted another plot cleared. The family worked every day in the summer, from just after breakfast until the sun began to set. They moved in an endless rotation, starting with the plot that had been tended last. Weeds grew swiftly around the Vine, as though they, too, wanted to be near it. The kids all had to work five times as hard as they would have had to work if they were growing corn or grain, or any other crop, to keep the space open for the Vine to grow.

When they got to the first field of the day, Letta was already there; Joanie and the baby were not.

"Come on!" she shouted, pulling Emil in by the arm as they approached. "Look sharp, especially in these first ten rows—there are already more weeds than I like to see. Y'all were slacking last time we came down here. All of the planting'll be wasted if the weeds drink up all of our water and work." The sun-warmed plot roiled with the twisting, newly growing Vine of Heaven. The Vine fenced away the earth, and the gaps between the finger-thick twists of plants were just wide enough for the children's hands.

The little kids knew which shoots of green were worth money, and which were the weeds. It was the first thing they were taught. Sil understood that the greatest value in their youth was the delicate size of their hands. Emil and Miracle drew the unwanted plants out gently, and didn't disturb the soil around the precious, striving, thread-thin roots the way a grown person's pulling would. It was the reason Letta and Sil took in so many kids at the garden. Sil said there were roots moving through the ground that couldn't be seen by the naked eye, that's how tender and new they were.

Miracle and Emil knew, thanks to Letta's snap of the switch, which plants to leave alone. They were smart, especially Miracle. She always knew what should get pulled and what should stay.

"Marcela," Letta continued. "I want you to follow Cello. He's setting up a new plot—help him."

"What?" Marcela whined. "Why can't Joanie do it? Can't I just weed with the little kids?"

"You're not a little kid anymore. There needs to be a woman at every new planting. You're a young lady now. You need to learn—this is your job in the family. Joanie and I can't do it forever," Letta snapped.

"Can I go with her?" Sabina asked quietly.

"Fine." Letta rolled her eyes. "Just get a move on before I start to get upset." Cello searched for any sign of suspicion in Letta's face or hands—when she was saving up a punishment, she flicked her fingernails against one another, like she was counting up how may minutes of suffering you were going to get.

Cello and the sisters hiked to a spill of land that Sil had chosen for the new plot. Marcela fell onto the grass and rested an arm across her eyes. Sabina waited, halfway between Cello's searching, tensed form and Marcela's collapsed one.

"Over here," Cello spoke, waving toward a line of trees. "We'll start here, and I'll mark it off. Sabina, go get the mower and drive it up to that hill." It was true, what Letta had said about each new planting needing a woman to turn the soil. If it wasn't done, the Vine wouldn't grow.

Sabina nodded, and nudged Marcela with her foot. "Are you alright?"

"Go ahead," Marcela said, her arm still over her face. "I just need a minute."

"Are you crying? Why?"

"I'm not crying. I just need a minute, I said."

"Alright." Sabina had always been the quiet one, the patient and obedient one; she saw and understood everything. Cello knew what Sabina saw—that Marcela's mind swelled with anger and worry. Letta hadn't given her this responsibility before, and Cello couldn't imagine what it would do to her. He was relieved not to know.

"It's okay, Mar. Rest a little—and don't worry, Cello won't mind that you're being lazy," Sabina said, giving Cello a soft, apologetic glance.

"Like I give two shits about what Cello thinks." Marcela rolled onto her stomach, hiding her face. "Why doesn't Letta make Joanie do it? She took care of all of the plots before the baby."

"You know the baby takes a lot out of her. It'll be okay. It's only one plot, and you're so strong. I'll be right back." Sabina gave Marcela another playful tap with her foot, and ran out into the warming day to collect Sil's mower.

Cello walked the edge of the field, pressing the long grass down in a footprint-wide path as he moved. He studied the hollows in the ground, and the way the wind moved around the earth there. Everything Cello knew about planting he'd learned from Sil—Sil, who could make anything grow. He could coax life out of places teeming with mold and rot.

The garden was a constellation of plots—some tiny, half the size of the kids' trailer, some large; the largest was almost three acres. Most fell somewhere in between, and it was Cello's job to mind the middling ones. The largest plot and the smallest were Sil's, the small plots were filled entirely with his experiments.

Sil taught all of the kids different things, but it was Cello who received the most instruction, because it was Cello who was most like Sil. Cello could also make things grow. He knew certain things, just by picking up a handful of earth—whether the plants were healthy, and thriving, or if they were not. Sil

taught him how to smell the soil for elements that were missing, and showed Cello how to add those things back.

"In farming, people will tell you to leave the topsoil alone,"
Sil had explained. "But there're ways around it. You can't till
the topsoil the way you'd need to for most crops, but for what
we're doing now, you can. You just have to plant around the
contours. You need to *strategize*." Sil tapped at his forehead with
a dirt-caked finger.

Cello couldn't remember his life before working in the garden with Sil, just that he was smaller than Emil, and had learned
which plants were valuable the same way. All of their harvests
were delivered straight to the Josephs. In exchange for the truck
beds full of cuttings they drove to the Joseph compound, Letta
took home envelopes fat with cash. He and Joanie had been the
only kids then, but as the Vine kept growing, and as Letta kept
planting, their ragtag family—and Letta's envelopes—grew, too.

Cello didn't fully understand the arrangement until Joanie
finally explained it one night, after she came back from living on the compound. It was late in the kids' trailer, the littlest
ones were in that stone-heavy sleep that only people who were
recently babies could reproduce. They hadn't had enough food
that winter; nobody was ever full.

"She's just cheap," Joanie told them—Cello, Marcela and Sabina were the only ones awake.

"What do you mean? It's not like they have jobs." Marcela
flipped onto her side—her voice sounded clear in the tinny dark
of the trailer.

"God, you're such idiots," Joanie said, her voice muffled
against her pillow. "What do you think the Josephs put in those
envelopes they give Letta? Stickers?"

"How would I know?" Marcela said. Cello could feel her
flash of irritation ripple in the air.

"The little kids are sleeping, you guys," Sabina whispered.

"Who cares about that?" Marcela said. "They sleep plenty. I

want to know how much money the Josephs could be paying for a bunch of flowers and weeds, is all."

"Yeah, what are they? Florists?" Cello had said, half joking, but still unsure. He had no idea how much money florists made. Could be millions.

"I can't believe I share a room with you idiots," Joanie said.

"News flash," Marcela shot back. "This is nothing close to a room. Just tell us what you know, if you're so smart."

"What do people pay that kind of money for?" Joanie asked. She let the question float there in the dark.

Cello turned to face the peeling laminate paneling on the wall. He breathed in the smell of lacquer and stale sweat from his unwashed sheets. Perhaps he had known all along that there was something dangerous about the Vine, how often they were warned not to break its skin or release its sap. But until Joanie's prompting he'd never linked the Vine to Marcela and Sabina's disintegrating mother. He'd never made the connection from the work they did in the garden to the empty-eyed tenants who waited by the Joseph compound gate. A tremor of panic glanced through him as he began to understand he knew very little about what the Vine could do—could there really be such dark, addictive power in it, such shadowy value?

Sil treated those plants better than he treated the kids. Cello had always partly believed it was because he was drawing magic from the ground, and that it was more about Sil's practice than about profit. Letta, on the other hand, had always seemed very mercantile-minded with their work. More scams than crimes, at least that's what Cello had believed.

Meanwhile, Marcela chattered in the dark. "Are you serious? Sabina, she's messing with us, right?"

"Please be quiet," Sabina whispered.

"Joanie? Are you serious?" Marcela repeated.

Joanie didn't speak again, and soon they all fell asleep, even Marcela.

After that, Cello watched Sil and Letta more carefully. He watched them especially on those regular visits to the Josephs'. They always left the little kids with Sabina and Marcela, and brought along Joanie and Cello, who sat in the back of the truck with the tarp-covered mounds of fragrant plants. They pressed their arms and legs down on places where the wind flipped up the tarp. For Cello, those afternoon drives were filled with the scent of languishing greenery and hot canvas, and the thrilling proximity of his limbs to Joanie's. The cuttings they brought to the Joseph compound were unloaded into a barn, in a kind of anteroom—a large, refrigerated metal compartment. No one let Cello see beyond that, but he knew that now Joanie understood exactly what happened there.

Cello shook his head to loosen thoughts of Joanie from it. *Just do your job*, he told himself. The plot he'd outlined flickered green and gold under the sun. Sil would be happy with this, he thought, surprised by how much satisfaction he felt. He knew it was pathetic to crave that approval, but he also knew he'd done well.

Cello felt the flush of his skin and the slick of sweat between his shoulder blades and across his chest. He wondered what time it was, and when Sabina would come back with the mower. Marcela still lay in the grass, curled like a sleeping fox kit.

"Hey, Marcela," he said, maybe too gently.

"What." Her face was buried in the crook of her arms, and her voice sounded distorted, like it belonged to someone different.

"Are you going to do it, or is Sabina?"

"I'm going to," she hissed. "As if I would make Sabina. She doesn't know anything about it. I'm not a monster," she said, with a look that sliced right through him.

"I'm sorry," Cello said, without looking at his foster sister. "I wish I could help you."

"No, you don't," she said. "Believe me." Marcela stood up

and walked the perimeter Cello had outlined. He followed her, a few paces behind.

"Can you get back, please?" she said, vicious. Cello stood still and watched as she crouched to the ground, her toes at the new plot's edge. She yanked fistfuls of grass out by the roots and tossed them to one side, exposing a bald ring of earth. She scratched at the tiny, living fibers with her fingers, turning the soil beneath them. Cello had watched Joanie and Letta do the same thing dozens of times, but there was something different, less resigned, about Marcela's movements. He wondered if it would even work.

"Are you sure you know what you're doing?" he called out.

"Of *course* I do! Letta makes us practice every month when we bleed."

Cello inched closer, split between curious and afraid. "I don't know—I think Joanie and Letta do it different. What happens if you don't do it right?"

"Oh, my God, I'm doing it *right*, Cello. Plus, I'm bleeding right now if you really must know, and that's pretty much a guarantee that it'll work."

"Oh," Cello said, flushing.

"Yeah, *oh*—why else would Letta make me do this today?" Marcela's hair hung around her cheeks in sweaty clumps, and her skin seemed to glow with concentration. She lifted handfuls of the soil out and around the shallow ditch she'd made, and pressed her fingertips around the insides, coating the interior with her touch. She spat once, and then again, as if to double down on the intention—but there was nothing loving or caretaking in the gesture. Sweat dripped from Marcela's face, tapping into the ground.

"Are you sure that's right?" Cello asked before he could stop himself.

Marcela glared at him and stepped over the boundary Cello had pressed into the grass with his feet. Marcela kicked the dirt she had removed, violent and sloppy, back into the shallow grave she'd dug for her saliva, and then stamped on the mound. Her skin flashed the scorched red of a sunburn, just as Letta's and Joanie's skin reddened when they did the Work, as though they were burning from the inside out. Marcela waited a moment, and then jumped on the pile of earth again. Her movements were the incongruous, joyful little hops of a small child, but her face brimmed with exhausted fury.

Cello held his breath and waited—each time he'd watched Letta or Joanie complete this ritual, the results were immediate—but there they stood, and nothing.

"Well?" Marcela shouted, not to Cello, or herself, or to any human being, but out to the world's widest parts. She was answered with a rumble. The earth shook gently beneath them, as though a massive swarm of bees bounced and buzzed on the other side of the ground. "You see?" Marcela said to Cello, accusing and out of breath. "I told you."

The swirls of grass and weeds within the new plot began to gleam. Marcela waited until the entire shape intended for the fresh planting was coated in a uniform skim of radiance before she stepped back, outside of the lines. Cello blinked, and the grass was just grass, lit only by the strong summer sun overhead.

"Wow, good job, Mar," he said, and meant it.

"Shut up," she replied, and plopped back onto the ground, scooting back into a cooler patch of shade. Her face looked suddenly drawn, and the space beneath her eyes formed two purple crescents, dark enough to look like some kind of injury.

"What does it feel like, when you do that?" He'd never asked Joanie or Letta. Cello had always accepted the Work as just another part of tending the Vine. It was a normal part of their lives, the same way he never asked Sil what it felt like to sink a new irrigation line. Marcela looked so different from her usual self that the question climbed out of his mouth before he could stop it.

"It feels like dying. Like the worst fever you ever had." Her breathing was audibly shallow, like a sick kid's. "Please don't tell Sabina I already did it, okay? Just say Letta wants to do it herself or something."

"Yeah, I will. If that's what you want."

"It's what I want. I also want some water. Please, I'm so thirsty." She turned her face away from Cello and collapsed back into the grass as though her body had been wrung out by the ritual.

Cello winced, and shaded his eyes against the sun, even though the sun had nothing to do with his grimace. "Okay, I'll get you some."

He told himself that by taking those cuttings in the early morning, he hadn't taken anything away from Marcela or any of his foster siblings—he had only really stolen from Letta. But as he watched, he began to understand how much, and from whom, Letta and Sil were stealing.

3

Joanie stood and swayed by the rusted water heater in the yard. She held the baby pressed to her chest, his body limp with sleep.

"Hey, you alright?" Sabina asked, jangling the keys to the mower.

"Shh, I just got him down," Joanie said.

"He's still so little." Sabina ran her finger across the baby's dangling bare foot. "You sure he's growing enough?"

"Of course he is. Why would you say that?" Joanie turned more deeply into a patch of shade. "He's fine," Joanie said softly, speaking against the crown of the baby's head. "Here, can you take him for a minute? I'm sweating like a hog." Joanie handed the baby off to Sabina, nestling him into the crook of her elbow.

"How could you not love this tiny thing?" Sabina fanned at his flushed face with her hand.

"Girls!" Letta's voice called out into the yard from her trailer's open window. Sabina and Joanie shared an efficient, worried look.

"I'll go—just wait here a minute. I'll be right back," Joanie said, striding across the grass. She knocked on the scorching trailer door.

"If I didn't want you to come in, I wouldn't have hollered for you, would I?" Letta said, her voice sharpened by some irritation other than the heat.

Joanie pushed open the door, turning her own anger up, too, just so she would feel stronger. "What is it?" she asked, sliding into the trailer's humid, stinking interior.

"Light one for me, baby, will you?" Letta gestured to the squashed pack of Grand Prix Mediums beside her linty, slippered foot.

"Is that what you called me all the way in here for?" Joanie stamped over and took up a lighter from the coffee table. She flicked one of the Grand Prix alive and passed it to Letta before lighting one of her own.

"No, smart mouth," she snapped. "Something is off today— do you feel it?" Letta massaged her jaw, loosening it back and forth. "I can feel it in my teeth. Like something's missing."

Joanie froze for an instant only, before blowing a concentrated stream of smoke in Letta's direction. "Nope," she replied—simply, harsh. "I don't feel anything like that."

"Then you're not paying attention." Letta prodded a magenta-polished fingernail between her eyes. "Try again. Really try this time."

Joanie closed her eyes, chilled. Had Cello followed her instructions early? Without telling her? It wasn't like him to be so enterprising. She hated these checks that Letta insisted on; she hated that Letta watched her. Letta started her foster daughters on these inspections as soon as they started bleeding, once they were old enough to give to and take from the Vine.

If she let her insides go silent, she could feel the faint outline of every plot in the garden—the ones she had tilled herself were brighter and more pronounced in that jigsaw legacy, but they were all there, if she was quiet enough. She opened her eyes. "Everything looks fine to me," she said, shrugging in Letta's direction.

Letta rested her head on one arm of the stained, sunset-colored sofa. "Try again, Joanie. You're being careless."

Joanie heaved an exaggerated sigh with her next exhale of smoke and tried once more, entering the perimeter of each plot in her mind as though there were a series of gates connecting them all. She waited until she felt the tiniest shock, like the prickle of static on a fingertip against a doorknob. It did feel strange and wrong, but small—like a tiny, dashed break in the perimeter of one of the plots.

"Okay, there's something," she conceded, opening her eyes, straining every muscle in her face to stay still and calm.

"Yes," Letta said, sitting up suddenly, "there is." Her eyes narrowed, but her smile was harmless, even sweet. Joanie shivered under that look, despite her best efforts at control. "Can you guess what's wrong?"

"Something's missing?" Joanie said, trying to stay angry, understanding that this emotion was the only thing keeping Letta's alligator-jaw suspicions away from her throat.

"Yes, honey, fucking bingo!" Letta stood up. "Something is most definitely missing. And I have to find it before Amberly gets a whiff that something's wrong."

"How're you going to do that?" Joanie said with a very deliberate and obvious eye roll.

"I think you know exactly how. I'm gonna go light me a fire." Letta took one last drag before stabbing her cigarette into the pink glass ashtray on the table. Fire was how Letta, how any of the girls, could get a closer look at the Vine. If it wasn't growing quick enough, they lit a fire; if the blossom's color appeared faded, they lit a fire. There was always some kind of answer waiting for them in the flames. Joanie clamped her fingers down into her palms before they could tremble and give her away. "Maybe an animal got into it," she said.

"An animal?" Letta smiled coolly, incredulous. "Honey, in the forty years I been tending these plots, no animal has ever been where it shouldn't have been." She tilted her head as she looked at Joanie. "No animal with four legs, anyway." Joanie stayed quiet, relaxing her mouth and resisting the urge to press her lips together. She waited for Letta to leave before she finished her own cigarette in a numbed panic and retreated to the yard where she'd left her son.

"What happened?" Sabina asked, holding the baby out to Joanie. "Did you get in trouble?"

"Why would you say that?" Joanie asked, mimicking Letta's incredulous fury from inside the trailer.

"Joanie, I'm on your side. I'm always on your side. If something happened, you can tell me." Sabina's face twisted with concern.

"Nothing happened. It's just this place. It makes everybody crazy." Joanie stared down at the baby's tiny, flushed face. "I'd do anything to get him out of here. I really would." She tucked him more securely against her arm, jostling him nearly awake.

Sabina jolted back, as though struck. "Do you really think it's that bad? Where else would we go?"

Joanie tried to force a kind smile for Sabina, but felt her face erupt, the tears already loose. "It's not that bad exactly. It's just… nobody has any choices here. Not even Sil and Letta, not really." Joanie pressed her lips together until they hurt, and tried to swallow down that stinging feeling in her throat. "You better go," she said. "Don't give Letta any more reasons to be mad."

"Can I just wait with you for one more minute?" Joanie nodded in response. The two girls bent their dark heads over the sleeping baby, and waited for a breeze to pass their way. Joanie waved Sabina along as soon as she detected the scent of smoke in the air.

★ ★ ★

Letta finally stalked back into the clearing in front of the trailers, a rough branch still smoldering on one end clasped in her hand. Her robe was covered in a milky layer of ash, and her face was open with active curiosity. Joanie wobbled with dismay at the sight of her—the Vine had shared a secret with Letta in that ritual fire, but Joanie couldn't quite tell what. Letta swiped a sharp, puzzled glance over toward Joanie and the baby and narrowed her eyes.

"You should take him inside. It's getting too hot," she said as she strode out beyond the trailers toward the Vine's first grove. She'd told Cello to take the cuttings at night, when Letta was tired and often drunk and wouldn't notice the Vine's throb of absence. Cello had taken something, but Joanie couldn't understand why the loss felt so slight. Maybe he hadn't taken as much as she had asked for. Joanie tucked the sleeping baby against her chest and trailed Letta into the oldest part of the forest, the place where the Vine had first climbed into their world. Letta stood among the cornstalk-height, mature plants and pointed the charred branch at the base of each one, directly, like a flashlight.

The baby began to fuss against her sweaty breast and Joanie bobbed a bit to settle him back to sleep. Letta muttered under her breath. One of the stalks began to glow wound-red, as though Letta had set fire to it. Letta threw the branch to the ground and looked down at her crossed arms, her mouth set in a stern line.

Joanie could feel the thrum of her heartbeat all the way up to her throat. Cello had done it, and hadn't listened to her. She would have to think quickly and act faster—it was only a matter of time until Letta pieced together what had happened. Joanie prayed that she would at least have until that night. She prayed to the Vine, willing it to jam whatever signal it had transmitted to Letta, begging it to understand why she needed this so badly. *I've served you my whole life*, she pleaded, tipping her face forward in a humble bend over her baby's head. *I just need this one thing.*

But she didn't feel that connection—the click of understanding was missing. Either Letta's appeal was stronger than hers, or the Vine was deaf to her feeble plea. Joanie pushed the panic away, breathing in the scent of the child in her arms. It would be alright. She traced her sign of protection across the baby's chest, and headed quietly back toward the trailers to salvage her plan—to salvage *their* plan.

That night, everything went wrong. Cello watched the flicker of Joanie's pale jeans dip and turn through the night-dark leaves and rolling-silver tall grass. She didn't turn around to speak or to look at him, but Cello knew what she was thinking because he was thinking the same: *hurry.*

Cello tucked the pilfered cuttings from the Vine down the front of his shirt while Joanie's baby mewled and clutched the folds of his blanket in the wooden crate.

Joanie drew her sign of protection across the box's splintery side. "We'll come back. I don't want any of the Lees to see him. Anyway, we'll be faster just us two," she said, her voice dull, her gaze unfocused like a sleepwalker's. It pinched Cello when she said it; everything about Joanie seemed suddenly so uneven. He tucked the crate into a divot between two blackberry bushes, camouflaging the dreaming baby beneath the stems drooping heavy with fruit.

Their race through the meadow beyond the garden felt endless—they didn't stop once. The scent of the garden receded as they ran through the ragged plots, and past Sil's creaking tractor shed, fragrant with diesel. Joanie had arranged the meeting with Franklin Lees, calling him from Letta's trailer earlier that day—Letta was elsewhere, occupied over one of her fiery concoctions. Cello could hear Joanie's jolt of satisfaction, even through her panic. Cello hadn't asked what would happen once the man paid Joanie.

Joanie's speed was meticulous—consuming. He could hear it in the rhythm of her breath. Every step away from the farm built something else, maybe something safer, something that was theirs. They would be fast; it was only three miles to the Leeses' farm. Their fast, though, wasn't fast enough.

Sil found them almost right away. He scooped them up in his truck on an access road off Route 9. He was rough but quiet, almost as if he'd known exactly where they'd be. "Where's the baby?" he asked, his face grim and hard.

"Over where the creek meets the road," Cello said softly.

The drive back was so quick it was like they'd barely left. Joanie didn't seem to care about the inevitable punishment—her feelings were elsewhere. Even the baby's stirring and fussing couldn't pull her back into the truck. Cello saw it in the radiant anger of her gaze when Sil pulled her down out of the truck bed. Sil had ruined everything, and she was furious. He pushed Joanie toward the light of the trailer, but held Cello back by the arm. "We'll let Letta have her turn with the princess here." Joanie slipped up and away, into the glow of Sil and Letta's trailer, and Cello buzzed with worry.

Letta knew how to hurt people, but not in the way that Sil did. Sil used his arms and legs, branches and belts. But none of that was as bad as the harm done by Letta. She could wrangle the darkest thoughts into a person's head and make them believe, *believe*, that they deserved nothing, or worse, that they deserved everything. People who walked away from a conversation with Letta were always a little bit worse than they'd been before. Cello worried far more about Joanie inside the trailer with Letta than he worried about himself outside with Sil.

Cello understood that he and Joanie could expect the most harm that both of their foster parents could give. He only hoped that Letta and Sil were the only ones who knew what they had done.

"Where's that worthless grub?" Letta growled out into the darkness.

Sil poked between Cello's shoulder blades, hard, but it wouldn't leave a mark. Saving his strength for the real thing, Cello thought. Letta stood in a pool of light streaming from the trailer's open door. She wore a long, blue dress, and a gold barrette clipped at her temple. "Betrayal in our own home," she said. "I didn't believe it—wouldn't believe what the Vine showed my own eyes and ears. How could you two?" She tossed her head in an exaggerated shake. "Give it back," she said, terribly quiet.

Cello reached for the bundle of cuttings that scratched against his chest and set it on the ground. Letta lifted it into her arms quickly, holding it like a swaddled infant. "Well, Sil, you found them so quick I think as a reward you should decide what's next for our Cello." Letta glared down from a full, glittery face of makeup. "What do you want to do with this ungrateful, skinny shit?"

"We could kennel him for the rest of the night." Sil swung an arm around Cello's narrow shoulders.

Letta nodded and smiled so that Cello could see the gilded fronts of her overlarge teeth. "I don't think that's quite enough. You know what you need to do, Sil. Just remember, the boy has to work tomorrow."

"If that's what you want," said Sil.

It began out in the still-hot grass beyond the trailer. Maybe there was blood; definitely there would be bruises. Sil finished up with the face, but only a few knocks—again, being practical, Sil aimed for Cello's cheeks and chin, leaving the boy's cranium alone.

Cello could feel Sil slowing down, could tell where he was trying to take a break, where his older body was beginning to argue with the exercise. When Cello fell against the grass for the last time, he breathed in the smell of earth and sun, still holding on to that feeling of being alone with Joanie, away from everyone.

"Now Joanie," Letta said, lighting a fresh cigarette.

"You sure?" Sil called. He didn't usually hit the girls, and never because it was his idea. Sil was sweating hard—Cello could smell it on him.

"I'm sure, honey," she said. The smoke fell to the ground around her in a gust of wind. "Come on now, Joanie," she said. "Your turn." Letta pointed to where Cello had collapsed, struggling to breathe evenly. Sil had knocked the wind out of him, and now his lungs pushed and pulled and stuck.

"Maybe tomorrow, Letta," Sil panted. "I wore myself out on this one already." He gave Cello one more smack on the back as he said it.

"No. It has to be tonight. Now." Letta pushed Joanie forward into the dim wash of light coming from the other trailers' windows.

"I don't know, sweet pea," Sil called. "She's too old."

"You're never too old to be put in your place," Letta said. "You—" she pointed at Cello's curled, exposed back "—move."

Cello shuffled to the side, but watched Joanie walk toward Sil. The waist of her jeans had slipped down low onto her hips, and the skin Cello saw there—smooth and moonlit—made him shiver.

Joanie stood in front of Sil and pulled her shirt over her head. Cello watched where it fell on the ground. "Go ahead," she said.

Sil turned his eyes up and away from her body, like he thought it shouldn't have been out in the dark like that. They all knew that Sil didn't think it was decent. Letta knew, but it was Sil's job to keep them at the garden—to keep the garden safe—and he needed his punishment, too.

"Before morning, Sil," Letta called, her voice flat and bored.

"I'm just working up to it, alright? Well, turn around, girl!" Sil hollered. "Have a little shame."

Joanie turned her back to Sil, and closed her eyes, waiting. Sil paced the yard in front of the trailer, his body lit and then hidden each time he walked past the open door. Cello didn't look at Letta, or even at Joanie. He only watched Sil.

Sil rubbed at his chin, and then ran his hands over his sun-wrecked face.

"Alright," he muttered, clapping his hands in a single smack of palms. He strode toward the nearest tree—a maple—and chose an impressively gnarled branch.

Cello hated his powerlessness. He hated that all he could do to help Joanie was endure the beating beside her. He wished that he was different and bolder—that he could be useful—instead of slouched in the grass beneath Joanie's struggle to stay silent.

"Oh, Sil," Letta said, shaking her head. "You're going to have to do better than that."

"Come on, Letta, I'm wore out," Sil pleaded.

"What, you want me to do it?" Letta's tone shifted to its familiar scattershot, flinty rage.

"Of course not. Give me a minute." Sil lowered the branch and tilted his neck from side to side.

"Hurry up," Letta said, lighting a new cigarette off the burning one between her lips.

Sil cleared his throat and began again, this time harder. Cello cast a glance at Letta, who was finally smiling a real smile. It would be over soon at least.

Letta's last satisfied look pried out an unexpected realization. Cello understood that they'd done him a favor. If he and Joanie hadn't been caught, if they'd been successful and escaped out into the world beyond the garden, Cello knew that Joanie would eventually peel off and away from him. That's how Joanie was. He wouldn't see it coming, either. Joanie loved secrecy, silence. If it weren't for Sil and Letta's intervention, and even the punishment, Cello would have been alone, and away from everything he understood. He had nothing outside of the predictable world of the garden and its inhabitants. Certainly, he had nothing to give to Joanie.

Cello felt sick as that combination of gratitude, disgust and anger mingled in his body.

"Now," Letta called from the trailer's low, steel steps. "I think you've done enough. Off to bed with you two. I better not hear any more about this. And keep it to yourselves. I don't want a soul to know the nonsense you tried tonight."

Sil, out of breath, dropped the branch and brushed his hands down the sides of his shirt. "Jesus, Letta," he said, hollering. He held his palms out to her like a surrendering man. "I got blisters now. Hope you're happy you got your way."

Sil disappeared into the dark and Letta turned, slamming the door to their trailer shut.

Joanie and Cello were left in the heavy night air, not looking at one another. They walked back toward the trailer where the kids were asleep, their eyes on the grass.

"What would happen if she told Mother Joseph?" Cello asked.

"She won't," Joanie said. "She can't."

Back in the kids' trailer, Cello and Joanie had to lie in bed on their stomachs. The stuffy air inside was filled with the night sounds and smells of the others. The kids had slept through everything; they gurgled and snored, and the tang of urine hung thick in the air—Miracle had wet the bed again.

Cello saw Joanie's open eyes stare out at nothing, definitely not at him, and tried to sleep. The baby cried out, and Joanie went to him. "I'm sorry," Joanie said, smoothing his little back. "I'm so sorry." Cello fell asleep to the sound of her low humming; the scent of the Vine and the earth he'd packed around it still clung, like a reproach, to his skin.

4

The next day, Letta behaved as if nothing had happened, though the other kids were unusually quiet. Sil and Cello walked in silence down the hill, and around the perimeter of the plot he and Marcela had started. Sil pulled a robust sip from the can of Crown Light held low by his side. Cello understood that Sil was prone to the same tides of emotion as anyone. He didn't always blame Sil for his spates of violence. They didn't seem personal, the way Letta's did. Sil just aimed to hurt—it was like the violence was still a part of him, just a fist, attached to an arm, attached to a man, attached to a heart. Letta aimed to hurt surgically, specifically—without emotion of her own.

"This looks good, son," he said, slapping Cello on the back. Cello winced as the force of Sil's friendly pat collided into what remained raw from the blows from the night before. Not that Sil noticed.

"Couldn't've done better myself. Mow this here, maybe three-quarters of the way up that slope, see?" Sil gestured ahead. "We don't need this much space on both sides. Shouldn't need it, if we do things right."

"Okay."

"And if you got time tonight, run the rototiller over it. I'm gonna see how the east plot's getting on. Make sure Marcela and Sabina pick up the scraps. I want those for compost."

"I'll be fine on my own," Cello said, brushing a fly from where it had landed, lapping up the sweat on the side of his throat.

"I know you will, but Letta wants the girls out here today. I'm sure they'll stay out of your hair. Just bring them back in with you before dark."

Sil paused, rolling the can of Crown between his hands. "I know it wasn't your idea, son, but what you and Joanie did put us all in danger. Mother Joseph'd kill every one of us if she knew. Think of the little kids. What'd happen to them? We depend on Amberly Joseph for everything—I'm not saying I like it, but that's just the truth. If it weren't for her, we wouldn't have a damn thing. No farm, no roof over our head—nothing. You know that, don't you?"

Cello nodded quietly.

Sil slapped a hand against the side of his leg. "Let's get to work, then. Make sure the girls help you, like I said. It's what Letta wants."

Cello worked evenly—not too slow, not too fast—and thought about what Sil had said and how the conversation had been a kind of apology. Cello knew he'd get nothing like that from Letta. He understood that Letta's punishment hadn't been meted out yet, and the wait made him itch.

As the afternoon slipped into evening, the air cooled. Cello hitched the tiller to the little tractor and noticed Marcela and Sabina under a low stand of pines. Their figures were dark shadows half-swallowed by the trees' deep green cover, straightening the piles of brush they'd moved out of the way. "Marcela, Sabina! Come help!" he called, surveying the rest of the broken branches and clumps of debris across the plot that needed to be cleared before tilling.

They didn't hear him, or pretended not to. As Cello strode toward them, he wondered what it would be like to talk to someone who shared the same blood with you. Maybe that person understood better. It seemed like that sometimes, with Marcela and Sabina. He walked into the midst of their conversation, noticing how naturally they hovered near one another like blossoms on a branch.

"What're you thinking, Mar?" Sabina smoothed her sister's hair back where it had fallen in her eyes.

"I'm thinking I need to get out of here," Marcela said, squatting down by the pile of rubble they'd collected, hiding, maybe, from Sil's eyes or Cello's. "I mean," she corrected, "*we* need to get out of here."

"Why does everybody keep saying that?" Sabina asked. "It's really not that terrible."

Marcela rolled her eyes. "You're only saying that because you're still one of the little kids."

"I am not!"

"That's how they all treat you. It's still safe for you. But look how Letta shipped Joanie off and what happened to her. She was my age when she got sent away."

"Letta wouldn't do that to you," Sabina said. "You aren't like Joanie."

"What's that supposed to mean?" Marcela crossed her arms over her chest.

"It's just…you're not trouble, like Joanie is." Sabina's voice was low, soothing. She cooed at her sister in the way she'd perfected over the years. Sabina could recalibrate her sister's emotions with a few words, and bring her back from the obviously dangerous idea she'd been circling.

"But I *am* trouble," Marcela said. "Maybe even more trouble than Joanie. I hate it here more than she ever did."

"I don't know—you don't always seem like you hate it." Sabina looked down at her hands.

"Well, I hate it now, and once they stop treating you so soft, I know you'll hate it, too. You heard what Letta said—I'm a young lady now. She could send me to Mother Joseph's anytime. I'm not forgetting what Joanie was like when she came back. Is that really what you want? Is that what you want for us?" Sabina didn't speak, waiting for her sister to finish. "I just want us to be ready. We got to make sure we have some money in case we need to leave quick. Letta's not selling me to the Josephs. I don't care what I have to do."

"Okay, Mar. Of course not. I'd never let that happen." Sabina looped her arm around her sister's waist and tucked her head against her shoulder.

Cello left them alone. He didn't want to ask anything of them right then—it didn't feel right to interrupt. So he kept on alone. The sun slowly disappeared behind the tree line. Cello breathed in the humid, grassy scent of the fresh soil he had turned up— the familiar smell undercut with a dense but comforting warmth. Despite the day and the night before, Cello couldn't resist the satisfaction he felt when finishing a job. It bloomed through him—not happiness, definitely not that—something more basic, like quenching a thirst.

He called out into the near-night for his foster sisters, and they packed up.

When they got back, everyone had already eaten dinner. Cello could see it in the way their listless bodies were sprawled around the trailers. The little kids lay on their backs in the grass, and Letta and Sil sat propped against their trailer sipping from sweating tallboys of Crown. Even Joanie was out, cooing at the baby propped up on her knees.

"Y'all are late," Sil said, flushed from the heat and the day of drinking. Cello didn't begrudge him any of it, really. The night before had done something to all of them, moved things around.

"Yeah, sorry. I wanted to finish up," Cello said.

"Did you?" Letta's voice poured out, caustic, like she hadn't spoken for days.

"Yeah."

"And what about you two? You do what Cello told y'all?" she asked the girls, rumpled as a pair of barn owls.

"Of course," Marcela said, and then yawned.

Cello stared as Joanie slipped back into the kids' trailer to put down the baby. He watched the door until she returned, her arms crossed, and sat on the step.

"We could've used your help here sooner," Letta said. "Feeding everybody dinner."

Emil nodded and lifted his tiny fingers into the air, tracing something only he could see in it. He dipped and turned his palm in the dark, a pink tip of tongue pressed into his nearly toddler-size lower lip. Cello felt a stab of tenderness for Emil. He felt that way about all of the kids, even Marcela. Leaving Letta and Sil would have also meant leaving behind the kids.

"Cello, go clean up the dinner things," Letta said. "Inside." She rapped the wall of trailer behind her, and it rattled a little. "I want to talk to you alone."

Cello felt a fresh layer of sweat bleed out through his skin. His punishment from Letta was coming.

Cello went immediately to the tiny sink, scrubbing the pans that soaked there. Letta leaned against the enamel-topped, miniature dining table and lit another cigarette. Her head tipped back when she exhaled. Cello tried to keep his eyes on the pans.

"I thought it would be good to clear the air," Letta said.

Wash, wash, wash, Cello repeated in his mind, trying not to listen too carefully to what Letta was saying.

"You're such a trusting boy," she continued. "Shame, since it makes you so dull." She paused, and Cello could hear the tap of her finger as she ashed her cigarette. "I don't really blame you. I mean, I blame you some, but it's mainly Joanie. She can be convincing. Probably told you she loved you, wanted to be with you forever. Maybe get married again. That's what she said, right?"

Cello didn't speak—he kept washing. *Wash, wash, wash.* He felt her approach, felt the shape of her scrawny body bump into his own. She stroked the back of his neck, like she was appraising the length of his hair. "Is that what she said, Cello?" He felt her file-tapered fingernails dig into the skin at the base of his skull.

He shook his head, and Letta chuckled, blowing smoke around his face and head. "I thought she would at least have promised you that." She moved away a little, and Cello took a deep breath, inhaling the harsh citrus scent of the dishwashing liquid.

"No guesses, then, about why Joanie just had to leave, and right away?"

Cello knew better than to speak.

"Sad, that you had to hear it from me. Mother Joseph wants another girl from us. I told Joanie about it. How I was thinking about sending her back. We'll keep the baby here, of course."

Cello's body trembled with alarm, but he tried not to betray his panic. "Wouldn't think she'd want Joanie, after what happened to Josiah." He struggled to keep his voice wooden and even.

Letta barked out another laugh, and Cello heard the flicker of her lighter as she inhaled on a new cigarette. "Wow, you're really trying to keep your cool, honey. I respect that," she said, though Cello knew, better than anyone, that she didn't. He kept his head down, scrubbing at a cracked plastic bowl. "No, I haven't decided who I'll send yet. But I'll surely let you know."

Something—large—clashed against the side of the trailer, and the laminate floor beneath Cello's feet trembled. Letta hurried to the door, and Cello followed, wiping his soapy hands on his T-shirt.

Sil's voice spilled through the open door.

"None a'that, miss," he said. "You'd think after last night you'd all be on your best behavior."

"What did happen last night?" Marcela asked, her mouth a snide little curve. "Is Joanie pregnant again?"

Cello and Letta clamored down from the trailer's sweltering interior into the cooling night.

Joanie's arms and legs seemed to stretch and grow longer as she reached for Marcela. Cello heard someone shouting his name. He tried to grab onto one pair of limbs belonging to the same girl. It was hard to separate them, because they'd twisted arms and hair and waists around each other.

"Jesus Christ, Marcela!" Miracle's little voice cut through the muggy evening air. It was like a clap on his shoulder.

Cello plucked at one of Marcela's skinnier, longer arms and clamped it still. She swore and tried to kick out at him, but he just held her wrist until she stopped, until Sil had pulled Joanie from the tangle. Cello held Marcela at arm's length until Letta grabbed her shoulders and nodded for Cello to let go.

"This is the hour, I guess, for y'all to test my patience. Joanie," Letta called to Joanie but didn't move her head. She looked straight into Marcela's eye. "Do you want to go back to Amberly Joseph?"

Cello took a covert look at Joanie through the dishwater-blond hair that had fallen across his face in the struggle. Her eyes were wide and startled, but the rest of her face quiet.

"Right," Letta continued. "I'll say this one more time, in front of all of you, so you don't misunderstand me. I see any more nonsense from anyone, everybody sleeps outside for the rest of the summer. Don't matter what weather, or bugs, or how sick you get. And, Joanie, if you can't conduct yourself like a lady, I will send you back, no question. We'll hang on to little Junior, of course, so you can give Mother-in-Law your full attention. She's sure desperate for another female over there." Letta narrowed her eyes as she examined Marcela's spotty complexion. "How about you, Marcela? Time to start thinking about marriage."

Marcela turned her head and spat. "Nice try, but Mother Joseph doesn't have any more available sons. Joanie killed off the very last one."

Joanie made a screeching sound in her throat, but kept her mouth closed. She'd come back from the Josephs' so different. It wasn't just because she was pregnant, either. It was like she'd lost her subtle Joanie-ness. Cello didn't care, though. It made him love her more, watching her move through that change. He wished, though, that he could make it easier for her.

"Oh, honey." Letta smiled while Marcela sneered. "She may not have any sons, but she does have that brother. And all the cousins. I mean, they're barely human the way Amberly lets them run around," Letta coughed up a strange laugh. "But they sure are there. And they're plenty available, as you say." Letta brushed off Marcela's shoulders. "Keeping all you kids is expensive. And Amberly does want another girl on the place." Letta took a deep breath. "Just something to think about." Cello shuddered at the declaration. "Come on, it's bedtime. We got to work tomorrow."

5

In the mornings, it was usually the sounds of the baby that woke Cello. Sometimes he'd be crying, sometimes he'd be crooning—looking up at the stained ceiling of the trailer, or at Joanie's sleeping, milky softness. But this morning was different. This morning was ominously quiet.

Cello immediately felt off by how naturally he'd wakened. There was no bleary longing for a few more minutes of rest—only a heavy, sated feeling in the full morning light streaming in through the trailer's windows.

Cello sat up, trying to recognize what was wrong. How long had they slept? Not too late, since Sil hadn't come by to bang on the door yet. He pushed the dark flannel blanket down his legs and stood up, scanning the trailer's guts from end to end. The kids were all asleep and breathing heavily. Emil had kicked his covers onto the floor, but the others were just as tucked in as they'd been the night before when Cello had collapsed onto his cot.

He moved to the kitchen counter, to the baby's crate. Was

he sick? Cello imagined resting a hand on the baby's belly to feel for the gentle fill of air into his tiny lungs. But in the crate there was no baby. Cello felt a shiver of worry, until he remembered that sometimes Joanie brought the baby to bed with her, if he'd been fussing.

Cello approached Joanie much more carefully than he would have come up to just the baby alone. She was asleep on her side, turned away from him and the baby's crate. He peered over the smooth fall of dark hair over her face and shoulder for the baby's diminutive sprawl. But there was nothing—or rather, there was only Joanie.

Cello gripped Joanie's arm—through her blanket—and shook it. "Joanie," he whispered, not wanting to wake the others. "Where's the baby?"

She murmured incoherently and turned onto her stomach. An arm darted out from under the blanket and then flopped down the side of her cot.

"Joanie," Cello repeated. This time he gave her arm a real squeeze.

Joanie's dark eyes popped open. "Ow! Cello!" Across the trailer, Miracle coughed in her sleep. "What?" Joanie snapped.

"Where's the baby?"

"Over there." Joanie yawned and waved at the crate in the trailer's narrow kitchen.

Cello shook his head.

"What?" Joanie sat up a little straighter, the blankets falling away from her body. She stood up and Cello looked at the stained carpet floor so that he wouldn't stare at her bare legs.

"Where did you put him, Cello?" Joanie's voice would sound bored to anyone else, but Cello heard the fear pressing through. "It's not funny."

"I didn't put him anywhere." Cello pulled on his jeans and Joanie whirled out of the trailer. She let the door slam behind her, knowing it would wake up the little kids. Cello winced as Emil let loose a little wail.

"What time is it?" Marcela called from under her thin camping pillow.

Cello kicked the side of her cot. "Get up. The baby's missing."

"Huh?" Marcela sat up and retied her ponytail. Sabina had already climbed down from her bunk and leaned over the empty wooden crate. Cello watched as she pulled away the small squares of blanket, and then the miniature mattress she and Marcela had made while Joanie lurched through the end of her pregnancy, swollen full of the baby.

"He's not in here," Sabina said softly, as though he were and she didn't want to wake him. She turned the empty crate on its side.

"No shit, Sherlock," Marcela said from her cot. "I'm sure Letta has him."

As though Marcela had called her inside, Letta burst in with Sil and Joanie. Joanie's feet were still bare and covered in dew and broken blades of grass.

"No one thinks this is funny," Letta began. "Marcela?" Letta hovered over to where Marcela sat, upper body folded over her legs, eyes still only half-open.

"What? I didn't do anything," she said coolly. Cello noticed that same fear pulsing under Marcela's studied evenness.

"Cello." He could smell Letta's pungent breath as she came up close to him. "What have you done?"

"Please," Marcela snorted. "Cello loves that baby more than Joanie. It's embarrassing."

Even Cello didn't see the slap coming. Letta spun at Marcela so fast that he heard the strike across her face before he understood what had happened.

"Shut your mouth, Marcela. I don't want to hear your voice until that baby gets found. Start looking, all of you." Letta tossed her arms around, as though trying to animate the kids from a distance.

"Do you mean we should look outside?" Miracle asked.

"Yes, very good, Miracle. Of course, outside. Go!" Letta shouted.

"But he can't even walk," Sabina protested.

"Go! I won't tell you one more time! Anyone still in here in two minutes is cruising for a bruising."

Sabina helped the little kids get dressed, and Marcela huffed her way into the trailer's only bathroom. Joanie, Sil and the truck were already gone.

Cello and Miracle worked together, walking in overlapping loops around the campsite. When their paths crossed for the fifth or sixth time, Miracle reached out to Cello.

"Do you think we'll find him?" she asked.

Cello nodded.

"Will he be dead?"

"No, he won't. He'll be fine," Cello said. He hoped hard that he was right. Miracle nodded back at him and lowered her head. Cello felt a rush of love for his foster sister, for the obvious concern that whorled across her face.

Cello's sneakers were soaked through with dew, even as the sun built its strength above them. Each time he passed Miracle, she looked more wilted.

"Go get a drink, Miracle," he said when he saw her next. They'd fanned out a little, but the trailers were still visible through the scraggly patch of woods where they stood.

"I don't think I should yet," she said. Her cheeks were red from the heat and her face shone with sweat. Cello swiped his hair away from his face. He felt the slickness on his own skin, too.

"Let's both go," he said. "Maybe Sil and Joanie brought help." Cello knew they weren't back, just like he knew there were no cops called. His hearing was sharp enough that it would catch the first crunch of gravel when Sil's truck turned from the main road onto the obscured track to the garden.

"Come on," Cello said as he caught on to Miracle's small, sweaty palm. "Let's see what's happening. Maybe Marcela and Sabina found him."

Marcela and Sabina hadn't found anything. Marcela leaned against the abandoned, rust-speckled water tank and drank from a plastic bottle, almost the same color green as the underside of the leaves above them. Sabina was entertaining Emil, and now the two were sprinting across the mowed rectangle of grass Sil kept short for their yard.

"Go get some water, Miracle. Where's Letta?" Cello asked.

"Lying down." Marcela nodded toward their trailer. "And no, they're not back yet."

"You think they went to the Josephs'?" Cello asked, holding out his arm, waiting for Marcela to pass him the green plastic bottle.

"I don't know, probably. You know if anybody took him, it has to be them." Marcela shrugged and handed it over.

"How could it be them? They don't even know Junior was born," Cello said, before unscrewing the cap and pouring the contents into his mouth. He coughed as a syrupy sludge undercut with alcohol stung the back of his throat and nose.

"Jesus, Marcela, what is that?"

"One of Letta's wine coolers." Marcela wiped the flat of her hand over her perspiring forehead. "She won't miss it today."

Cello drank again, swishing the sharp citrusy liquid around in his mouth. "You really think they went over there?"

"To the Josephs'?" Marcela asked as she snatched back the bottle. "I don't know. I mean, they went *somewhere*, didn't they? It's the first place I would check."

Cello nodded. "You and Sabina didn't find anything?"

"What were we going to find? Clues?"

"I don't know," Cello muttered. "Just something." He flushed under the layers of frustration.

"Well, we didn't. Ask Sabina if you think I'm lying."

Cello squinted across the yard where Sabina and Emil played tag. Even though the sisters were three years apart, Sabina was the slightly taller one. Their silhouettes were almost identical, though Sabina was leaner, almost bony. If it had been a hazier day, Cello wouldn't have been able to tell which girl was chasing Emil. Emil's squeal of laughter punctured his thoughts, and Cello turned back to Marcela.

"What? No, why would I think you're lying?"

"Whatever. I'm going to check on Miracle." Marcela left him alone by the old water tank. Cello could feel their anxiety, all of it pressed together, like they were animals in a pen. Miracle had been terrified on their hunt, and even now, Emil's screams sounded more hysterical than joyful.

Even Sabina, who consistently exercised a poised calm—in the ways she spoke and moved—seemed broken up somehow. Cello closed his eyes against a sudden vision of Mother Joseph's hands on Joanie's baby. He quickly tamped down the possibility that Junior was under the Josephs' roof, and blotted out what it would do to Joanie—to all of them—to lose the baby to her.

Cello pushed his hair off his forehead, and left his hands stacked on the top of his head, letting the breeze fill all of the space around him.

6

Joanie hunched over the dashboard, holding her back away from the scorching vinyl upholstery of the car seat left to broil in the sun. Her body knew this shape—the shape of fear, the shape of violence. Joanie longed to be in some other body, away from the garbled panic coursing through her. As soon as she realized the baby was missing, she knew that, somehow, Amberly Joseph was to blame. If her baby had been stolen and taken to the Joseph compound, he would cease to be hers. All of the Josephs' poison would leach into his tiny body, and by the time he spoke his first word, he would be one of them—he would belong there instead of with her.

At first, Joanie believed that her life would be better as a Joseph. Something would happen, some ascendance, and she would have what she wanted, would say what she wanted. She'd only known them from a distance—they were wealthier than Letta and Sil; they controlled Letta and Sil. More importantly, Amberly Joseph controlled the Vine of Heaven; she would answer the questions Letta couldn't. Joanie imagined the Vine's power looming and opening before her; she imagined controlling Letta and Sil, too. At her most daring, she imagined controlling Amberly Joseph.

But, looking back, she couldn't be expected to have known the scale of the Josephs' dank secrets. She might have guessed or suspected that the Josephs weren't any happier, or really better off, than Letta and Sil and their collection of kids. There was no guarantee that living with the Josephs would be an improvement, only that she would be more powerful among them. It was all that Joanie saw in the beginning.

And the Josephs were powerful. It was Mother Joseph who chose Joanie from the girls. If she'd wanted Marcela or Sabina, she would have waited. But it was Joanie she wanted, because she knew Joanie was Letta's favorite. Because she wanted to show her power over Letta. And Joanie went willingly because she, too, wanted Letta to feel her strength.

Remembering her life with the Josephs made Joanie wince. It was a reflex now, an involuntary, conditioned response, as reliable and acute as an animal's under the whip. There had been real pain in the Joseph household. And at first, Joanie had been a little fascinated by it.

That third morning at the compound, she went to sit with Mother Joseph on the mildewed lawn chairs out in front. Even though her thighs were bruised by her excitable new husband, and the shower smelled different, and she couldn't think about or touch Josiah without feeling a mix of contempt and curiosity, she felt an unexpected wash of peace.

The early-morning quiet, the sensation of half her face in sunlight, the sitting; it was luxurious. *What is this feeling? Is it because I'm not a virgin anymore? Because I'm married? Because I'm sitting drinking coffee with the most powerful person I know?* She was nearly happy, preening under Mother Joseph's attention.

"How're you settling in, baby?" Mother Joseph asked her as she crunched on a piece of toast.

"Fine." Joanie pitched herself toward her new mother-in-law, the cup of coffee just against her lips. She admired the bronze angle of her bent arm, and imagined, for a minute, that they were two women breakfasting on a European piazza.

"That's good, very, very good. You know Letta was worried about you coming here. But I know one of us when I see one of us, and you, baby, you're one of us."

"Thanks," Joanie murmured against the ceramic lip of her mug.

"To make it official, though, I'd appreciate it if you'd do me a favor."

"Sure." Joanie dropped the hand holding the cup into her lap.

"Now, you're not the type to have a weak stomach, are you?" Joanie shook her head.

"I need you to pull a tooth for me."

"What, your tooth?"

"Lord, no!" Mother Joseph laughed and the movement rippled across her body—from the soft spills of flesh at the openings of her neon green housedress to the thick calves she'd propped up on a milk crate. Joanie watched, captivated, as the woman's laughter took her over, absolutely possessed her. *This isn't normal*, Joanie thought, but wasn't disturbed. Instead, she was curious.

Joanie knew she wasn't good like Cello. She knew she wasn't shrewd like Letta. She began to wonder if maybe she was like Mother Joseph.

"Whose tooth, then?" Joanie's voice was cool, easy. She knew her mother-in-law was trying to unsettle her. But Joanie had lived with Letta her whole life, and knew exactly how to react.

Mother Joseph's full, body-vibrating laughter slowed to a subdued hiccup. "I guess you do have a strong stomach, Joanie. The last man who came near my mouth walked away short a ball."

"Well, I'm not a man." Joanie kept her gaze level, just at the older woman's ragged hairline.

"No, I guess not. It's Cher's tooth that needs to be pulled."

Mother Joseph whistled through her teeth. A large brindle mutt loped over to the cluster of decaying lawn furniture. Cher was Mother Joseph's personal pet. It was a test, Joanie knew. In a way, pulling Cher's tooth was a greater show of confidence in Joanie's potential than marriage to Josiah.

"Now?" Joanie asked, easing her body out of the chair.

"Course now—isn't that right, my lamb?" Mother Joseph reached for the dog's muzzle, pulling it wide-open, even as the animal whimpered and trembled. "That one, you see? In the back, bottom left. It's all black."

Joanie set her coffee cup on the ground and squinted inside against the animal's foul, hot breath. "I see it. You gonna hold her?" she asked Mother Joseph without looking at her, while staring into the filthy, dark cave of Cher's mouth.

"Sure, I'll hold her."

"We could always tie her down." Joanie knew she sounded cruel. She wanted Mother Joseph to know that she, too, could be cruel.

"Oh, I couldn't do that to Cher." Mother Joseph cooed and stroked the dog's back.

"Fine. You got pliers?"

Mother Joseph nodded toward the slat-patched, corrugated metal shed beside the driveway.

"I'll be back in a minute. Calm her down, I guess." Joanie removed the open padlock that looped a chain keeping the door shut. The dim light inside shook something out of Joanie—a realization that something was really changing. Now she was really part of the Josephs' domestic snarl. A quarter-size spot of pain formed in the center of her forehead, and she rubbed at it with the heel of her hand. *Pliers, okay, here we go*, Joanie thought. She took the least-rusty-looking tool from a shelf tacked to the wall and closed the chain with the padlock.

She swiftly walked back to the woman and the dog, her steps evenly spaced and graceful. Mother Joseph had gathered Cher up against her chest. When Joanie saw that Cher's body was clamped in place, she moved right up to the dog's limp, pink tongue, pressing it down with her thumb. She took Cher's snout, squinted at the fuliginous tooth, clamped the pliers on it and drew it out with a jerk, along with her hand.

The animal wailed, a horrible sound that made Joanie sick with guilt. She tried not to show it, though she couldn't help turning her face away from the whimpering dog, and the blood streaming from her mouth. She knew Mother Joseph was watching her. Joanie threw the pliers, still clasping the dripping tooth, to the grass at Mother Joseph's feet. "If you need anything else," she said, "you know where I'll be."

"I knew you'd have a steady head. You did good, girl!" Mother Joseph called after her. "So good, I'm gonna let you decide from now on whether Josiah gets his medicine or not." Joanie froze at the thought, but also thrilled at the possibility of what it would mean to shoulder one of Mother Joseph's tasks. It felt to her like the beginning of something important—the beginning of some transfer of power. Joanie shivered as she walked away, and Mother Joseph's voice softened as she crooned to the trembling pile of dog in her lap. "Didn't she do good, honey? Oh, you're alright, quit the fuss."

This makes me one of them now, Joanie thought as she walked away. She stepped firmly, trying to press back the nausea she felt with each footprint.

Joanie thought she was going to feel like a Joseph on the day of her wedding, but she didn't feel anything at all. Instead, she numbly observed the differences between her old family and her new one.

In the chill of the courthouse hall, Joanie looked not at her future husband, but at her future mother-in-law. Set against Letta's rangy height and gaunt face, Mother Joseph was substantial, significant—a monument in some ancient city that had weathered thousands of years filled with storms and riots. Standing, Mother Joseph seemed biblically enormous—wide and tall, swollen with matriarchal importance.

Joanie studied Josiah's pinched carp's face, the tiny pointed nose and chin that swam up out of the fleshy pond of his cheeks and thick forehead. She looked for a trace of Mother Joseph's grandeur in that face, and saw none. Mother Joseph hadn't given her a prized family possession—she realized quickly that Josiah was a trap, insurance. Josiah brought nothing to Joanie. It was Joanie who now belonged to them. It was through Joanie that Mother Joseph would collar Letta even more tightly.

And Joanie smiled, straight into Josiah's bloated face, because she knew that she could help Mother Joseph. She wanted to help, because when, really, would she get another chance to put Letta in her place?

After that third day, she wasn't so sure. Obeying Mother Joseph—submitting in a way she had never submitted to Sil and Letta—and pulling the dog's tooth had shaken something loose in her. She didn't like how changed she felt, as though all the molecules in her body had been rearranged.

Mother Joseph moved them into their permanent room the morning after Cher's procedure. Until then, they'd had a sad, shambolic honeymoon in the Josephs' single guest trailer set back in the woods.

The room was cold—Joanie felt the keen autumn air slipping through the unsealed window by the bed. It was only going to get worse; she decided to fix it before the first rain or snow. The scent of mildew and traces of sweat hung thickly around them. Joanie's bag was already on the bed. She grimaced when she thought about Mother Joseph, or any of the others, touching her things.

"I don't know how Letta taught you to set up house, but I like things neat. You take something, you put it exactly back where you found it. I don't wanna have to go looking for things. Don't make me do that."

"No, Mother Joseph, I won't." Joanie stood quiet, a few feet away from Josiah. His tiny eyes incrementally widened in the late-afternoon gloom. He clutched a glass aquarium against his chest, swaddled in an old towel that had been washed so often that it had lost all color.

"You keep your creepy-crawlies in your room, Josiah. It's only since you're married now that I'm letting that goblin in the house."

When Josiah set the aquarium on top of the room's rickety dresser, Joanie didn't know what the creature inside would become to her. It would be her anchor, that turtle, when the worst of it started—when Mother Joseph became fully disappointed in her new daughter-in-law. When Joanie ceased to be herself, it was Josiah's pet trapped in the aquarium that got her off the floor. The last, full-brained thought she'd had was about that poor turtle, its warped shell clamoring against the glass aquarium tank.

That her baby was half-Joseph, Joanie couldn't undo. But he was half her, too, and she'd do whatever she could to find him. She knew there was no question of them going to the police, and doing whatever it was a regular mother would do under the same circumstances. She knew that there was only one place for them to go.

Sil had been driving, directionless, for the better part of an hour. He kept looking at her, giving Joanie nervous part-smiles, part-grimaces. He was waiting for her to say it. She knew that Sil was too soft to force her back to the Joseph compound. He hadn't forgotten the state of ruin she had been in when she left.

"I guess we better check out the Josephs' place," Joanie said, watching Sil's hands on the wheel.

He didn't turn to look at her, his eyes on the windshield. "You sure about that?"

"What else can we do?"

He nodded and slowed the truck, then made a U-turn in the middle of the road.

Joanie tried to remember what it had been like to feel the

way she'd felt on that third morning—powerful, commiserating. She could at least try to fake it, to unnerve her former mother-in-law. Under no circumstances would she let Sil in alone. Joanie was the only one who would know if Amberly Joseph was lying.

Sil pulled the truck into a little dusty polygon where the Josephs parked their scabby assortment of vehicles. Joanie opened the passenger side door and slid to the ground, relieved that none of her former family were standing around and smoking in the lot as they often did. She felt that dangerous shimmer in the air, too—one of Mother Joseph's protections.

She and Sil walked the winding gravel path to the main house, the house Joanie had lived in, been hurt in—the house she thought she'd die in. Sil walked slightly ahead; maybe, Joanie thought, to protect her, maybe to show the Josephs that he was in charge. Once they were in front of the peeling white painted door, Joanie was the one to knock.

When the door creaked open, Joanie slouched in relief; Harlan, one of the cousins, and not Mother Joseph, answered the door. Harlan had never frightened her, even when he'd meant to. He was ancient compared to the rest of them, with a body covered in patches of thin, white hair. Harlan had always disgusted her, not least of all because he was one of Mother Joseph's favorites.

"Well?" Harlan said as he eyed them there on the porch.

"Lady of the house in?" Sil asked.

"No, gone on an errand." Harlan looked straight at Joanie. "Didn't expect to see you again," he said to her.

Joanie gave him a thin smile. "Me, either." She leaned in toward the open door, testing the thickness of the air. Joanie thought she would be able to taste if her baby was inside.

"Can we come in and wait?" Sil asked.

"'Fraid not. After the trial, we weren't supposed to see this one again." Harlan pointed at Joanie in a sideways thumbs-up.

"We'll wait out here. On the porch," Joanie said quickly. She felt fury bloom in her very pit. Harlan, always so loose-brained, had let slip one thing Joanie hadn't known. Mother Joseph didn't want her back—didn't want to even look upon her. Letta had lied. There was no chance of her coming back. Staring through the open door where Harlan stood, she felt light-headed. The familiar smell of the house, and the shadows of the objects that belonged there, struck her in a suffocating wave. The last time she'd been inside was the trial Harlan had mentioned, her trial.

"Fine by me," Harlan said, closing the door and keeping them out.

"You didn't hear anything, did you?" Sil asked. "I mean," he said, lowering his voice to an exaggerated whisper, "no crying or anything like that?"

Joanie shook her head. She wanted to sit, but didn't want any part of her body to touch anything that belonged to Mother Joseph. Sil saw the plume of dust in the driveway before Joanie did, and squeezed her arm a little.

"Should we go on out by the car? Quick getaway and all," he said.

"No, let's wait for her here." Joanie walked down the decomposing steps into the front yard so she wouldn't be trapped on the porch.

Joanie could smell Mother Joseph before she saw her lumbering up the gravel path. The unmistakable scent of the old woman's perspiration and Pert Plus carried into the yard. Joanie set her hands on her hips, and felt the heat from Sil's body as he edged in toward her.

Mother Joseph stopped abruptly as soon as she saw Joanie, and dropped the blue-and-white plastic bag in her hand. Two of Josiah's cousins who had accompanied Mother Joseph on her errand flanked her.

"Cy," Mother Joseph said, talking though her teeth. "Get my gun from the car."

"No, no, no," Sil called, waving his hands in the air, forcing a chuckle. "We're not here for any trouble, Mother Joseph."

Joanie noted that Cy disappeared despite Sil's protestations.

"Silvanus, I don't want to hear it. I told y'all I didn't want to set eyes on this child again. She should be dead," she added. "She's a demon. Only reason she's still living and breathing. If you bring a demon to me, I'll fight it." She nodded at the man beside her. He lunged at Joanie, and she felt, before she really understood the physics of his attack, his hands at her throat, a single plastic bag, now empty, its contents scattered on the grass, wrapped around her neck. Joanie noted the specifics of the pain—the hard bite of the plastic against the soft part of her throat, and the burning in her lungs as she pulled deep from the air around her to get enough to keep her standing on her own. She felt something like a laugh caught between those lungs and that throat, because whatever this was, it was nothing compared to what she'd already endured on the Josephs' place.

"Let's all just stay calm," Sil said.

"Calm! After that demon slaughtered my boy?" Mother Joseph looked back to the space where Cy had returned, training his weapon on the visitors.

"One of our valuables went missing," Sil said, clipping each word off so that there could be no misunderstanding him. Joanie watched Mother Joseph's incredulous reaction—rage was the only emotion that splashed over her features. There was no complexity to that particular brand of anger; Joanie knew from experience. It was a basic, unforgiving heat.

"And you thought you'd just drop by and throw around accusations?" Mother Joseph yelled now.

"Nothing like that, Mother Joseph. Only we thought you might've heard something. From one a y'alls…tenants." Sil shifted his weight over his two feet, back and forth, as though his boots were a size too small. Tenants—a generous word, Joanie thought, to describe the users who flocked to the Joseph place. They slept in the woods at the edge of the property line, working whatever odd and unsavory jobs the Josephs needed done. They haunted the perimeter of the compound, willing to do anything, to ingratiate themselves in any way, in return for a taste of the Vine and Mother Joseph's benevolence.

"Get off this property, Sil," Cy said.

"Shut your mouth, Cy," Mother Joseph said. "I know that Letta didn't tell you to come out here."

"No, ma'am," Sil lied. "Just looking for some information from our nearest and dearest."

"Well, what I can tell you is that I always thought you were a slimy piece of work, and Letta must've lost her mind playing house with you." Mother Joseph pointed an arthritis-warped finger at Sil. "What I can tell you is I don't want you coming around here again. In fact, I can't be sure I can do business with y'all again." She nodded at Cy, and he released the safety with a click. "Maybe I'll pay you all a visit and pack up what's mine. What I gave you out of the kindness of my heart. Familial love."

Sil dipped his head and looked toward the ground, his forehead creased. "No, no need for that. We'll be on our way, Mother Joseph. We won't bother you no more." Sil took Joanie's arm, firmly, eyeing the hands at her throat.

Mother Joseph tilted her head to the side and whistled. "Shoot," she said. "You really think you'll be 'on your way.'" She aped Sil's cadence, putting a whine on it. "Just like that? Cy, shoot him in the leg."

"Sil's got something new for you, though," Joanie said, her voice struggling into the sound. The man behind her tightened the plastic, and kneed her legs open. He pulled her harder against his body, and she felt the rot of him all over the backs of her bare legs.

"That's right," Sil said, his palms turned up and outward in supplication. "Brand-new product. It was supposed to be a surprise."

"By the heavenly Vine." Mother Joseph propped her hands

on either side of her impressive belly. "Y'all are almost too pathetic." She rolled her eyes, head tilted back, for an instant like a woman seized.

"No, ma'am, I really got something. I been working with the Vine and some of my jimsonweed. A hybrid—it's beautiful. Lots of stalks and blossoms on these, and they need less space. I been trying them out in one of my test plots, and it's coming up beautiful." Sil gestured eagerly, as though trying to paint a visual aid onto the air. Joanie wasn't sure if Sil's reply was just for show, or if it was genuine.

"Well?" Mother Joseph said, turning back to Cy, one of her wiry eyebrows raised. Cy shook his head.

"Couldn't hurt to take a look." The man holding Joanie spoke. His voice, Joanie could hear and smell, was wet with dip. His hands sagged a little as he turned to inspect Sil. Joanie took a full breath as the plastic around her throat loosened.

Sil nodded. "Usually it's real finicky. But this batch come up perfect, I mean picture-perfect. My boy and I've been using something special, and the Vine's loving it. Mixing it into the topsoil. It's got a couple of different kinds of fungus, and—"

"Lord, give me strength!" Mother Joseph called up into the sky. "I don't give a solitary shit what you cocksuckers're doing with your topsoil. Bring it 'round next delivery and I'll try it."

Joanie could see Sil's body sway with relief.

"No, never mind, I don't mean that." Mother Joseph guffawed and bent double in her amusement. "I never want to see either of you out here again. Send Letta with it. 'Cause if I do happen to see you again out here, y'all can count on being shot on the spot. Shot on the spot, shot on the spot." She clapped her hands along with the rhyme. "What do you think about that?"

Cy giggled nervously behind her.

"Alright, alright, let her go." Joanie fell forward a step when she was released. Mother Joseph backed up, reflexively, at Joanie's sudden movement toward her. Joanie couldn't suppress a familiar pinch of excitement, the kind she got when she'd won something, even something as small as a step.

Sil tugged at her arm, and soon they were stumbling away, not quite running, but almost. She felt the Josephs' eyes on her all the way back to Sil's truck.

Although it had been terrible, Joanie felt incrementally lighter. Mother Joseph didn't want her. *Never wanted to see her again.* While most of her was relieved, she was still outraged. She couldn't come back to look for the baby. She couldn't come back to challenge Mother Joseph ever again. Which meant that her mother-in-law had disqualified her from whatever game they'd been playing and won by default. She'd disqualified Joanie because she was afraid. Amberly Joseph was afraid of *her*, of what she'd done at the trial.

That Josiah was dead, though, wasn't exactly Joanie's fault. Joanie's insides contracted in a dark minute, all of her muscles clenching and aching. Her body betrayed her as it flashed back to the panic she'd felt as she repeatedly pressed her palms into Josiah's chest trying to revive him.

She *had* tried to save him, she told herself, shaking away the sticking guilt. She tried to save him, which was more than Mother Joseph or anyone else in that family had done.

Joanie slammed the door to the truck, crossing her arms and legs, folding back into herself.

"Let's get the hell out of here," Sil said as he backed the truck out of the compound's lot and drove away. "I'm sorry, Joanbug," he said, wiping sweat from his upper lip with a shaking hand. "We shouldn't have gone."

"Yes," Joanie said. "We should have." An optimistic thought, tiny as a seed in a pod, tapped out at her. If she was powerful enough to frighten Amberly Joseph, she was powerful enough to find her child.

7

When the truck rolled back up the lane, Cello could see the hot blush of Joanie's face. He could see it all the way from where he stood by the abandoned water tank. There was always a pull toward her. All the siblings felt it, but Cello felt it the strongest. Cello had to force his feet still, to push back against the compulsion to go to her. His first memories were filled with that feeling, needing to stay as close to her as possible—him and Joanie, running around the garden like twins, like they shared the same heart. He could tell, from Sil's heavy step, and Joanie's blotchy face, that no baby had been found.

Letta swayed out of her trailer, clutching Miracle's hand as she descended the abbreviated, rusting stoop.

"Well?" she asked.

"Well, nothing," Sil answered, kicking at the whirring sound of a bug flitting between them. "So what now?"

Letta looked over to the truck encapsulating the still-silent Joanie. "I don't know." Letta seemed muted, less than what she usually was.

"Don't you think we ought to report it, honey?"

"Oh, Sil." Letta turned her gaze to the cloudless sky, Miracle clutched to her front. "You know we can't. First place they'll come looking is here. You know we can't have that."

"Well, this doesn't feel right," Sil said, jabbing at the air with a pointed finger. "Somebody's got to know a baby's gone missing."

"We know he's gone. Nobody better to look for him than his own family. Isn't that right, Miracle, honey?"

A melting cherry Icee dripped its scarlet syrup onto Miracle's fist, and she licked it off. Letta took it for a nod of agreement.

"This is serious now," Sil said. "We need help looking for him."

"Are you saying you're going to call the law in on this?" Letta spat.

"I don't see why not. I could—I don't know—hide what we got going on."

"Please. You're embarrassing yourself, Silvanus."

"You know what's embarrassing?" Sil's voice pitched high and hysterical. "You! That is a living child out there somewhere! We got to do all we can to make sure he gets found. Can't you do something? With the girls? I bet y'all could track him down. Maybe with a fire?"

Letta shook her head. "You know we can't. The Work only protects the Vine, not the people who grow it."

Joanie straightened her back, cool and silent as water while Sil's and Letta's voices pinged around the yard. To give her some room and keep himself from moving toward her, Cello walked to where Letta and Sil argued.

"I'll go in," Cello said. "I'll tell the cops about him."

"You?" Letta's voice was shrill now, matching Sil's wavering panicked tones. "And who are you? You think anybody's going to listen to you? You're nothing to that baby. Why, you'd be the first suspect, I bet. Go on." Letta waved her arms like a terrible sorceress. "Run along and report it, Good Citizen Cello. I have a feeling we won't see you again for quite some time." Her voice brightened with falseness. Letta wrenched the half-eaten popsicle out of Miracle's hand and threw it at him.

Cello ducked, but the Icee still clipped his ear. He felt a buzz of cold at the side of his head.

"Leave it alone, Cello," Joanie said. She leaned out of the truck's rolled-down window, and rested her head against the door frame, closing her eyes. Cello took a few steps toward her.

"It's not right," Cello said quietly, just for her. "Listen to Sil, please."

"I never thought I'd hear you say that," Joanie answered, the words floating on a strange and dark current of humor.

"Please," Cello whispered, wanting to touch her, to squeeze the message into her palm.

Joanie nodded. "I think Letta's right. We can find him probably better than anyone, even if we can't use the Work."

"What does that mean?" Cello asked.

She didn't answer. Locked away behind her unfocused eyes, Cello could see her growing something, an idea.

Letta's and Sil's voices erupted in front of them. They started circling one another, with Letta looking for more objects to throw. Miracle had been pushed away, and ran into a huddle with Emil and Sabina.

"Did you go down there?" Cello asked quietly, looking at Joanie with magnifying-glass intensity.

Joanie nodded. "Mother Joseph said if I come back, she'll shoot me. Sil, too," she said, all calm.

"Do you think the baby's there? You want me to go back and look? I'll be quiet—they'll never see me, I promise."

"I don't know," Joanie answered. "I didn't feel anything while we were there, but now that I'm home, I don't know—it feels like I left him there. She has to have my son. Who else would take him?" She crossed her arms over the window jamb and rested her head on her soft pile of limbs.

"I'll go tonight," Cello said.

"Okay," Joanie replied, her voice slow and mixed with strangeness, like she'd been drugged. "I'm going to stay here for a minute. You can go. I'm fine, really. I just want to think for a while." Cello turned away, trying not to feel wounded by her dismissal. He tried not to remember what it had felt like before her time at the Josephs', when Joanie told him everything.

Letta and Sil had quieted down, and stood close, their whole bodies touching. Cello strained to hear their lowered voices.

"If she knows what Cello and Joanie did the other night, this isn't the end of it," Sil said.

"I know," Letta answered, clinging to Sil as their bodies bent together.

Sabina and the little kids were gone, disappeared either into the woods or into the kids' trailer. Marcela smoked out in the grass. Cello walked over to her, and from there, he could see Sabina's shadow flickering back and forth across the grease-clouded windows of the trailer.

"Want one?" Marcela saluted him with her cigarette.

"Sure," he said. They stood side by side under the blaze of the midday sun. "I'm going out to the Joseph place after dark, and I really think you should come with me."

"Ugh, I knew you were about to say something crazy like that. Who do you think we are? Batman and Robin?" Marcela threw her cigarette butt to the earth and stomped on it vigorously.

"Fine, if not for the baby, aren't you curious about what they do over there?" Cello said, letting the smoke push out and against the soft caverns of his lungs, steadying his breathing. "You've never been to the Josephs' and you might end up living there."

Marcela hung her head, quietly examining her extinguished Grand Prix.

"And think about if we actually find him. This may be the most important thing we ever do," Cello said.

"Please, if this is the most important thing I ever do, kill me."

Marcela sauntered away, and Cello thought over what he remembered about the Joseph place.

What he knew from helping with deliveries wasn't much. Mostly, he'd waited in or by the truck while Sil or Letta got out to negotiate with Mother Joseph. There was one night, though, when he'd seen more. When there was more to see.

That night, it was understood that there might be violence. Letta sent them off, just Sil and Cello alone. Her face was tight, all the other kids asleep in their beds. They'd heard from Mother Joseph earlier in the day—a single, brief phone call. Letta winced into the phone, just nodding, and then, "Okay."

"Josiah's dead," Letta told them once she'd hung up the phone.

"Big Josiah?" Sil had asked, eyebrows arched against his bald pate.

"No." One word, but that's all it took to make Sil grimace and Cello soar. With her husband gone, Joanie would come back to them, back to Cello.

"How'd it happen?" Sil asked.

"I don't really know. Amberly's upset—said Joanie probably did it."

"What do you mean, did it?" Sil asked, agitated. "You mean she killed him?"

"That's what I said," Letta replied evenly. "Amberly put on a trial. For Joanie."

She and Sil looked at each other, and Cello could barely keep still. He wanted to run, to find Joanie, to haul her back.

"You boys'll go get her tonight."

"Is she alright?" Cello asked.

"It doesn't sound like it, honey. Like I said, there was a trial. You go get her, now—quick, before Amberly changes her mind."

A single nod, and they were on their way. Cello knew that dangerous people swarmed the compound, and that most of the wild Joseph cousins were grown men. He knew that if they wanted to fight, they could kill all three of them—him, Sil *and* Joanie. Cello was never foolish about the things that bodies could do.

The truck's headlights bobbed in the dark like two pale fish, swimming ahead. Sil drove, and Cello tapped his foot.

"Jesus, son, quit it! You'll drive us both crazy with that wiggling and waggling."

The lights from the Joseph place were bright smudges in the evening fog. Sil pulled up slowly, and parked in their usual spot—the place they parked when they stopped for trade. Cello got out and felt the sting of the cold night air, and the frozen mud under his feet. It was almost spring, but the nights still felt like true winter. Cello let Sil go ahead, slinking behind and hunching his shoulders in his oversize sweatshirt.

All of the Josephs appeared to be in for the night—strange for a group in mourning. Any death in their network of families meant drinking and fighting, or wailing and laughter. Before a body was burned or buried, it was surrounded with surges of emotional excess. The only burning Cello had ever seen was Sil and Letta's grown daughter's. It had happened when he was small, and all he remembered was the noise—all that wailing, and crying, and singing, and commotion over the body. He'd hidden at the edge of the garden until it was all over, and when Sil finally returned from the compound exhausted and limping, they'd just gone back to work like it had never happened.

This evening was different. Josiah must have been dead for a while. Maybe he was already buried. Sil knocked on the main house front door, respectful. They knew Mother Joseph would be inside.

A thin little boy opened the door, and Cello's heart beat hard. Long, tangled hair hung around his gaunt face. He was one of the tenants' kids. Cello stared at the boy, trying to imagine Emil in his place. It wasn't the first time he wondered if being separated from your parents could be a good thing. Amberly Joseph's overwhelming bulk suddenly filled the door. Her face was pasty and made-up, a strata of smeared eyeliner and mascara ringing her eyes.

"Sorry for your loss, Mother Joseph. We just came for Joanie, and we'll be out of your hair."

"I'm not the keeper of that trash anymore. So don't come up here asking after her," she coughed out at them into the night, horrible and phlegm-flinging.

"Now, now," Sil gentled. "I know you're grieving, but you sure wouldn't have called Letta and had us come all the way out here if Joanie was, well, if she had gone anywhere."

"You're a real genius, aren't you? You heard that?" Mother Joseph called into the belly of the house. "Einstein came to pay his respects."

A tall man, almost as wide as his sister—for there was no mistaking their relationship—met them at the door: Big Josiah. His face was contorted and half-frozen, like a stroke victim on the TV hospital shows.

"What? They came for the widow?" he asked.

"That's right," Sil answered.

"She's out in the shed," said the man. "Grab her quick. Can't vouch that she's still alive. Y'all should've come sooner."

Cello moved away before Sil could stop him. He hadn't seen Joanie since she'd become a Joseph. Mother Joseph talked to Letta sometimes, for practical reasons. Once in a while she'd put Joanie on the phone, but only for a minute, and only with Letta. Cello went from knowing everything about Joanie—how she'd slept and what she ate—to knowing nothing. He was anxious to pull her back, to gather up everything he had missed.

He paced circles around the Josephs' outbuildings looking for a shed. He didn't actually think Joanie would be dead, just hurt and scared. He grimaced into the night; it pained him to think of someone like Joanie being scared. She'd always been the most fearless among them. That sly bravery was what he loved first and most. It was too dark to see much, but the smells of the frigid night were powerful. The scent of cats hung in the air—

their fur, their piss, their very cat-ness. Cello thought to follow the smell, since it was likely that a shed was where they slept.

He heard Sil run up behind him—could tell it was Sil by the pattern of his breaths and the singular jangle of the keys in his pocket. Sil blew a low whistle, and Cello slowed and crouched in the grass.

"Let's make this quick. Mother Joseph is none too pleased with her daughter-in-law."

"What happened?" Cello asked.

"Well, let's see about that when we find Joanie. She's the one we should be asking."

Cello nodded, acknowledging the truth of it. "I think the shed's over there somewhere." He pointed out toward a stand of sappy pines. They walked quietly, a few arm's lengths apart, just so they'd have a better chance of spotting it.

Sil knocked into it first, swearing and tumbling. He shook out his rolled ankle and tapped gently on the door.

"Joanie," he called softly. "It's Sil." He looked over to the boy at his left. "And Cello. We're here to take you home, honey."

There was nothing but the sound of small animals breathing and shuffling around grime with their paws.

Sil pushed against the door, but it was locked—by a looped chain welded shut on the outside. Cello heaved a shoulder against it and the door bent, almost comically, under and around his weight, like some soft cartoon barrier.

"Jesus, Sil, help me, will you?"

They ran at the door together and it buckled under the force. The sound of wood splitting cracked out into the night.

"Easy does it," Sil warned. "We don't want no more trouble here."

"How else are we supposed to get her out?" Cello tried not to shout, but the swell of volume in his throat was already beyond what he could control. "What if she's dead, Sil?" That, he whispered. He didn't want the fullness of the idea out in the air like that, like keeping his worry quiet would make it less likely.

A rustle from the shed's innards turned their heads. Cello put one palm flat against the cracked wood of the door.

"Joanie?" he whispered.

Sil spat onto the ground. A loose metallic clank sounded as the hinges split from the frame. The door rattled and opened onto a shadow, dark even against all of the other darkness.

"I'm not dead," she said. Her voice was exactly the same as it had been when they'd left her with the Josephs, months ago— strong and full.

I love you, Joanie, Cello wanted to say. *Never leave me again.* But he didn't. Instead, he threaded his arm through the narrow opening and reached for her.

"I see you," she said.

Cello pulled back and pried open the door the rest of the way so that Joanie could get out. Sil left his arm out there, too, in case she needed help to steady herself. When she finally had enough space to step out, both of the men had to stop themselves from scooping her up in their arms, anything to hold her up. She was so gaunt Cello thought she might need to be carried. A lurid purple blotch flowered over her shoulder, down her arm and even partway up her neck.

"What did they do to you?" White-hot anger pooled inside of Cello's head.

"Son, don't get worked up. Keep your wits together, alright? We just got to get home in one piece."

Joanie took a few slow steps—she was obviously weak and malnourished, probably dehydrated, too—but she moved with languor, like the pace was deliberate and enjoyable, and not painful or necessary.

All of the anger tearing through Cello's body melted into those familiar feelings for Joanie: pride and desire, and also shame, because she'd ended up like this and he hadn't been able to help her.

Sil and Cello hovered on either side of the rickety girl. They passed through the Joseph property without a sound. Sil lifted

Joanie into the truck, and Cello swung in beside her. He wanted to hold her hand, to hold her entire body. Sil started the truck and let out an audible lungful of air when the engine turned over.

"It's over now," he said.

"For you, maybe," Joanie muttered.

Once they were home, it all fell out of Joanie. She was tucked up in Letta and Sil's trailer, and Marcela fed her canned soup from a mustard-yellow mug. The little kids dozed on the bed around Joanie's feet. Sil waited outside; Cello thought he probably didn't want to hear about it. Letta sat on a stool at the doorway of the bedroom and waited. When Joanie started to talk, it was like she couldn't help herself; the words ran out of her mouth in all of their snarled ugliness. Mother Joseph had treated her like an animal. Josiah had been wretched, but she swore she hadn't killed him. When Letta pressed, Joanie refused to talk about the trial. She'd stopped bleeding, she said, and then went quiet.

Marcela and Letta looked at each other. Even Cello knew what it meant.

"When, Joanie? When did you notice it?" Letta asked.

"Two months, probably. I was hoping it would die. Or maybe I would."

"Just stop that." Analetta's tone was sharp. "Whatever happened, at least you came home with something."

"Nothing I asked for," Joanie muttered.

"I mean it, Joanie. Stop that."

"Will you tell the Josephs?" Marcela asked.

"Have you lost your natural mind, girl? I wouldn't let Mother Joseph get her hands on a *dog* I liked."

"Thanks, Letta," Joanie said through a twisted, caved-in smile.

"You know that's not what I meant." Letta leaned in to inspect Joanie's injured neck and shoulder. "This looks like something I've seen before," she said, squinting at the elaborate pattern of swirling discolored skin. Letta's mouth turned down abruptly. "Amberly seen this? In the light?"

"I don't know." Joanie shook her head. "Probably not."

Letta set a towel filled with ice over the mark and smoothed Joanie's hair back. "Really, honey, what did you do? They aren't *evil* people."

"They aren't?" Cello's voice felt too loud again. He crossed his arms over his chest tightly, trying to stand still.

"Get out of here, Cello," Marcela said.

"This is only for women to talk about," Letta added.

"No, I want Cello to stay."

Cello couldn't be sure Joanie had said it. Maybe all of that longing had sent him spinning into hallucination. Nobody looked at him. "I'm not going anywhere," he whispered down at the peeling laminate floor.

Cello knew that he should be sad for Joanie. And he was—he was sad and angry that others had hurt her, that her body had been insulted in so many ways. But his thrill at her return was a euphoria unlike any feeling he'd ever known. It felt like everything was going exactly right, exactly how it was supposed to go. Even as he watched Joanie's body swell and her moods plummet and darken, he felt that there had never been such perfection in the world. Everything he did, he did more easily.

When Sil made him pack up the truck before the sun was out, it was like flying. The work in the cold, fingers numb with it, shivering out under the weak sunlight in the middle of nowhere—it was paradise as far as Cello was concerned. Because Joanie was back.

Cello sifted through the night he and Sil had taken Joanie home, scanning it for anything that could help him find the baby. He couldn't dip into that memory, though, without feeling flooded with relief. *I want Cello to stay,* she'd said. His impending covert visit to the Joseph place seemed suddenly less risky, backlit as it was by that honeyed recollection. All he wanted was to bring the baby home. All he wanted was for Joanie, for all of them, to come back to themselves.

8

Cello and Marcela set out just as the sun began to drift out of sight behind the ragged mountain skyline. When Cello told Sil he was going back, that he needed to check again, one last time, Sil had only nodded. When Cello and Sil were on the same side of something, Cello could almost see the harmony between them. Sil told them to leave before dark so that they wouldn't have to switch on the truck's headlights. He even suggested they walk part of the way to make sure they weren't seen.

"I didn't agree to walking," Marcela said.

Despite her protestations, Cello parked half a mile out on the unlined access road covered by a dense cluster of pines. He pulled an empty milk crate from the truck bed and carried it along. The night was thick with the sound of insects. It swelled and pulsed around them, and Cello considered the thousands of tiny, brittle lives dipping into and dropping out of the world. He prayed that the baby's life was still lambent among them.

As they walked, Marcela was completely silent. If Cello hadn't known that they'd driven there together, he would have wondered if he imagined her presence beside him. His own feet were clumsy, knocking stones out of place—but nothing, not even the sound of breathing, came from Marcela.

There was no plan, really. They were simply there to observe, to look and listen for anything out of the ordinary. Not that they knew what was ordinary for the Josephs. Not that anything they were doing, or had done, was ordinary. A sagging, chicken-mesh fence laced with barbed wire ran around the perimeter of the property. Cello stomped down into the hip-high trough of the fence segment with his work boot, to give them a little room, and then pushed the empty crate up to it. He hopped up and over it, grimacing at the noise he made when he fell to the other side.

Marcela jumped over after him, and a flare of light spat out around her feet and then instantly disappeared, as though she'd dropped into a temporary, glowing puddle. Cello raised his eyebrows and she shrugged as they moved forward with care.

Cello's thoughts were now on the underfed dogs that patrolled the tall grass. The windows of the main house were still lit ahead of them. Cello pointed farther left, and Marcela nodded, clutching on to a scrap of Cello's shirt. They moved slowly, together, Cello willing Marcela's silence and ease of movement to cloak him, too. They were hunched over, and for a moment Cello wondered if one of the Josephs would mistake them for a beast—a renegade deer or horse—and shoot them. He decided the Josephs would probably shoot at them even if they knew they were people.

The outbuildings were completely dark: black holes in the night. Cello listened. For a moment he thought he heard a cry. Marcela mirrored his pause, then touched him lightly on the shoulder. He looked at her and saw her pointing up, toward a swoop of bats wailing out around one another. He nodded and they moved on to the first outbuilding. It was an abandoned smokehouse. Cello smelled the stench of mold and decaying rodent carcasses. He pressed his hands into the rough, fieldstone wall in front of him, hoping they could set up some kind of base behind it. He motioned to Marcela to stay put, but she shook her head, and followed him inside.

Cello left Marcela by the door. He scanned the low-ceilinged room for movement, for a fresh, living scent, anything. He realized, with a terrible sinking feeling, that if the baby was anywhere—that is, if he were still alive—the only place he could be was in the main house. Not even Mother Joseph would leave the baby in a place like the smokehouse, or the shed where they'd found Joanie all those months ago.

Cello circled back around to Marcela and spoke, but just barely. "We have to check the main house."

He saw the flicker of Marcela's loose hair as she violently shook her head. He leaned back in. "It's okay, you wait here. I'll go." He felt her small, strong fingers pinch a layer of his skin as she grasped his shirt more tightly. He felt, rather than saw, her repeated, vehement refusal. Cello moved toward the doorway, and Marcela followed. Cello paused when he heard the sound of alcohol-slurred voices, and the yelping of a dog.

"What's that, Win, what'd you hear?" Cello couldn't be sure which Joseph the voice belonged to, but lucky for him and Marcela, it sounded like it came from an old one. They could outrun one elderly, drunk Joseph, he thought with a burst of relief, but stiffened again when he considered all of the weapons the Josephs kept on their place. Maybe they'd be lucky. Maybe the old Joseph would be too drunk to aim; but then that noise would lead to other, more able-bodied Josephs giving chase, maybe aiming better. Cello squinted hard, trying to pick out shapes in the night. He couldn't really see around the door, and the squinting made his head ache.

Marcela plucked at his forearm, forcing him to turn toward her. She pressed a nail-bitten finger hard against her mouth, and then tugged on her ear. He saw her eyes, wide as they could open, willing him to understand. She tugged on her ear again, and then mimed rocking a baby in her arms.

Cello nodded. She was right—if the baby was there, maybe the old, drunk Joseph would talk about it. They waited, and the stiffened backs of Cello's leg muscles quivered. Marcela was like nothing, just air behind him.

The old man whistled bright little scraps of songs that Cello didn't know. They waited a long time—long enough for Cello's legs to tingle with numbness, and he knew if they didn't hear something about the baby soon, they'd have to find a way to disappear undetected. The smokehouse stank of decay, and as his eyes adjusted, Cello saw the outline of low piles of debris, studded with the bright outlines of small, linked bones. Mice, or rats, Cello thought—more than one would expect in a space so small. What had happened in this room? he wondered.

Marcela glided toward the ramshackle pattern of bones, circling it. She paused in two places where the chalky outline broke. She crouched down and swiftly replaced the bones that had rolled or shifted out of order. He squinted into the dark, trying to make out whatever pattern she'd seen there. Cello stayed put, shifting his weight from foot to foot, when the old man began to sing to his dog.

The song, if it could be called that, ran from wrong note to wrong note; the singer's broken voice, veined with hundreds of thousands of cigarettes, drove the dog to wailing. Cello saw the flash of the animal's tail, as it whisked in and out of sight. The dog sidestepped away from the man into full view of the deteriorating smokehouse and its missing door. The dog stilled, bristling from end to end. The old man interrupted his song to speak to the dog. "What is it, boy? Possum?"

The dog lunged into the doorway, and Cello and Marcela fell back against the wall. Cello hoped getting up to investigate would be beyond the ancient singer, and was relieved when the old Joseph began the irregular melody, picking up where he left off.

The dog leaped straight toward Marcela, who had clamped a hand over her mouth to stop herself from shouting out. She locked her other arm against her body and Cello kept his stance loose and neutral, balling his fists. They'd grown up outside. Marcela and Cello knew what to do if an animal wanted to hurt them: nothing. Cello kept his gaze down, away from the dog's, and made a low, nonchalant humming sound in his throat, the way he'd heard Sil do it. The dog seemed well-fed, which meant they'd probably be fine, but Cello saw in its form that nervous forward lean, typical of a creature subjected to regular abuse.

"Get out of there!" grumbled the old man. "I'm talking to you." Marcela's eyes squeezed tight, and a pale glow flared out from the pattern of bones, swift as a blink.

In his peripheral vision, Cello saw the dog seize up, as though shot or struck, before he turned around and scampered out. When the dog cleared the doorway, Marcela lunged for Cello, pulling him away from the door.

"Let's go," she hissed.

Cello nodded, but still strained to hear the old man's voice. If they could only wait a little longer, he thought. Marcela prodded him, hitting a bruise left over from Sil's disciplining. Cello jumped a little and kept himself from crying out. He leaned forward, hands in the dirt, and fell onto something. It was about the size of his palm. He lifted the object into the weak light coming through the doorway and saw that he held the case of a turtle's shell. It was not alive—the creature inside had been dead a long time. The shell, though, had been defaced—carved into. Cello traced the grooves and discovered a series of letters roughly scratched into the shell's uneven surface. The muddled letters and strange symbols were illegible, except for a small crawl of undulating, linked semicircles. Cello knew that drawing. He'd seen it drawn into the mud, etched into the kids' trailer wall, permanent-markered onto T-shirts. The pattern was Joanie's sign of protection.

"Okay," he whispered.

They pushed out a solitary half shutter in the smokehouse's back wall and slithered out of the narrow opening.

"What was that?" Cello asked, once they were in the safety of the truck's sight line.

"What was what?" Marcela asked.

"That thing, with the bones. What did you do?" Cello opened the door, illuminating a small patch of night.

Marcela's expression hardened. "I don't know, I just did it. I couldn't help it." She climbed into the truck and crossed her arms, clutching her opposite elbows as though for warmth.

"Whatever it was, I think it saved us." Cello squinted into the night and tried to be grateful that he and Marcela hadn't been hurt or seen. Mostly, though, he was furious—the kind of furious that brought tears to his eyes. They'd found nothing, and he had failed Joanie and her baby again.

Back at the garden, Sil was not surprised by their failure.

"Least you didn't get caught," he said when they returned. Sil—and only Sil—had waited up under the light of a bug lamp.

"I'm going to bed," Marcela said, her face still tight from their errand. She breezed past them into the kids' trailer.

"Don't wake them up, Marcela! Have some decency at this hour," Sil called after her.

"Uh, you're welcome," Marcela said, and slammed the door shut.

"That girl is going to be more of a problem than you and Joanie put together." Sil pointed his burning cigarette squarely at Cello. "Really, y'all didn't find anything?"

Cello shook his head.

"Well, okay." Sil pulled a squashed pack of Grand Prix from his back pocket and passed it to Cello. "Go to bed—we got an early day. I want to take up some of that hybrid in the morning."

"You think it's ready?" Cello asked. "Could use a couple more weeks. Even just one week would do it good."

Sil shrugged. "We'll see. Josephs want a batch. You and Letta are gonna deliver it, okay?"

"If that's what you want." Cello paused, nearly leaving his next question unasked. "What do we do now? About the baby?"

"Well, shit. We just got to keep going like normal, I guess," Sil said. "Letta's right about this, like she always is."

"And is that alright with you?" Cello asked. He tried to keep his voice calm, but his hands trembled, and the Grand Prix between his teeth wouldn't catch the quavering flame.

"No, it's not *alright*," Sil said. "I love that child same as the rest of you. But what else can we do? Can't call the authorities." Sil's voice was pitched high, but he wasn't quite shouting.

"There's no guarantee they'd come here," Cello said as he scratched his neck in the place where it disappeared under his frayed T-shirt collar. "They could still look for him, you know—" he gestured with his cigarette beyond the garden "—out there."

"Course they'll come here! Don't you understand how it works?"

"I'm just worried about him." Cello flushed; maybe it was from anger, maybe embarrassment.

"We should just try to forget him for now," Sil said. The way he said it, it was like the words hadn't come from his own mind. It was like Sil had snatched the thought out of the air before him.

Cello looked away and they didn't say anything else, only letting the night close in around them until it was too much, too heavy. Cello went for a walk and smoked under the clear sky, checking on each of the lush, curling plots. He squinted in the dark at a narrow groove in the grass at the edge of the property line—some unfamiliar track. He couldn't tell if it was human made, or how old it was, but he knew he would investigate it. Anything to find the baby.

9

The sky was lit by a plump, white moon. Joanie swam under its light, crowded with thoughts. The water was too warm—the day had been long and the sun strong. The creek was the temperature of other bodies, of the blood suspended in those bodies. Joanie ducked her head under the surface, and tried to conjure up the winter. She imagined the stripped branches and her nose running from the cold. She tried to place herself anywhere else. On a mountaintop, a pair of heavy boots on her feet, the baby bundled close against her chest. She felt a hysterical gurgle at the base of her throat, and the burn of keeping it silent. Everything had been ruined so quickly.

When Joanie left the Josephs' that winter night a year before, she really believed it was for the last time. That she'd returned to their compound—voluntarily, and ultimately for nothing—hurt. It was her fault now, if whatever dam she'd built against Mother Joseph's influence had disintegrated. Joanie knew the garden wasn't safe for her and the baby. She needed to get away.

Mother Joseph would always be too close, and she would never forget about Joanie, about what she was.

She remembered the first Sunday after Cher's procedure, when Mother Joseph led her into the smokehouse. She'd flicked on a fluorescent strip of overhead lights and illuminated a fireplace wide enough to lie down in. Over it, on a nineteenth-century iron hook and ring, hung an enormous steel pan. Piles of the Vine, prepared by Joanie and her foster siblings' hands—and other hands like theirs over the ten-mile network of farms Mother Joseph reaped from—were stacked beside a wooden trough that had been pushed up against one wall.

"Now," Mother Joseph said, clasping her hands over her belly. "It's the Sabbath so we're not doing real labor today. I'm just giving you the tour."

Joanie nodded, eyeing the bright green tangle of the stacked cuttings.

Her mother-in-law reached for the pile and unraveled one of the plants, holding it up in the fluorescent light like a necklace. Joanie had always known the Vine—she'd tended it since she was a toddler, watching its looping leaves filigree through one another and crawl across the ground, coiled in the grass like a nest or a serpent in repose. She'd watched the enormous brilliant blue blooms teeter up into the sun, and even then, only a little girl, she knew there was real charm in them.

"You know what's in here?" Mother Joseph asked. "Heaven." She snapped the Vine in half, and Joanie gasped at the sound and the fresh scent that wafted between them. Breaking a perfect cutting—harvested from the base of the root to the carefully intact blossom, every drop of sap sealed inside—it was the worst that the kids, or even Letta and Sil, could do. They'd treated each such infraction as a small death, burying the ruined slip of green in its own, individual grave. At the garden, breaking open the Vine roused the kind of guilt Joanie associated with real crime. Mother Joseph, though, didn't look guilty at all. She smiled at Joanie's shock.

"Letta's done a good job with that at least," she said. "Making sure you kids respect it." Mother Joseph let the sap run over her fingers, and Joanie watched the fluid drip into her palm, greener than anything she'd seen in the garden. "Try it," Mother Joseph said, holding a single, sap-coated thumb in front of Joanie's mouth. Joanie didn't know if it was a trick, or another test. Was she supposed to take it, or refuse? She stared into Mother Joseph's small, dark eyes and saw no clues there. Joanie was trapped, but also beguiled. She swore the verdant liquid beckoned to her, lured her tongue closer, until she felt the rasp of Mother Joseph's calloused finger in her mouth.

At first, Joanie was startled by the bright, sweet rush of juice. Her heart beat like an engine turning over in her chest—it was not only the ferocity she noticed, but also the thrill of a beginning and the movement that followed. Joanie was gathered up in a near-physical motion where everything was soft, warm and floating. The world around her was not blurred, though. It became an unblemished, sharper version of itself. She watched Mother Joseph's mouth move quickly, nearly out of sync with the words she spoke.

"You never knew, did you?" she asked. Joanie couldn't tell if she was disappointed or pleased. She held a hand out and clutched her mother-in-law's upper arm, to steady herself. "Easy now," Mother Joseph said. "The harvest from Letta's is always the strongest." She detached herself from Joanie's grip and moved toward the trough.

"I don't know if Letta told you, but our grandmother found the Vine of Heaven when she was a girl. She ran and told her mama about it. Great-grandmother Joseph had never seen anything like it, and she knew this land like the back of her hand." Mother Joseph plucked cutting after cutting from the pile and tossed it in the trough. "It's hard to grow, but that's one thing you do know. And it's not like anything else. It only grows on Joseph land, so our family, and only our family, is responsible for it—time you knew that. Yes, through the growing, but also the Work. What you girls do with Letta is just the beginning. This plant is our partner, a member of our family, too."

Joanie stared at the flashing leaves that seemed nearly alive, winding over and around each other in the trough. "What do you do with it all?"

"We sell it, girl." Mother Joseph chuckled that full-body laugh. "Family takes care of each other. But I bet you already knew that much, too." When the trough was almost full of perfectly sealed stalks, Mother Joseph pulled up on a wooden lever. The trough contracted, and Joanie thought it looked as alive as the plants within it. It crunched down the layers of Vine, pressing the juice out. Mother Joseph pulled out a section of wood, a disguised, narrow channel, and directed the extracted liquid to the pan in the fireplace. She switched on the fire, an industrial kitchen-size natural gas flame. The green liquid began to bubble, and as it heated, the scent changed from organic and grassy to sharply mineral. Joanie shook her head clear of the smell, though the taste of the fresh sap remained in the back of her throat.

"How? Where do you sell it?"

"You think I'm going to tell you all my secrets? For now, I want you in here, anytime we get a delivery," Mother Joseph said, switching off the flame.

"Why me?" Joanie asked, the words unspooling from her throat in an amber swirl.

"'Cause you're a real Joseph now—it's your responsibility, too. This is one of the most dangerous parts, adding the heat," Mother Joseph said. "You heat it too much, and it's ruined. You don't get it hot enough, and, well, that's another story."

"Is this what the tenants buy off you?" Joanie asked. She knew the question would make Mother Joseph angry—she knew they were never supposed to ask about the tenants. Whatever Mother Joseph did to adulterate the sap in that smokehouse was a perversion of the Vine's true power. Joanie had always known that Mother Joseph's greed and not the Vine itself destroyed the tenants and others like them. She inhaled the fumes of transformation from the divine to the basely narcotic, and understood that her mother-in-law bore the shame of that greed, and hated to be reminded of how she had contorted the Vine to serve only herself.

Mother Joseph let loose a thick laugh. "You sure are a ballsy one, I'll give you that. How about you don't worry yourself about what the tenants buy off me? Y'all are so interested in the tenants!"

"Who else is interested in them?" Joanie asked.

Mother Joseph abruptly fell silent, like a fan switched off. Her arm was a blur, but Joanie knew she'd been struck. It didn't hurt; the Vine seemed to have changed the way her body was feeling things, but she tasted blood.

"Maybe you should just pay attention to what I'm showing you, miss." Mother Joseph held her sap-coated hands in a prim clasp at her waist. "Repeat what I told you."

"Put the cuttings in here." Joanie pointed to the trough. "Get out the juice and then heat it up till the smell changes."

Mother Joseph nodded. "That's right. And you put all the cooked juice in here." She opened a narrow door made of a few roughly nailed-together rotting planks of wood. Behind it was a polished steel tank, with a small hatch built into the side. Joanie wondered why her new job involved so many layers of camouflage in the ancient smokehouse, but clenched her jaw closed against the question.

"Pour it from the pan right in here?" Joanie asked, fiddling with the hatch's silver handle. "When it's hot?"

"Yes! Lord, you can be simple, child." Mother Joseph slapped

Joanie's hand down, and used the hem of her housedress to rub the handle free of fingerprints.

"Then what?" Joanie asked.

"Don't worry about 'then what,' worry about right now. You do alright, I'll show you what comes next."

"How long exactly do I cook it for? Am I just supposed to leave it in the tank? What do I do when it's full?" Joanie tried to swallow down the last traces of sap, sucking it out of the little pocks in her molars. She felt trapped by it—after that initial rush of pleasure, it made her throat itch. She coughed, hoping it would help. Mother Joseph laughed and smacked her on the back.

"I know you didn't ask Analetta this many questions. She never liked that! When we were kids, she'd rather bite her own tongue off than answer anybody's questions. One more thing, about Josiah's medicine." Mother Joseph paused to bite off a hangnail. Josiah had always been sickly—he'd been born too early. After the wedding, her mother-in-law had flashed the yellowed photos of his withered, newborn body in front of Joanie to prove it.

Mother Joseph spat the sliver of nail on the smokehouse floor and pulled a brown glass bottle from the pocket of her dress. She pressed it into Joanie's hand, but kept her eyes away from Joanie's face. "Since you're Josiah's wife now, you make sure he gets his medicine every day. To keep him strong and healthy," she said. In the dim light of their musty bedroom, Joanie had watched her new husband swallow down the daily doses his mother administered. She'd thought then, maybe it was some kind of vitamin. She understood, now, in the clearer light of the smokehouse, that the medicine he took morning and night was the Vine's green sap.

"You can get it yourself, in here—when you run out. Make sure you only give him the fresh, not the cooked," Mother Joseph said, not quite looking Joanie in the eye. "I don't want to hear you told Josiah about where you got it, neither. The boy doesn't have self-control. You're responsible for him now, too."

Mother Joseph never showed Joanie what came next, though. She kept Joanie in the smokehouse, blindly working that one step, over and over. Joanie was meant to be a babysitter: a babysitter for Josiah and a babysitter for the Vine press. After weeks of her new life's routine—of hunching over the trough and the boiling pans of sap, waiting for the scent to change, of Josiah trying to get her pregnant, of dodging the ravenous eyes of the other Josephs on the compound, of ignoring the tenants haunting their side of the gate—Joanie got angry. She didn't gain anything from this marriage—not the power she thought was coming to her, not even the chaotic but occasionally soothing family life she'd had at the garden. She was wasted there, in the cramped, hot smokehouse, and she hated it. The Vine seemed to seethe with her in encouragement and solidarity. Its bright green had the urgency of a traffic light, pushing her toward action like a palm at her back.

She was so angry that one morning she refused to give Josiah his medicine. Josiah's dose the evening before had been the last in the bottle, and Joanie had not refilled it.

"Where is it?" he asked, sitting up in bed. Joanie averted her eyes from the sprinkle of acne over his widening, hairy gut. She pushed away the memory of Josiah's scabrous belly slapping against her back.

"It's empty," she said as she pulled a faded, lavender shirt over her head.

"You gonna get more?" Josiah asked.

"Nope." Joanie tossed the empty bottle onto the stained quilt.

"You have to get more," he whispered. "I can't get out of bed if I don't get it."

"Then I guess you know where you'll be all day." Joanie combed her fingers through her hair and turned to leave their room, but looked back when she heard a thud from the bed.

Josiah rolled and kicked at the blankets, and then the wall, finally falling to the floor in a sweaty, bulbous heap.

"Mama'll get it for me. And then she'll whip you."

"Yeah, no. I don't think she will. It's not up to her anymore if you get it or not." Joanie pulled her hair into a bun off her neck, anticipating hours of sweating over the fire. "It's up to *me*."

"Why are you being a bitch about this?" he moaned. "I need my medicine."

"Josiah, it's not complicated. You give me something, and I'll get you what you want."

Josiah stilled and looked up at her from the floor. "What do you mean?"

"I mean," Joanie said, kicking his flopped open thigh out of her path to the door, "tell me something I don't know. No." She bent at the waist and squinted down into his pasty, perspiring face. "Show me something." If Joanie could see the full, closed circuit of Mother Joseph's operations, then maybe one day she could take it over—or dismantle it.

Josiah let her into the barn that night, flicking a flashlight's beam around the perimeter of the open space to make sure they were alone. She could smell the clamminess of his skin from where she stood.

"If somebody sees us, Mama'll kill you," he said. His hands trembled after his enforced day of abstinence, and he nearly dropped the flashlight.

Joanie shrugged. "If somebody sees us, we'll tell them we're fucking." She plucked the flashlight out of his hands and left him at the door. Two stainless-steel tanks stood in the center of the room. Joanie walked around each one, looking for markings, but saw nothing. She was sure, though, that the green sap she extracted in the smokehouse was being transported here. Cardboard boxes were stacked on either side of the room. One stack looked empty, and the other towered with boxes that were already taped shut.

Joanie moved the flashlight to her armpit and illuminated the seal. She plucked an end of tape up and peeled the strip back. Josiah yelped at the scraping sound.

"Hush up and come hold this," Joanie whispered. Josiah shuffled toward her and held the light as she opened the cardboard flaps. Inside, the box was filled with row after row of tiny brown glass bottles. Joanie picked one out and held it up in the light.

"You can't do that—you didn't say you were going to take anything," Josiah whimpered.

Joanie turned to face him in the dull glow of the sagging flashlight. "What is this?" she asked. "Is it the juice from the Vine?"

"I don't know," Josiah said, trying to hand back the flashlight.

"Well?" She threw the bottle at him and he barely caught it. "Why were you bitching about it all day? You could've come in here by yourself and got it anytime. I don't get why you're still sick."

Josiah rolled his eyes involuntarily. "No, just look at the bottle," he insisted.

Joanie snatched back the flashlight and trained it on the container. It was a modest, four-ounce round bottle, all very ordinary. The label, though, was a surprise.

"Where's she selling these?" Joanie asked.

"Catalogs, mainly. Stores where rich people shop. Places you go for vitamins," Josiah said. "Now you gonna help me?"

"Catalogs?"

"Yeah, like the natural foods ones, the ones yuppies get," Josiah said, scratching at the front of his throat.

"Who's buying it?"

"I don't know, people!"

"How much do they pay for it?"

"I don't know—a lot! Come on, Joanie, I showed you—you promised me."

"Yeah, okay," Joanie said, slipping the bottle into the waistband of her pants. "Close that box, then I'll take care of you."

In their room, Josiah was spirited into a heavy sleep. Whatever else skipping a dose had done to him, eventually getting his spoonful of jade liquid turned him into a snoring, unmoving mass. Joanie switched on the lamp beside the bed and sneaked the bottle out of where she'd hidden it, in one of her shoes under the bed. She knew she'd have to get rid of it soon, but wanted to make sure she understood what she'd seen in the barn.

The label was simple—across the front in bold, gold capital letters it spelled HELEN'S CORDIAL. Underneath ran a thin line of italics: *Our elixir made from an old family recipe with organic ingredients to improve vitality, fertility, appetite, aches and pains, and speed weight loss.* The back of the label listed the ingredients, nothing else: water, sugar, natural flavors. She untwisted the black plastic cap, and poured a drop of liquid onto a fingertip. It wasn't the near-glowing green, syrupy substance she had come to know so well at work in the smokehouse. It was the color and consistency of black coffee. She licked the elixir from her skin, and tasted nothing of the transcendent, grassy sweetness of fresh Vine extract. It was bitter, like the concentrated herbal tea Letta brewed for the kids when they got sick.

Mother Joseph had severely diluted the sap, but Joanie understood that it was still there—she could hear it humming through the glass bottle. The effects of the Vine had to be mild enough to keep the Josephs from suspicion, but Joanie knew that the plant's seductive magic still twinkled in the murky brown liquid. She wondered exactly how much these people were paying for it, where the money was going and how much more there was. If she could intercept it somehow, both the lives she'd known—sweating in the sun at the garden and sweating over the fire in the smokehouse—could be over. Joanie didn't know what next life, exactly, she would choose, but she knew it wouldn't involve sweating for anybody else.

She hadn't known then that she would become pregnant. That the baby would change everything. Living at the garden after he was born had felt more like a dream than anything else. Joanie knew they couldn't stay there forever, but she hadn't felt strong enough to move along. The half-formed plan she roped Cello into was proof that she was still not herself, that her good sense had been overtaken by desperation. Joanie pedaled at the water, willing the warm river to restore some of her old self.

She hadn't done any real worship since her return home, and she wondered if her weakness came from that arrested practice. Joanie flipped onto her back, allowing the fluid to fill all of the space around her, leaving only her nose, mouth and eyes open to the air. She reached out through the water, through the soil, through all of the stones and roots in the way, to the Vine and asked a question: *Can you help me?* She kept thinking about what Letta had said, that the Work couldn't protect people; it could only protect the Vine. But she wondered, with the night sky breathing down on her, if she could bend the worship to help her son. As she floated, she held the question lightly in her mind, waiting with her water-filled ears. Joanie had always believed she and the Vine were connected, that the Vine's power favored her over anyone else—but after her failed attempt at escape, she wasn't sure.

She'd been wrong to think Mother Joseph could remain ignorant of her grandson's existence. Then there was the enormous and sickening chance that Mother Joseph knew about the attempted theft, too. Joanie chased the thought away by ducking her head under the tepid water. If life at the Josephs' had been bad for her, it would be worse for her son. She didn't want Mother Joseph's dark influence over his rapidly growing brain. She didn't want his wide, newborn eyes to ever see what Mother

Joseph offered. Joanie didn't want her child to see the inside of that house, and hoped, if he was there, that she could find him before he could remember anything about it. She prayed in the river, believing the water would amplify her plea. *Help me*, she begged, tugging insistently, experimentally, at her connection with the Vine. *Help me get him back*.

She couldn't think about the Joseph house without thinking of the trial. It was the day they meant to bury Josiah's body, and the house rumbled with guests who'd come to attend the burial. Mother Joseph decided to hold the trial the same day, to have as many family members in attendance as she could.

Joanie remembered how it felt, that many-months-ago morning, when she was tied to a straight-backed chair in the main house's front room. She remembered the weight of the serpent box in her lap, the way it was still warm from the heat lamps in the cellar. The witnesses—ten at least, Mother Joseph had been adamant—staggered around the chair. Some, barely awake after the funeral festivities, others still in the grip of the Joseph family's darker brand of refreshments.

Mother Joseph was fully untethered and under the Vine's influence. Of all of the guests, she was the farthest away from herself, and from her good sense. Joanie had significantly weakened by then, denied food and water. A cleansing, Mother Joseph explained, her grief-razed face split open into something too terrible to be a face. Harlan wrapped the cord around Joanie's waist, so her hands would be free. This was the way they'd always done it. In all serious family matters, particularly when crimes were committed inside the family, guilt or innocence was determined by serpent.

Josiah had been the one who explained to Joanie the origin of the serpent, the evolution of the Work and the beginning of the family's unusual brand of worship. Before Great-grandmother Joseph's vision, the women in the family had done the Work without knowing it—somehow compelled by the Vine to give it exactly what it needed. They tended the very first grove like women under a spell. It wasn't until the vision that everything began to make sense.

Great-grandmother Joseph had been a moderate woman. It wasn't common for hallucinations to accompany a taste from the Vine of Heaven, at least none that a person could clearly remember. The old woman's vision came to her after a drowning, after a different burial, decades before.

Great-grandmother Joseph ladled the sap into her mouth, more than she usually took, smacking her decaying gums and yellowed teeth as it went down. She was in her sorrow, Josiah had explained, that's why she'd taken so much. She lay in the front room of the house, the same place Joanie waited for the serpent's justice, as though dead herself. Mother Joseph was a girl then, but she remembered it and passed the story down. She remembered Great-grandmother Joseph's labored breathing and cold, still figure laid out on the floor for a full day. She woke up, gasping, like a body pulled from the water and revived. The old woman drew across the skin of her forearm, a wavy line with her finger, over and over.

When speech returned to her, she tried to explain—a dream of a garden, gold and green, the Vine of Heaven twisting and glowing under a clear day. A clap of thunder pulsed through the vision. The vines moved quickly, the stems and leaves braiding into a sinewy coil, the bright blue blossoms sprouting fangs and tongues. The garden filled with snakes, slinking and hissing. Great-grandmother Joseph didn't recount the story with fear. The serpents were benign, benevolent even. Every whisk of their jade bodies against her skin was a gentle caress. Josiah had held a hand to his cheek, miming the way his mother had shown him.

It was this vision that elevated their simple tending, to what Great-grandmother Joseph called the worship. For decades, the Josephs fostered this connection between the Vine and its reptilian counterpart by keeping a serpent in the cellar of the main house. It was a spiritual creature, Josiah explained; it provided a charge of gratitude. Keeping a serpent in the earth along with the growing Vine drew more power into the crop. And, when the time came, Mother Joseph used the serpent to mete out justice, the same way her ancestors had.

In the light of eleven in the morning, Joanie waited, slumped in her seat. She stayed still, too weary to struggle against the cords that bound her. Mother Joseph's black dress gapped down the front where several buttons had come undone, and as she leaned over the chair, Joanie saw the clot of gold chains that had formed between her wrinkled breasts.

"Well," her mother-in-law slurred. "Take it up." The woman's pupils were two enormous blots. Joanie understood, but her body was slow to comply. She contemplated her wrists, so thin and useless. She doubted she could even open the box.

"Hello?" Mother Joseph yelled, her face close to Joanie's. "I said, take it up!"

"She doesn't look so good, Amberly. Maybe give her a sip of water," Big Josiah, her brother and one of the witnesses, said.

"Shut your fool mouth, Josiah!" Mother Joseph flung her body back, rising up on her toes, her arms straight up in the air. She looked more like a black bear than a human.

Mother Joseph's massive body contracted around Joanie again, so close she was like the white to Joanie's yolk. The inappropriate observation startled Joanie into a sudden smile. At that, Mother Joseph drew in a breath. "A real-life demon, you," she said. "Take. It. Up." Mother Joseph thumped a heavy hand on the box with each word. Joanie felt the snake's frantic movement inside.

Joanie moved her hands to the box's screen lid, and lifted it. The creature lay coiled inside, golden as an autumn leaf. Joanie marveled at the copperhead's circular, glinting beauty.

"What did I say?" Mother Joseph screamed from the back of her throat.

Joanie dipped her hands into the box, and scooped up the animal. She didn't understand it then, but she began to laugh. It wasn't hysterical, half-sobbing laughter that poured from her throat. It was joyful, as though it came from someone else, and she delighted in the sound of it coming out of her mouth. The snake's winding body was so warm, and it moved over her hands and around her forearms like it knew her. She felt a reassuring, almost tangible tug from the Vine, where it lay stacked in the smokehouse only yards away. Joanie stared down and shook with laughter. Holding the creature was like dipping her hands into some strange water, the way the golden body rippled and swam across her skin. Joanie's laughter was the only sound in the front room.

When she looked up, to see if she hadn't just imagined it, to see if maybe she really was alone, Joanie saw only Mother Joseph's face. What Joanie saw there wasn't anger—it was terror. Joanie laughed even louder, with honest delight, as the snake wound away from her hands and up to her face. The serpent's flat little head nuzzled her chin, and Joanie dipped her face forward with affection.

"How much longer, Amberly?" Big Josiah said. She followed the serpent, moving her head as languidly as the copperhead, as though they were two halves of the same creature.

"Till I say stop!" Mother Joseph snapped, but kept her distance. Joanie felt a sudden coolness around her. She wasn't sure if the snake had cooled, or if Mother Joseph and the other witnesses had backed away, opening a halo of space around the chair. Joanie leaned forward and into the plastic cord, toward the serpent.

"This girl ain't right, Amberly, look at her. Just take a knife to her if you're that upset."

Mother Joseph flashed into Joanie's line of sight, her hands hovering over the animal, as though willing it to strike out at Joanie.

"No, I'm doing this the right way," Mother Joseph said. "How we've always done it."

Joanie heard their voices like a language she didn't know— they were speaking too slowly, opening their mouths too much. She heard an argument grow around where she sat, but it felt far away. A fresh, grassy scent hung in the air, as though the animal had been perfumed. The serpent coiled around her upper arm and shoulder, pressing into the side of her head. She allowed it to push her, leaning so far down the chair began to rock forward. Joanie heard the voices, louder now, and the serpent box as it clattered to the floor. She leaned over, more, and slid her tied feet through the chair legs, letting herself fall to the floor— as that seemed to be the copperhead's intention.

When the snake finally bit her, it was only once, on the shoulder. She heard Mother Joseph whoop, calling in more witnesses, the room suddenly hot and filled. Joanie couldn't see the snake anymore. She couldn't see anything. She tried to blink the room into focus, but every sweep of her eyelids seemed to worsen the blur. Her body was being moved, she didn't know by who. When she was finally flung down, after an endless, lurching journey, it was in a place with a familiar smell. Joanie rubbed her cheek against the ground, and knew it to be the earth and not wood or concrete. She was in the toolshed, she thought, the one behind the crumbling old smokehouse. The place where she had gotten the pliers the first time Mother Joseph had commanded her to a task.

Joanie knew she was going to vomit. She crawled until she could get a hand up on a wall and lifted herself to her knees. A bucket, she thought, or at least a corner. But there was nothing to really come up, since they'd kept food and water from her. She heaved out an unceasing, acidic dribble until she stopped remembering things.

Joanie woke up in the night to the quiet of the compound. She didn't know what day it was, only that she was cold, that the guests from the burial must have gone home and that she was supposed to be dead. So, she stayed quiet, pretending to be dead.

It had hurt to go back to that house.

Joanie swam through the heat of the creek, and swore her baby would never know life as a Joseph. If her baby was alive, somewhere, she'd get him back. And if he wasn't alive on this earth, she would still find him. He was something other to her than a child. Something more, something stranger. Through the months of corrosion, through her strangling pregnancy, Joanie had fought to be a mother. Her body had fought for it. And when the baby was born, and drank from her, her mind fought to be a mother, too. All of those first, soft brushes of something so new, the times she held that fresh, sleeping creature in the crook of her elbow and he practically glowed—Joanie had felt something growing. The times she had rested a hand on his tiny chest and felt the astounding flicker of his heartbeat in her palm, she'd been terrified. Joanie believed these moments with her son were openings into something else, a portal to a different life.

A flash of coolness glanced through the water, like dropping a handful of ice cubes into a glass. Gently, the Vine tapped back a message to her through the lapping stream. It was a message of seduction, as obvious as opening a window. Mother Joseph, the compound, the serpent's bite, even the nursing of her baby—they had all weakened her. If Joanie repaired herself and renewed her devotion to the Vine, she could grow stronger than Mother Joseph—stronger than anyone. A person like that could recover anything she'd lost. A person like that could make something new.

Joanie tested this idea, beneath the slow caress of the river. She willed each ripple of water to press what she was missing back into her, to restore the balance in her blood and bones and muscle. She understood that she had not been paying attention, dream walking through her second life at the garden. She had allowed her cracks to widen. She had allowed herself to become brittle and drained, drained of milk and empty, her monthly bleeding suspended since the birth. The water crept back in through each tiny skin cell, and she understood, as clearly as a whisper in her ear, that the restoration of these powerful fluids would please the Vine, and make her a sound vessel for the worship.

Joanie's time as a Joseph had marked her, maybe it had even marked her baby. The only way to keep them both safe—to restore them both—was to fill her body and mind with all of its dormant potential: to triumph over and erase Mother Joseph. Joanie tilted her head back, submerging her hair in the water, her body covered in the dark liquid, drinking it in.

10

C ello followed the strange groove in the grass. He couldn't tell in the dark, but it was too even and uniform to be a track made of footprints. It seemed more like the work of a single wheel. Cello conjured an image of an invader, one of the desperate tenants from the Joseph place maybe, bundling the baby into a wheelbarrow and tearing him away in the night. It couldn't be a coincidence, the baby's disappearance coordinating so perfectly with the appearance of this alien path.

Cello willed the track to cross a fresh, muddy place, so he could see more clearly who or what it was that had trespassed, but it faded out, disappearing in the layers of brambles that separated the garden from the unused access road. Cello doubled back, scanning the grass for any sign of the intruder—maybe he'd dropped something, or left a set of footprints Cello had missed. Even though it was dark, the moon was bright enough for him to spot anything obvious. An unusual sound broke the stillness of the night, interrupting Cello's search.

It was the sound of a body in water. He turned to follow it, heading for the same bulge in the creek where the kids swam. He approached silently, barely moving through the lush sprays of green brush bordering the riverbank. He shuddered, imagining the baby falling through the murky water. Had the kidnapper done worse than steal the child? Was the thief—perhaps murderer—still there?

Cello searched the ground for fallen tree limbs or stones, anything that could be used as a weapon against whatever it was swimming in the river. He crouched low, feeling through the grass for any hard, heavy object. A flash of an arm glistened, caught in the bright moonlight. Cello froze, because it was an arm he knew—it belonged to Joanie. He stood and put his hands to his face, breathing in the scent of late-summer grass, half dried out by the sun, half violently growing. He shook his head, trying to separate the sinister thoughts of drowning, and kidnappers with wheelbarrows, from his—their—Joanie.

"Joanie? Is that you?" He stood still, apart, an almost tangible veil of seclusion suspended between them.

"It's me," she replied, her voice layered over with the kiss of water on skin.

"You alright?" He hung his head and nearly turned his back to the river, feeling compelled to give her some bit of privacy.

"Go home, Cello. I'm fine." He tried to respond, but his mouth hung heavy on his face.

"Be careful," he said, so soft he was sure she couldn't hear it. Cello walked away, toward home and the kids' trailer. An uneasiness coursed through him, and Cello tried to think of something else, about the plot he'd prepared, or Miracle's perseverance as she'd looked for the baby, but his mind would not be cleared.

The next day, nobody spoke about the baby. They all knew not to mention that they were one less, but even outside of this loss, Letta was not herself. Her nastiness, her joking affection, all of it was blunted by the sudden change in their number. She sent them off to work in the morning half-heartedly, and with an uncharacteristic flash of kindness. "Let the little kids come back at noon for lunch. Sabina, you take them. I don't want anybody wandering off. I'll let Joanie sleep till then, and send her back out with y'all."

Cello didn't ask her why Joanie had been up so late, knowing that he wouldn't get an answer. He didn't ask Sil any questions, either.

Sil, too, worked as though he were in a trance, barely speaking. Sil's usual, cheerful pedantry, and his running commentary on "the way things are done," were suspended. It left the air around them silent. The bees that flickered around their hands and mouths, and the hollow calls of the sparrows, were eerie in Sil's stern, focused quiet.

When Emil and Miracle noticed they could get away with it, they ran to the shade of a set of beech trees and raced between them. Even their little child shrieks didn't stir Sil, wherever he was. No one could pay attention. Cello understood that Sil's silence was easier to endure than his anger, and was happy to keep silent, too. Marcela, though, wanted to talk. He could see that her forehead creased whenever she stooped closest to the earth, like the gravity there was pulling together all of her thoughts into a denser and greater mass.

Cello and Marcela harvested the elongated, sealed stems from the Vine with efficient, practiced slices of their utility knives. As they worked, Cello could feel the conversation they were going to have, hanging between them like the humidity.

"The Josephs took him, right? Don't you think? We just didn't see him, that's all." Marcela stopped sweeping her fingers over the feathery young plants. Sabina had quit working, too, and hovered nervously near her sister.

Cello shrugged, his eyes still slightly unfocused, searching for more stems ready to be cut. "I don't know." He closed his mouth, keeping the strange tracks—and Joanie's oddness in the water—safely inside of his head.

"They wouldn't hurt him, right? He's only a baby," Marcela said.

"Since when do you care?" Cello knew it sounded severe, but Marcela's chatter made him impatient.

"Of course I care! Jesus, Cello, how could you say that? Didn't I risk my ass going out to the Joseph place in the middle of the night with you?" Marcela stamped her feet, but just barely. The long grass at the edge of the plot bogged her ankles down. Cello knew it would have to be cut down soon with a hand scythe. The space between plots here was too narrow for machines. They turned toward Sil at the same time expecting some sort of scolding, but he hadn't heard them—he kept on working. Sabina reached for her sister's hand, and raised her eyebrows at Cello.

"No, you're probably right," Cello said, his voice spackled tight with guilt. He knew he should tell someone about what he'd seen, about the strange track, but he couldn't do it. "If they took him, they wouldn't hurt him. I mean, especially if they figured out the baby was Josiah's," he murmured to Marcela weakly.

"Well, what else would they think? That it's yours?" Marcela was trying to hurt him, he could tell. Just like Letta.

"She doesn't mean that," Sabina said quickly.

"I don't understand. Why can't she just call Mother Joseph?" Marcela's voice was higher and louder than usual.

"She who?" Cello asked.

"It doesn't even matter who! Letta, Joanie, Miracle, I don't know! Just someone." She kicked at a clump of curled thistle.

"You?" Cello asked. He stood up straight and looked at Marcela. Her eyes were dark, like Joanie's, but they weren't alike in any other way. Marcela's hair was violently curly; even tied back the way it was, Cello could see the defined shape of each twist of hair. Her eyebrows were thick and dark, giving her expressions their own unique and urgent punctuation.

"Yeah, me," she muttered. "I found out how useless we both are last night." Sabina rubbed her sister's back, but Marcela shook her off.

"Well, Marcela," Cello began. "If they didn't take him, us calling up and saying, 'Hey, did y'all steal Joanie's kid?' is going to make them ask where that baby came from. Letta's right about that at least. If they don't know about Junior, we don't want to tell them."

"That is enough," Sil said, his voice thin, not quite right. "Just leave it alone. None of this is up to us." He adjusted the worn blue baseball cap on his head, and leaned back down into the garden. "Come on, now—get to work."

Cello figured Sil was probably right, at least until he could get a better look at the foreign tracks and determine their origin.

Cello did leave it alone, but only until the messages began. The first one came four days later, on Miracle's birthday.

11

It happened early in the morning. A padded mailing envelope sat in the grass in front of the kids' trailer, soggy with dew. Cello opened the door and stepped out toward the melting cardboard.

"Don't touch it." Letta was already there, leaning over the delivery, smoking.

"Maybe it's garbage," Cello said.

"It's not garbage. It's from *them*."

Cello and Letta both understood *them* to be the Josephs, or whoever it was capable of stealing a baby. Them.

"On Miracle's birthday, too." Letta shook her head and smoke streamed from her nostrils. "Are the kids still asleep? Is Joanie?"

"Yeah," Cello said, and crouched over the lumpy package. "You going to open it?"

"I'm not touching it. Fingerprints."

"So? You don't want to call the cops," Cello said, prodding the bundle with his shoe.

"No shit, Sherlock, but sooner or later, somebody's gonna

come snooping, maybe ten, twenty years from now. I don't want my DNA anywhere near that thing."

"You watch too much TV, Letta." Cello picked up the envelope and peeled away the seal at the top.

"Well?" She leaned in close, her nose practically touching the Bubble Wrap innards.

Cello reached deep inside and withdrew a single sheet of lined, yellow paper. It was taped to something—a plain, white envelope.

"Go on," Letta said, lighting a fresh cigarette off the old one. Cello opened the package and they both winced and turned away at the same time. The envelope was filled with nail clippings—tiny, miniscule, nearly translucent nail clippings. They had congealed in a loose, spiky clump at the bottom of the paper envelope.

Letta put a hand to her mouth. Cello turned the yellow sheet of paper over, and they read the note together. It was a few lines, scrawled in blue ink, in looping—almost childish—oversize cursive.

Leave $100 at the Stuckey's on Route 9. Put it in this envelope and stick it behind the Crown Light sign in front of the dumpsters. If you don't, somebody's getting hurt.

"It's a prank," Letta said.

"What if it's not?" Cello asked. "How could it be a prank? Nobody knows the baby's missing except us."

"Even if it's not, you aren't supposed to negotiate with these people. Everybody knows that."

"We should call someone," Cello said, turning the envelope over, tucking the flap inside and hiding away those tiny slivers of baby fingernails.

"Who should we call?" Letta took an especially deep drag and blew the smoke back around them, like she was trying to obscure what they'd found. "I want you to throw that away, and I don't want you running your mouth about any of this, neither. I don't need Joanie in more of a mope than she's already in." Letta turned her back to Cello—and the package—but didn't move away. "Do it now," she said.

Cello knew Letta wasn't heartless. He knew that she really had cared for the baby, and that she would worry about the package and its contents. But life at the garden wasn't like life anywhere else; it didn't come with the same protection others had.

He stuffed the envelope in his back pocket and shaded his eyes against the white light of the cloudy, already warm morning. This was something he could do, find a hundred dollars—he knew he would find it, even if he had to steal it, even if he had to leave the garden to do it. If all he could do was put money behind a dumpster at the Stuckey's, then he would do it, happily. He only had to decide if he'd do it alone, or ask Marcela or Sil for help.

Sil and the kids lounged under a chestnut tree eating the birthday lunch. Miracle smiled shyly into her peanut butter sandwich when she saw Cello.

"See, I told you he'd be here in time," Sil said as Cello stooped over Miracle to hug her little shoulders.

"Happy birthday," Cello said, straightening the little girl's skewed ponytail.

"You ready, Marcela?" Sil asked.

Marcela sat a little behind them, in the deepest shade of the tree, her body curled, hiding something.

"Happy birthday to you," Sabina began, her voice the best and strongest. Marcela maneuvered a cardboard box into the middle of their picnic. In it, a rosette-speckled, store-bought cake bristled with candles. They all sang, even Cello. Miracle was flushed, and grinned wide as she blew out the candles. Marcela sliced up the cake, and Sabina handed it around. No one cared they didn't have plates; they just ate from their hands.

The smell of sugar and melted wax mingling in the air, and all the smiling, made Cello almost forget the gruesome souvenir in his back pocket.

"Fancy," Cello said, pointing at the cake. "Where'd you get it?"

"Store on Route 9." Sil beamed as the kids giggled and licked icing from their hands.

"What?" Cello was chilled.

"The Stuckey's on Route 9. Are you deaf, son?" Sil smacked the back of Cello's head. Hard, but still playful. "Sabina picked it out, though. Ain't it a beauty?"

Cello nodded, stunned, and shivered out from under Sil's reach. "I'm real hot—I'll go wash up in the creek while y'all eat."

"Well, hurry back, Jesus. You'd think we were running a four-star hotel. Take your swim before lunch," Sil said in an attempt at a British accent, miming a monocle over one eye, the can of Crown Light dangling from his fingers precariously.

"Yeah, just got too much sun. Happy birthday, Miracle." Cello started off toward the strip of river that wound through the property.

"Get back here right after!" Sil called. "You're making the run to the Josephs' today."

Cello froze. "Letta know about that?" He hoped none of the birthday celebrants could hear his alarm.

"Oh, sure," Sil drawled. "Letta knows all, ain't that right, kids?"

Cello hadn't meant to actually go to the creek, and he was surprised by the cool, green scent of it as he came upon the rocky bank. He felt disorganized and a little frantic. Something was going on with the surprise delivery to the Josephs'. Cello was troubled by the symmetry of the envelope's arrival and the unexpected visit to the Joseph place. Under all of the morning's surprises pulsed the question of money. How was he going to get it? Letta wasn't handing it over, and Sil wouldn't if Letta wouldn't.

Cello peeled away his sweat-dampened clothes and swam out into the river. The cool water pressed into the healing welts from Sil's punishment, into the spaces between the hair follicles on his scalp, around and through his fingers. For a while, Cello just swam, hoping to find an answer to any of the questions beating behind his eyes in the clear, honest river.

He felt something move against the side of his leg, and he turned first toward it, and then away from it, before he broke the surface of the creek. The water dribbled into his eyes, and he moved closer to the shore until his feet found the muddy bed.

When he saw what had touched him in the water, he stopped breathing. There was Joanie, easy and naked as he was, swimming, in the same even pattern he had favored. Like she'd been following him. Cello's stomach lurched as he sank into the water, crouching down until he was covered up to his neck.

He watched the shape of her body flicker in and out of the different shades of light and disturbances in the water. He desperately wanted the river to stop moving, so he could really see her, but he felt an equal and opposite gratitude that it was moving so swiftly, that there were tangles of leaves and branches floating around it, obscuring both of their bodies.

Joanie lifted her head out of the river; her hair was slicked back and darkened by the water. The fierceness of her gaze physically hurt Cello. He crumpled over, even more ashamed of how he must look beside her, ashamed of the way she looked at him, ashamed at how he'd failed in trying to help recover her son. *Not anymore*, Cello thought. *This one thing, finding money for that envelope, I'll do. It won't hurt anybody.*

"How come you aren't at Miracle's birthday?" he asked, eyeing his pile of sweaty clothes on the opposite bank.

"Didn't exactly feel like celebrating." She swept her arms out, swimming toward him. "I've been swimming a lot. I think it's helping," she added. Cello felt the heat in his skin, a blistering flush covering him as she moved closer. "How about you? Why are you out here in the middle of the day?"

"I had a problem," he blurted out, not sure if he wanted to drive her back or lure her forward. "I thought a swim might help me figure something out."

"What?" Joanie ducked her head a little, surprised, maybe even a little pleased, by his response, as though she had sent him a silent message that he had understood. He was warmed, comforted even, by this glimpse of their old rapport. "What's your problem?"

"I just need some extra money."

"Why?" she asked, moving a dripping piece of hair out of her eyes, her arm lifted so high that Cello could see the top of her breast swell out of the water. He felt the violent beat of his heart everywhere.

"I just need it, okay?" Cello wondered how long they could stay in the water like this.

"You should probably ask at the Josephs'. Since you're going over there today." He heard the dip in her voice, a studied casual droop in her tone, as she glossed over the word *Josephs*. The way she said the word sounded like a scratch.

"Did Letta tell you we were going?" Everyone had known but him.

"No. I could just tell," she said with an odd satisfied smile. "When you go—" her voice was so quiet he could barely hear it over the sluicing of the creek "—you'll have to go without Sil."

"Oh." It was all Cello could do to take one breath after another. He was startled by her strange calm, and overwhelmed knowing that Joanie was naked—that he was naked—that he could just swim over to her if he wasn't so chickenshit.

"I knew every time you came to the Josephs'," she said. "While I was over there. I could always tell. I wonder if that's why I can tell now, or if it's something else." She moved away and swam upstream, toward her own pile of clothes. Cello stared as she climbed out of the water. The way her body looked and moved, it was like part of the river had come alive and was moving up onto the ground. The soft lines of her thighs moved and split as she bent and reached for her clothes. She turned and saw him watching before he could cover his eyes, do anything, to not seem like a disgusting pervert.

"It really is working," Joanie said, holding a bundle of clothes loosely in front of her, inspecting the stretch of an arm. She spoke more to herself than to him, but Cello could see something different, another shimmering dimension to her skin. Her distracted gaze sharpened toward him, and he could feel her attention as viscerally as a fingertip pressed against his forehead. "When you're there, ask one of the cousins. They always know where to get a little extra money. Come here," she said. He swam forward, looking carefully at the space above her head. "Give me your hand." Joanie pulled his outstretched palm closer and flipped it over, efficiently, impersonally. Cello watched, fascinated, as she dipped her forefinger inside of her mouth, and scraped it against the inside of her cheek. He almost jerked away as she lowered the dampened finger to his skin, and began to write on it. He squinted, trying to pay attention to the pattern, but all he could feel was Joanie's touch. "There," she said, satisfied. "See if that helps. But be careful." Her voice slipped into a flat, bitter pitch. "Make sure you watch the tenants. Stay away from them if you can." Cello wondered what she'd done, what they'd made her do, maybe for extra money. Before he could ask what had prompted that flare of anger, she disappeared from Cello's sight.

He unfurled, and pulled his body into the deeper water, into the same place Joanie had waited while they spoke. He swam and swam in the same pattern she had used, an elongated triangle. He swam, repeating the shape, until his body burned with activity, and not shame or wanting. He swam until he knew he was late, until he knew the birthday lunch was long over, probably earning yet another punishment. He swam until he could put a single thought next to another single thought, until a relative calm replaced the various frenzies and extremes he'd felt over the course of that strange, jagged morning.

Only then did he heave himself out of the water, breathing hard from the work of swimming. While he got dressed, a single purpose fused in his heart—to get that money and, in some way, protect the baby.

When Cello got back to the plot, he was late, but not as late as Sil was drunk. Marcela shot him a gloomy look, and Miracle had been crying. The little girl was curled up in Sabina's arms, her small, dark head resting against her foster sister's shoulder.

"Where've you been?" Marcela asked.

"Swimming," Cello answered, pulling his hands through his damp hair. His gaze darted around the yard—was there anything of value that wouldn't be missed? The old water heater, the rusted-out husks of cars—Sil had combed through their guts, harvesting and selling their parts: both useless.

Marcela's voice startled him out of his proto-calculations. "Well, thanks for giving Sil all of that extra time for birthday fun. Letta's trying to sober him up enough to figure out what y'all need to bring to the Josephs'."

"Oh."

"That's right, 'Oh.'"

When Sil and Letta eventually stumbled out of their trailer, Cello had inventoried any items of potential value at the garden that could be sold, but he came up short. The farming equipment would be missed—it would be needed. There was a TV in Sil and Letta's trailer, but where would he sell it? He certainly wouldn't get enough money for it, or any of the other derelict housewares that littered their domestic lives.

"Cello!" Letta called. "I've been hollering at you for five minutes! You finally go off the deep end?"

"Sorry," Cello said. Letta shook her head as she climbed behind the wheel of the truck. Cello loaded in the delivery of the Vine and Sil's prematurely harvested hybrid cuttings. His eyes hurt from straining for a glimpse of Joanie, but he didn't see her anywhere.

12

Their truck rumbled down the Josephs' drive, two gravel ruts split in two by a bright stripe of grass. Cello sat in the bed of the truck with Marcela, the sun-hot black plastic burning his thighs through his pants. This would be Marcela's first delivery, so Cello hoped it would be a quick and easy one.

Letta shouted out of the truck's open window. "Keep an eye on her, Cello. We can't lose a single stem on the road. You know that."

Marcela's haughty indifference forced Cello to work twice as hard as he'd had to work with Joanie. Joanie had been just as vigilant as Cello, maybe even more careful, tamping down a corner of tarp with her foot, or catching a loose tangle of green before it flew off into the afternoon. Marcela sprawled across a pile of cuttings, but seemed to do it more for her own comfort than to keep the wind at bay. Cello did the work of two people to keep the cargo in the back, squinting out into the cloudless bright day.

"Marcela," he called as the wind picked up around them. "Can you just sit over there? On the edge of that blanket?"

Marcela huffed and moved around a bit.

"Marcela," Cello repeated as he repositioned himself on the tarp.

"What?" she snapped.

"You don't have any money, do you?"

She laughed, her voice cracking against the wind. "Please, do you think if I had any money I'd still be living with Sil and Letta? Why?" She leaned in, so close Cello could smell the oil from the pores of her skin. "What do you need money for? Or is it Joanie who needs it?"

Cello felt the blood press up against the insides of his face.

"Of course Princess Joanie needs money. You know if you give her anything, she'll run off and she won't take you with her. Could you live with that, Cello?" Her voice was suffused with mock sympathy. "I don't think you could."

Cello didn't answer as Letta made the final turn on the Josephs' long driveway. He knew the feel of that turn in the truck bed, clear as a road sign. He stared down at his legs as they waited for the herd of tenants that lurked in front of the gate to separate and allow them to pass. At every visit, he tried to forget them. He watched the laces on his boots until they were through.

"It's not for Joanie," he said as the truck lurched to a stop in an enormous, muddy puddle.

One of the younger Joseph cousins stood in front of a sagging shed, a bright green hose wound through his hands.

"Letta," the young man said, nodding as Letta climbed down from the truck.

"Nice to see you, Frank," Letta said primly. "Your auntie at home?"

"Out back," Frank said, gesturing behind him with the hose, as an arc of water looped across the sky.

"Thanks. Marcela, you come with me. Wouldn't be proper if I left you alone with these boys out here. Stay with the truck," Letta said to Cello without looking at anyone, her gaze exploring beyond the trees that rimmed the Josephs' wide yard.

Cello climbed down and stood at the puddle's murky edge, looking from the colony of mosquitoes skimming the water's surface to Frank's dark silhouette.

"So," Cello began, eyes on the water. "How's business?"

"Alright," said Frank. Cello was relieved to hear the lazy ease in Frank's voice. He was relieved the question wasn't a dangerous one.

"Maybe you could help me out." Cello looked over at Frank, but didn't move, still unsure. "I'm looking to pick up some extra money."

"Oh, really?" Frank scratched at the significant stubble on his chin. "How much you looking to pick up?"

Cello looked down at his hand, where a mosquito had landed. He slapped the insect dead. "Not sure." A spark of warning accompanied the insect bite.

"I guess better question is how much trouble you want to get into?" Frank dropped the hose on the ground and moved closer to Cello. The running water pooled around them, flowing into the puddle, scattering the mosquitoes with sudden, violent ripples.

"Not too much, I hope," said Cello, concentrating on Frank's face without looking into his eyes. Cello didn't want to know what lurked there, didn't want to know if the man he was speaking to was someone who'd hurt Joanie, who'd stolen the baby.

"Well, you sure are a delicate one. The way I see it, the more trouble you're looking for, the more money you make. I'll let you know if I need any extras done," Frank said with a shrug.

"Alright. Thanks." Cello turned back to the truck and opened the back. He slouched under the disappointment. If he'd been bolder, would Frank have offered him some kind of deal right off? Cello pretended to be busy, and lifted the tarp to check on their haul. There were still eleven bundles although one had loosened. Cello took a roll of twine from the cab and retied it.

"Looks a little lean today. Y'all having trouble out there?" Frank asked. Water still ran from the hose at his feet. Cello shrugged, his mind on Letta, on her hands, on the money Mother Joseph would count into them, on the Stuckey's on Route 9.

"We're fine," Cello said, still busy with the twine. "This is just some extra we had to bring. Something special."

"Something special?" Frank grinned.

"Sil's project." Sil had loaded it lovingly into the pickup— he'd even buckled one small crate of the best-looking cuttings into the passenger seat.

"Huh. You tried it?" Frank asked.

Cello shook his head.

"No, I guess you wouldn't. Sil and Letta are training you up right. You could give me a little out here. Free sample before they weigh it?"

Was Frank negotiating with him? Could he risk selling some of Sil's Vine to Frank—maybe they could work something out that way. Cello paused and shook his head, just once. An unfamiliar feeling rose in his chest—not anger exactly. It was more akin to frustration. If he was being tested, the consequences would be far worse than a beating from Sil. But he needed the money—and there was no way around that.

"Where's your bathroom at?" Cello asked. A high-pitched ringing began in his ears as he organized his thoughts around a new idea.

"What, pissing in the woods not good enough for you?" Frank said, the water still flowing. A pert-eared mutt danced around his legs, rhythmically picking its paws out of the mud.

"No, I just… I had a stomach bug and, you know, it ain't all clear." Cello clutched at his stomach, trying to make the urgency look authentic.

Frank looked at him through narrowed eyes. "Well, sure, if it ain't all clear, you can use the outhouse." He gestured over his shoulder to a half-collapsed wooden structure.

Cello jogged off toward it, masking his disappointment. He thought if he could get into the house, or *somewhere*, he could lift something worth a hundred dollars. Maybe he could leave that—some kind of jewelry, anything—at the Stuckey's, if he couldn't actually get the money. He opened the outhouse door to a space thick with cobwebs. He glanced back at Frank, whose gimlet eyes were still on him. Cello stepped inside and closed the door, looking around for another exit. The slats in the back were nearly rotted through. Cello pressed his fingers into the soft wood, manipulating open a space the width of his hand. He folded the rest of the plank back easily. He slipped through and pressed the plank back into place.

The stretch from where he stood, hidden, to the main house was long and unforgiving—there was nothing but open, mowed lawn, not even a shrub to duck behind. Frank's back was turned, for the time being. Cello ran, willing himself invisible. He couldn't be caught—this was the only thought he had as he ran. He tried to remember what Letta taught the girls about tending the Vine's power, and wished he knew the words that could conjure the right kind of help. But boys were forbidden to learn, so he did what he could—running swiftly, optimistically—praying that Frank wouldn't see him, that no one would see him, that he would find everything he needed.

Cello pressed his back to the side wall of the boxy main house, his lungs heaving with the sudden burst of effort. He waited for a minute, for the sound of being followed—a dog's bark or an outraged human voice—but he was still alone. Cello crept along the outer wall, looking for a way in.

But at every window, he heard the flurry of voices. He propped his chin up over a peeling sill and spotted Letta's bored profile. Marcela's eyes widened out at him through the glass, and she tilted her head forward, urgently—*Get out of here*, she meant. Mother Joseph's heavy step rattled the windowpane, and Cello ducked down, thwarted. He wasn't going to get in this way—maybe the basement, he considered. He looked for an opening near the ground, crawling close, his hands in the dirt and his right side scraping against the house like a beast trying to get inside.

A narrow rectangle gaped out at him. Cello pushed a hand against it—a flap of galvanized steel gave at the pressure. Some kind of a vent, he thought. He didn't know if he would fit, but decided to try. Cello slid feetfirst through the opening, like a letter in a mail slot. He moved his feet and legs experimentally, surprised not to feel the twists and obstructions of ductwork, only plain opening. He slipped down, letting himself fall.

Cello slid into darkness. A spherical orange glow appeared suspended in the middle of the space. He waited, still and silent, for the sound of discovery, but again, nothing. The light pulled him forward to a glass tank lined with leaf-green gravel. A snake lay nestled in the stones like a brass ring. Cello tapped the glass, and the snake lifted its lazy gaze toward him. Cello's eyes adjusted to the dimness. The cellar floor was packed earth—he could smell it. It was easy to move over, and forgivingly muffled any sounds that would have echoed on poured concrete. It was surprisingly tidy. A line of assembled folding tables had been arranged on the wall opposite the snake. It looked like they had been set up for the creature to guard.

Cello heard footfalls of activity overhead. The crash of a slammed door burst through the orange quiet. Someone was leaving the house. Cello hurried to the tables, squinting in the gloom. He swept his hands over the surface of the table, and felt the scatter of filled, hand-size plastic packets slipping over and under his fingers. He grabbed one of the heavier ones, and brought it under the light of the tank. He unzipped the opaque plastic envelope, and from it spilled a stream of bills. His heart chugged with the thrill of it.

He scooped up the fallen slips of paper and shoved them back in the envelope. There were mostly twenties, but larger bills, too. He shoved a handful into his back pocket, and zipped the envelope closed. Cello threw it back onto the line of tables; there was no time to try to resettle the strange buffet of tiny plastic bags that he'd discovered.

He felt a glimmer of pride—he had done something of value for two people he loved. He had to get out, back to the out-house, all quickly, all without being seen. He couldn't remember where the slot was, and even if he did, he doubted he had the upper body strength to heave himself out. Cello crept up the stairs, past the serpent's illuminated tank. He pressed an ear to the door and heard nothing. He twisted the handle, but the door had been locked from the outside. Breaking it open wasn't an option. Cello wasn't trying to create an obvious problem—if the Josephs did notice an interference in the basement, he didn't want it to coincide with his foster family's visit.

Cello ran lightly back into the cellar and paced in panicked laps, looking up at the dark smudge where the wall met the ceiling. He looked at the light attached to the snake's tank and wondered if he could detach it and use it as a kind of flashlight. He was near nauseous with gratitude that snakes didn't bark. The back of his hand itched and stung where Joanie had drawn on it; the sensation was uncomfortable and frightening. It was in that strange instant that he noticed the serpent's head had moved dramatically—the triangular jut of its snout holding still, its entire body pointing like an arrow to a very specific place. Cello followed the snake's direction and reached a hand up, feeling for the flap. He felt nothing at first, and then jumped, getting a little higher each time; he was so eerily certain the snake was communicating with him.

He gasped with relief when he felt the slip of steel duct on his fingertips. Cello leaped, grasping at the opening. He didn't know if it was adrenaline or something stranger, but he caught on and lifted himself to the opening on his forearms. He tried to crawl out without banging against the steel flap, and his muscles burned and struggled against the impossible task. He plunged out into the sunlight, ungainly as a birthed calf. Cello didn't wait for any signals of detection this time—instead, he sprinted to the nearest spot where the woods edged up against the Josephs' lawn and ran in their prickly cover, back to the outhouse, back to where Frank was eternally watering. Cello collapsed on his knees in the yellowing grass, wiping the sweat from the back of his neck.

"You weren't joking," Frank said, his mouth awkwardly moving around a burning cigarette. He took a few steps back from Cello. "You look awful, brother."

"Yeah," Cello breathed out, trying not to smile, striving to contain his triumph.

"They shouldn't let you out like that," Frank said, sparing a pat for the dog. "Could be catching."

"Got to work," Cello said, shrugging.

"Really pulling through, huh?" His eyes half closed and he flicked his cigarette butt into the grass—not exactly at Cello, but near enough to be some kind of message. "Next time you come around, I'll have something for you," Frank said. "Always can use an extra, uh, hard worker."

"Yeah, okay, thanks," said Cello. A sudden swarm of gnats whorled around them in a gristly mist. He stretched his arms behind his back. The muscles there still quivered.

Marcela reappeared at the edge of the clearing, sour-faced, eyeing them both with her arms crossed over her chest.

"Nice to see you again, Amberly." Letta's voice carried from beyond the overgrown row of scrub oaks.

"Wish I could say the same." The other woman's voice fell raspy and thick over the clearing. Even the gnats fled from that sound. Cello dreaded meeting Mother Joseph at these deliveries. Whenever he saw her pocked, nicotine-yellowed face, he ran to rage, remembering the listless Joanie they'd collected from the sagging shed—the exact shed he could see now behind Frank as he kept on wasting water.

"You should turn off that hose," Cello said, before the older women came into sight. Frank raised his eyebrows, but said nothing. Letta's knifelike figure approached; Mother Joseph lumbered beside her.

"This boy of yours is fresh," Frank said.

"I hope you been minding your manners, Cello," Letta said.

"Quit gabbing and unload the truck," Mother Joseph snapped.

"Marcela?" Letta called, keeping her voice sweet.

Marcela sauntered over and held out her arms for the first bundle. Frank's lewd gaze ran over her body.

"Come on now, Frank. Don't be inhospitable." Mother Joseph flicked her fingertips out toward her nephew. The rest of her was still as the moon, her thick legs adhered to the ground in their baggy, faded jeans. Cello wondered what it would be like to pull out tufts of her voluminous but slovenly graying hair, to see her face twist with pain. Mother Joseph moved only her eyes to stare back at Cello, and smiled, as though she'd read his thoughts.

Cello and Frank loaded out the truck, while Marcela leaned against it.

"And how is your Joanie? We had such a nice visit last week," Mother Joseph said, as though remembering Joanie for the first time. Even the dullest among them, even Frank, could read the artifice there. Marcela stiffened midlounge, her body pressed awkwardly against the side of the pickup.

"Oh, Joanie's Joanie," Letta said, her voice like a whistle.

Frank and Cello had picked up the pace. Everyone wanted it to be over.

"Boys, you about done?" Letta asked, crossing the lawn to the driver's side of the truck.

"Yeah," said Cello.

"Nice seeing you again, Frank," Letta said, delicately shaking his hand.

"You, too, ma'am. And don't forget what I told you, man. Next time." Frank nodded a goodbye to Marcela.

She and Letta shared a look between them, then Letta smacked the dusty side of the truck with an open palm. "We'll see you again next month, Amberly," she said.

"Yeah, well, we'll see about that," Mother Joseph muttered.

Cello and Marcela scrambled into the now-empty bed of the truck, and the engine turned beneath them.

"What'd he mean by 'next time'?" Marcela asked, everything crossed now, arm over arm, leg over leg.

"For that extra cash."

"Oh." She blew a wisp of dark hair out of her eyes. "What about me? Did you ever think I might like some extra money? Jesus, I'd like some money, period." They were silent—Cello knew they were both thinking about the last time one of them had asked Letta or Sil for money. It ended with Marcela kneeling on a raft of broken branches for an afternoon, her bare kneecaps bloody for days, and her muscles spasming from holding the tensed position for so long.

"What happened in there?" Cello finally asked. "Did you pick up on anything?"

"What? About the baby? I don't think Mother Joseph even knows about Junior. I'm starting to think it's not them."

"I don't think it was *them*." Cello moved his arm, demonstrating an inclusive rounding-up. "Maybe just one of them."

"Whatever, I don't know. They barely talked at all. Why were *you* sneaking around the house?" Marcela asked.

Cello shook his head. "Just trying to look around a little more. Hoping we missed something last time, I guess."

"It's disgusting in there. All those old drooling people lying around—I don't know what Mother Joseph's doing to them, but it's zombie central in that house. And it stank like adult diapers. I thought we had it bad. I don't know how Joanie ever put up with it."

"She didn't, I guess," Cello said. It had been barely a year, and already Marcela forgot what Joanie had been like coming home—a creature, not a girl.

Cello reached over and knocked at the window of the cab. "Letta?" he called.

"What?" her muffled voice asked.

"I need to stop at the Stuckey's, okay?" Letta turned her head sharply, slowing the truck and pulling it to the side of the road. The engine idled beneath them as she looked from Marcela and back to him. "I sure hope you didn't do something stupid," she finally said.

"What?" Marcela asked as Letta pulled into the cracked asphalt lot of the Stuckey's.

"Nothing," Cello answered. Letta opened the driver's side door and began to speak over him.

"Go get some milk," she told Marcela.

Marcela eyed them both, arching a dark brow. "Okay," she finally said. Letta slapped some money into her palm, and Cello watched his foster sister disappear under the gabled entrance of the convenience store. Letta stared ahead through the windshield, holding up her hand like a traffic cop. "I don't want to hear nothing about it," she said. "If you're going to do what I think you are, go do it and don't waste my time." Letta twisted a brassy loop of hair around her finger and tied it in a knot. Despite her refusal to actively help, Cello saw her carefully controlled optimism in that single nervous gesture.

Cello hopped out of the truck bed, his mouth curled in a partial smile. Despite how useless he'd believed he was—to Joanie, to the baby—he'd done it; he'd met a demand. Maybe he was even saving a life. Cello was filled up with something then, that same magnificent power he felt coaxing something new from the dirt—what he was doing felt right. It felt good.

He jogged around the deserted gas pumps and up to the empty side of the lot. A yellowed sign—Broken—was pasted over a collection of miniature vending machines, their clear bellies filled with faded plastic toys. Cello considered his other visits to the Stuckey's on Route 9. Those had always been covert affairs, where he'd huddled in the cab of Sil's truck while the older man pumped gas. Sometimes Sil would fling a five-dollar bill at him and send him into the too-bright store for overpriced peanut butter, or a pack of Grand Prix. He'd conducted those transactions like a fugitive, never looking the clerk in the eye, and avoiding the gazes of other customers. Once, a woman—wiry and blonde with a set of small children swarming around her and pulling at her clothes—had asked him to reach for a package of toilet paper from a shelf above the refrigerator cases. He remembered how startled he'd felt, being spoken to directly like that.

In all of these visits, he'd never once noticed a Crown Light sign. Cello felt for the envelope in his pocket and the money from the Josephs' cellar. He withdrew the little packet of nail clippings and tried to feel grateful that the baby was still alive. That he was still healthy enough to be growing nails. For a moment, Cello was tempted to cast the cloudy, hardened slivers onto the cracked asphalt of the lot. Instead, he put them back in his pocket. He smoothed the crinkly backs of the stolen twenty-dollar bills before sliding them into the creased envelope.

He waited for Marcela to leave before going into the store, thinking the sign might be inside. He slid a glance toward the woman behind the counter. She wore glasses with enormously round lenses, and her frosted hair had been processed into a voluminous helmet. She clutched a yellowed paperback, and didn't look up from it when he came in.

Cello walked to the back, to the beer cooler. He scanned the row of gold Crown Light cans, looking for something, some signal from the thief who'd taken their baby. He ran a hand along the bottom of the case, but found nothing. He rubbed his chilled palms together and let the door slam shut.

He looked up and around—there were signs and cutouts, displays of all kinds, but nothing about the refreshing virtues of Crown Light. Cello knew he didn't have much time. He paced back up to the register, and cleared his throat.

The woman's eyes flicked up from her book. "Can I help you, hon?"

Cello looked down at the blue linoleum tile as he spoke. "Ma'am, do you all sell any other beer than what's here, in the back?" He shuddered as the words fell out of his mouth, clumsy and too quiet.

"You got ID?" she asked, a corner of her mouth turned down.

"It's not for me—my uncle wanted to know."

"What we got is all there." She looked at him from under the shade of her hairdo. "You gonna buy something?"

Cello shook his head, and she pushed her stool farther away from the counter with her knee, drawing the book back up toward her face. He pushed the glass doors open. One more look around, he promised the baby.

On the other side of the store he found a stack of lumber and an ice machine, greasy with handprints. Cello searched on, circling around the restrooms that stank aggressively, even through the closed metal doors. Cello's mood plummeted. All he could feel was the inverse of that initial accomplishment—that tickle of rightness, of goodness, it was all gone. It was all nothing. Cello plodded back toward the truck, back to Letta's disappointment and Marcela's questions.

He stumbled over a chunk of fieldstone, and looked down to kick it aside. The gold crescent moon of the Crown Light logo winked out at him through the crackling leaves of a dried-out azalea bush. A cardboard sign advertising a deal on twelve-packs was propped against the convenience store siding at the parking lot's edge. Cello's body buzzed with the discovery. He leaned down and carefully peeled away a corner of the sign, found nothing, and peeled some more. The space behind the sign was empty, except for a divot in the mulch. Cello scraped away at the spot and uncovered a plastic sandwich bag. He brushed off the dirt—the bag seemed new; the stripe of green and blue that sealed it closed was neon-bright. Something white had been folded into a square inside.

Cello quickly dropped the cash-filled envelope into the hollow in the mulch and covered it until it would be invisible to anyone but the thief. He slapped the sign back up and retreated to the truck.

Cello shook with the achievement, and a mix of triumph and terror. He climbed into the cab, leaving Marcela alone in the back. Letta saw him, beaming all over. She shook her head, but her mouth moved in an involuntary, small smile. She started the truck, and Cello clasped his trembling hands in his lap over the plastic bag.

Letta stopped at the solitary light on the way back to the garden. "What is it?" she asked, nodding toward his hands.

"I don't know. Something they left for us."

"Not for us," Letta said, waving a bony finger between them. "For you."

Cello pried the bag open with one hand. Inside, there was a folded-up paper towel. He felt Letta shift closer, felt her breath on his face. Cello opened it gently, revealing an oily blotch at the center, and a line in Sharpie written across the top: *Another $100.* Cello suppressed the sudden rage that flowered in his chest. He had been naive to think this would be the end of it.

A horn sounded, and Cello looked up; the light was green. Letta swore and the truck heaved forward. He held the paper close to his body so Marcela wouldn't see it. He looked from the message in his hand and back to the road in a kind of trance. He kept looking, back and forth, until something cleared in his mind. Cello spread the towel over the space between his hands and felt like an idiot—a terrified, ashamed idiot. He understood the oily blotch for what it was, and what the thief had done to put it there. There, filled in the familiar scent of motor oil, was the distorted stamp of a baby's tiny footprint.

"It's his foot," Cello whispered.

Letta coughed into the crook of her elbow, clearing her throat. "This isn't right," she said, banging her hand on the wheel with each word she said. "I don't want you messing with this no more."

"But if we don't do anything, they might kill him," Cello said, stabbing each word toward the driver's side.

Letta clenched the steering wheel and glared out at the road. "They probably killed him already. And now they want to play games with us."

Cello's eyes itched with tears. "No, Letta," he rasped out. "They still got him. He's alive. I know it."

"No, honey," Letta whispered back. "They don't. Let it alone." Cello couldn't look at her after that.

13

The sun beat down overhead and warmed Joanie's hair dry. It was too hot for what she wanted to do, but she was running out of time. The sooner she began the worship, the sooner she would get her son back. The path leading to the old grove circled around their kitchen garden. A figure leaned down among a swath of cucumbers. A fissure of irritation broke through Joanie's determination. She hadn't wanted to see anyone; she didn't want the complication of another person's desires and purpose to disrupt her own.

"Joanie," Sabina called, and then straightened. "What happened to you? You missed Miracle's birthday cake."

Sabina looked so tall, so suddenly grown, that it occurred to Joanie that the girl's active growth—all of that voraciously expanding bone and skin and muscle—might help to amplify the worship. The idea drifted over her, like it had belonged to someone else first. "Lost track of time," she lied, shrugging apologetically. "Hey, can you come help me with something?"

Sabina's eyes narrowed, unusually suspicious. "With what?"

Joanie knew how she must look, how she must seem. She kneaded her knuckles against the sides of her waist, reminding herself of the body she occupied at the garden, that she was still a sister capable of exchanging sisterly compassion.

"I know I've been distracted, and I'm sorry. I'm sorry I wasn't there for Miracle, and I'm sorry I haven't been there for you."

Sabina's surprise and obvious softening made Joanie's throat tight with guilt. Even if she meant what she said, she was plainly aware of her manipulation.

"I know you're worried about the baby." Sabina took a quick breath, as though she was going to say something else, but turned her face away from Joanie toward the rows of vegetables.

"Listen, there's something I need to do, and I know you might not want to, but you'd be helping me a lot."

"Helping with what?"

"I'm going to set up something important. A worship, like I used to do over at the Josephs'."

"Why?" Sabina's voice was open and doubtful all at the same time.

"Because it'll make all of our lives easier."

"A worship? It's not like..." She paused plucking the right words out of her mind. "It's not like what we're supposed to do in the fields, is it?"

Joanie shook her head. "No—it's better. Come on. I'll show you."

The girls walked together to the site of the Vine's first planting. It smelled different than anywhere else in the garden, metallic, like a handful of coins among the flowers. The heat of the morning concentrated the scent, and Joanie said, "Can you smell it, too?"

"I don't think so." Sabina's forehead compressed in confusion.

"It's special here," Joanie clarified.

Sabina nodded carefully. "I think maybe I can feel that."

"I knew you would." Joanie broke into an encouraging smile. "Hold still a second." She traced out a path, following the demands of the Vine, riding the strong currents of its insistence with the soles of her feet. "Right here." Joanie pointed at a curve of blackberry branches at the edge of the grove. "We'll build it here."

"Build what?"

"A chapel. A little space for the worship." Joanie knelt down, and sunk her thoughts down into the earth where the Vine's roots twisted and stretched. *This is our secret,* she explained. *Don't tell anyone.* She separated a long strip of the Vine, the way she would during a normal harvest, and Sabina gasped at the snap.

"What are you doing? Letta's going to murder you!" she said, her body pushed and pulled by the dual impulses to stop Joanie and to remain frozen.

"It's okay," Joanie murmured, soothing both Sabina and the Vine. "Letta won't know." She lifted the Vine with the same care she'd used to move her infant from place to place, and carried it to the little cove of blackberry bushes. "Come over here, Sabina. I'll show you exactly what to do." Sabina blanched, but she obliged, and crouched beside her foster sister.

Side by side, the girls wove strand after strand of the Vine through the twiggy bases of the blackberry shrubs, building a little green cavern. The opening faced the old growth Vine. It seemed to Joanie that the plant pulsed with pleasure; she could feel the sap that ran through the walls of the newly made chapel hum in response. She held her hands against the woven walls, giving whatever the Vine needed to take, as she drew the patterns for worship against them. Joanie's palms burned with a violent pins-and-needles sensation. The setup exhausted her, but she was satisfied, fulfilled, even as the Vine pulled what it needed from her body into the woven wall of stalks.

"Joanie," Sabina said, tugging on her elbow. "I have to take a break—I'm so thirsty." Sabina's face was mottled and red.

"Of course you are, I'm sorry. Let's go get a drink and rest some. Working with the Vine always makes people thirsty." When Joanie swallowed, her throat scraped with discomfort, too, only she hadn't noticed. She'd been so absorbed by the pattern she wound into her chapel. Joanie caressed the walls in farewell, and led Sabina back out into the hot, white summer light.

"How come it does that? Make people thirsty?"

"Marcela hasn't told you anything? About the Work?" Joanie couldn't disguise her surprise. The sisters were so close; it didn't seem possible that Marcela would keep such a thing from Sabina.

"Not really. All I know is Marcela doesn't like doing it. I know it makes her tired and thirsty, same way it makes you and Letta tired and thirsty."

"Well, we do the Work so the Vine will grow."

"I know that," Sabina replied, wrinkling her nose playfully.

"Okay, okay—sorry," Joanie said. "The way Letta first explained it to me is that the Vine needs human watering. It'll take anything we can give it, like spit, blood, sweat, everything."

"Everything? Even pee?"

"Even pee."

"Why?"

Joanie hesitated, not wanting Sabina to know too much before she needed to know it. "The Vine needs to feel connected to us. This is the only way it understands. The idea is to make it want to grow because we're here." As she explained, she felt the optimism well up behind her ribs like an extra set of lungs. If her worship appealed to the Vine's desire for connection, it wouldn't be able to resist restoring the broken bond, snapping back the missing part of a whole family.

The kids' trailer was empty and cool. Joanie took a tube of frozen orange juice concentrate from the freezer and sliced off two disks into a glass. Sabina watched her like a hungry cat, her usual even calm debrided by thirst and exhaustion—and by some other irritation Joanie couldn't identify. "It'll be just a second." Joanie mixed the juice, thrilled and unsettled at the same time by Sabina's odd expression. Had helping her build the chapel shifted something in her foster sister? Was she responsible for a change like that? Did she really have that kind of power? Joanie jabbed the dissolving orange crystals harder, and the spoon clanked against the glass, disrupting the dim silence.

"Here," she said, quickly pressing the drink into Sabina's hand. "Orange juice after is always best. Anything cold and sweet will get you feeling back to normal. A little extra sleep is good, too." As Sabina drank, Joanie massaged her neck and shoulders, trying to shake a little more energy into them. She could feel her muscles seizing up. Making the chapel had drained her entirely. Joanie ran the cold water and lowered her mouth to the tap.

"How come only girls can do it?" Sabina asked quietly, her eyes, her face, everything settled back into their usual, pleasing lines. Maybe she had only been thirsty and tired, nothing more.

Relieved, Joanie wiped her mouth with the back of her arm. "Why do you think? Girls can grow things—we're designed to make things grow. We can grow whole people, like it's nothing." She couldn't resist imagining her son's soft little body, and bit on her cheek, suppressing a hot stab of grief. "And because we bleed every month. The Work, the worship, everything, is more powerful when you're bleeding. Letta would've told you all this, once you started bleeding."

"Why does Letta have to wait until I start bleeding to tell me? Do you have to be bleeding already, to do this?"

Joanie shook her head. "It's safer, though. Then the Vine can't take too much. While you're bleeding, you're strong. Stronger than it, even. I think."

Sabina's mouth twisted in a skeptical frown. "Why? What can it do if it's stronger than you?"

"Don't worry." Joanie took her hand and squeezed it. "As long as you're helping me, I won't let anything bad happen." She just hoped she was telling the truth—a tickle of uncertainty scratched into her thoughts. "Why don't you lie down? I'm going to rest a little bit, too."

When Letta, Cello and Marcela came back to the garden, the others were mostly asleep. The little kids had crashed after all of the cake, and a wilted-looking Sabina had packed them into the trailer for a nap. Joanie was stretched out on a blanket on the lawn, her head resting on her folded arm. She yawned up at the truck's return, and then flipped to her back, casting a hand over her eyes. Cello bit down on the insides of his mouth to keep from telling her what had happened.

"So, what? Y'all just thought you'd call it a day?" Letta said, exiting the driver's side and crashing the door shut. "Sil!" Letta called out as she fumed toward their trailer, where he was sleeping off the remaining daylight. Letta shook her head, and then pointed at Cello and Marcela. "You two are the only ones still standing—go down the hill and pick some vegetables for dinner."

"You're standing, too," Marcela said, pointing back at Letta. "Maybe we should all go."

"Hush up with that attitude," Letta snapped. "Now, hurry. And don't forget to take the crate! We're feeding half of the goddamn county here."

Marcela let out all of the air in her lungs in a creaky moan.

"Would you quit whining!" This from Joanie, followed by a projectile clump of earth. Cello circled around to the back and took one of the plastic milk crates stacked there. He slung a look back at Marcela. "You coming?" he asked.

"Yes, fine. God." Marcela ambled behind him, down to the large kitchen garden. This small stretch of earth was the least tended of all of the plots. Sabina was the only one who remembered the garden that fed them—she was usually the only one who watered and pulled the weeds in the underappreciated spot. Cello sometimes sensed little ripples of irritation from her when someone else had been there. The way they lived, he didn't blame her. It was hard to make anything your own and keep it that way.

"So what was that all about? That whole emergency stop at the Stuckey's."

"Nothing," he said.

"Don't lie to me, Cello. You're shit at lying."

"I am not," he said, dropping the crate in the grass. "Letta needed milk, just like she told you."

"No, there was definitely some other reason." Marcela wrinkled her nose and artlessly wrestled a dozen, semiripe tomatoes from the closest plant.

"Sabina's gonna kill you," Cello said. He separated runner beans from their stems with the same care he'd use petting a cat.

Marcela snorted and they worked on. "You know," she said, interrupting the silence. "You can trust me. If there's something going on, you can say so."

Cello looked at her extravagantly open face. He felt guilty, leaving her out of everything. Before he could answer, the sound of a bicycle's wheels rushing through the grass interrupted them. Cello turned his body toward the invisible bike. "Hell, no," he said, and dropped their dinner harvest to chase after it. The rider, whoever it was, was not supposed to be there. Protecting the borders of the garden was like a reflex, and Cello and Marcela followed the fresh serpentine track pressed into the grass almost without thinking. As Cello stared down, he noticed that the print of the tire was identical to the track he'd found in the dark.

"Look," Marcela panted, "they turned here." She pointed to a small smear of trampled grass and then she was leading, Cello running after her. Who could it be? Cello wondered. Some idiot tourist trying to mountain bike? They'd definitely found a bewildered one of those before, shirt dusted with pollen, sweat running freely from a too-tight helmet. More likely, Cello thought, filling with anger, it was the kidnapper.

Marcela broke through the layer of camouflage first. Cello saw the lengths of cable twined with leaves before she did—a crude screen. Marcela tripped and fell on her knees, all of her hair flopping forward over her face. Cello slowly stepped through the gap she'd made, thinking maybe something bigger than they'd imagined was going on. Maybe it had nothing to do with the missing baby. Maybe it was a secret hustle arranged between Letta and one of the other farms in Mother Joseph's bailiwick. The glint of the toppled bike drew Cello's eye. Behind the bike stood a boy, a boy Cello had never seen before.

He was suddenly overheated, an unfamiliar mist of emotion suspended around him. Had the boy come for Joanie? Had he taken the baby, and just now come back for her? A haze of jealousy tinged that other, strange, tropic acknowledgment. Marcela stood between them, suddenly blocking the boy from view. Was the boy there for Marcela? It seemed unlikely, but Cello was smart enough to understand the coexistence of all the small hidden things that whirled a family together—even if the family wasn't a real one.

"Um," the boy began as he took a step toward them. This boy wasn't some lost tourist—he had none of that blithe, entitled belonging. He looked at Marcela and Cello like they were stray dogs, with respect and care, but also with assured superiority. His head tilted, exposing a smooth, square jaw and glint of cheekbone that had been hidden beneath hair as long as a girl's. Both Marcela and Cello followed the movement with the kind of attention reserved for dangerous things. This boy, whoever he was, was not like them.

"Who the hell are you?" Marcela said. "What are you doing back here?" The three of them moved slowly, swirling like sluggish, muddy water around rocks in a river.

"Um," the boy said. "What are *you* doing back here?" There

was a hint of a smile in this voice, an unsophisticated attempt to smooth them back, Cello noted.

"We live here, asshole," Marcela answered.

The boy was incredulous. "Really? You live here?" He looked around the immediate surroundings, as though searching for a hidden door in a scooped-out hillside. "Where?"

"That's none of your business. Who are you?" Cello said as he squinted at the stranger, searching for some familiar Joseph feature. The boy's face changed a few times, taken over by several different answers. He stepped forward, reaching out for a handshake.

"I'm Ben," he finally said. Marcela and Cello looked at his proffered hand and then at each other. Ben let his hand drop. They shifted a little, tightening the space between them.

"You armed?" Cello asked.

"What? No!" Ben fell back in alarm.

Marcela and Cello shared another, this time relieved, look. Whatever he was, this stranger didn't belong to the Josephs.

"What's this all about?" Cello asked, waving at the primitive screen of camouflage hanging around them. Ben moved toward his bike, but Marcela darted forward, tripping the stranger and pouncing on the bicycle. She righted it and got on, balancing her elbows on the handlebars. Her pleased little smile lifted Cello's mood. There had been a bike at the garden once, a long time ago. All the bigger kids took turns riding it, but it had been left out in the weather and rusted into oblivion.

"Listen, guys, I can just get out of your hair here," said Ben, standing and brushing himself off.

"I don't think so," Marcela said, glee plainly shimmering in her answer. "I think you're going to tell us what you're doing out here. And about your little campsite, or whatever this is."

"Trust me," Cello said with a sympathetic shrug. "If you have something to explain about this setup, you should be real happy to be explaining it to us and not the others." Cello sensed some sort of moneymaking scheme was at the heart of what was going on—the planting was too organized, making the most of the smallest amount of space. Whatever the boy was doing, it wasn't something for his own, recreational enjoyment. Ben considered Marcela's colonization of his bike, and looked suddenly devastated, as though he'd been given terrible news.

Cello shook his head. "If Sil knew you been coming around here, he'd be doing a lot worse than running you off right now."

"He your dad?"

Marcela and Cello looked at each other, their goofy smiles nearly identical. "Absolutely not," Marcela said, her voice bright and wavering. It felt forbidden and thrilling, sharing this information with a stranger, Cello thought.

"Well, if he's a reasonable man, surely he can understand my predicament here." Ben looked at them, from one to the other.

"Well, he's not. Reasonable. And you kept your predicament to yourself so far, so hard for anybody to understand it. But if you're looking for understanding, you won't get it from Sil. He won't think twice about shooting for trespassing," Cello said. He had started to enjoy the questioning, once he was sure that this boy knew nothing about them, nothing of their work at the garden, nothing of the missing baby.

Cello watched the stranger's decision surface around his eyes. "Well," Ben began. "You guys ever heard of senging?"

"Huh?" Marcela asked as she hopped on the bike properly and began to pedal a narrow trough through the tall grass.

"Senging," Ben repeated, looking after her, and the bike, with longing. "Picking ginseng."

"No," Cello answered. "Never."

"Well." Ben put a hand to his throat as though feeling for his pulse. "Some people pay for it, for wild ginseng. Mostly buyers from China."

"What?" Marcela said, flying past the two boys on another lap.

"You find it in the woods—it likes the shade?" He motioned

to the homemade canopy. "Has to be organic to get the best price. I found this little patch growing here, and thought I'd take care of it. Keep an eye on it until it's ready to pick."

"So that's what you're doing here?" Cello said. "Stealing our wild ginseng?"

Ben flinched at the mention of theft. "Look," he said. "I had no idea this was your property."

"Obviously," Marcela said. Tiring of the bike, she stopped beside Cello.

"No, I mean, I thought this land was abandoned or something." Cello saw the sincerity in the other boy's face and sucked his teeth against the insides of his mouth, hoping he looked menacing.

"Man, this kid is an idiot," Marcela said gaily. "Look," she continued, this time directly to Ben. "If you just give us what you made off what wasn't yours, we'll let you go." Her suggestion was underscored with an imperious pointing, a gesture so like Letta's that it made Cello shiver.

"No, no, no," Ben said, waving his hands like he was trying to clear away what Marcela had said. "I mean, I'm sorry and everything, but you can't hold it against me. I didn't know!"

"Offer us something else, then," Marcela said with half a shrug.

"Okay, okay, okay," Ben stammered, turning his back to them. "I mean, it's usually too early to sell now, but I know a guy who buys it year-round." He turned around, looking at them with what looked like an entirely different face—a face swarming with insincere charm. "We could do, like, a group project. We can all go looking for it and triple the profit."

"A group project? What the hell is that?" Marcela said.

Cello crossed his arms in front of his chest. "How much did you get already?" he asked, thinking of that envelope buried behind the Stuckey's.

"Nothing," Ben said. "Really, nothing!" He repeated this for

Marcela's benefit. Cello could feel the icy glare she was aiming at Ben. "We'll start off on the right foot and everything. Teamwork, you know?"

Cello and Marcela looked at one another, considering the measure of this unusual boy.

"We might consider giving it a try. But we're going to need some goodwill. From you," Marcela said.

"Like how?" Ben asked.

"You think we're soft in the head?" Marcela continued. Her voice was cool and even, and, Cello thought, absurdly confident. "You give us a nice bonus for using our property, and *then* we're starting on the right foot."

Ben put his hands in his pockets and rolled his shoulders. "Fine." Cello noticed the resignation in Ben's face. "I don't have it now, though."

"Of course you don't." Marcela rolled her eyes. "I guess we'll just have to tell on you, then."

"No, I mean, let's meet up here tomorrow morning, okay?"

"You've got until seven a.m.," Marcela said with an irritated little wobble across her brow. "You don't come back with our money by then, we'll take up all of what you spent so much time watching here, and find somewhere to sell it ourselves."

"Fine," Ben said. They waited him out, staring as he retrieved the bike and sped away.

"Wow, Marcela, you were great," Cello said. "Maybe Letta should have you do all the talking next time we go out to the Josephs'."

"That's hilarious," Marcela said, reining in a beaming smile. "But it looks like you got a way to make that money you need."

14

Joanie watched Cello and Marcela leave early in the morning, their whispers bouncing like moths against the trailer walls. She squirmed away from them and curled her body around the crescent of empty space where her baby sometimes slept. Cello's goodness had once been reassuring and familiar—growing up, she'd felt it spill over onto her every now and then with a kind of celebratory affection. But his naive optimism wouldn't erode any of her problems now. Joanie shut her eyes and allowed herself to be sad about that, too, just for a minute. Her missing son, her broken body. Growing her energy was her singular focus now.

Marcela and Cello tried not to slam the door, though Joanie could hear that Sabina was already awake. The new duo was gone again, on some other hopeless adventure. Joanie wondered if her sister's shifting alliances hurt Sabina. Joanie tried to imagine the wound, that separation, an unexpected bright flash, and was nearly knocked breathless with the force of it. Her emotional link with Sabina was a natural, lingering effect of setting up the worship together, that was all. She chased away the thought that it might be something bigger with the sweep of a hand over her hair. She pressed the empty spot on the mattress beside her, and thought about going out to the chapel again.

She considered the shape of the worship she'd learned at Mother Joseph's. It was nothing like worship on TV, those waves of pressed, sweating people, dripping with lace, heaving as one under the glass bell of a massive church far away, nor that soft, child's lisping begging for a small and simple thing. The worship she'd been taught at the Josephs' was different, bigger than the Work Letta taught her, and she was pulled—maybe pushed—toward the plausible conclusion that there was some other, bigger form of worship that the Josephs hadn't worked out yet. A form that only she was meant to discover.

Joanie remembered the first time she'd been taken down. It was in that brief but electrifying period where Mother Joseph had come to trust her—or, if not exactly trust, to treat her as a creature of value. They filed down the groaning steps, Mother Joseph first, then old Harlan, and finally Josiah, who led her into the cellar with sweating hands. In the basement of the main house there was a secret place. An arched opening that yawned from under and behind the stairs, itself like the wide jaws of a serpent. It smelled different from the rest of the house, verdant but also dusty. Mother Joseph switched on an old floor lamp with a singed yellow shade, the cord trailing like a rodent's tail to an outlet in the basement proper.

Joanie squinted against the strange, dusty light, at the walls filled with woven thatch coverings. The scent of the room was familiar, because the coverings were desiccated stems from the Vine. Joanie wondered who had woven the elaborate, quilt-like patterns around them. She was certain it hadn't been Mother Joseph.

"You remember coming to this chapel?" Mother Joseph asked, fanning herself in the room's heat. Joanie shook her head and pressed a hand against the wall. It was the first comforting texture she'd felt in her new home, like the rasp of one of the old chestnut trees at the garden. "We brought each of you down here, me and Letta, once we got you. For your baptisms. You," she said, pointing between Joanie's eyes, "were a trade. From one of the tenants."

Joanie tilted her head back, like she was swallowing medicine. The reality of her origins hit her with the force of a slap. When she was very little she wondered about her parents. In the privacy of her mind, she employed them in ridiculous, rococo ways—they were dentists, or witches, or hairdressers. They were always beautiful, incandescent as shampoo ads. Nothing could be further from what she'd imagined than those apparitions that stalked the gate. If there was any consolation, it was that no parent of Joanie's could possibly still be alive, so miserable and doomed were those bodies she tried not to see as she walked to her work in the smokehouse.

"You were only two, I think. Look, that's you over there, on that side." Mother Joseph leaned against the wall she was closest to, and nodded in the opposite direction. Joanie moved to where her mother-in-law's chin pointed, to nearly a dozen ghostly chalk outlines of miniature bodies. The figures were cartoonish—like an iced gingerbread man parade along the wall. She counted the outlines and wondered where the rest of the traced children were.

"Which one is me?"

"Should say on there," Harlan said. The thought of Harlan's hands on her infant body locked up Joanie's throat.

"This one," Josiah said, tapping at one of the figures.

"Don't touch it," Joanie snapped, pulling his hand away.

Mother Joseph produced a laugh that transformed into a phlegm-riddled cough. "Nice to see you got the right attitude. This is where we worship. Took a while to come around to it myself, but my great-grandmama started these traditions, and say what you want—it works," she said. "And now you're one of us, I expect you to worship here, too."

"What do you mean?" Joanie asked.

"Well, you don't get something for nothing. It's up to you to come down here and pay the price," Harlan said, leering.

"You'll be expected to do some Work down here, like all the women in our family have done over the years," Mother Joseph said.

"Don't worry," Josiah whispered, giving her arm a clammy squeeze. Mother Joseph lifted her lime-green housedress up to her waist. Joanie, stunned, tried to brace herself for whatever was coming. She imagined the very worst; her mother-in-law wobbling out of her clothes—all of them—enormous, drooping breasts, wiry gray hair squashed in a matted nest at her crotch and ringing her withered nipples. Joanie averted her eyes from Mother Joseph's varicose-veined legs, and covered her mouth, as though breathing in the old woman's exposure was dangerous. Joanie tried not to imagine what horrible thing would come next.

She heard the slap of palm on flesh and winced. Mother Joseph had dropped her dress back down and let loose a corrosive tumult of laughter. "You should've seen your face," the old woman said, leaning against Harlan. "You see that, Harlan? Thought we lost her there for a minute." Mother Joseph seemed off—a little vacant, as though not quite fully in her own, powerful body.

Harlan nodded, his expression stippled with distinct, animal lewdness. Joanie wanted to scratch at them both, wanted to call the blood up from their swollen cheeks and sagging throats. She sauntered up toward that feeling, cool and slow, restoring herself as best she could.

"We don't have all day down here," Mother Joseph snapped at Josiah. He moved past Joanie, flashing her a bloated, apologetic look.

Joanie bit down on the insides of her cheeks and stared evenly at Harlan and Mother Joseph, who closely watched Josiah fossicking in a small cabinet behind her. She resisted the urge to turn and watch him, too. The feeling that Mother Joseph and Harlan planned to pounce on her, overtaken by some deranged whim, was too strong. There was a strange feeling twinkling in the air around all of them. Joanie watched them closely, prepared to fight.

"Here," Josiah said as he nudged a navy blue box of salt into her hand. "You just spread it over the floor." He waved his arms around the space, his shaking hands little smudgy blurs of flesh.

Mother Joseph made a sound in her throat. It startled Josiah and he dropped his arms to his sides with an exaggerated slap. "As usual, son, you haven't made a drop of sense. Give her the book, Harlan." Mother Joseph shifted the bulk of her body from foot to foot, swaying with impatience. Harlan disappeared and quickly returned with a stack of notebooks held together by a crumbling leather belt. Joanie lifted it into her hands—it was still warm from the heat lamp over the serpent's tank.

"This is what Letta and I trained on—this is some of what she showed you and the other girls at the garden. The basics, I guess you could call it. But what's here is the whole enchilada. You keep up the worship down here, the better the Vine'll come up everywhere. That's all you'll need from now on," Mother Joseph said. "You're ready for it, I can tell. Josiah and Harlan'll be outside till you're done—just out the door here." Mother Joseph walked backward through the arch. "This is your job now, every Friday at sundown. You don't wanna disappoint me."

Joanie shook her head.

"Alrighty, see y'all at dinner." Mother Joseph clapped her hands together with an odd, violent cheer. She vanished in the cool dark of the cellar, and Joanie was alone with the two men in the chapel.

"You all leaving or what?" she said.

"My, my, ain't we eager?" Harlan said, pulling Josiah along

with him toward the door. "No breaks, now, not till you're done. We got to make sure you don't disappoint."

Joanie rolled her eyes and shut them out of the warm little room. She heard the thud of their bodies collapsing against the wall and floor. She allowed herself the rush of relief at being by herself, at being spared a more gruesome or repulsive task. Joanie believed she could do anything difficult, as long as they left her to do it alone.

Opening the books was easy, as natural as taking a drink when she felt thirsty. Closing them would be much more difficult. That day in the chapel, Joanie felt a new presence come over her, something outside of Josiah's sweating bulk beside her in bed, or Mother Joseph's constant obstacle course of tests. She felt something *good*. Mother Joseph meant for the work in the chapel to be another trial, another way to rough Joanie up, to subsume her in the smells and bodies—the living and the dead—of her new family. Her mother-in-law had catastrophically missed the mark.

The chapel did not torture Joanie. In the chapel, Joanie found a reward, peace. The notebooks, along with what information she had forced from Josiah, unfolded around her in a galaxy of possibility. Great-grandmother Joseph's handwriting raged and slithered across every page. The cover of each book was printed with her name in jagged peaks of irregular capital letters: HELEN JOSEPH. Joanie understood she was meant to be disturbed by what she saw there. Instead, as she followed the pages through to their outrageous conclusions, she felt soothed. Comforted even, like Great-grandmother Joseph had written directly to her. She knew she was meant for those notebooks, the same way she knew not to touch a hot thing—*she just knew*.

Joanie heard Harlan and Josiah on the other side of the door, their lazy conversation seeping through the woven chapel walls. But their presence didn't distract her or make her nervous. Rather, their existence on the other side of the door seemed diminished—they were nothing, those two. Equivalent to clumps of dust and hair to be swept from the baseboards.

Great-grandmother Joseph had drawn illustrations, too. Faded colored pencil filled in the inky outlines of recognizable copies of the Vine and its flowers. And there were patterns—pages and pages of colorful patterns. They weren't quite geometric. They were globular and sprawling, like they had grown out of the earth under the house and had pressed through the floor, then the table, then through the book, up to Joanie's eyes. She couldn't look away—as though some invisible hand was trained at the back of her neck, daring her to stop reading.

Helen Joseph's captions alone were instruction enough for the worship Joanie was meant to begin that day. Joanie knew to pour the salt on the floor, then to scoop and sift it into one of those patterns. There were pages of patterns for every day—not just the seven days of the week, or even for the month, but patterns for every day of the year. Friday patterns were more elaborate and repetitive, filled with curling swirls and curved, teardrop shapes. Joanie's hands were scrubbed red as she moved the salt against the earth all afternoon. Perhaps her mother-in-law had meant to frustrate her with the monotony and apparent uselessness of the chore. Mother Joseph couldn't have possibly imagined what Joanie would eventually extract from those notebooks.

Joanie slid her finger across the pages, and found that in every pattern, one feature was repeated: an arched doorway—just like the door to the chapel. As she poured the salt from the navy-blue box over the floor, she thought about what the shape had meant to Helen. She thought about it as she pushed and scraped the flecks of salt into the circles and loops of Helen's drawings. She understood that she'd been wrong. Mother Joseph wasn't the powerful one. Whatever power she held was a watery copy of what had rushed through the channels of Great-grandmother Joseph's mind. With every scratch of her palm in the salt, Joanie felt the staggering strength of it moving through her—through her tissues and hair and teeth. The air around her thickened and blurred. She felt taken over, like her hands were moving without her mind, like her mind had lifted up through her head and out into the chapel. Like that arched doorway was letting something in. Joanie had never felt like this in the rudimentary Work she'd done with Letta. And just like that, at the thought of Letta and her old life, her body and mind were snapped back together. The walls settled and solidified back to their familiar woven shape around her, and she stopped pushing and pulling at the salt to consider what had just happened. She sat back on her heels and understood. This chapel was a place to find comfort and grandeur in what she thought was a small and rude life. In a corner of the salt sculpture, Joanie traced in her own sign of protection, the way an artist would sign a painting. It was one of the things Letta taught all the girls along with tilling—to create their own talismans against potential danger to the Vine. It felt right to add hers to Helen's Work; it felt like growing. In the chapel, Joanie would not be wasted. In the chapel, Joanie would transcend.

In the muggy trailer, Joanie tingled with the secret that she and Sabina had built. She had a proper place to trace the limits of her own power, and perhaps to exceed them. She would make a new way to get what she needed, and she knew the Vine would help her. The Vine would not be able resist helping her. Joanie felt a surge of optimism; she could feel the shape of her baby beside her, and smelled his faint, sweet scent. She would build upon Helen's work and, a green whisper in her ear explained, she would lift off.

15

It was still dark when Cello woke Marcela. He rolled out of bed and dressed. The empty envelope and the Stuckey's on Route 9 jutted sharply into every thought. Marcela wasn't as quiet, and Cello could tell that she'd woken up her sister and Joanie, too. He felt Joanie watching them as they slipped out of the trailer. He wondered what she thought, and was skewered by the thin, hopeful impression that she could possibly be jealous.

They trekked to the camouflaged spot behind the vegetable plot, expecting to arrive first and catch which direction Ben cycled in from. The stranger had beat them there, though; he was already waiting, sitting cross-legged in the wet grass. The boy's long hair was damp, and slicked back in a dark knot behind his head. The face fully on display was older, sharper, than it had looked the day before. He slouched wearily over his lap as he waited.

"You're early," Cello said, itching at a bug bite on his leg. Ben's gaze flickered toward them.

He shrugged. "Guess so."

"So, where's that money you promised us?" Marcela elbowed into the clearing behind the leaf screen. She rubbed her eyes with sleepy languor, and pretended nonchalance while Ben handed her a fold of cash. She didn't even look at it, just passed it back to Cello with the casual flippancy used in yard games of hot potato. Cello wanted to count it, to chaperone it back to the Stuckey's where he could throw another mantle of protection over the baby. But he understood that he couldn't break whatever air of confidence that Marcela had cultivated.

The fresh dynamic unfolding between the three of them made Cello a little delirious. If they made their own money, maybe Cello could save enough to lure the kidnappers out, to truly restore the baby. With enough money, he imagined being granted the power of a real father; together, he and Joanie and the baby could be their own family. He imagined the baby's soft cheek on his shoulder, and Joanie's relieved smile. At least he hoped. He hoped so thoroughly he practically lurched with the want of it.

"Better get started, then," Ben said. Cello noted Ben's stare and shook himself back into the conversation in the clearing.

"Okay, let's go," Marcela said, swinging her arms as she began to lead the way.

"Wait—do you know what you're looking for?" Ben asked.

"Figure we'd just watch you do it." Marcela reached up and pulled a spray of leaves from the strung-up wire.

"Hey, don't touch that, okay?" Ben said, reaching to secure a dangling slip of greenery back onto the fretwork.

"Why not?" Cello asked.

Ben shook his head, and covered his face with both hands. "I can't believe I'm doing this," he said, his voice muffled. Ben's hands fell away, and he untied his hair, shaking it out to dry. Cello was startled by the familiarity of the gesture, something his foster sisters did all the time. Under Ben's hands the motion was inverted into something else, some other magnetic thing.

"The plant we're looking for is about a foot tall." Ben held his hands up, dragging shapes into the air. "There's a stalk, and then a couple of prongs. Only a three- or four-pronger is worth digging up. On each one you got five leaves, two little, three big. Sometimes you'll see red berries in the middle, not always."

Cello nodded, and Marcela widened her eyes and churned the air with her hands in a move-along motion.

"The stem's soft—make sure it's pliable before you dig it up, or else it's not ginseng. You want to keep everything, the whole plant, but especially the root. Please, please be careful when you dig it out. Can't sell broken roots to my guy." Ben shook his head. "Beginners always fuck up the dig-out."

Marcela's face was bright with a triumphant little smile. She looked over at Cello, sharing a knowing glance.

"Alright, let's go." Cello led the way out of the clearing and Marcela followed. Ben hung back.

"I'm going to look on my own. Better haul that way," he said.

"Fine," Marcela called without looking over her shoulder.

As they walked, Cello realized he was enjoying this new camaraderie with his foster sister. It was nice to get a sense of Marcela alone. She was always so forceful within the group of kids. Cello thought that maybe he should explain to Marcela about the note and the package, and why he was really there, but quickly covered over the idea. This Marcela seemed so much happier—he didn't want to stain that feeling. They hiked across the property to the line of wooded hills that edged the south side.

Cello knew the garden. He understood its obvious strengths and weaknesses, but he also knew its secrets. Ben had described the ginseng plants the way someone would describe a mutual acquaintance, and as Cello ran through the stranger's rough picture, it caught—a vision, a snap, of exactly where he'd seen plants like that before.

"Come on," Cello said to Marcela, who was already lagging behind him.

"How far? I don't want to be out here all day." She slapped a mosquito dead against the side of her bare calf.

"Will you hold this?" Cello shoved the crate they'd brought into Marcela's hands. "I'm running up the hill a second." Before she could push the crate back to him, Cello sprinted toward the spot where he remembered once seeing one of Ben's plants. He skipped over the brush carefully, not wanting to fall and come back bleeding. Cello was halfway up the hill, in a dark-damp cluster of climbing bramble. There, at his feet, were the hand-like leaves, waving from atop their prongs. Three prongs, like Ben had said, and a bright clutch of crimson nestled in the centers.

Cello crouched over the plant and moved the soil away with his fingers, gently, the exact way he'd removed weeds from the earth when he was as small as Miracle and Emil. The root emerged like any other, like the finger of some long-dead creature. Cello loosened it until it came away from the ground completely, and he shook it out, the smell of damp soil radiant under the heat. Cello laid out the plant on the ground, like a tiny body, and stood to show Marcela.

"God, it's early as butt," Marcela muttered, unimpressed. "What time should we head back?"

Cello shrugged. "We haven't even got started yet and you're already trying to head back?"

"Give me a break. I'm just trying to—you know—get a sense of the day. I don't want Letta to be missing us."

"Uh-huh."

"Ugh, shut up."

Cello pretended to be annoyed, but the attempt evaporated under the hot promise of their successes. They worked and the pile grew. They hiked up the incline farther into the woods until Cello caught another flash of red. He blinked hard. They'd hit upon what looked like a flattened ray of space filled with ginseng plants. About half were too small to harvest, but there were plenty to dig up. Marcela preened with delight, bending down to check that the stems were soft. It was very suspicious, Cello thought, this profusion of wild ginseng just there for the taking—growing so neatly and abundantly. It had the familiar order of one of Sil's plots. He knew Sil hadn't planted it; Sil told Cello about each of his new plantings—the locations and instructions for care. "In case something happens to me," he'd said. But maybe Sil hadn't told him everything. Maybe Mother Joseph had set up another satellite farm and hadn't told Sil or Letta. He didn't like the idea of another of Mother Joseph's gardens closing in on theirs.

Cello ducked away from the sinister shape his thoughts were circling. Marcela began to piece together her own suspicions as she walked through the line of plants.

"What the hell?" Marcela said.

Cello shook his head.

"It isn't Sil's, though?"

"No."

"You sure?" Marcela picked at the dirt from under her fingernails. "Wait a second." Her gaze moved from the ground to the top of the tree cover. "Again with this?" Cello followed her eyes to the edge of the makeshift plot. She hooked a finger around a piece of thread-thin wire—another curtain of camouflage. "It's that Jesus-looking stranger's, of course. How long has he been doing this?"

"Doesn't matter. Anyway, I guess it's ours now." Cello and Marcela bent to the ground and started to dig. They dug with their hands and the blunt, tin spoons all of the kids carried during delicate harvests at the garden. The roots were elegant and jagged, but not difficult to free from the ground intact. Cello smiled as he recalled Ben's despair at being at the mercy of a couple of ham-fisted beginners. Marcela started up a thin, cheerful whistle. Cello breathed a lungful of clean, cool air, and kept working.

"What's going on over here?"

Cello and Marcela paused, their hands lifted from the plants they'd been working loose. Their heads turned toward to the source of the voice. For one awful moment, Cello thought the voice was Sil's. When he stood, he saw it was Ben, a hand half covering his yawn.

"Look what we found," Marcela said. Each of her words had the jab of a pointed finger.

"Wow, this is really lucky," Ben answered, skittering away from the accusation in her tone.

"Isn't it?" Cello said, unexpectedly enjoying the other boy's discomfort.

"Wow, you guys already got a lot," Ben said, the genuine surprise in his voice an obvious swerve from his carefully guarded earlier tone. He moved toward the pile of roots that loomed out of the ground between Cello and Marcela. Marcela put her hands on her hips, and Ben stood still. He looked closely at Marcela, and then at Cello—at their hands and faces and bare arms flecked with dirt.

"Okay, so what's your deal? Are you all farmers?" he asked, looking from one of them to the other.

"Not exactly." Marcela laughed and coughed at the same time.

"Is your family really into gardening, then? Are you brother and sister?" he asked, raising his eyebrows.

"God, no!" This time, Marcela coughed more than she laughed, so that it sounded like she was choking. Ben reached out and gave her back a couple of solid thumps, but watched Cello the whole time. Cello stepped more deeply into the shade of one of the large oaks curling over them.

"None of your business," Cello said.

"How long have you been doing this?" Ben gestured to the pile of roots and leaves warming under the sun. Marcela moved away from his hand still on her back.

"You ask a lot of questions for a trespasser," she said. Cello winced as a vivid surge of doubt beat against his chest. This stranger showing up with convenient solutions right when they were needed—even Cello couldn't be optimistic enough to ignore the darker explanations looming underneath.

Ben shook his head. "No, you're absolutely right. Sorry." He turned a bright look on Marcela and then at Cello, too—an obvious attempt to charm. "I think we have enough here, between what you pulled and what I got. Besides, if this batch gets a few more months, it'll be more valuable. I can take what we have over to my guy this morning."

"Ha!" Marcela released a single cackle. "That's funny. We'll be coming with you, of course." She pulled on Cello's arm so that they faced out, side by side, like a pair of athletes on the same team.

Cello leaned in closer to Marcela. "I think one of us needs to stay back. We can't both disappear all day."

Marcela slouched away from him and averted her face, her temporary good cheer punctured. "Mind giving us some space to discuss?" She directed the question to Ben, but Cello felt the force in it that was meant for him.

"Go right ahead," Ben said, warming and loosening up under their impending skirmish.

"No, you can go right ahead." She raised her eyebrows and tilted her head toward the tree line.

"That's fine." He held his hands in the air and started to walk off.

"And stay gone until you hear us call for you," she called.

"Okay, sure." The smile in the boy's voice was obvious.

"Seriously? You're gonna leave me here?" she said.

"Why? Do you want to go? You know I'm coming back with our money. You got nothing to worry about."

"Right, of course you'll come back because Joanie's still here." Marcela rolled her eyes and shook her head at Cello.

"That's not the only reason." Cello crossed his arms over his chest, and remembered the sleep-warmed weight of the baby there. He needed to be the one to go, and he needed to go alone. Even if he told her, Marcela wouldn't care about depositing another payment at the Stuckey's—she'd say he was better off throwing his share away, or giving it to her. "You know I'll take care of it. And somebody's got to get back before everyone's up. You can cover for me. I don't think you should be alone with this guy. Unless that's what you want?" Cello wiped the sweat from his face. It was getting hot as the morning swelled.

"Um, no—thanks, anyway. Don't fuck this up. Make sure you follow him the whole way—I don't want him running off with my share. He seems like kind of an asshole." Marcela tossed her head, and the musty smell of their blankets filled the space between them.

"Well, that I know how to deal with. Hey! Man!" Cello shaded his eyes with his forearm. As Ben ambled toward them, Cello noticed how Ben's body looked like it, too, was part of the earth, like it had grown and morphed from the layers of soil and shale. It was the way his feet connected with the ground as he moved, like the land came out of him and grew down through the soles of his feet. Cello tried to remember where he'd felt that before, and then flushed when he realized it had happened with Joanie, with her naked body moving from the river.

Cello cleared his throat. "Okay, I'm coming with you."

"Sounds good to me," Ben said, smiling widely as though he'd known exactly what Cello and Marcela would decide.

"I'll see you at home, Cello," Marcela said. "Be careful."

"You, too." Cello and the stranger packed up the harvest in silence. Cello followed along as Ben brushed the crusted soil off the roots and plaited the stalks with the skill of a produce packer. Cello studied the neatly folded burlap bags Ben set at his feet. Nothing about this venture seemed spontaneous or amateur. Ben worked well and quickly, surprising Cello. He was used to working this way only with Sil.

That kind of communion was what Cello thought you might

find in a church; it was one kind of devotion. Harvest, and planting and tending, all of those, for Cello, were a conversation with greatness. Coaxing something beautiful and living from something so vast and complicated, well, it didn't really feel like toil. He knew it wasn't like that for everyone, but it was for Ben—the familiar, content respect for that work streamed off his shoulders. It was a curious, close feeling, almost like holding hands with someone.

Cello shook his head, shuffling the reason for this errand—a tiny baby on his own—up to the front of his mind. "So, we're pretty close to done here, right?" he asked.

"Yeah, I guess. How come you didn't want your friend to come?"

Cello was quiet, gathering the little plant carcasses, careful of the brittle, delicate strands of roots. "None of your business," he finally said.

"That's like your catchphrase, man. Tell them to put it on your tombstone." Ben held his hands up, like a film director setting up a shot. "None of your business." Ben rolled his eyes, an impressive echo of Marcela's merciless teasing.

"Well, it's not," Cello said. "How much are we getting for this? And don't lie now, 'cause I'll be right there watching you."

"Forty a pound. That okay with you, Mr. None-of-your-business?"

"Yeah, it's okay," Cello said. He tried to stay relaxed, as loose as a layer of cloud cover, but in his mind, the possibilities erupted and multiplied. "Let's go now." He skimmed the eagerness out of his voice. "I can't be gone all day. I've got work to do."

"Fine. When do you need to be back?" Ben dusted off his hands over the pile they had gathered.

"Noon."

"Well, I rode my bike over. I usually borrow my roommate's car, but he's using it today."

Cello worried his lip with his teeth.

"What, you don't have a car, either?" Ben asked.

"Nope." Cello shook his head. "How far is it? Can we walk?" He looked at the pile of filled sacks and felt his optimism trickling away.

"Not if you want to be back by noon," Ben said.

"Alright, I guess I'll try to get Sil's truck, unless…" Cello looked the other boy in the eye for the first time. "Do you have another bike?"

"No," Ben replied, his voice flat, dry.

"Well, shit. I guess I'll sneak out the truck. I'll meet you by the road." Cello gestured to where the county route access road pressed a rim up against the garden's edge.

"I'll take the plants," Ben said.

"No, *I'll* take the plants," Cello corrected, pleased by how uncompromising and serious, even mature, he sounded.

"That makes no sense." Ben sighed. "Why don't you just take half, and I'll take half?"

"Doesn't seem fair. Our deal was me and Marcela get two-thirds, right?"

"Fair? Dude, if it weren't for me, you wouldn't be selling this at all."

"Fine. Half. Ten minutes, down there, the first place you run into the road."

Cello held the pile of plants against his chest and ran. He was already late to work in the garden; he hoped Marcela came up with something believable to tell Letta. Taking the truck without permission would be bad. The beating he got for running away would feel like a nap compared to what Sil would do if he found his truck missing. Maybe he could tell Sil he needed to haul the tiller down to the new plot. If Sil was still hungover and taking it easy, he wouldn't notice the time.

Cello paced around the back of the trailers, straining his eyes for the metallic flash of the truck. If Sil had taken it out already, there was nothing Cello could do.

"Where you been?" Joanie's voice sliced through the humid, late-morning air. She pulled her loose hair over her shoulder, and her deeply tanned throat, glimmering with perspiration, shone out at him.

"Nowhere," he said.

"Marcela said you had the runs. Letta bought it, but the rest of us know she's the one full of shit."

Cello flushed, felt all the blood in his body pushing up against his skin, trying to get out. "I—I need the truck," he stammered.

"What for?" As Joanie moved closer, he felt his muscles contract. He looked up, met her dark eyes with what he hoped was confidence.

"Just something."

"What are you and Marcela up to?" she asked. "You're not gonna tell me?" Joanie's breath was warm against the side of his face.

"Nope," Marcela interrupted. She shuffled through the grass, noisy as a creature alone at night. "What's going on, Cello? How are you feeling?" she asked.

"A little better. I wanted to take the truck to get something. For my stomach."

"I'm sure Letta's got something for you. You know they won't let you take the truck out alone." Joanie looked from Cello to Marcela. "I'll go ask Letta and see what she's got."

"No," Marcela said, too loud.

"No?" Joanie repeated, challenging.

"Why aren't you working?" Marcela asked.

"Me?" Joanie said. "Why aren't you working?"

"It's an emergency. Believe me." Cello looked right at Joanie when he said it, willing her to understand the importance of this trip.

"Go on," said Marcela. "We'll cover for you. Right, Joanie? Just go, Cello. Go now." Marcela raised her eyebrows and gave him an encouraging, emphatic nod.

"Right, okay. Tell Sil I needed the tiller down the hill at the new plot. If he asks." Cello darted back to where he'd stashed the burlap sacks of prepared ginseng, begging God or anyone to keep this part of his day quiet. He opened the door to the truck's cab and piled the bags onto the cracked vinyl bench seat. He put the truck in Neutral and circled to the back, heaving a push against it. It took a few tries, and more strained and protesting muscle tissue—Cello was sure he'd be counting bruises on his upper arms and shoulders later—until the truck began to roll. He skipped back as it veered slightly off the drive, but came to a jaunty stop at the base of the second slope of gravel-covered lane. He didn't want to start the truck until it was too late for Sil or Letta to stop him.

Cello thought he heard voices, but hurried after the truck, anyway. *Better to ask forgiveness later than permission now*, he thought. He couldn't remember who had said that to him, but it was from a long time ago, from someone who'd cared about him—one of those memories so far down in the mulch of his mind something twisted in him to think of it.

He turned the key in the ignition and hoped the robust sound of birds and animals chattering would mask the sound of the engine. He hoped Sil had already tied one on this morning, his senses blurry and sluggish. He hoped Letta was still upset about the baby's motor-oil-dipped foot, that she was distracted and cowed by someone whose cruelty was greater than her own.

As the engine gnashed and caught, Cello was surprised to discover he was more proud than afraid. He was alarmed but also buzzed by his boldness. With a small, satisfied smile, he pulled the truck forward.

16

Joanie felt the change in the family—of the garden—like a missing tooth. *It isn't just me*, she thought. The removal of the baby, the breaking away of Cello and Marcela in some mysterious alliance, even her own postnatal weakness, had all destabilized the garden. She could sense the Vine testing their reliability, their suitability, every time she closed her eyes. This uncertainty terrified her; if she ever needed the Vine to cooperate with and trust her, it was now.

Joanie left Marcela in the yard and peeked into the kids' trailer where Sabina, Miracle and Letta were playing cards.

"Hey, Sabina, want to come with me? Gonna take that walk now," she said, careful to keep her voice neutral and easy despite the panic she felt.

"Where, exactly, are you two going?" Letta asked, smoke streaming out of her nostrils in a suspicious flare.

"I'm going to teach Sabina a couple of the basics," Joanie said, clearly, confidently. "I need a little help with the Work. An assistant."

Letta's mouth turned down in a skeptical twist. "She's not ready. And I can tell you're up to no good."

Joanie shot Letta a cool stare. "She is ready."

"Oh, I guess you know best."

"We both know I know more than you."

Letta, stung, looked hard at her foster daughter. "That's what I'm afraid of."

"Don't be afraid. Everything I do will be for this garden, and nothing else." Joanie reached out for Sabina's hand, to help her off the floor. She felt a pinch of worry as she found herself already standing over Sabina without even realizing she had moved.

"This won't bring him back, honey," Letta said, soft and sad, as Sabina clamored to her feet. "It's too dangerous."

"You don't know that, Letta. What if it can?" Joanie gave her a defiant shrug. "And if you're that worried, you can come help us. See exactly what I'm doing."

Letta curled herself around Miracle, as though she didn't want Joanie to take her, too, and lit a cigarette. "I don't think so," she said with a deliberate look at Sabina. "It's not really safe if you're not bleeding—yet or anymore."

"I can keep you both safe," Joanie said.

"No, thank you." A nervous tremble undercut Letta's voice. "I'm not good at it anymore. I was never any good at it. And anyway, if you know everything, then you know it's a young girl's game."

"It's not a game at all. The Work I'm doing, it's something different." Joanie saw Letta lean back before she understood that she was pressing herself toward the older woman. She was so stunned and thrilled to be the stronger one that she didn't question what force had bullied her forward against Letta.

"Sabina, you don't have to go with her," Letta said, but made no movement to approach Sabina, or to hold her back.

"I want to help. I like doing it," Sabina said quietly, eyes cast down.

"Fine. If you two hurt yourselves, don't come crying to me!" Letta shouted, crossing all of her limbs, and closing Miracle and herself away from the two girls.

The chapel was different, charged. Joanie could sense it immediately, even before she caught the green glow of it in her sightline. It responded to her. The verdant call of the chapel reached out, near desperate, to fold her into the woven little cove. The longing was violent, and it produced an urgent answering inside of her—a mother's frantic compulsion to feed her hungry child.

Joanie clutched Sabina's hand and pulled her forward in a half run.

"Ow, Joanie, don't yank on me like that," Sabina said, withdrawing her fingers from Joanie's insistent clasp.

Joanie forced her pace to slow. "Sorry." But she wasn't sorry. The Vine was loosening its hold on the garden because it was tightening its bond with *her*. Helen had never mentioned anything like this in any of her notebooks.

"Well," Sabina said. "What do we need to do?"

Joanie knelt in the chapel and began to trace Helen's patterns for worship over the walls. Instead of drinking the patterns in, the Vine seemed to press out against them. It wanted something else, and Joanie needed to find out exactly what. "We need to come back. With something more," she said.

Cello knew moving slowly wouldn't make the engine's growl any quieter, so he sped off to the meeting spot he'd arranged with Ben, finding the boy by the side of the road. He stopped the truck without pulling over. "Get in," he said, though Cello wasn't sure if Ben could hear him through the window glass.

Ben moved efficiently and, with more grace than Cello expected, he settled his bike into the back of the pickup.

"Go on," said Ben, throwing his share of the haul on top of the pile between them. "I'll tell you when the next turn's coming up."

Ben led them to a neat, compact neighborhood. All of the houses were symmetrical, matching pieces, painted the color of seashells. The lawns were uniformly shorn, and the hedges and mailboxes were all the same height. Cello was surprised by the neighborhood's respectability and permanence. The house number—232—was stenciled on the curb in navy blue. As he drove, Cello's eyes repeatedly flickered to the rearview window to make sure Sil hadn't somehow followed him.

They parked on the street a few houses down. Cello was used to subterfuge, to confusing people. Even if this was legal, and he wasn't sure it was, it didn't feel right to drive up and approach the house like a guest. He thought back to all of his family's transactions with the Josephs. Those had felt nothing like this.

"Wait here," Ben said.

"What? No—that's not what we agreed."

"There was no deal about this part. My guy will get nervous if he sees me bringing people up here. This is his home," Ben said.

"So?" Cello climbed out, holding an armful of overfilled sacks to his chest. "You don't let me come in, I take our share back."

Ben cranked the passenger window up. "Fine. You better not fuck this up, man. Just let me talk, alright?" Ben asked. He stood close, too close, Cello thought as they walked up the brick, her-ringbone-pattern path to the front of the house.

Cello stared at the pristinely painted white door. Even the doorknob seemed too nice for him to touch, all glossy and shining.

"Do you think there's a back door, or a garage or something? It doesn't feel right for us to be here."

"This is how I always do it." Before Cello could stop him, Ben reached forward and pressed the doorbell. He practically leaned into it—surely, Cello thought, maximizing the sound inside. He winced, imagining Mother Joseph's response to this kind of salutation.

The man who opened the door was older, middle-aged—not

too much younger than Mother Joseph, but the comparisons to Joanie's former mother-in-law ended there. He was short and fiercely sunburned—his eyebrows like two bleached-blond fuzzy caterpillars on a red stone. He adjusted a dark, wool cap, moving it farther down his creased forehead.

"Benjamin," he said. "I see you've brought a friend."

"What's up, Dr. Santo?" Ben said with a perky little wave. Cello stared at Dr. Santo's thin, cashmere sweater, and felt the dampness of perspiration under his soiled T-shirt.

"You had better come inside," said Dr. Santo, scratching an arm through his sweater.

"Want me to bring this in?" Cello asked, lifting the fragrant burlap-wrapped plants up a little.

"No, I want you to leave it outside," Dr. Santo said, like a robot, Cello thought. "Better yet, just throw it into the street."

Cello's eyelids stretched open all the way, until the corners of his eyes hurt.

"Just come in, man," Ben said, and his hand between Cello's shoulder blades pushed him gently forward.

"Not the sharpest tool in the shed, is he?" Dr. Santo motioned them into the house. In the living room, everything matched: the sofa, the coffee table, the armchairs, even the curtains. Cello was stunned, like he'd fallen into someone else's body. It couldn't be him, Cello, standing in this harmonious and beautiful, sweet-smelling house. He looked at Ben, helpless, with the filthy sackcloth in his arms.

"Yeah, I'll take that," said Ben. "In the kitchen, Dr. S?"

"That's where the scales are, Benjamin. Would you boys like a lemonade?"

"Sure, that'd be great," Ben called from the brightly lit, gleaming white kitchen that Cello could barely see. *It looks like heaven in here*, he thought.

Dr. Santo left and returned with three glasses on a tray. He handed one to Cello. "It's sweetened, I hope that's alright. Just with a little agave."

Cello took the glass, and examined the scrollwork etched into the rim. Little shreds of green floated among the ice cubes. He didn't want to put his mouth on it. He looked at Dr. Santo and then at Ben, waiting for them to drink first. *Maybe this is a trick*, Cello thought. He recalled Letta's warning never to take anything from the Josephs, not to eat or drink anything they offered.

Dr. Santo disappeared into the kitchen, and Cello followed, not wanting to stand alone in the pristine living room shedding dirt and mud onto the freshly vacuumed floor. In the kitchen, it was clear to Cello that Ben had been here before. Probably many times before. He gulped from the cold drink and Cello watched the other boy's throat move as he swallowed. Cello felt an odd compulsion, to switch glasses with Ben and drink out of the half-filled glass, to put his mouth on that glass instead of the one in his hands. He looked over at Dr. Santo, who was openly studying him with narrowed eyes.

"What did you say your name was?" he asked.

"I didn't. It's Cello." Cello watched Ben's hands untangle the stems and leaves quickly but gently, bunching the ginseng together into weighable piles with similar-size roots.

"Like the instrument?"

Cello nodded.

"Huh. And how do you know Benjamin? Are you also a student at Grove?"

"What?"

"Grove College. Are you a student there, too?" Dr. Santo spoke slowly, as though trying to communicate with a speaker of some other language.

Cello shook his head and tried not to look too dazed.

"I guess not, since I'd probably know you, or at least about you, if that were indeed the case." Dr. Santo directed his speech at Cello, but Cello got the sense he wasn't actually being spoken to. That Dr. Santo conversed with some quiet person seated in a corner of the room. Cello looked around quickly, just to be sure.

There was no other person, but something suspicious, something colorful, caught his eye. A car seat patterned with yellow and green cartoon animals rested at the foot of the carpeted staircase. It made him nervous—it was the only trace of a baby in a house where no baby should be.

"Nice sweater," Cello said, and flushed as red as Dr. Santo's sunburn.

"Thank you. I got it when I was working with the peace corps. In Romania."

"Oh," said Cello, looking from Dr. Santo to Ben. Ben caught Cello's eyes and smiled—the smile made Cello half-angry. Of course Ben was making fun of him; Ben wasn't like them, all desperate and grasping. He was privileged, smart. He knew where the paper towels were kept in a kitchen like this.

"Dr. Santo was my history professor last year."

"You were a brilliant student." Dr. Santo shook his head and looked sadly into his lemonade. "I'm so sorry you didn't enroll for next semester. Such a waste."

"I've got a lot going on, Dr. S," Ben said, removing a fallen, yellowed leaf from the front of his shirt.

"Yes, yes, I know. The hard sciences," said Dr. Santo contemptuously, looking again at Cello. "And where are you in school, Cello-like-the-instrument?"

"I'm not," said Cello, taking a careful sip of his drink—mint, that was what the bits of green were.

"Did you graduate? You look a little young—still in high school?"

Cello shook his head, chewing a sliver of mint.

"Where are you enrolled?" Dr. Santo persisted.

Cello gave Ben that same look from the doorway before they'd entered this strange, snow globe of a place.

"I think Cello was homeschooled, right?" Ben had emptied

the sacks, and carefully refolded them. He washed his hands and gave Cello an odd look.

"Yeah," said Cello, deciding that it was mostly true.

"Hmm, I see." Dr. Santo tipped his head back and finished the last of the lemonade. Cello stared at the older man's upper lip where bits of mint had lodged in his stubble. "Are you saving for college as well, young man? I like to think that our work here enriches all sorts of lives, even though it isn't strictly under the law. But then so much of our Constitution is open to interpretation. Meant to be a flexible, living document, you know."

Cello watched Ben dry his hands on a beige-checked towel with words printed on it. *A towel with words on it,* was all Cello could bring himself to think in that moment.

"I think we're ready for weigh-in, sir," said Ben.

"Very well, then." Dr. Santo turned his attention to the piles of plants. He pulled a sleek glass-and-chrome scale from some secret compartment in the heaven-kitchen and began to weigh the piles, writing numbers down on a little pad by the scale. Cello was surprised, indignant even, that Ben was just letting this old sweater-wearing history teacher write whatever numbers down that he wanted. Cello tried to lean nonchalantly over the counter, to make sure the numbers on the scale matched the numbers Dr. Santo scratched onto the pad. He felt Ben looking at him, looked back and saw the trace of a smirk. Dr. Santo worked as quickly as Ben had, and soon his lips were moving as he added the numbers in his head.

"Six hundred and twelve. Does that sound right to you, Benjamin?"

Ben leaned over and looked at Dr. Santo's paper for barely a second. "Looks good to me."

Dr. Santo reached into his pocket and pulled out a bulging wallet, a thick, juicy pear of a wallet, Cello thought. He plucked a stack of bills out and counted out six hundred dollars. Cello watched Andrew Jackson's face flashing continuously out until

Dr. Santo stopped and looked up. "Don't think I have the twelve. Okay if I get you next time?"

"Sure, Dr. S." Ben nodded, smiling a cheerful, calm smile.

Cello thought maybe he should say something, like: "Absolutely not, give us our twelve goddamn dollars." But he stayed quiet, understanding in a new and complete way his ignorance about what was happening, how people could behave this way with each other. Cello was stunned by the realization that he probably had no idea how most things happening in that house could be happening—how a floor could be so clean, how so much furniture could fit into a room and look beautiful and not stupid, what the peace corps was. He felt himself being ushered out, and shook Dr. Santo's hand, bewildered. This, at least, he understood, he thought as he remembered the thousands of handshakes between Sil and the Josephs, between him and Sil even.

Back in the truck, he waited for Ben.

17

Joanie paced between the trailers, hoping the physical movement would propel her toward an answer to her problem.
She needed to give the Vine some form of nourishment, something that would soothe it, and make it fully open to her. Joanie
stopped, and stretched out on the ground; she closed her eyes
and begged for a solution to materialize. She felt Letta before
she saw her; the old woman pushed her foot against the side of
Joanie's leg. Joanie sat up, wiping away the grit left behind by
Letta's shoe.

"I don't know what you been doing, but I need you to get
back to honest work. Now."

Joanie lowered her head between her knees. "Letta," she
began. "You need to tell me what you remember about the worship you used to do at the Josephs'. I know I can do, well, *more*.
But I'm stuck. You have to know something that could help."
Joanie could hear a frenzied, devout heat swelling her voice.

Letta cleared her throat, shifting her hands from her hips to
clasp in front of her chest. "Got in trouble, didn't you? Isn't that

what I said would happen? And why on earth would you think I know anything about *more*?" Letta said, her voice hard.

"Mother Joseph told me you had us all baptized in the chapel. So you know something." Joanie pushed her hair away from her face, and gathered it behind her neck into a rough braid.

"Well, that's different. I've never been one to take Helen's ideas to heart. Why do you think I'm all the way out here while Amberly's in the main house?"

"I just know you can help." Joanie took a deep, deliberate breath. "It could help me. And you owe me, Letta, after all I went through."

"*I* owe you? I raised you like my own." Letta moved a garish cocktail ring Sil had given her, back and forth, from one finger to another. "You, miss, owe me right now. You owe me hours and hours of missed work. You know I can't keep covering for you. It barely works for me anymore, anyway. And the migraines that I get after don't go away for days. The Work is *your* responsibility, as the oldest girl. Concentrate on that, instead of *more*."

Joanie stood and moved to where their work boots were all lined up beneath the kids' trailer step. She was calm, she thought, reasonable. "Well," Joanie said, "if it's my responsibility as the oldest girl, then it should be my choice how we tend to the Vine here. If it's my responsibility and I think we need to do more, then we need to do more. If you help me do that, I can help you, too. You don't know half the things I learned at Mother Joseph's. You don't know half the things I'm learning now." She pulled the laces on her work shoes tight.

Letta put the heels of her hands to her forehead. "I don't need none of that trouble," she said. "I need you to do what we've been doing for years—and right now, I need you clean up all of what we picked. Go on out to the tent."

"Think about what we could do," Joanie said, pinning the long braid up off her neck. "What I could do."

"I can't go against Amberly like that," Letta said, chewing on her lip. "It's too dangerous."

"Are you sure?" Joanie leaned in, relishing the few inches of height she stood taller than her foster mother. "Just think about it." She left Letta beside the trailer, scratching nervously at an old mosquito bite. "Just see what you remember."

Joanie walked to the patch of milky plastic under a blackening sky—the unmistakable crackle of a thunderstorm hung in the air. The tent was stuffy and warm. In that heat, surrounded by fragrant cuttings, Joanie was filled with a transcendent optimism; Letta's fear felt like confirmation that she was on the right track. Surrounded by the humid embrace of the Vine's cuttings all around her, she focused her mind, dived down into her gut and found that her instincts pointed to a solution as clear as a turn signal on the road. Joanie would prepare a recipe in the chapel, not one of Helen's, but one of her own. A gift, to persuade the Vine to let her further in. *It would work.* She could feel the Vine's affirmation all around her. If she could coerce her way more deeply inside of the Vine's mysteries, she could persuade it to do anything she wanted—even track down her son.

Mother Joseph would never have dreamed that Joanie could make the worship belong to her. Mother Joseph would never have dreamed that any person could make the worship her own. Her mother-in-law's worship was an unquestioning child's devotion. But Joanie was curious, like Helen had been. Joanie traced the borders of the Work and understood how she could transform them. Mother Joseph had opened a secret door into the Vine's power, leaving Joanie alone with those ragged books inside of the chapel.

She remembered the books being warped and rippled with damp, their cardboard covers mostly gray. Any trace of color had been leached out over the decades. When Joanie unbuckled the belt that held them together, she noticed they had been stacked in a deliberate order—the oldest ones on top, and the newest ones at the bottom. Reading through them had been like walking alongside Helen Joseph—witnessing her discoveries and theories about the Vine as she made them.

As she ransacked each book for secrets about her new family, Joanie came to a very clear and surprising realization. Helen believed that she was some kind of priestess, and that the line of Work she described could not be broken. Helen filled her books with warnings about upholding the practice, and the dangers of abandoning it.

One night, Josiah asked her about the hours she passed in the cellar. "You don't have to do that every day," he'd explained. "You just can't skip Fridays. Mama's strict about our Sabbath—she's very superstitious."

"How come?" They lay back on the pile of mildewed pillows, Joanie with a cigarette in her hand, Josiah with an oatmeal cream pie in his.

"It's 'cause Letta's sister died doing it different."

"How?" Joanie turned to watch him explain. The pillows were ice cold against her cheek.

"I don't know," Josiah said, pressing the rest of the cookie into his mouth.

"You can tell me. We're married now. I should know, right?"

Josiah chewed with his mouth open. The powerful chemical odor of factory-made cinnamon extract settled over the room. "She was doing the worship. Aunt May—Letta's twin. What you've been doing, down in the cellar."

"Yeah." Joanie reached over Josiah's body to ash her cigarette into an empty orange soda can. She felt Josiah reach up for her, but slapped away his sticky cinnamon grope. "Not now, Josiah. Finish telling me."

"Then?" Josiah asked.

"Maybe." Joanie lit a fresh cigarette off the old one and raised herself onto her elbows.

"Grandmother said she did it wrong."

"What did she do wrong?"

"I don't remember. Just something different. Not like how she did it before. But Aunt May told Mama whatever it was, it was out of our hands, and Aunt May couldn't disrespect the worship without paying. And then she just died, right there in her bed—just, like, blood coming out of her mouth."

Joanie winced and put a hand to her face, as though checking to see if all of her features were still there. "What happened? Did she get sick before?"

"No." Josiah shook his head and she felt the entire bed wobble with the vehemence of his denial. "Just dropped dead out of nowhere. It's why Mama's making you do it. She doesn't like to do it herself if she don't have to—she's scared."

"Huh." Joanie filled her lungs with smoke and then exhaled all of the heat back out into the winter-cold room.

"How come you don't want me?" Josiah asked.

"What?"

"You never want me."

"Quit whining, Josiah. Things would go a lot easier for you if you didn't whine all the fucking time."

"You're just saying that because you're the one who gives me my medicine now." As he sulked, his body sank down into the sag of the mattress. "And I got to keep reminding you."

"Well, Jesus—whose fault is that? If you didn't need your medicine so much, maybe you wouldn't be bitching all the time, would you?" Joanie stubbed her cigarette out on the wall on her side of the bed so she wouldn't have to touch Josiah again.

She had never suspected that their conversation that night would precede Josiah's death by just a few weeks. Joanie wondered, if she'd known then, if she would have done something else. Would she have tried to protect him? Would she have done more for him, if she'd known their child was already a furiously expanding mass of cells inside her?

Joanie shuddered away from the thought. She hadn't done differently, and he was dead. She couldn't have helped Josiah by way of the worship, or otherwise. He was beyond help of that sort. Josiah was too empty. Too dependent on the Vine in the wrong way. Joanie knew whatever magic was in those books wouldn't work in a vacuum. That power needed fuel, juice of the heart—it required a material of substance to catch and burn.

The power in those books, and those callous and fascinating lists of ingredients within them, had charmed her. She hadn't made any of Helen's recipes while she stayed at the Josephs', though she considered it constantly. She thought about how easy it would be to tip the ingredients into the pan in the smokehouse.

Easy, because the worship worked.

One morning, Joanie asked her mother-in-law—from the kitchen where she scrubbed the breakfast pans—if there were more books. Splinters from the decaying floorboards poked through the thick socks on her feet, and the hot dishwater steamed in the freezing kitchen.

"More books?" Mother Joseph repeated. She was half-gone, drooping over a glass of whiskey. "You don't have enough to keep busy downstairs?"

"I was just wondering if there's any more. Those last ones get a little fuzzy." Joanie heaved her weight into scraping off the scales of dried eggs.

"Those *last* ones?" Mother Joseph shouted. "Don't be worrying about them. You just do what we've been doing for a hundred years. Those last books aren't for you."

"Who're they for?" Joanie asked. Was there something she'd missed?

"For people who want to die. Now hush up and finish that. You still got to take the laundry out."

Joanie nodded and kept washing. Before she went out to hang the laundry, she refilled Mother Joseph's glass. She pulled on one of Harlan's old jackets—it stank of sweat and smoke, but it was warm. On the porch, Joanie hauled out the clump of wet clothes from the washing machine and set it on the grass under the line. She thought about what Mother Joseph said, that the books were for people who wanted to die. Did she want to die? Was a divine discovery worth it? Her back was warmed by the sun, even as her reddened numb fingers worked slowly, clumsily prying apart the wooden pins and pinching the sodden fabric to the clothesline.

Maybe, she thought. *Maybe.*

When she was finished, Joanie retreated into the cellar. Just to take another look. Out of all of Great-grandmother Joseph's illustrations, the final pages scratched through with images of a crossroads chilled and intrigued Joanie the most.

The crossroad drawings were deliberately singed, nearly a third of each page disappeared into the air. Helen must have tried to use a fire to ask the Vine what came next. Elongated bodies looped and uncoiled from the burned edges. The faces of some of the figures were blacked out, others had gaping mouths full of sharp teeth. In the center of each corrupted page there was a rough pencil sketch of an organ: a heart, a lung, a kidney, a brain. The papers were bordered by chains of not-quite-connecting crosses. There were no captions for these drawings, like there were for Helen's other illustrations, but on the back of each page—some smeared with charred, sooty fingerprints—eight words were neatly printed in giddy, almost childish loops. A PLACE WHERE LIVING AND DEAD CROSS PATHS. Joanie sensed the danger in those scalded pages, and understood these last books were a place where one might find another level of power. She could feel the tingle of that promise rising up through the paper to meet her fingertips.

Had Letta's sister been the last one to read these? Joanie wondered if she progressed in the worship did it mean she would die, too—like Letta's sister? She approached the idea cautiously, warming her hands at it.

Death would keep her out of the dank bedroom she shared with Josiah. It would keep her away from the gate, and the guilt she felt at the sight of the tenants in their listless all-bone bodies. It would keep her away from the stinking house, and Mother Joseph's unpredictable orders. And if she didn't die, she would become something else, something even Helen Joseph hadn't imagined.

The recipe pages in Helen's books were extensive, although most actual measurements were obscured; fragments of words were piled one on top of the other, towering across the height of the paper. The handwriting was small, two or three layers of writing stacked on each line. Each list of ingredients was strange and incongruent—chamomile leaves, one-third of a railroad spike, turmeric, nettles, rainwater. Joanie ran a finger over each ingredient, remembering it, guessing at its location at the Joseph place.

Joanie lifted the thin cardboard cover of the very last book, exposing the final drawings there. Helen had carefully labeled sketches of what she called the Vine's Heart Cycle: a sinewy loop, serpent to rodent, rodent to seed, seed to soil. All of the sketched creatures climbed and wound around in a circle—a delirious whorl of life.

This was definitely a book for someone who was obsessed, a book made by someone who was testing her limits, Joanie thought. And she wondered if she was like Helen enough to pick up where she left off. Could continuing what Helen began result in the birth of something new?

Joanie devoted her days to studying the worship. As soon as she finished a boil in the smokehouse, she came to the cellar to salt the floor. If there were no cuttings to boil, she came to the chapel straight from her bed, a tap on the turtle's tank her only greeting for the day. Joanie memorized the contents of the books, whispering over them in the dim cellar.

Leaving the Josephs and having the baby had meant a long pause in her worship, not its abandonment. Under the bubble of the tent where she sorted and sponged off the harvested lengths of the Vine with outward calm, she wondered, desperate, how she could reach the Vine in her new chapel. There was nothing in Helen's books about recovering what was lost, but maybe Joanie could build a recipe for that. Bring back her son.

She pulled on a pair of yellow rubber gloves and took a stalk of the Vine from the freshly cut pile in its usual bin. Joanie settled the razor in her hand and, despite the bulk of the glove, shaved deftly away at the browning leaves, leaving the bright green loop of stalk intact. She had always been swift and precise in this work, never accidentally discarding any healthy bits of the plant, or puncturing the cylindrical, fluid-filled stem. She could almost feel the stalks moving, they were so vivid and alive. Joanie pressed her plea into each stalk, and felt an answering squeeze, like the grip of a hand.

She listened to the muted crunch of her rubber gloves compressing and expanding around her fingers. Joanie was swept under the work in a kind of grisly meditation. She imagined the texture, a sinewy slip, of her uncoiling organs through her fingers—like the cord that had connected her baby to her body. She imagined that she was part of the Vine, and that it was a part of her, a part of her baby, too. She urged it along, willing it to stretch further and longer, to wrap all the way around her, to wrap around her baby. Her baby who was gone, torn away like a piece of her flesh.

The Vine called to her, in response to her jolt of loss. It called out from where it lay piled around her; it called out from where it twisted between her fingers. *I will give you more*, it crawled. She pierced the stalk of the Vine, and a glimmering slick of sap oozed out onto her fingers. Joanie lifted it to her mouth.

She drank a single, long sip and tipped her head back, feeling the thick, green scent in the tent cover her. She had only drunk from the Vine that one time with Mother Joseph. This was different—it was much more than the floating ease she had felt at her mother-in-law's elbow. The sap offered her something bigger, an invitation. The Vine's power wound around her like a pair of arms; it lifted her out of the tent and set her by the side of a road. The cartoonish cross of white and yellow painted highway lines glowed bright. She saw the unmistakable outline of Mother Joseph on one side of her, and the impression of her tiny son, on his back on the pavement, kicking his legs joyfully, on the other. Across from her another figure, unfamiliar, wavered and glistened. The Vine lifted her up, so that she could see all of them, even herself, from above; they were arranged just so, four stars in the grisly constellation Helen Joseph had drawn in her final book. A crack of thunder outside the tent broke her vision in half. As it fell away, Joanie found herself on the ground, cradled by the soil as it drank in the water from the storm.

When the rain stopped, she stood, fully back in the tent, hazily taking in the surroundings she had left. Her discarded clippings had already filled the blue plastic tub on the ground. Joanie hadn't remembered skimming off so many leaves, and she wondered how long she'd been in the tent. She ducked outside to empty the tub onto the mulch pile, the storm gone as quickly as it had come. The earth was spongy with water, and the rain caught in the leaves of a colossal maple, shuddering with tiny downpours at every residual gust of wind.

When Joanie turned back inside, she nearly stepped on the bloated body of a dead rat, overcome in the storm. The shape of it struck her suddenly like an answer—an ideal fit into one of Helen's asymmetric, bubbling drawings. She felt a stirring alignment with the decaying animal, and she dropped to the ground beside it. She pressed into it with the flat of her hand, and felt a connection. She rolled the still-warm body over, a key turning in her mind. It was like Helen had delivered the animal herself from the beyond, a creature bridging her world and Helen's, to bless the junction of her last recipe and Joanie's first.

Helen's gift was perfect. Joanie knew exactly what to make— to find what she had lost. She would take the silt-thick liquid from the creek. She would mix in the ash of burned, precious things. She would infuse it with the husk of the creature before her. She would boil it in a great fire and then she would take it to the crossroads she had seen. Joanie understood where she had to go if she wanted to find her son.

She left the drying tent, determined. She abandoned the slick, shorn stalks of Vine and her rubber gloves on the ground. In the kids' trailer, she collected the baby's crate, and began to fill it. Even though they weren't there, Joanie could feel the presence of her foster siblings. She could hear them, and feel their cravings all through the bits of debris they left in their communal sleeping space. Joanie touched their pillows and blankets with the same fondness she would have used to touch their shoulders or cheeks. She paused by her cot, and slipped the top sheet off her bed. It was coated in skin cells, she thought, the cells that belonged to her and her baby. She folded it calmly and settled it into the crate with a little pat.

What Joanie needed most wasn't in the kids' trailer—it was in Letta's. The night that Sil and Cello had brought her, half-dead, back to the garden, she remembered the floor, the way all of her bones seemed to rest atop it in a careless pile. She remembered being alone with Letta, Letta stripping her naked. The smocked peach dress she'd worn to the trial was filthy and reeking, covered in vomit. Letta sliced the dress off her with a pair of kitchen scissors, but didn't ball it up and throw it away. Instead, she held it up cautiously, as though it were a serpent, too. Joanie wasn't sure if she dreamed it or not, but it looked as though Letta held it up to her face. Close enough to see the stitching. Then she folded it and closed it away in some cabinet or case, as though quarantining the garment. Only then did she wash Joanie and dress her in familiar things. Letta settled Joanie into her and Sil's bed, and fed her a warm tea. She hummed as she cleaned and dressed the festering snakebite.

At the time, Joanie hadn't understood why Letta had saved the dress, but now it was clear. The Vine's sap lingered in her body and tapped a message through her. The dress had power—

it was filled and saturated with it. The sweat from Joanie's pores as she'd handled the serpent, and the creature's poison that had been retched back into the world, all of that mystical fluid vibrated in the fibers of that destroyed dress. The Vine was giving her directions, the same way Helen had sent her a sign.

Joanie didn't bother to knock at Sil and Letta's door. She pushed through, unafraid. Letta was there, smoking on the sofa, ashing into an upturned doll's hat nestled between her ribs.

"What is it? One of the kids?" Letta's voice was tense, but she made no movement to hoist herself to standing.

Joanie shook her head. "Where's my dress?" Joanie's voice was hoarse.

"What dress?" Letta exhaled and the trailer filled with smoke.

"My dress from the trial," Joanie said, calling it up in her mind.

"Whatever would you want that for?" Letta's voice hardened, shutting down any suggestion of affection. She knew Joanie hadn't come to apologize.

"Did you think about what I said?" Joanie asked.

"Why can't you leave it alone? I said I'm not interested." Letta ashed her cigarette and covered her throat with a skeletal hand.

"We're on the same side, Letta."

"You're on your own side," Letta said, dragging heavily from her cigarette. "Do you even know what you're throwing away messing around like this?" Letta stabbed her cigarette out in the little plastic hat.

"I just want my dress. It's mine, isn't it?" Joanie kept her voice low.

Letta dropped her head into her hands, as though protecting herself from an invisible blow. "I can't stop you now. I can see you already got started. But I won't help you." Letta looked up, her mouth turned down in a mournful purse. "Promise you won't hurt any of the kids. Or me and Sil."

"Of course I won't," Joanie said, stung.

Letta looked at her hard. She pulled a fleck of loose tobacco from her lip, and pointed to a bank of cabinets. "Up there," she said.

Joanie pulled the large, overturned plastic bin Sil and Letta used as a coffee table against the wall and climbed onto it.

"Did Amberly say anything about the mark on your shoulder, from the—the bite?"

"What? No." Joanie opened and closed the thin fiberboard doors with purposeful viciousness.

"Because there's something you should know, before you go too far." Letta paused and shook her head.

"Well?"

"That mark you had, when you came back to us. My sister May, she had it once. Like a rash. She told me and Amberly it meant one of us was going to die."

"So? Neither of y'all died from it. I almost did."

"Amberly and I were fine, but May wasn't. What you're doing—this Work—it's dangerous. I mean, life-and-death dangerous. I'm sorry, honey," Letta said. "About Junior. I really, really am. But this won't help him." Joanie froze, and tried to really listen, to comb through each of Letta's elongated syllables for any trap she'd set there. "Did you hear me? This won't turn out the way you want," Letta called loudly, her voice abuzz with irritation.

"I heard you," Joanie said, and kept looking. The dress was on the top shelf of the center cabinet. She snatched it up. It was stiff with her year-old vomit.

"I know you won't listen. Lord, help us." Letta canted her head a few inches, and squinted one eye closed, focusing her gaze on Joanie.

Joanie climbed down from the bin and stuffed the dress into the crate. She took a plastic bag for the rat from beneath the sink, and left the trailer, the filled crate tucked under her arm. She stepped out into the humid afternoon with a grim giddiness, a premonition that she was at the beginning, instead of the end of something.

18

Cello rubbed at a small crack in the windshield, reaching over the wheel. The plastic ridge pushed against his ribs. Ben climbed into the truck. His face had lost the practiced cheer on display in Dr. Santo's absurdly bright kitchen. It was warped into something else, a new, unfamiliar look. Cello was surprised by all of the work that had to be done when meeting someone new—noticing moods he didn't understand, and figuring out how they might affect him. He wondered if Joanie would have navigated this new predicament more easily, but he was uncomfortably grateful she wasn't there, in the cab of the truck. He shuddered away from the idea of Joanie meeting this attractive stranger, or walking through Dr. Santo's immaculate house.

"Thanks for the ride," Ben said. "Do you mind driving me to my dorm?"

"How far is it?" Cello asked, feeling immediately chilled beside Ben, no longer interested in his particular moods.

"Just about eleven, twelve miles. I can take the bus, but it barely ever comes, you know?" Ben's face transformed again, this time near sticky with supplication.

"Which way?"

"Back east."

Cello nodded. He was overwhelmed by the bizarre stretch of hours that had passed—not overwhelmed exactly, more like overfilled. Cello didn't think he could take in another unexpected piece of information. He would do the right thing, take Ben home, drop off the next payment at the Stuckey's on his way back and return Sil's truck. He just had to keep remembering himself. He wasn't like Ben, or Dr. Santo. Cello would never have a life like theirs. He'd hated that untethered feeling from inside the house, like he was a moth or some other pest who'd connived his way indoors—that he was a creature who didn't belong there. It made him wonder what kind of life this extra money could buy. What kind of life would suit him better than his life at the garden?

Ben buckled his seat belt, and Cello turned the key with a little shake of his head. "Wait, don't you want you guys' money?" Ben asked.

"Oh, yeah."

Ben counted out his and Marcela's share onto the space between them on the vinyl seat. As Cello folded over the bills and tucked them underneath his thigh, he did his best to hide his humiliation. He'd been so blinded by Dr. Santo and his home that he hadn't even thought to ask for their money—he'd had to be reminded.

"You okay, man?"

"Sure," Cello said, winding through the neighborhood's neat, freshly paved drives. "Just to the college you said, right?" He was caught in separate tides of worry. One current pulled at him, away at his understood life, peeling back those small routine comforts and exposing other questions and desires. The other current pushed him, toward the Stuckey's, toward his obligations to his family, to Joanie.

"Yeah, thanks. I'll show you when we get closer. Or actually you can just drop me there. I have class soon," Ben said.

The college wasn't too far from the garden, but Cello had never been there. Until he'd met Ben, he had never seen anyone from there, either. In the rare times he'd ridden past the campus, it flashed by quick as a photograph—fleeting and flat. It might as well have been Mexico, or the moon. Of course, Cello knew how to get there. The college was famous for practically straddling two states, his own and Maryland, another place he only knew through its fields on visits undertaken with Sil to buy specific types of seeds or supplements for the soil.

"What kind of class you got?" Cello asked.

"Renaissance drama."

"Huh. What's that?"

"It's plays. Written around the time Shakespeare was writing plays, but not Shakespeare."

"That doesn't seem useful to anybody," Cello said plainly.

"No," Ben laughed. "It's really not."

"I thought college was expensive."

"Oh, man, you're killing me. I have practical classes, too, but I let myself take one I like every once in a while," Ben said, putting his feet up on the dashboard.

"Don't do that," Cello scolded.

"Sorry." Ben resettled himself on the bench and slapped his palms on his thighs. "It was actually a pretty good day, don't you think? We got a lot of work done—you guys did well. You're so fast."

"I guess." Cello scratched an itch on his chin with a T-shirt-covered shoulder, keeping his hands on the wheel. "Is that why you're doing what you're doing? To get money for college?"

"Sort of," Ben said, tucking his greasy dark strands of hair behind his ears. Cello was suddenly aware of Ben's smell filling the cab of the truck—it was mostly sweat, but there was something else, some strange and not unpleasant scent spilling from his pores. A kind of melting, minerally sunscreen. Cello cracked the window, letting the vegetal fragrance of summer pour over him and dissolve Ben's scent.

"What about you?" Ben asked. "What are you using the money for?"

"Not for Shakespeare class," Cello said.

"No, seriously, why? You got a girlfriend you're trying to impress?"

"Sort of," Cello said. A thought of that terrifying morning discovery jolted through him—the pained twist of Joanie's face and the mussed blankets in the empty crate.

"That's what I thought," Ben said, half smiling out of the passenger side window. "What's her name?"

"None of your business," Cello said.

"There it is again," Ben said, his smile widening. "The old 'none of your business.'"

"We meeting again tomorrow?" Cello asked.

"Your girl must have expensive taste, if that's not enough to tide you over." Ben tapped the space next to Cello, where the money lay in a lump under his thigh, skimming his leg.

"Yeah," Cello said, leaning forward. He sped toward the college, suddenly desperate to deposit Ben where he belonged, so he could get to the ancient, falling-apart Stuckey's where he was supposed to be.

It was well past noon when Cello rolled the pickup back into its customary spot worn into the earth ruts beyond the kids' trailer. He grimaced at the creak that erupted when he pushed the door just wide enough to slide through. He hastily brushed the dirt off the seat and closed it with his back. Cello folded the paper towel into quarters and tucked it gently into his pocket. Leaning against the truck's hot, metal side, he waited.

He was still simmering from his unsuccessful visit to Stuckey's. The sinister dip in the mulch hadn't been touched since Cello's last visit, and the money from earlier was still there. He left the Crown Light sign as it was and added the extra hundred, agitated by the slow-moving thief and his own wasted time. He mulled over the kidnappers' bizarre and apparently sluggish behavior, and admitted it seemed typical of Mother Joseph.

Before he could suss out Sil's reaction to the missing truck, Sabina came running out to him from the tree line, shielding her eyes from the sun. "Where you been, Cello? You took the truck?"

Cello nodded. "Sil know?"

"No, he doesn't. Already passed out thanks to his precious new experiment crop."

"Letta?"

"She's with Joanie." She looked at Cello carefully. "Did you say something to her? To Joanie?"

"Why? What's wrong?" Cello pitched himself away from the truck's dusty side.

Sabina shook her head. "She's not right."

"Of course she's not right—somebody took her child!"

"I know, but—" Sabina paused, looking somewhere beyond Cello's ear. "This is something else. You better come. We need help."

Cello turned to look where Sabina had gazed off. A thin smudge of smoke hung in the air. He started toward it, and Sabina followed, wincing down at the ground as she ran. Maybe Joanie had hurt herself, or one of the little kids—the smoke, though, was what worried him. If Joanie had damaged the garden, that would bring the fury of not just Letta and Sil, but Mother Joseph.

The source of the smoke, Cello noted with relief, wasn't one of the plots. It was a small bonfire with everyone but Sil gathered around it. This fire was much larger than the ones Letta sometimes set to check in on the Vine. Only one figure moved around the chest-high flames. Cello would've been able to spot Joanie from the sky, that's how well he knew the boundaries of her body. As he and Sabina got closer, he saw that Letta stood off to the side, Emil clutched in one arm, and the other clasped against Miracle's small shoulder, holding her close. From that distance, it looked half like Letta was trying to protect them from harm, and half like she was about to sacrifice them to the fire.

Marcela hovered nearer to Joanie. Joanie's body was angled now, toward the flames. There was momentum there, something coiled and wild, so sudden and violent that Cello believed she might pounce on the fire herself. Cello and Sabina fell toward them, Sabina joining her sister and Cello closing in on Joanie.

"Cello will help me," Joanie said, nodding at him over the crackle and hiss of the fire. Cello noticed, now that he was close, that the fire burned through a large crate—a large, very familiar crate. He looked away as the baby's former little bed burned.

"Cello understands, don't you, Cello?" Her voice turned soft as she swiveled toward him and gripped his forearm. Cello knew it shouldn't feel thrilling, her hands on him this way, but it did. It wasn't the usual thrill he felt at Joanie's touch; Cello's chest burned with fear. "He'll do anything I say." She said it so the sound of the fire and the wind covered it over for everyone else. She'd meant for only Cello to hear.

There's no getting out of this, her hot, dark eyes said.

"Joanie," he said, "what are you doing?"

"A worship." Her hands still held his arm, but loosened a little. They loosened enough so that he could get away if he wanted. But he didn't want to; Cello stayed still as an obedient, leashed animal.

He stared into Joanie's face, trying to pass through the frenzy he saw there. "What? Is this something you're doing for Junior?"

She turned her head sharply away. "Don't call him that," she said.

"You know I'll help you, of course I will. Just explain it to me." Cello's eyes darted to the others arranged around the fire, willing Marcela or even Letta to lead them back to the trailers, away from the fire. "Isn't there some other way to do this? A safer way?" Cello leaned over her, the fire scorching beside them.

"No, there's *no* other way. I don't really even understand it myself. All I know is that it's going to work."

"Work for what? To do what? Joanie, you could get hurt, or hurt one of the kids," Cello said as his knees buckled and his body suddenly drooped toward her.

She stepped away from him sharply. "I would *never* hurt one of the little kids. How could you say that?"

"No, I mean, of course you wouldn't. Not on purpose. But there could be an accident." Cello pointed to where Letta held Emil and Miracle. "Look how scared they are."

"I didn't tell them to come down here, Cello." She moved closer to them, closer to the fire. "Tell Letta to get them out of here."

"What if the fire spreads?" Cello said, backing up to where Letta stood with the kids.

"You think I don't know how to control a fire?" Joanie sneered at him, snapped back into her new, terrible purpose.

Cello motioned to the others, still frozen where they stood, to get back, to disappear. Marcela and Sabina got the idea and started to pull the little kids away, only they had some trouble moving Letta along. Letta was unusually stiff, gaping at Joanie. Cello turned back to Joanie with the same gentleness he'd used with her infant.

"But what's all this for? What're you *doing*?"

"It's going to tell me where my baby is," she said, grabbing onto his wrist.

"Who's going to tell you?"

"The Vine," she snapped. Joanie dropped her hand and Cello felt his body suddenly very hot in the place her skin had touched his skin. "You going to help me?" Her voice was less, somehow—not just quieter, but drained of that single-minded aggression.

"I'm with you, Joanie, I'm always with you. But first, let's do something about the fire," Cello said.

"I'm going to put it out," Joanie said. "I need the ashes."

Cello thought of the scrap of paper towel tucked into the pocket of his jeans that bore the footprint of her baby. He thought for an instant about showing it to Joanie. Almost immediately, he thought better of it. He didn't want to push her any further. Joanie moved to a bank of blackberry brambles and pulled a shovel from the ground. When she'd returned to the blaze, she began to shovel soil onto the flames. Cello took the shovel from her when she slowed and quickly got the fire out.

Joanie watched silently. "Can you get something to hold the ashes?" she asked.

Cello nodded, but waited for the fire to go entirely out. He felt the charred earth's heat through the soles of his shoes as he tamped out the last of the flames. He left Joanie leaning against the shovel, and headed up to the trailers. Cello didn't see anyone outside, only Sil, snoring in a golden nest of spent Crown cans.

He knocked on the door of the kids' trailer and then felt embarrassed about knocking and just pushed his way inside. Marcela and Sabina sat on Miracle's bed. Both girls shone with sweat, and sat the exact same way—one leg tucked underneath, the other foot on the floor.

"What the hell happened? Did she set that fire by herself? Where's everybody else?" Cello asked. The girls looked at one another and then lifted their faces toward him.

"It was so weird," Marcela began.

"Joanie started that fire, and just kept adding stuff to it. Our stuff," Sabina said. "And Letta didn't say a thing. She was the one who seemed scared of Joanie."

"Why?" Cello asked, running a hand over his rib cage where

the bruising from his last beating still lingered. "Why didn't she wake up Sil?"

"You should be kissing the hem of Letta's garment for not waking up Sil," Marcela answered. "Hell, at first I thought Joanie was covering for your ass, distracting them, throwing that fire together. I was like, man, she's dedicated. Maybe she really does care about Cello."

"What're you talking about, Mar? Why would Joanie need to cover for Cello?" Sabina turned a confused face on her sister.

"Nothing, don't worry about it." Marcela patted her sister's leg, but Sabina seemed more irritated than calmed by the gesture. She muttered something and turned to face the wall. "But that fire." Marcela nodded as she spoke. "It was just weird. Do you think Joanie's possessed?" she asked. Her eyes were wide, her fingers twisting through one another.

"People don't get possessed." Cello snorted. "It's not like that at all. She's just upset about the baby," Cello said, trying to keep his voice kind.

"That's the thing, though," Marcela said, so slowly that Cello could practically see her choosing her words. "She doesn't even seem upset exactly. She's focused. Too focused. Like she's trying to do something that can't actually get done."

"Like get back Junior?" Sabina asked.

"I don't know, probably," said Marcela.

"Where is she? She still by herself?" Sabina stood and headed to the door. "You shouldn't have left her alone, Cello."

"She sent me up here to get something," Cello said, his voice rising. "You could have gone down there to stay with her if you're so worried. Y'all can't expect me to do everything."

"You're right—I'll go," Sabina said quickly. "What'd she want from in here?"

"Something to hold the ashes. She wants to use them for whatever this is." Cello pressed a weary palm against his forehead. "I don't know." He sat on Joanie's stripped cot, setting his hands on either side of his legs and pressing into the thin mattress. His body ached with the extra labor of the ginseng harvest, and his eyes were gritty with not enough sleep.

Sabina reached under her bunk and pulled out an old faded pillowcase. "Y'all should check on Letta, too." Sabina kept her eyes on the fabric in her hand as she folded it into a neat square. "Help her with the little kids. Let's try to keep her in some kind of a good mood."

"You're sure bossy today," Marcela said, her voice quiet, her words not quite a joke.

"You're bossy every day—how about that, Mar?" Sabina rushed out of the trailer, slamming the door behind her. Cello looked at Marcela, and they both looked toward the still-banging door.

"So?" Marcela said, holding out a palm. "Where's my money?"

"It's here." Cello reached into his pocket and peeled out Marcela's share, counting it into her outstretched hand.

"Wow," she whispered down into the cash.

"You got four more coming."

"Four *hundred*?" Marcela squealed.

"No, four regular. Four, like, dollars." Cello peered through the window for signs of movement, or the silky flash of Joanie's hair.

"Still, that's pretty good. Are we meeting back up with Ben? What was his guy like, the guy you sold to?"

Cello remembered the bright clean kitchen, and the way Dr. Santo and Ben had spoken to each other, so easily and precisely, like people in a training video. Cello didn't tell Marcela about that.

"I don't know, he was a guy. I told Ben we'd meet up again tomorrow—but I don't think we should be making any plans with Joanie like this."

"Come on, we all know Joanie can take care of herself, even

if she's, you know, not exactly all there. Do you think Joanie would give a rat's ass if one of us was in a mood?"

"Course she would." Cello recited it only out of loyalty. He knew that if Joanie were in Cello's place, she'd meet Ben and his guy until she made as much as she needed. He knew that with the caustic certainty he knew someone had dipped Junior's thin-skinned baby foot in motor oil. He imagined the skin, so sensitive it couldn't be in the sun, flaring red and blotchy from the slick, chemical contact.

"Everyone's been acting weird, and I hate it," Marcela said.

"Let's try to get everything back to normal, alright? We're supposed to pick the rest of Sil's hybrids today," Cello said as he and Marcela left the trailer, fanning out toward the largest Vine plots. "He won't like this."

"Sil's got bigger problems. Anyway, he'll just make us work extra tomorrow. Letta will make sure her money keeps coming. She won't let anybody get in the way of that, not even her precious Joanie."

"Maybe." Cello frowned.

"Hello? Have you lost your mind, too?" Marcela scolded. "You wanna split up—I'll go check on Letta, and you get moving on Sil's plot?"

"Sure," Cello said, peeling away from Marcela.

"Well, bye and good luck to you, too," she called.

19

The silence after the fire was enormous; all of the birds and squirrels nearby had fled the intrusion. Joanie waited by the pile of ash, stamping at the places that still winked out at her, smoldering. She squinted up at the figure marching down the hill toward her—it wasn't Cello, and the figure didn't move with Marcela's loose swagger. It was Sabina; she could tell by the carefully controlled, uniform steps. Sabina held out a square of folded cloth, her head down.

"You okay, Joanie?" she asked, eyes still averted.

"You can look at me, you know. There's nothing to be scared of." Joanie tried to make her voice kind, inviting. But it wasn't coming out right. It was like the intensity of the fire had leaped straight into her throat. "Listen, do you want to help me? Cello said he would, but you're here now. I think it's better if you help, anyway."

"What do you mean?" Sabina looked up, her face open, maybe even a little pleased.

"I mean, the Vine knows you now. And it's better if a girl

helps. Here, let's get all of the ashes into this bag." Joanie knelt down and began sweeping the fire's warm residue into a pile. "What're they all saying up there?" She tried to make it seem harmless, a perfectly normal question.

Sabina crouched down and joined her in scooping handfuls of ash into the bag. "Mostly everybody's confused. Why didn't Letta get mad at you?"

"Because I'm doing something even Letta doesn't understand. And if it works, she'll be better off." Joanie brushed her hands clean on her denim shorts. "Come on. Let's go to the chapel."

Sabina followed behind, matching her stride so that their two sets of legs left a single set of footprints. The little green cove they had built together was almost invisible, but the atmosphere was thicker.

"Go grab a cutting for me, and meet me back over here as quick as you can."

Joanie circled the tiny chapel, searching for the creature she had hidden. It was exactly where she left it—it looked like a bright, white stone in the grass. Joanie clutched the plastic bag with the rat's body inside, tying it closed more tightly against the scent of decay.

"Joanie?" Sabina untangled and handed over a twist of the Vine. Joanie accepted it, looking for the best place to break into it.

"Here, come closer to me." She waved Sabina beside her. Joanie snapped open the Vine so that only a trickle of sap emerged.

Sabina gasped as the green bleed perfumed the chapel.

"What're you doing?" Sabina asked.

"Hold it for me while I drink. Don't let me take too much. And as soon as I'm done with it, bury the cutting right away. Right here." She pointed to the ground beside the chapel wall.

"How much is too much?" Sabina asked, uncertain.

"You'll know." She put a hand on Sabina's arm, not sure if

she was steadying herself or her foster sister. "The Vine will stop you. It doesn't want either of us to get hurt." Joanie cleared her mind, opening it wide to whatever the Vine had to show her. Sabina took the cutting, as carefully as Joanie had taken up the serpent during her trial, and held it to Joanie's lips.

Joanie lapped at the broken cutting like an abandoned kitten drinking from a rag soaked in milk—careful at first, then taking more, and much more. A thirst overtook her, and she swirled into a vision of kneeling beside a river, drinking down as much water as she could. As she drank from the river, she grew stronger; her vision was sharper, her hearing almost painfully keen. Her skin tingled, like it was answering back to the river she had drunk. Everything went quiet, as quiet as the clearing after the fire, and Joanie's arms were suddenly heavy with the weight of her baby. A wash of green tinted her vision, and she sank into it, gratefully. For a moment, Joanie couldn't find her way out of this soft merging with the Vine; she had never felt so close to anything. From far away, Sabina was shaking her. Just before Joanie lifted out of the vision, she saw a dark gap in all that jade—the dark shadow of Mother Joseph.

"Joanie?" Sabina said, pulling her back into the little chapel with both her hands clamped on Joanie's arms. "What happened? Are you alright?"

Joanie felt a swell of tenderness for the girl, and wrapped an arm around her, pulling her into a hug. The momentum of the embrace swung the grisly plastic bag against the sides of their bodies.

"I'm fine—don't look so worried. I know what I'm doing, I promise. Every time I come to the chapel, or use the Vine, I understand it better. It wants me to be with my son again. It wants us all to be happy. Can you feel it? I'm going to make things better for all of us. I'll take all the harm far away from here."

Sabina pulled back, a little stiff. "Take the harm away?

Shouldn't we take *ourselves* away from the harm?" She rubbed at her eyes, at pollen or tears, Joanie couldn't tell.

"You know, I used to think that was possible." Joanie smoothed the younger girl's dark hair off her face, astonished by how tall she suddenly seemed. "But the kind of harm that's all over this place—that's over all of Mother Joseph's places—it's the kind of harm that follows you everywhere."

Sabina nodded, her face wet. Real silent weeping—Joanie thought, *This is why. I'm doing this for all of us.*

"I used to feel exactly like you do, but I don't anymore. You know why? Because now I'm not powerless." Joanie closed her eyes and reached out along that tingling connection she felt with the Vine. "I'm gonna make it better, baby. You'll see." Joanie used the hem of her T-shirt to wipe Sabina's face. "Do me a favor?"

Sabina nodded, her eyes everywhere except on Joanie.

"Go get me a couple more cuttings. For later. And keep Sil and them away, alright? What I got to do next is big. It might seem scary, but you shouldn't be scared." The words bubbled out of Joanie's mouth as naturally as a spring from the earth. She could *feel* the ease they would bring Sabina. She could feel the green pulse of truth in her promise. The garden would be better; *she* could make it a peaceful place, a safe place to raise a child, a safe place to grow up.

"Okay, Joanie." Sabina turned, running her ash-covered hands through her hair as she walked.

Joanie packed the extra cuttings and the bag of animal remains into the pillowcase filled with ashes. She swung the bundle of treasures by her side and headed to the cover of the blackberry bushes where she'd hidden the rest of her supplies; it was also the place she'd hidden her baby weeks ago. The decoy fire had worked. Letta would believe she was all finished now. Joanie imagined her, collapsed in relief on her bed, a cold compress on her head and a drink in her hand. The first fire hadn't been entirely for show. She needed the ashes for Helen's recipe.

She paused, hearing the whisper of the Vine all around her, and corrected herself—*she needed the ashes for her own recipe*. Joanie's thoughts began to lap one another, moving more quickly than she could track them. Maybe she had taken too much from the Vine; maybe she had pushed too far in. Joanie felt different, like the molecules of her body were arranging themselves in a new way.

Whatever was happening to her had already half-happened, she decided. She wouldn't leave it unfinished. Joanie headed into the woods, the brush thick, catching and scraping her skin. She walked as though following an invisible trail, a path that had existed before the woods had even grown. The pulse of the Vine drew her forward. She didn't stop, or slow, or hesitate. She was already far from where her foster family hid in their trailers.

Joanie stopped, her bare legs plunged into a thicket of swamp roses. She saw the blood well up on her skin from the deepest of the thin scarlet scratches, surprised that she hadn't felt a thing. She pushed a wave of fear back.

Joanie reached into the back pocket of her shorts and removed an X-Acto knife. She slid the knife open and began to slice shoots and branches from the thicket. She held up a clump and turned it around, examining it from all sides. She held the bundle, separating it into three pieces, and wove the sections into a crude braid in the shape of her sign of protection. Her hands bled and stung, but the pain gave her a little jolt of satisfaction. She could feel the sap from the Vine glimmer with approval through her veins. Her blood would only make the worship more powerful.

Joanie reached into her back pocket for the plastic lighter she'd stashed there. Another fire out here would be trouble, and not just with Sil and Letta. A fire here, with all of the brush and woods surrounding it, would be massive: an important sacrifice of the trees in the equation of her worship. The Vine's demands were as clear and insistent as the demands of her own body. She would give it whatever it wanted in exchange for her baby, in exchange for that new surge of strength. It would be only a matter of time before the volunteer fire department arrived. She knew that—a current of reason still ran underneath all of her delirious preparation. *But for how long?* Joanie wondered. When would she forget herself?

She was dizzy with the heat and the thrill of her act of creation, but took a breath. She knew, despite everything, she was calm—her face still, composed.

"I know what I'm doing," she said out loud. She didn't know if the reassurance was meant for Helen Joseph, or the Vine, or herself.

Joanie emptied the plastic bag and the rat fell onto the ground in a small, wet heap. She lit the woven swamp rose, shaking away the lighter when the skin at her thumb began to blister from the heat. Joanie dropped the burning branch onto the furred, dead body and stepped away. She couldn't name the sensation that swelled through her. She could only identify that it felt like *more*.

The blaze grew in the span of a few breaths. It caught on and lingered over the rat, the smell of burning hair and fur, along with burning flesh, hung in the air. It didn't take long for the fire to jump from the pile to the surrounding brush. It was already too big for a single person to manage. The Vine's approval beat out from the flames.

Joanie worked quickly, using a fallen branch to scoop some of the burning debris toward her. She beat down the orange glow to ash with her feet, and the scent of melting rubber compounded with every stomp. She scooped a few handfuls of fresh ash into the half-filled pillowcase. Joanie mixed the two sets of ashes through the cloth carefully, oblivious to the blazing danger growing around her.

★ ★ ★

Sabina hurried to the trailers, her movements frantic, half starting and half stopping. Cello watched her from where he worked, her jerking motions like a rabid animal's.

"Sabina!" he called. "You alright? Where's Joanie? I thought we weren't going to leave her alone."

Sabina shook; Cello couldn't tell whether it was anger or fear that drove her trembling. "No, you should go get her. She sent me away. Joanie needs you. She's not herself." Sabina pushed him down the slope.

"What about you? Are you alright? Did she say something to you? Did she do something?"

Sabina shook her head, her arms out, setting a perimeter around herself. "I'm fine, I'm fine," she repeated. "What is that? Do you smell it? Is there a fire?"

Cello tried to approach her slowly. "Sabina, take a deep breath, okay? In through your nose, out through your mouth. We put out the fire, remember? I saw it myself."

"Cello," Sabina said, her eyes wide, her body suddenly still. She raised her arm and pointed to something behind him.

Cello turned, and saw a dark plume of smoke rise up from the base of the hill. Then he ran, calling Joanie's name as he fled. He ran straight through the heaving layers of smoke to the source, because he knew, as surely as he knew the contents of his heart, that Joanie would be there. She was completely still, as though snared in a trance. He nearly crashed into her, unable to control his speed. The sky above them simmered with dark clouds, and the loom of a thunderstorm snapped in the gusting breeze.

Joanie jolted at his arrival, and something behind her eyes flickered. Cello waited for her to tell him what was wrong, what she needed. In those few silent moments, the fire grew, catching onto an old oak tree. The sound of an animal crashing through the woods rumbled toward them. Cello and Joanie turned, expecting a lurching deer or bear, but staggering up to them and to the fire was Sil. He was screaming, too, though Cello couldn't quite understand him. The dry heat blossomed around them, an eerie counterpoint to the humid summer air. Cello reached for Joanie as Sil lurched toward them, his arms waving furiously.

"Get her out of here!" Cello heard through the gold curtain of the blaze.

But Joanie, in the middle of the fire's fierce grip, didn't look like she needed anyone to get her out of anywhere. Cello thought she looked calm and powerful, like she could walk through the fire and away from the danger. Sil reached them, stinking, so saturated with drinking that Cello thought he might just be flammable, too.

"Get back, Joanie!" he screamed. "Cello, help me!"

Cello watched Sil's feeble attempt at stomping out the flames in the gusting wind, and he knew there was no chance that they could all put the fire out together. The forest was beyond their help.

They stood off the side as Sil danced along the fire's edge. Joanie's lips were pressed together in a little satisfied smile. She watched the fire, and nothing else. The blaze grew out and away from them, the smoke billowing across the darkening afternoon sky.

The distant call of sirens from the nearest access road propelled Sil away, though he still hurled his arms and stomped the ground like a madman. When Cello saw him start to run toward them, he also began to run, pulling Joanie along with him. They ran, sometimes tripping and slowing, but faster than Sil, who staggered along after them, repeatedly falling to his shins and swearing. Soon, he was so far behind them that Cello couldn't hear him anymore.

He didn't know what to do. He didn't want Joanie to suffer more punishment. *He* didn't want to suffer more punishment. Maybe Letta would send Joanie away again. Maybe she'd send

Cello away. Outside of that threat, another foreign compulsion swept through him—to be alone with Joanie, not to bask in her presence, but to force an explanation. More than anything else, Cello was desperate to understand her the way he did before her stay at Mother Joseph's.

He remembered the money in his pocket, and veered away from the path that led to the garden. They wouldn't go back, he decided. He pulled Joanie along toward the road, toward Route 9. They slowed down, but half skipped and half walked along the edge of the faded asphalt, ducking into the cover of the tree line when a car or truck sped along.

They rounded a curve in the road that bulged out into the back lot of the Stuckey's. The weathered vinyl siding of the convenience store drew Cello forward like a light blinking out a message. He wanted to see if the money he left had been taken. In a flash of selfishness, he thought maybe he would take it back. It would help him and Joanie get farther away.

"Let's take a break," he said to Joanie, stretching his arm out, almost touching her.

Joanie looked up at him, her eyes bright. She followed him to the small stretch of littered sidewalk and sat down on the curb. Her skin glowed eerily under the fluorescent light of the Stuckey's.

"Wait here, I'm gonna get us a drink," Cello said.

He returned with a bottle of bloodred energy drink, but not before checking on the envelope buried beneath the Crown Light sign; it still had not been taken.

"Here," he said, passing Joanie the bottle. His throat was dry from the walking and from being so close to the fire, but he let Joanie drink first. He couldn't help himself. Taking care of Joanie had been a reflex his entire life. Even now, when he couldn't make sense of her or his shifting feelings, he couldn't help it.

Joanie's scraped-up arms looked sinister, almost angry, clutching the cold, red bottle. "Can I get you something else?" Cello pointed back toward the convenience store. "For those cuts?"

"No, thanks," she said between swallows. "It'll work better like this—being open." Cello sat down on the sidewalk beside her, and she handed him the rest. Cello finished it off, tapping the empty plastic cylinder against his knees. He forced away the swell of fear Joanie's words pulled out of him.

"What do you want to do?" Cello asked. "We can't go back right now. Letta and Sil would kill us."

"I know." Joanie paused and her focus shifted, as though she was listening to someone who wasn't there. "I need to get to a crossroads," Joanie said.

"What? What're you talking about?" Cello stared at her, wondering if something in her was really gone, burned away in the fire or before.

"I didn't do all of that Work for nothing, Cello. There's a plan I need to follow."

"If you want me to help you, you need to tell me more than that."

"If I don't get to a crossroads, everything I did so far will be a waste." She stood up and scrubbed at her face with her filthy palms. "Let's keep going," she said.

Cello stood and they walked on until the day stretched to its end. They'd made it almost eight miles from the garden, to where Cello hoped they'd make it before dark—a garishly lit, lemon yellow motel near the exit to the interstate. He tugged on Joanie's arm, pointing her toward the pool of light streaming from the place.

"We can't go *there*," Joanie said, shaking him off.

"Yeah, we can."

"They're not going to let us stay for free," she said, and kept walking.

"I have money," Cello explained.

"Really." Joanie stopped, and faced him. "Since when?"

"I'm working on a special project. Letta and Sil don't know about it."

"Then you should save it. We can sleep in the woods tonight, or keep going till we find something better," Joanie said.

"No, we can't. We tried that already and Sil found us in a minute." Cello was shocked that he'd spoken to her that way, surprised by the anger that leaped up in him and made each word rasp with harshness.

"I don't think Sil's looking for us yet," Joanie spat, her eyes narrowed. "That fire kept him busy, I know it."

"Well, he won't be looking for us in motels—he doesn't know we'd be able to pay. And anyway, if we go around looking like this—" Cello pointed lamely at their filthy, smoke-drenched clothes and faces "—somebody's going to put two and two together and call the police."

"I can't stop now, Cello." Joanie kicked at a loose knot of asphalt in frustration, sending it in an arc into a patch of dirt nearby.

"Look, you're exhausted. Whatever you're trying to do, you'll do better once you rest. We can get inside, and figure out how to get to your crossroads or whatever. And maybe what comes after that." Cello exhaled all of the air in his lungs and wondered, What *could* possibly happen next? He didn't have that much money.

"What comes after? I'm going to get him back—that's it. But I think you're right. This'll all work better in the daylight. Let's just get inside," Joanie said, abruptly turning, walking quickly toward the motel lights, her limbs propelled by adrenaline or some other mysterious burst of energy.

Cello followed her, though his movements were imprecise, like he was wearing another person's body as a biohazard suit. Normally, he would always find pleasure in helping Joanie. But there was no pleasure in this. He thought about what Sabina had said; Joanie was not herself. Maybe he wasn't helping Joanie at all, just a blurred copy of her.

★ ★ ★

Joanie waited outside in the dark while Cello paid a leering clerk in exchange for a sticky brass key. Cello unlocked the door and let Joanie in first. The room was dark and cavernous compared to the packed and stuffy kids' trailer. Cello didn't feel like one of the kids in this room.

Joanie flipped the light on in the bathroom and closed the door. He heard the shower run and quelled the alien impulse he felt to run. Where would he go, anyway? Cello pinched his arm, focusing on the sliver of compressed skin. He cared about Joanie, and worried about her. They were both just overwhelmed. Clearly the loss of Junior had sent Joanie over the edge. He thought about the folded paper towel in his pocket, and what would happen if she knew about it. Maybe it would divert her from this path of destruction. To wherever it led. She would see there was something real to be done. Maybe Joanie would even go to the police, if she knew they had something to go on.

Cello felt the darkness hanging thick around him, and switched on the TV as a distraction. The eleven o'clock news glowed out in a muted blur. Cello started, his throat tightening, as he began to recognize the woods being shown on the screen. It was the fire, or rather, it was the charred remains of the fire Joanie had set. A doughy volunteer's face stared gravely into the camera, his mouth moving soundlessly. Cello fiddled with the knob on the television set but the silence remained. He read the line in bold white typeface beneath the firefighter's head with some difficulty: COUNTY-WIDE ARSON INVESTIGATION.

He was shot through with an icy panic. What would happen to the kids? To all of the plots? If the police found Joanie, would she go to jail? Would he? He knew what Joanie did hadn't felt right, but to have it aligned with this twisted, capacious word transformed it into something else. Joanie had dragged him into the sinister maze of this word: *arson*.

When Cello thought about life outside of the garden, he thought about someone like Dr. Santo, or Ben. Someone un-afraid and far away. But looking into the fireman's full, smudged face, he saw real despair, a kind of despair he understood. He looked at the door to the bathroom, limned with light, and the shushing of the shower within. Would he tell Joanie or would he turn off the TV and pretend he hadn't seen it?

The door abruptly opened, and Joanie walked through the murk wrapped in a thin, gray towel to where he stood. She looked at him, and then at the lit screen.

"It's on the news," he said, his eyebrows drawn together. "I have to show you something." He reached into his back pocket for the grimy paper towel and unfolded it between them.

"What is it?" Joanie asked, her hair still dripping from the shower.

Cello sighed, not sure how he should tell her. He opened his mouth, and everything he tried to say, to make his story gen-tler or easier to hear, just fell away.

"Letta and I found an envelope, on Miracle's birthday. It was from whoever took the baby. Asking for money."

"Wait, what?" Joanie put a hand to her temple. "Why didn't you tell me?"

"Letta said not to."

"Who gives a shit if Letta said not to? You should've told me, Cello. He's *my* baby." Joanie snatched at the paper towel, tearing it a little as she pulled it away from him. The footprint had bled into a cartoonish shape, but five distinct, miniscule toe prints were still recognizable as human. "Did this…did this thing come with it?"

Cello shook his head. "No. I brought some money to the spot the note told me to go, and this was there. Asking for more money."

"*Letta* gave you money for this? Or was it Sil? Do you still have the note?"

"No. Not Letta, and Sil doesn't know. I got the money my-self."

"Jesus," Joanie murmured as she touched the oil stain with an extended fingertip. She sniffed at the square of paper. "What're they doing to him?" She traced the scrawl of looping black script at the top.

"I don't know, but he's alive at least. We'll get him back, Joanie. Don't worry."

"Cello." Joanie's voice was cold and hard—the resigned voice of a much older person. "This is Mother Joseph's handwriting." She sat on the edge of the bed, and Cello wondered if he should sit down with her.

"What? Are you sure?" Cello's stomach lurched with nausea.

"The thing about all this is," she continued, "I'm not even surprised."

"What do you mean?" Cello watched the light from the muted TV cast shadows among the curves and hollows of her face.

"I mean," she said, looking up, right at him, "nothing good can ever happen in a world like this. Now do you understand why my plan is so important?" Joanie brandished the torn paper towel. "I don't want to live in a world, or raise my son in one, that has people like this in it! I'm going to get him back, no matter what I have to do. *We* are going to get him back." Joanie looked out past him, determined.

It was the melody of that declaration, its cool mournful dip, that shook something loose in Cello. Like he'd been struck, and that movement sloshed his feelings over the edge of their containment. He was suddenly light-headed, impelled toward Joanie, toward his own idea about *something good*. The family he imagined they could be: him, Joanie and Junior. He would tell her how much he loved her, would kiss her and hold her.

More than anything, Cello wanted to show himself that his feelings about Joanie were the same they'd always been. He almost didn't feel his body moving in toward her, and nearly missed the sight of her face contorted in disgusted alarm. Before he could put his mouth on hers, Joanie blocked his body with her forearm and pushed him away. "No, Cello," she said firmly. "Not that. You know I love you, but I don't want that."

Cello straightened and stepped back; a rush of humiliation ousted all of the hopeful feelings he'd wanted to channel into Joanie. He ducked his head down, waiting for whatever else she was going to say. He hated himself for the tears he could feel forming. There was so much injustice between them, Cello thought, not just the injustice of Joanie never really loving him, but the injustice he'd just subjected her to—being loved when you don't want to be. He felt his way through that bog of sorrow, understanding that he had reached the end of something, the oldest story he'd told himself.

"I should have thanked you for getting us here, and making me rest." Joanie's tone was soft and careful. "Where did you get the money?" she asked quietly.

Cello tried to keep the emotion out of his voice when he answered her. "I met a guy. We've been senging—digging up wild ginseng. We sold it to some other guy."

"You took it from the garden?"

Cello nodded. "It was wild, though. Nobody knows." He didn't tell her his suspicions about Ben's arrival at the garden right when Junior went missing, and he didn't tell her about Dr. Santo.

"Then we have to go back. Or at least you do. We're going to need more money. How long do you think I can stay here?" Joanie asked. "I don't know how much time I'll need." Joanie stared off toward the corner of the room, squinting at something Cello couldn't see. "Is there enough for a week? Two?" Cello was heartened by her sudden flash of practicality. It was like the real Joanie had been called back up.

"I'm not sure," Cello answered. "Maybe. I can figure it out."

They both breathed several lungfuls of mildew-tinged air before Cello spoke again. "How do you think she got him?"

"Doesn't matter how she got him—the point is, she has him. And now I know exactly how to get him back." A sudden dark splash of liquid ran from Joanie's nose, splattering the bath towel over her ribs.

"Joanie, you're bleeding," Cello said, running to the bathroom for a clump of toilet paper. She made no move to stop the flow, but let Cello press the tissue to her face. They sat quietly, waiting for the bleeding to stop.

"I'm sorry, Joanie, about that. What happened before. I shouldn't have tried to—"

Joanie lifted her palm to him, facing it out like she was casting a protective spell. "We're not gonna talk about that again. I'm sorry, but I can't—I can't talk about it again."

Cello nodded. "You still need to get to some kind of crossroads?"

She nodded back—a single, firm dip of her head. "Yes. But we'll figure it all out tomorrow," she said, not looking at him. "When you come back with more money. I'm not sure yet, what all else I'll need."

"When will you know? How will you?"

Joanie stood and moved around to the side of the bed, still gripping the foot-printed paper in her fist. "I just will." Her voice was hard, different from before. Cello couldn't explain why, but he believed her. She pulled the blankets down and slipped between them.

Joanie's refusal clung to him in the dark motel room, in the TV screen's thin light… Cello wondered if that life he'd imagined—the three of them as a family—could ever have existed.

He shivered away from those thoughts and switched off the TV, taking his turn in the shower. He fell asleep in the other bed thinking not only of Joanie and the baby, but about how he would find Ben again, without running into Marcela or any of the others.

20

In the morning, Cello left Joanie asleep. He hadn't seen her sleep so soundly since before she'd left for the Josephs'. He locked the door as quietly as he could, and walked back toward the garden, hidden in the curling branches of a long row of horse chestnuts. The long grass and bald dandelion stems flicked out at his bare ankles with every step. When he got dressed, he couldn't stand to put his filthy socks back on. Cello knew he was getting close to home when he smelled the char on the air.

He walked toward the dark seam of the burn that led back into the wild ginseng field where he and Marcela had dug up that first harvest. Cello was surprised to find Marcela, and not Ben, seated curled over her knees on a flat rock.

"Oh, hi. Nice to see you," Marcela said icily, lifting her chin in Cello's direction.

"What happened? You alone?" Cello didn't approach her.

"Yes, I'm alone. You think Sil and Letta hired bodyguards to accompany me places now there's a lunatic on the loose setting fires?"

Cello could feel the understanding between them, like a light patter of rain, about who that lunatic was.

"Do they know it was Joanie? Did the police come?"

Marcela hesitated, stuck her pinkie finger in her ear and twisted it. "They came."

"Did they find anything? Any of the plots?"

Marcela shook her head. "Sil's not sure, but probably not. He stayed by the fire, said he was hunting and smelled it. They didn't care about anything else, he said. Just the fire. They didn't follow him home."

"They'll be back since it's easy to tell somebody set it. For the investigation," Cello said, wooden.

Marcela nodded, inspecting the extracted wax on her finger.

"Will they come up to the trailers?"

"Probably. Letta thinks yes. I wouldn't go back there if I was you. I wouldn't go back there if I was me, but... Not like I have a choice." She stared out at Cello, grim. "Unless I make some more money."

"That's what I was hoping for today, too." Cello stepped closer to Marcela but didn't make any move to be chummy or affectionate.

"Where'd you and Joanie go?" Marcela brushed her hands together and looked up at him.

"I'd rather not say."

"Yeah, I bet!" Marcela let a sharp laugh into the air. "You're probably in seventh heaven."

"Not exactly," Cello murmured. Joanie's frightening hot-bright eyes, and her mysterious plan, flashed through his mind.

"Who's in seventh heaven?"

Marcela and Cello turned together. Ben had snuck up on them from behind, and Cello felt a yearning lean toward the stranger. Cello envied the other boy's clean clothes. A visible smudge of sunscreen streaked the side of Ben's neck. Somebody should rub that in, Cello considered, but then quickly slapped away the thought.

"Cello. He's snuggled up in a love nest with Joanie," Marcela taunted, flipping a wave of dark hair over her shoulder, twinkling out at Ben. But it wasn't Marcela Ben watched. Cello realized the stranger was staring at him.

"She the girlfriend?" Ben asked.

"She's our sister," Marcela said, delicately wrinkling her nose.

"She's not anybody's sister," Cello said, just to Marcela, not looking at Ben. "Anyway, are we doing this?"

"Let's split up," Marcela said, giving him a sharp look. "We'll get more done that way."

Cello liked that he didn't have to rush back to follow Sil's instructions, or explain his absence to anyone. He could just work for himself. He let himself wonder: What would he do if there were no Joanie, no kidnapper, no garden?

He could go somewhere nobody knew him and have a fresh start. He would still work outside, but he would live alone. He could eat the things he grew, and sleep when he wanted to sleep. No one would hurt him. If he got tired of being alone or needed something, he could sell the things he grew, and use that money to buy whatever he wanted. He could go to the movies, and choose his own clothes. He could move forward.

The cool, shady calm he felt in this separate place—away from the garden, even away from Joanie—was disturbed only by Ben. He felt Ben shadowing his searching, assessing the spaces beneath logs and around clumps of rock that Cello had already checked. It wasn't just that he could feel Ben; he could hear him, too.

"You didn't grow up outside, did you?" Cello asked the other boy, who trailed about fifteen feet behind him.

"What? Who grows up outside?"

"You're really loud."

"Excuse me?" Ben's voice lifted in pitch, incredulous.

"Not much of a hunter, are you?" Cello said. "Deer would hear you a quarter mile off."

"No, I don't hunt." Cello was amused to see the stranger lift himself onto tiptoe, as though that would dull the noise he made.

"You go to class every day?"

Ben nodded, still looking down, presumably working, but Cello could see that he wasn't really looking, that he was more with Cello than he was senging. "Practically."

"Must be a good school. That teacher has a real nice house."

"It is a good school," Ben said. "They expect a lot from us. I have a scholarship there. To study chemistry."

Cello tossed another body-shaped root onto their pile. "That doesn't sound very easy."

"It's not. Really, I'm interested in history, and I'd rather be studying that. But, you know, jobs in that field are harder to come by. Not to mention they pay way, way less."

Cello nodded like he did know that.

"You hear about that fire?" Ben asked.

"Yeah, on the news." Cello shrugged, trying to keep his movements calm and smooth.

"Said they didn't catch the guy."

"Yeah, I saw. Sure it wasn't you?" Cello asked, trying on a playful smile, the kind he might share with Sabina.

"No," Ben said quietly. "I wouldn't do something like that." Cello watched the stranger from under his practiced harvest slouch. He seemed sincere, kind even, in his declaration. Cello hated what it said about Joanie. "Would you?"

Cello boiled under the question—would he? He'd never harm the garden or the land in that way. He'd been trained to feed and fuel the soil, not destroy it. It hurt him to think Joanie capable of such destruction.

"I don't think so," Cello answered.

"Yeah," Ben said. "I don't think so, either." He pulled a root from the ground, replanting the seeds in the socket of earth left behind.

"Can I ask you something?" Cello said.

"Sure." Ben dusted his hands off and held his arms in front of his body, expectantly, like a waiter on TV. He was so confident and easy, Cello thought—the realization streaked through with envy.

"You planted that plot yourself, the one me and Marcela found. Right?"

Ben twisted his mouth into a soft lump of lip. He nodded. "Yeah, I did. I didn't want to say anything because I thought it'd get me into more trouble. Your sister seems very…litigious." He shook his head, smiling at the ground.

"She's not my sister," Cello said. His heart beat with a ferocity he only knew from extreme fear.

"Wow, you live with a lot of girls who aren't your sister." Ben smiled, and Cello caught a dull white flash of teeth.

"Yeah, I guess," Cello said. "It's not like that, though."

"Like what?" Ben asked.

"It's not really like anything. I don't know how to explain it." Suddenly, though, Cello wanted to try—he wanted to tell someone about the garden and its clusters of tragedies. The things he and the rest of his foster family had felt, it all just kept running through their closed circuit—each one of them passing similar thoughts and emotions over and onto each other, recycled and stale. It was a thrilling novelty to have a fresh heart and mind right there to address and engage with. It was seductive even. "There was a baby," Cello began, "who lived with us. He got taken."

"What?" Ben's brow creased and he stepped a little closer, as though trying to make out what Cello had said over a wide distance. "You mean like by the state?"

Cello shook his head. "One morning he was just gone."

"Oh, my God," Ben said, reaching out, putting a hand to

Cello's forearm. "What happened? Was he okay? Was it—" he bobbed his head a little to catch Cello's gaze "—was it your baby?"

"No." Cello shook his head and looked away from the stranger's eyes. "It was Joanie's." He felt his eyes heat with tears and was humiliated—he didn't want to cry in front of the stranger, and held it back the best he could. "The people who took him, they're bad people. The money, all of this—" Cello waved vaguely toward the ground "—I was giving the money to them, so they wouldn't hurt him. I wanted to help him, to just do whatever I could." He cringed, remembering Joanie's face when she'd identified Mother Joseph's handwriting. Why hadn't Letta seen it, and he wondered in a single dark instant—did she have something to do with it, too?

"Sure you did, man," Ben said, putting an arm around him awkwardly. "I'm sure you tried to do the right thing. Can't you tell the police, though?"

Cello shook his head. "It's complicated," he explained. Cello wiped his dripping nose with the back of his hand. He didn't like the way Ben was looking at him, all wincing sympathy, tinged with a sour note of judgment. He was suddenly desperate to change the subject, to escape this sudden, forbidden confession. He had no right to tell a stranger about what happened at the garden. It wasn't Ben's place to know, and it wasn't Cello's place to tell.

"So those plants you've been watching, and all the rest of this." Cello gestured out over the shade-dappled ground. "This is just you? Nobody's helping you?"

Ben shook his head and abruptly paced a little farther up the hill. "Come on," he said. "Let's check up here." He turned and looked straight at Cello. "You coming?" The stranger's open face had shifted, sliding into the flat, calm surface of a pond.

There, Cello thought—Ben was lying.

21

When Joanie woke up, she saw that Cello had gone. She stood and moved around the room, considering the items that occupied it. It was wholly unblemished by other lives and bodies. The room was unlike any place Joanie had ever been; every other place had been indelibly marked by the people or creatures who lived in or used it. Whatever had happened before in this place was meant to be erased. It was perfect and clear, just as Joanie was, away from the garden, away from the Josephs. She was free of all former tangles of emotion; she was open and new. She was ready to *make* something new, and the room's clarity magnified her purpose.

But she needed a place to start, a door to open, to let the Vine in. If Joanie didn't have access to Helen's cellar chapel or her own at the garden, she would simply build another, a better one, in the crumbling motel room.

She began with the sheets and the blankets. All of that cotton had come from the ground, after all. She stripped them off the mattresses and onto the floor. She pushed her bed against the wall, and Cello's bed against the door—they would be the pillars supporting her arched doorway. Joanie formed the blankets and the sheets into a thick, lumpy rope. She wound the rope around the wooden legs of the motel beds, connecting them, pulling the rope into a half circle. She stood and looked down at her feet in the center of that arch. Joanie tore one of the sheets into long strips and began to mold the thin fabric into one of Helen's patterns inside of the arch. It felt so different from using the salt or even twisting the Vine—every step, every adjustment, was a caress, not a scratch. She felt the Vine's approval from where it lay in the pillowcase on the carpet.

Joanie lifted out of herself and into the perfect blankness that materialized through the repetition of her hands and eyes as she worked. She gripped a loop of the Vine in her hand and snapped it open, dipping her finger into the sap. She painted it on her lips, like a balm, and used it to draw her sign of protection across the skin of her forearm. Everything she did felt smooth and guided, until the sound of a baby jolted Joanie out of the worship.

She heard a thin, short wail, the cry he let out when he was having trouble settling to sleep. Joanie began to search the room for him, turning over pillows, rummaging through piles of wet towel, checking and rechecking the bathtub. Was he dead, Joanie wondered, was that it? Had the arch she built let through his small, shivery spirit? She shuddered and reached under the bed against the wall, repeatedly scraping her palm against the floor. Maybe he'd shrunk down, she thought. Maybe he was so tiny that he was caught between the hardened fronds of carpet. She plucked at the spaces between the carpet's bristly surface, and slithered under the bed. *I need to check every corner*, she thought.

Joanie's hand slid over something slippery. She gripped it with her fingertips and pulled it closer—a piece of paper, a folded, glossy sheet. Joanie slid back out and held the colorful pamphlet up to the light. The pamphlet glowed in her hands, and when she licked her lips, the Vine sighed through her. The photograph on the front was filled with trees, green and verdant, with a calm, wide river running through the center. In the middle, was a stone bridge. Three arches, exactly like the ones woven into the walls of the chapel, supported it. Across the page, bold white letters leaped out from the green. Antietam Battlefield: The Bloodiest Day of the Civil War.

On the back, there was a map of the battlefield. Lines in garish yellows and reds illustrated the crossed paths of the opposing battalions, lines that wound over and across each other. Perhaps, Joanie thought, that wail hadn't belonged to her son at all. Maybe it was the Vine. Maybe it was Helen giving her another message, just as she'd reached out to her through those books, and through her vision in the tent. Joanie felt like Helen really was there, along with the Vine, handing over a final slip of direction.

Joanie's hands trembled, and the map moved under her fingers as though the fields were quaking. She understood, with electric anticipation, that these crossroads, not only of paths long ago taken but of lives torn from their bodies, would be the setting for Helen's final ritual, and Joanie's first. Joanie returned to the worship, keeping her mind on her baby. Almost reflexively, she considered her son's lost father. She pushed her palms into the stiff carpet, scraping away her guilt as she worked.

As Joanie spent more and more time in the cellar chapel, Josiah wanted more and more to impress her. She was certain that this first attempt to wean himself from the sap of the Vine had been meant solely to please her. The first time he refused the dose she offered, he looked at her with a craving, expectant face. Joanie knew he wanted her encouragement, but she muted her reaction. She made a small sound of surprise and then put the bottle away. She knew it was cruel, and she didn't care. Apart from her time spent in worship in the cellar, these small cruelties were her only source of pleasure. She tallied them up—not only in her interactions with Josiah, but with Mother Joseph, too. She didn't care about Josiah's self-improvement, or her mother-in-law's twisted, venal commerce. The only Joseph she cared about was Helen.

When Josiah's fevers began, no one associated them with withdrawal. Mother Joseph blamed Joanie for these spates of illness. At first, the accusation spouted from her in the form of lewd humor. "I guess you've been wearing him out at night, is that it, Joanie?" Mother Joseph asked, her mouth wide with laughter, the odor of her rotting teeth blustering out.

"That must be it, Mother Joseph," Joanie said with a stiff, obliging smile.

The best part of Josiah's giving up the Vine was his listlessness day and night. Joanie was relieved to be left alone. She certainly wasn't going to tell Mother Joseph about Josiah's new sobriety. Joanie had lived long enough with her mother-in-law to understand the value of a secret.

Joanie's sudden devotion to the Joseph ancestral sacraments repelled her mother-in-law to an almost suspicious degree. Joanie didn't know then whether Amberly was jealous of her connection with the Work or afraid of it. The distance was soothing, and Joanie appreciated every instant alone. The only ongoing dangers Joanie feared were Mother Joseph's unexpected and unchecked rages. Once she was angered, she couldn't stop, or even slow herself down. It was all ugly, dripping chaos until the anger was burned away.

One night, in the thick of Josiah's spell of fevers, he couldn't wake Joanie. She'd been dutifully soothing her husband during this period, and bringing down his temperatures when they were at their highest. Joanie tended to him the way she tended to her foster siblings when they were sick—layering his forehead and neck and wrists with cool compresses that she soaked in vinegar, changing the sheets when he sweated through them. Usually the fever broke after midnight, and he'd fall asleep. But before the break in those fevers, Josiah roiled with delirium. He chattered to Joanie, making no sense, or groaned as though he'd been shot, curling his body like a poked caterpillar.

It was only delirium that could have propelled him into his mother's room in the middle of the night. Joanie had been so tired—she'd nodded off and slept too soundly for Josiah to wake her. She didn't know then, but she was exhausted because the baby was already growing inside of her. Fever-crazed, Josiah had gone to his mother for help.

Mother Joseph stormed into their room, pulling the sweat-damp blankets off the bed. When Joanie saw her, she thought she must be dreaming—her mother-in-law clenched her teeth in the moonlight, a ratty lace nightgown billowing around her, and her long gray hair twisted into an incongruous, girlish side braid. Joanie sat up, stunned as though she'd fallen through a dream.

"You're both useless," Mother Joseph howled. "Good for nothing garbage." She dragged them both by the arms. Joanie was always surprised by the old woman's physical strength. "Garbage stays outside." She opened the front door and flung them onto the porch. She watched as Josiah collapsed onto the rough, splintering planks.

"Not there. *There.*" Mother Joseph pointed to a pile of broken-up fieldstone. Earlier that week, one of the cousins had carted the stone over to use for some repairs to the main house chimney.

Joanie followed Josiah, helpless as he stumbled toward the pile. Even in the fever's grip he knew to listen. He'd grown up with these punishments, and understood them as part of the natural course of life. Joanie felt a sudden stab of compassion for her husband, and shook with indignant anger. *How dare she*, Joanie thought, skewering Mother Joseph with all of the poison she could scrape into a single look. Mother Joseph felt it, and her rage ballooned to an unfathomable and unexpected extreme. She broke into incoherent snarling and pushed her son and daughter-in-law onto the mound of debris.

As Joanie and Josiah lay on the pile of stones, Mother Joseph stacked more rubble on top of their bodies, pressing and tucking the fragments into their skin with short, vehement pushes. Josiah whimpered beside her, but Joanie kept quiet. "There," Mother Joseph said when she was finally satisfied. The jagged clumps and plates of rock pushed down on her so forcefully Joanie could barely breathe. "Snug as two bugs in a rug." Mother Joseph's voice grew softer, and Joanie realized she was walking away, and leaving them alone. "See y'all in the morning."

Joanie dug herself out first, and then Josiah. They didn't dare go back inside, so they waited out what remained of the night crouched on the pile of broken stone. Joanie put an arm around her shivering husband and gave his shoulder a few sympathetic pats as though she were a different, caring person. Mother Joseph was asserting her place. Joanie understood that, but she was revolted by her own powerlessness in the situation. She hated that she was out in the cold night against her will, that she was stranded on the Joseph compound, with Josiah like an unwelcome barnacle.

After that, Josiah got worse. He began soiling himself and vomiting constantly. Mother Joseph wasn't just angry anymore—she was worried, too.

"What's wrong with him?" she yelled at Joanie while they ate dinner in the front room. Josiah had already left the table, his bulbous body now weakened by the constant purging of shit and vomit.

Joanie shrugged, ladling the salty potato soup into her mouth. She couldn't help herself. As much as she wanted to protest her life at the compound, to waste away and turn useless, to throw the food back in Mother Joseph's face, she couldn't. Joanie was overtaken by the compulsion to care for herself. She slept whenever she could. She ate everything she was given, and more—

everything Josiah left on his plate, she moved to hers. Joanie's anger was still there, but it was suppressed by the pregnancy flourishing inside of her, making its own demands.

"Well, go check on him!" Mother Joseph shouted, slapping the spoon out of Joanie's hand. "When did you turn into such a pig? Leave something for the rest of us."

Joanie stood and drank from her water glass, staring at her mother-in-law over the rim.

"Go!" Mother Joseph's color deepened, and Joanie noticed the sweat breaking out on her forehead and jaw.

"Yes, ma'am, I'm going," Joanie said, first setting the glass down and giving her mother-in-law a long, satisfied look.

Joanie was tired, and moved up the stairs slowly. She clung to the banister to ease herself forward with some of her upper body strength, but still had to stop a few times. At the top of the stairs, she shuffled to their drafty bedroom at the back of the house.

"Josiah? What's going on up here?"

When she found him on the ground at the top of the landing, she wasn't surprised. He'd grown so weak she expected to find him passed out on some surface. "Come on, now," she said, kneeling on the ground, reaching for an arm to hoist him up.

"Josiah," she hissed, pulling on the indifferent limb. "Come on. Let's get you to bed, alright?" Joanie pulled with no result, and then moved to her hands and knees, searching for something to bolster his body with. Her palms, though, didn't feel the rasp of splintered wood—instead, she discovered that the planks were slick with syrup. At first, Joanie thought it was blood, but when she peered over the bulk of Josiah's body, she saw the puddle of green. Josiah's brown-glass medicine bottle, the one she hadn't filled in nearly two weeks, lay empty on its side like a sinister, dark shell.

He heaved up to his knees, the pupils of his eyes dilated wide as coins.

"Josiah," she said, holding him by the elbow. "Can you stand?

We have to get you to bed. Come on, please, you've got to try and stand. I can't carry you there myself." Joanie pulled at his arm, feeling him move with her. She got him fully upright, though his body swayed.

"There," she said, patting him on the shoulder. "You did it. Now just a few more steps, and then you can go to sleep." She should have known what would happen. If she hadn't been so distracted, dulled even, by the pregnancy, maybe she could have stopped it. Maybe she could have thrown her arms around him just as his knees buckled, and pulled him back to the floor of the landing.

Instead, he fell. He fell, not like a human being who fells, and twists and protects the soft places of the body to survive. He fell like a thing, a heavy chest of drawers, thumping and cracking its way down the stairs. Joanie felt her own hand on her mouth, her gaze on Josiah's mangled form.

His body began to move. Joanie climbed down the stairs toward his convulsing figure and wiped her palms on the front of her shirt. Vomit and green foam frothed from his mouth and onto the floor. Joanie leaned over him and pushed down into his chest, the way she'd been taught as a little child. There weren't any hospitals or doctors at the garden, and Letta made sure all the kids knew CPR if only for her own longevity and protection.

She counted and pushed as her hair fell into her face. It clung in sticky clumps to her forehead and cheeks. Her skin and clothes were spattered by the spray from Josiah's mouth. Joanie stopped the compressions when she felt Josiah begin to involuntarily retch under her hands. She waited for it to pass and kept on pressing. She worked on him in silence. Later, she wondered why she didn't call for anyone. She wondered why she didn't even scream. By then, it was too late, anyway. Josiah was dying, and her hands were the last to touch him.

When Mother Joseph finally made her way to the back stairs of the creaky old house, after eternally hollering up for them to answer, all she saw were Joanie's hands on her dead son. She pulled Joanie away herself, calling for Harlan and Frank, and the rest of the cousins. They all put their hands on her, grabbing onto whatever they could touch. Then they locked her away, completely alone—or so they thought.

A pounding sound jolted Joanie out of the memory. Someone was knocking at the door of the motel room. She stood up, rubbing her tingling palms together, and peeked through the slats in the blinds. She saw an elderly woman with a housekeeping cart outside. The woman's head was bent with impatience, her curly yellowed-white hair held away from her face with an array of red plastic butterfly clips. Joanie climbed onto the mattress that barricaded the door, latching the discolored, greening chain. She knelt on the mattress, and waited for the knocking to stop.

But the knocking didn't stop—it moved. The sound jumped from the door, to the room, to the bathroom door. A slip of the mind, Joanie thought as she massaged her scalp with cold fingertips. She stood and switched the light on in the bathroom. It was too bright. The bulb had been dull and yellow the night before, barely illuminating the hot and cold taps in the shower. But now, the light was almost silver. The knocking continued all around her, growing in volume until the sound was coming from inside of her head. A push from behind drove her out of the bathroom and the door slammed behind her.

Joanie hunched down, trying to make herself smaller, to disappear. A figure stood in the room with her—the watery, ultra-blurred shape of a small woman. The face was familiar. The swollen lower half—the cheeks and chin—those were all Joseph. The figure stepped on the pamphlet Joanie had found and slid it forward with its bare toes. Joanie knew it was Helen. As the figure approached, she became clearer, lovelier. She looked not much older than Joanie herself. The Vine's presence hung between them, a bright cord linking the two women through space and time. Helen tapped and tapped her toes on the folded piece of paper on the floor. Joanie would've thought it was a dream, but the sound of calloused skin on the stiff, glossy pamphlet was so specific and clear she didn't think her subconscious could've dredged it up out of nothing.

Joanie tried to look at Helen, trying to piece together the right questions to ask. But the harder she looked, the blurrier Helen's outline became, until she dissolved back into the room. When Joanie looked down, she saw the folded brochure was already in her hands. It was a benediction, a reminder, a confirmation that this was how she would find her son, that her worship was working.

Urgency bloomed all around her—because of Helen, or the Vine, or finally having a specific place to go, Joanie wasn't sure. She only knew she had to leave right away, that her son's life depended on it. She gathered up the white cotton pillowcase full of ashes and the now-quiet loops of the Vine. She folded the map and put it in her back pocket and left, hoping for Cello's sake that he'd kept the key.

22

Cello and Ben harvested another section of the ginseng plot, even after Ben begged Cello to give it more time.

"You're killing me, man," Ben said, shaking his head. "If you'd even give it a couple more weeks. Do you know how long I've been waiting for this one to come out right?"

"How long?" Cello snapped, daring Ben to detail the length of his trespassing.

"Fine, never mind." Ben sulked as they took up the rest of the harvest. "But I really wish you could've been more patient."

"It's not about me being patient!" Cello said.

"What's it about, then?" Ben looked at him with frustrated concern.

"Nothing, don't worry about it," Cello muttered, sorting the stack of roots. When they were finished, they went looking for more wild plants, climbing up a rocky incline. Cello trailed Ben up the slope, scanning for dashes of red in the shade of darkened grass.

"Tell me more about why you're so good at this. How'd you learn so much about planting?" Ben asked.

"Why don't you tell me more about how you started doing this," Cello said. "Lot of work you did up here. How long did it take you to make those screens? Somebody had to help you."

"I told you, man. This is a solo project. Or it was." Ben smiled—it was uncomplicated, good-natured. The antithesis of the smiles Cello was used to seeing at the garden. There, a smile—if it wasn't cruel or mocking—was always restrained, always a lesser thing. To feel joy or pleasure was not the point, nor was it the product, of living at the garden.

"What made you pick this spot near us?" Cello asked. "Is it the only place you're working off of?"

"It's weird, but no. I tried a few different places at first. It's my third year senging. The other places did okay, but nothing like up here. I don't know what it is, if it's the shade or the moisture, or what—"

"It's the soil," Cello said, interrupting. "It's…" He paused, not sure what or how to explain their work with the Vine to Ben. "It's special."

"What makes it special?" Ben asked, eyebrows raised.

Cello was silent, just watching Ben, distracted suddenly by the glimmer of sweat at his throat.

"Let me guess, it's none of my business?" Ben said, smiling.

"Yeah, pretty much," Cello answered, returning Ben's smile, looking half at the other boy, and half over his shoulder and away.

"You won't tell me about the special magic soil, you won't tell me about your girlfriend—what're we supposed to talk about, man?" Ben gave a little laugh, and Cello was surprised by how his mood had lifted over the course of the morning.

"Why don't you tell me about your girlfriend, then." Cello was stunned by how light and teasing his voice was.

Ben stopped walking and shook his head, his mouth still fixed in its full smile. "Don't have one. Back to you, I guess. Joanie, right? How long have you been together?"

"It's not like that. Joanie is..." Cello paused, panicked by the involuntary and unfamiliar unsettling wave of emotion her name stirred within him.

"She's what?" Ben asked.

"I don't think it's right to talk about." Cello stooped down to a patch of moss, pretending to look for more plants. He didn't even know what Joanie was anymore, and it hurt like a blistering sunburn to admit it.

"Why?"

"It's just not." Cello turned away as the tears began to melt out of his eyes.

"Hey, it's okay," Ben said. He put out his hand, reaching toward Cello's forearm.

Cello stepped back a little, but it didn't stop Ben from holding on to his arm and swiping at a smudge of dirt with his thumb. Cello watched the other boy's hand on his body, and the way Ben's thumb smoothed away every trace of dirt until he was only smoothing Cello's blond arm hair. Cello couldn't look away— he couldn't move at all.

Cello watched Ben slide a hand up the rest of his arm, over his shoulder and catch on to the side of his neck. Cello liked it— the warmth, the deliberate gentleness. People didn't touch him that way, affectionately. No one recognized him outside of the tasks he performed. It was strange, the look and the contact. It was intimate and visceral, like Ben had summoned Cello's heart to climb out of his mouth.

Cello pulled away and turned around, his hand plastered across his forehead, like he was pressing back a headache. He didn't understand why he was sharing so much, so bluntly, with this stranger. "Are you okay?" Ben asked.

"I'm fine. What I was saying before—it's just that I love

Joanie and want to help her get her kid back," Cello said, more to himself than anyone.

"God, yes, everyone knows you love Joanie, Cello. Jesus!" Marcela stomped toward them through a swath of overhanging branches. "Uh, what's going on? Are y'all even working or what?" She shot Cello an accusing look.

"Of course we are." Ben waved an easy hand toward her. "Everything's fine."

Cello felt his face flush, and turned it away from Marcela, trying to collect himself. He didn't want her to see him so unsettled. Cello cleared his throat and wiped his forearm across his face to erase any sign he'd been about to cry, hoping it looked like he was just wiping away sweat.

"Let's go unload this batch. I got to get back." Marcela crossed her arms over her chest and looked from Cello to Ben and back again. "Seriously, what's the holdup?"

Marcela's raised voice shook Ben and Cello out of whatever moment they had, and they all went to pack up the morning's harvest.

Cello knew he had to stop at the Stuckey's, to check under the Crown Light sign, but he felt a growing urgency to get back to Joanie. He'd go to Stuckey's first. Maybe there would be some new message at the convenience store—anything that could point them toward the baby. He could pick up food there, too. They'd brought nothing with them and he could imagine Joanie's growing hunger.

Cello was chilled to find another gruesome delivery behind the hedge-obscured Crown Light sign. In a crumpled, cloudy, reused Ziploc bag, there lay a tiny sock, drenched in red liquid. Cello could feel the wetness through the plastic, and ran both thumbs over the macabre lump. Cello couldn't be sure, but he thought it was one of the socks Junior had been wearing the last night he was put to bed in his crate. It was too terrible to really look at, so Cello unfocused his eyes, allowing his vision to blur.

Cello didn't want to hold the bag anymore, but knew he couldn't leave it there. Maybe it *wasn't* blood, he thought. Or, if it was, maybe it wasn't the baby's. He held the plastic square lightly, at one of the top corners, and took another payment out of his pocket. He eased around to the back of the hedge and dropped the money down, kicking the mulched earth over it. He tried to hold the bag as far away from himself as possible without leaving it unattended, like an ersatz guardian for an ersatz baby.

On the long walk back to the motel, Cello considered disposing of the bag somewhere, throwing it into the woods so Joanie would never see it, so he would forget about it. But he couldn't go through with it. The way his face twisted and his breath staggered, it felt like he was crying, but he couldn't be sure.

Getting to Joanie would normally have settled him. Thinking of her alone somewhere, waiting for him—that would, only days ago, have filled him with happy purpose. But as Cello paced the parking lot, he felt the inverse of happiness. What would he tell Joanie? How would he explain this new sign of her son—could he tell her anything?

He knocked on the door to their room, but there was no answer. He tried the knob, and it turned easily under his hand. The door didn't open all the way. The path of its swing was blocked by some mysterious bulk. The room was dark, but he knew Joanie had to be in it because he could smell her everywhere. Cello knew all of Joanie's scents—he knew the way her sweat smelled, he knew the way her skin smelled, he knew the way her hair smelled when it was dirty and when it was clean.

He flicked on the overhead light, and was shocked by the room's transformation. He squinted around, expecting to find Joanie's shape fitted into some corner, but the room was empty. She was gone. He checked the bathroom, the closets and even under the bed. Cello held the bag out in the buttery light of the chipped glass sconce, his face smeared with crying, broken open under the heavy strangeness of the room.

He still felt responsible for Joanie, for the baby. He opened the Ziploc seal, forcing himself to closely inspect the contents. He saw rather than felt that he was shaking. He inhaled a burst of chemical odor—paint—and then pulled the sopping, scarlet baby sock out of the bag. He wasn't sure if he should feel relieved that the red fluid wasn't organic, or if it was a sign of certainty that it was some bitter practical joke. It didn't seem like the work of Mother Joseph; Mother Joseph had no time for practical jokes.

With a twist in his gut, Cello realized that if it was all some strange con, it had been planned by someone who lived at the garden. By someone who knew that the baby had gone missing. By someone who knew the baby existed at all.

Cello sealed the bag closed and set it on the bathroom sink. He washed his hands and face, scrubbing at the dirt and sunburn there. He wanted to ring out the last few weeks from his body, to sleep and then wake up cleaned of them. He turned off the lights and locked the door. He settled himself on the bed closest to the entrance and fell asleep as sounds of night insects echoed through the walls.

Cello sat up, his sleep disturbed by the sound of a thunderstorm beating out from a distance. A figure sat at the foot of the bed, but Cello wasn't afraid or even startled. He knew Joanie would come back. Cello looked into her face, trying to find the Joanie he loved and understood. He got up to sit beside her.

"What's happening, Joanie?" he asked.

"It's okay," she said. "I'm going to fix everything. You don't have to worry anymore, Cello." Joanie moved toward him, a sudden viciousness all over her. Cello hopped back a little, preparing for a physical attack. It wouldn't be the first time Joanie had come at him with violence. Even before her time at the Josephs', Joanie had occasionally reacted toward him with anger.

Almost always, Cello was the wall she railed against until whatever seethed inside her could subside. Cello never really minded. Only when she was pregnant—because then, he had to make sure the baby was safe, too. She never actually hurt him during these episodes, her heightened energy being its own release.

When she came at him now, Cello put his arms out to catch her. He was stunned when she slid through the gap between his hands, and pushed her body against his. He felt her mouth, her tongue, something, on his throat. He banged his elbow against the doorjamb and winced. The small pinch of pain was all he could feel, so foreign was this affection from Joanie.

Cello wasn't sure what he'd expected finally arriving at this longed-for convergence with her. Cello let himself feel everything that was happening—Joanie's shirt sliding over her head, the waistband of her denim shorts pulled down over her hips and off.

This is a dream, he thought. How else was it happening? But, unlike the other dreams he'd had, waking or sleeping, Joanie was not sweet with him, or loving. He had the feeling that she was excavating something, pillaging his body for a purpose unknown to him. The viciousness she wielded many times before at the garden was flooding them both.

Joanie slipped her leg between his thighs. Her skin was as silky as a fish in the water. Cello imagined it that way, the dart of her thigh between his like a sleek glimmering fish sliding through the waves. She turned him and pushed him forward onto his stomach so that he fell onto the musty, bare mattress of the stripped bed. Joanie had taken her shirt off. Her skin was there, against his clothes. The softness of her chest, the jut of her hips, the shallow curve of her waist; he recognized each of these parts of Joanie.

Cello turned into it, into her. Joanie didn't look happy or angry, just focused, like she couldn't break her concentration.

He stilled his body, suddenly feeling the enormity of what they were doing, feeling his own reluctance.

"Wait," he said, half sitting up. Joanie did not wait. Cello put his arms out, trying to hold her back. "Joanie, please stop." She moved away slowly, her eyes still viciously alight. Joanie was making him nervous in a new way, and Cello didn't understand how or why. He only knew that he had to resist her. Cello tried to catch his breath. Something had changed. What had always been between them—Joanie leading the way, and Cello, helpless, running after her—was over.

The storm dashed down over the mostly empty motel and Cello woke up in earnest, shocked to find relief instead of disappointment that being with Joanie had only been a dream.

23

Joanie squinted into the full sun of the day. It was a long way to Antietam, especially if she intended to walk. At almost forty miles, it would take days. She started down the road, the pockets of her cut-off shorts jammed with the small items she required to carry out her plan. She held the sack filled with ashes and Vine cuttings looped over her elbow. It was hot, and she hadn't brought anything else, not water or food. She pulled the pamphlet out of her pocket and flipped it over and searched for the winding blue line of the Potomac. If she followed its edge, she'd be led to the place where a filament-thin stream of the Antietam Creek split off, guiding her into the heart of the battle.

Down by the water, she crossed over mosaics of moss and removed her shoes. She thought about leaving them there on the riverbank, but plucked them up off the ground in a sudden panic. Joanie discovered, terrified, that she couldn't abandon anything else, least of all the shoes that had never done her any harm, only protected her. She thought about her baby, alone, withdrawn from her care. She couldn't help but imagine his little face, twisted in fear and hunger, and her legs burned with the urgency to go to him.

The trees were so healthy there by the water. They curled ardently over the river, shading Joanie with their overhanging branches. She walked all day, crouching by the river to drink from it when she grew thirsty, and soaking her feet in the rushing water when they started to ache. She walked through the long, stretched-out day, strengthening her purpose with every step. When it got too dark for her to see, even squinting her hardest through the dark, Joanie had to stop. She flattened a stand of reeds into a little palette and settled the pillowcase of ashes under her neck. As the stars swam out at her from the darkening sky, she spat in the palm of her hand and marked her body with protection symbols. The practice was comforting and familiar. She drew one of the symbols into the grass, willing it to pass through the miles of soil and roots, up through ground to wherever her son lay. Joanie reached out for the Vine, for reassurance that she was going the right way, but it felt faint and distant in the dark. As she twisted to sleep in the reeds, she begged Helen for more help—a way to strengthen her power for the Work she was about to do.

Joanie dreamed deep, her sore body following her into sleep. She dreamed of a collection, of plucking minerals from the earth, of pulling beans from their shells, of yanking a strand of thread from its spool and walking and walking away. She dreamed of the motel room, and the worship within it, and she dreamed of Cello.

She woke up under a slap of rain, and felt the thunder from the storm resonate all around her like some mountainous embrace. She stood up and huddled against a tree trunk until it was almost light and the storm had tapered off. That morning she moved along the Potomac slowly, too slowly. She couldn't be sure how long she'd been walking, only that her clothes had dried and then had been soaked through again with sweat. She felt her body fading, and began to panic. She couldn't do her Work in a weakened state.

Joanie opened the pillowcase she carried and considered the two remaining cuttings that twined among the ashes. She knew the Vine would help her, but she was afraid to use it too soon. She knelt by the riverbank and rinsed the cutting in the active water. She looked at the loop of green in her hands, like an absurd, neon doughnut, and bit into it.

As she crunched the bitter stalk between her teeth and drank the silky sweet liquid, she felt the Vine jolt awake inside of her. *I need help*, she asked. *I need to be stronger.*

An understanding careened up from the back of her throat and through the top of her head. Joanie felt like a toddler wobbling up and figuring out how to walk. She was acutely aware of the blood in her veins, of the water in the river, of the sap coiled inside of the Vine in her pillowcase. All of the fluids were connected, part of the same mystic pattern, and Joanie could use them all. She could draw power from these charged, living liquids everywhere, just as the Vine had drawn them from her, and others like her. *You can take what you need and release what you don't*, it tapped out in her mind, a lime-bright staccato. The Vine guided her to the road, pushing her ahead, feeling out a faster way forward.

Joanie knew, at least, that the sun was still out, and that people would be driving. She only needed to find one—one willing person. There was no way of knowing how far she had already traveled—ten miles, fifteen? At the edge of the asphalt, Joanie slid her shoes back on, leaving the gravel where it stuck to the bottom of her feet. When she walked, she felt the bite of the journey in each step.

She saw a cool rush of blue winding down the narrow road in the distance. Something about the car's pace and swerve recalled the movement of the river. She waved, and the sun winked back off the hood of the car, cheerfully. The car, a well-kept, old periwinkle-blue Volvo, slowed, stopping just beyond her. Joanie jogged to the passenger side and knocked on the window. The driver, a middle-aged, sunburned man with a prominent pair of bleached-blond eyebrows motioned for her to open the door.

"How can I help you, young lady?" the man said, pushing the edge of his knit cap higher up his forehead.

Joanie held the pamphlet up near her collarbone, underlining her face.

The man leaned over and squinted. "Ah, Antietam, yes. Not too far."

Joanie nodded.

"Well? Hop in." He gestured to the passenger side door, waving her forward.

Joanie smiled to herself—surprised by the perfect ease of the errand, at how neatly it had fallen together. "Thank you," she said—to the driver and to the Vine—and slammed the door, sealing them both inside.

"So," the man said, "what brings you to one of our most notorious battlegrounds?"

Joanie buckled the seat belt across her lap. "Thought I'd check it out."

"I must say, I admire your inquisitive spirit." Joanie felt his gaze roving over her body, and turned her face to the window, rolling her eyes. Of course it wouldn't be that easy. It didn't matter, though, she told herself. She calmly stared back at him. He was the first to look away, turning his eyes back to the road. Joanie was satisfied when she saw him swallow with discomfort. She felt the Vine's approval in this small flex of her power.

"What's your name?" he asked.

"Lorena."

"What a beautiful name." It *was* a beautiful name, Joanie thought, the name she'd always given her imaginary mother. "I'm Ray," the driver said, extending a hand out for her to shake. Joanie ignored it, and he dropped it back into the space between them.

"You know," he continued. "The battle at Antietam was the bloodiest day in American history."

"How did you know that?" Joanie asked, her voice wavering with suspicion. Perhaps she didn't have the upper hand in the car, after all. This man could be a monster, too.

"I'm a history professor. I have to know that. It's a pretty big one to know."

"That's what it says here, too," Joanie said, tapping at the brochure resting on her knees. "But how can we really know? How can anyone really know? How many gallons of blood was it? A swimming pool full? A river?"

"I mean, in terms of volume, no one can say exactly." Ray cleared his throat.

"Really? No one can say," Joanie repeated.

Ray nodded. "Other than the people who were there, who died there, I suppose."

Joanie leaned back into her seat. "Have you ever seen a dead person?" she asked.

"What?" Ray's eyes widened, and he looked over at her, his gaunt, sunburned face broke open. "I mean, I must have. At funerals, perhaps. But I get the feeling that's not precisely what you mean."

"I have. My husband."

"Your husband? You certainly don't look old enough to be a widow." Ray shifted behind the wheel, and he scratched a spot behind his ear repeatedly, like he was counting. "How did he die?"

Joanie set her hands on either side of her throat, trying to hold the skin together there. She was suddenly terrified that if she talked about it, she would break up into nothing, just dissolve right into the air inside of the Volvo. "An accident." She felt the word floating on the stream of her voice, nearly saw it, glowing, out in front of her face.

"That's terrible. I'm so sorry."

"His mother blamed me. Thought I was responsible."

Ray cleared his throat. "Were you?"

"Not exactly."

"Are you, I mean, do you need help? Are you in some kind of trouble?"

Joanie shook her head.

"I see. Should we move on to sunnier subjects?" Ray asked as he crossed the dotted yellow line dividing the road and passed a Toyota Tacoma.

"No," Joanie said. "Let's be quiet for a while." She concentrated on his flushed red face, and the blood that pooled under the skin there. She could feel the pattern of the platelets rushing, and reached out as the Vine might, to infuse herself with the driver's vital blush. But she couldn't catch hold of it, as though some slippery layer prevented her from finding a way in.

Ray looked at his watch and then back to Joanie. She felt his prodding looks, and felt her irritation increase with each one.

"Are we close?" Joanie asked.

He nodded. "Getting there. There's a spillover lot a few miles up ahead on the left."

"I can get out there," Joanie said, pressing a finger to the glass of the passenger side window. The muscles in her face tensed into a grimace as she considered her next step.

"If you are in some kind of trouble, maybe I could help," Ray said, moving his hand to signal before the turnoff. He reached across to where she sat and gave her shoulder what he probably meant to be a supportive squeeze. Joanie didn't answer, but felt his hand there. He stroked down her arm in what some girls would have interpreted as reassurance. Not Joanie. She knew exactly what he was doing, what he was looking for, what mealy, pedestrian fantasy he nursed picking up a young girl off the side of the road. She narrowed her eyes at him and wanted nothing more than to use the new power growing inside of her. An undercurrent of encouragement from the Vine shuddered through her. She reached her own hand down through the space that separated them and grabbed ahold of his thigh.

"What do you want me to do for you?" Joanie asked.

"What do you mean?" Ray shifted in the driver's seat.

"Nobody does anything for free. You're a history teacher. You should know that better than most people." Joanie looked at his miserable little goatee and felt a wild strength swell in her arms and hands and chest.

"That's not always true," he said, but he turned the car just short of the overfill lot under a dense spray of branches. He turned the key in the ignition and the engine fell silent.

"Do you want to fuck me?" Joanie said.

Ray jolted a little, and Joanie felt his discomfort shooting out at her, pushing her away. "Um, no," he said, his eyes moving over the empty parking lot in the distance.

"No," she said, and the rush of the Vine's power beat in her ears. "I really don't think you do." She moved even closer, so that she was on her hands and knees, half of her body in the passenger seat and the other half on the driver's side. She planted her forearm between his legs and felt him getting hard. She reached out again, the way she reached out to the Vine, and felt the driver spill open like an overripe melon.

"You do want something, though," she said, tilting her head. She looked at Ray, his head pressed back against the glass, as far away from her as he could get while still sitting in the car, his breathing almost a pant.

Joanie closed her eyes and inhaled Ray's scent of wool and patchouli, and with it, the nourishment her worship demanded. She felt another hand on her shoulder, a familiar one this time, almost like a push: Helen. There *was* some message here, some other thing she was supposed to collect.

Joanie looked closely at her driver and tried to match his wide-eyed terror and excitement with an act that would confound and distress him the most, to extract more of the power she desperately needed for the Work ahead.

When it clicked into place, she smiled. "I'm going to pee on you."

"Young lady, I think you should get out of the car now." Ray had squeezed his eyes closed tightly, but he was trembling and made no move to unlock the car, his erection through his pants now pitifully visible.

Joanie climbed over until she was straddling him. She unzipped her shorts and pulled them off one leg. She watched his labored breathing; she was thrilled and disgusted at the same time. The power she felt, though, overwhelmed every other sensation. It was difficult to get going, and Joanie realized she hadn't had anything to drink in a while. She wondered if she should waste her limited fluids on Ray like this, and nearly laughed.

Ray had opened his eyes, and one of his hands had already reached between them, trying to open his pants. Joanie released a trickle of hot, pungent liquid. She felt the steam of it between her legs. He grimaced and tilted his head back. Joanie abruptly stopped, and moved her shorts back in place. She climbed back over to the passenger seat and opened the door, confident she had denatured something in the dull and grasping little man and siphoned it off for herself. He had deserved it; it was another simple act of balancing.

She separated herself from the car as though she were leaving another planet, a place with its own laws of physics. She felt better, bigger, charged with supernatural energy—fortified for what was to come.

The sun was at late-afternoon height. It was hot, and there was no breeze to cut through the stifling warmth. Joanie walked along until she reached a bus loading area. Packs of kids climbed on and off buses of various sizes, and Joanie watched them with consuming fascination. Ultimately, she lurked around a group of high school students finishing their lunches at a row of wooden picnic tables. She studied them, the girls and the boys, and wondered, sincerely curious, how their mouths moved like that—so easily around laughter and words and food. They were so obviously having a good day, and Joanie hated them. She experimentally widened her mouth in a smile, mimicking the laughing, chatting, crunching students.

She slid next to a girl in a yellow-striped T-shirt, one of the quieter ones. The girl's face softened toward Joanie once she realized she had a seatmate.

"Anyone sitting here?" Joanie asked, the false smile already gone.

"Oh, no, please, go ahead." The girl bobbed her head, and her light brown ponytail swung along with her head and neck.

"You must really like horses," Joanie said as she picked up the girls' mostly untouched sandwich.

The girl gave a muted gasp, and leaned back a little in her seat. "How do you know that?"

"Well, don't you?" Joanie said as she chewed.

"I mean, yes, but how would—"

Joanie shrugged, and unscrewed the cap on the glass bottle of pink lemonade beside the girl's horse-silhouette-flecked lunch bag. She drank nearly the whole bottle, jolted cool by the long, sweet drink. Joanie wondered if her son had eaten yet that day, if he had been changed and washed.

"I just…that's weird. I didn't think I gave off that kind of vibe—you must think I'm a baby."

"What's your name?" Joanie asked, too loud—elevated by the hydration and sucrose she'd stolen from this nervous, horse-loving girl.

Startled, the girl blinked several times before answering. "Amy."

"You're not a baby. There's nothing wrong with liking horses." Joanie smoothed her shoulder and swung her leg over the bench, heaving herself away to leave.

"Wait, aren't you going on the tour? Which bus did you come on? Hampshire County?"

"Oh, yeah," Joanie said, wishing she weren't so dirty and sunburned, wishing for a brief moment that she could just get on the bus from the Hampshire County district and see what happened.

"They say the girls at Hampshire are bitches, but you're so nice." Amy tilted her head, her ponytail bouncing off the side of her throat.

Joanie laughed, and again felt powerful, just as she had felt with Ray. She let the laughter in, lining her insides. "Oh, Amy, that's cute."

"Want to walk with me on the tour?"

Joanie felt a little guilty—the girl in the yellow T-shirt had no idea what was going on. She understood nothing; she understood less of the world than little Emil, and suddenly Joanie felt a flash of tenderness toward her. "Of course. Let's go." Joanie picked up the other girl's half-full baggie of apple slices and started to eat them as they walked toward the group congregating by the parallel lines of parked buses, not in the least surprised by how closely Amy trailed her.

Joanie reached back and threaded Amy's arm through hers, so that they looked like a pair of young women in one of Letta's magazines—smiling, sunning themselves in admiration. Amy flushed, and looked at the other clusters of students, a pleased little smile on her lips. Joanie knew she'd be found out, that she'd stick out by being on her own. She'd latch onto the girl and get to the right spot unobserved this way.

"So are you in AP History, too?" Amy asked.

"Oh, yeah, love it," Joanie said, sighing over the glazed gold of the wheat fields. *There is something in here*, she thought. "I have a son," she told Amy, turning to look at the girl's shimmering ponytail. She couldn't hold back saying it, compelled by the glinting crops.

"Wow, really?" Amy tried to pull back a little, but Joanie held her arm firmly. "Um, how old is he?"

"About four months."

"Oh, wow. We should probably go over where people are gathering—you know, for the tour."

"Yeah, I know." Joanie looked at the girl beside her and wanted to snatch the ponytail off her head. How could a person be so nothing? Their feelings so easily pushed and pulled around? Was this what she would have been if her mother had been some nice, responsible Amy? She felt a rush of gratitude for her baby, and relief that she was his parent and somebody like Amy wasn't. Even if their life at the garden fell short in some ways, at least it didn't produce people like this. Joanie wondered if all of the clumps of students eddying around them were equally dull and impossible. Was she the only hot creature in this swarm of nothings? Joanie suddenly felt bored with the girl beside her, but couldn't abandon the cover she provided. Instead, Joanie focused on the other girl's body, collecting energy from her like the Vine would.

Joanie leaned into Amy a little, taking the warmth from her, making herself feel a little more golden. For what she was going to do, she needed all the strength she could gather. She imagined building a tower from the horde of young bodies and climbing to the top like a warrior. What could she do then? she wondered. Joanie gave Amy a cool smile. She imagined threading the girl's limbs through the limbs of some other sweaty nothing. Amy shifted from foot to foot.

"Ready?" Joanie asked, her voice bright as she dragged the girl along to the meeting point where the guide stood on a large stone, waiting for the crowd of lunch-sated youths to settle down.

"Eyes on me, p-people," the guide stammered into the wind. He swept his arms through the air, accidentally knocking into a tree branch shading Antietam's visitor center. "Please," he added, "keep it to a dull roar. What we're about to see is some somber stuff. I'd hope you could all be a little more respectful." The guide raised his eyebrows meaningfully at one of the teachers, a petite woman in a floral sundress.

"Settle down, everyone," she said half-heartedly.

The guide looked up to the sky, as though asking for divine patience, and continued. "Almost 26,000 lives were lost here, in a period of twelve hours. Indeed, the bloodiest day of the Civil War. That's more people killed in one day than were killed in the entire Revolutionary War and the Mexican-American War combined."

Suddenly, Joanie needed to know, was consumed by the need to know. "Ask him," she whispered to Amy. "Ask him where all the blood went."

"What?" Amy released a nervous, little laugh.

"Ask him." Joanie squeezed her arm, but only a little. She knew it would be enough to bully the other girl into speaking. Amy raised her hand, meekly, just barely clearing the top of her head with her fingertips.

"Yes, you there in the yellow." The guide wiped the sweat from his upper lip.

"Um." Amy looked at Joanie quickly and then back to the guide. "Where did all the blood go?"

"Where did all the blood go?" the guide repeated in surprise.

A murmur began to stir through the group of kids—they chorused, "Yeah!" and "Good question!" and Amy once again looked pleased, shining a smile out at Joanie.

Joanie stared hard at the guide as he tried to piece together an answer. "Well," he said finally, looking around at the swells of the bright green and gold hills around them. "I suppose it was absorbed."

"Like into the ground?" a girl shrieked. "Like into these crops?"

The guide paled and looked to the corners of the group where the chaperoning adults all seemed to be looking elsewhere.

Into the ground, Joanie thought. All of the elements of Helen's recipe were there, burned in the sack she carried, or there beneath her feet. It was falling together better than she had imagined. It was all there in flawless balance. She felt a shimmer in the air, a blessing from Helen, she thought. The tour wound through a grassy path that sliced through a field of wheat. The guide stopped to speak, though the students were still in a frenzy over the blood in the soil.

"This is the location of the fight for the cornfield. It took place early in the morning, approximately between seven and seven forty a.m. Imagine—it was foggy, the two armies set up on either side of this cornfield, this thirty or so very acres where you children are standing. The Confederates fired, and here you have the Federals advancing toward their fire. Can you see it, children? Lines and lines of doomed men marching through the corn."

Joanie could certainly see it, and for an instant it was as though shadowy figures clamored up and out of the earth. Joanie understood why Helen had scratched the crossroads into her notebook, why she had been so insistent; the power here, where the dead broke through, was undeniable. She could feel their decomposing hands clutching out at her living ones, and the echoes of their noises—retching, weeping, laughing, begging—rearranging her cells. All of their lives, compressed down into the earth, sang out at her. She fell back into their miserable wailing and closed her eyes—just like with Amy, and with Ray, she had the feeling that she was being charged with some essential energy. She waited toward the back of the group as the tour advanced, holding her arms around herself.

The guide led them to a bridge—the bridge on the pamphlet—another place where thousands of men had died. Joanie could see it, the bodies and blood in the water, turning the Potomac the muddy red of menstrual blood. She pressed her hands against her eyes—this…this was the place the Vine had shown her.

There was a little asphalt path just before the bridge that crossed a wide ditch—natural or manmade, Joanie couldn't tell. As the group moved on, she dropped down into the trench. She huddled under the suspended path, pressing herself against the gravel and dirt, waiting to begin.

24

Cello woke up in the undisturbed room knowing he was alone. Still, he scoured it for Joanie. The dream was not like any dream he'd had before, and Cello was troubled. Had she been trying to tell him something? He sat up and opened the blinds, staring out at the forest that bordered the motel lot. It was not only that Joanie was gone. Everything was different.

What would it be like between them if she'd been there, waiting? But every minute he adjusted to the emptiness in the room, the more he believed that Joanie had truly disappeared, that this time she had run off without him, without anyone. It wasn't so crazy to believe that he'd never see her again. The possibility did not fill him with the kind of anguish he expected, only a dull sadness.

If he couldn't help Joanie, he could still help Junior. Cello rolled into his clothes and started the walk back to meet Ben for another day of senging. No matter what happened with Joanie, he had to do his best for the baby. Somebody had to do their best for him. The morning was at its coolest, but parts of the road's asphalt shoulder were soft from the heat wave the day before.

Ben was already waiting for him in their meeting place, the ginseng plot where Cello and Marcela first discovered the stranger.

"Hey," Cello began. "Can you help me out? I need a favor."

"What kind of favor?" Ben asked.

"Remember when I told you about Joanie's baby who went missing?"

Ben nodded.

"Well, it's about that. I need some company while I wait. For someone."

Ben's forehead creased. He opened his mouth to speak, but then pressed it closed. "What do you mean?" he finally asked.

"It's hard to explain. I just...need a friend there," Cello said. Even though it wasn't exactly right he hoped at least that it was partly true.

"Okay. Can't say no to that."

They took Ben's bike, Cello standing behind on the back bar, his hands on Ben's shoulders. He was relieved not to have to make the walk again, concentrating only on the breeze over his face and chest, and his wild heartbeat. Cello gave directions as they sped along, leaning down closer to make his voice heard on the windy ride.

When they reached the convenience store lot, business had picked up. There were even a few cars waiting for the pumps. Cello watched the drivers and the passengers, wondering about the mornings they'd had. A deeply tanned balding man in an orange T-shirt stared at Cello appraisingly as he filled his gas tank. Cello turned his attention away from the man's intense gaze and squinted through the glare over the windows of the waiting cars. He wondered if any of the people inside of them lived like he did—if any of them had ever felt so outside of everything. Ben walked very close beside him, so close that their hands touched.

"What exactly are we doing here?" Ben asked.

"Shh, just follow me." Cello stepped to the side and led Ben around to the Crown Light sign. Cello signaled to Ben that they should move to the space behind the defunct ice bin. It was hot even in the shade behind the scaling white-metal shell. Cello could already tell it was going to be another blistering day.

"Uh, I think maybe it's time for you to tell me what this all is about," Ben said.

"How come you lied to me about the ginseng you planted?" Cello was surprised, the question out of his mouth before he could stop it.

"What?" Ben leaned forward, as though he'd misheard.

"You lied to us. How come?" The question, a slash in whatever rapport they'd been building between them. Cello decided to press it. He wanted some kind of answer. He'd never pressed anyone this way and understood this was how Letta must feel all the time talking to the kids, thinking two steps ahead. "You lied. You didn't do all that work alone."

Ben slid to the ground, his back to the mold-stippled brick. He put his hands up to his face and rubbed his eyes.

"I started out senging with a couple of guys I know from Grove. It was too many people." Ben's voice faded and he shook his head. "They didn't know what they were doing. Not like you all." Cello could tell that Ben had meant for him to feel the compliment squarely, to soften his story.

"So?"

"So, there was all this fighting—and, I mean, we tried everything. A chore wheel, for fuck's sake! But they couldn't get it together. The guy we were selling to—"

"That teacher?" Cello asked.

"Yeah," Ben said, looking down at his shoes, and toying with the laces. "Dr. Santo wasn't thrilled with the results, and you know, he took me aside when he saw that I was the only one who really understood what was going on. Told me we had to remove those other guys from the situation. They were expecting to get paid, too. And they weren't *doing* anything."

"What happened to them?" Cello suddenly felt chilled, shocked that something in Ben's life could be so similar to something in his own. Ben must have read the look there, and his face relaxed into a smile.

"Dude, nothing bad." Ben scratched at his temple. "Dr. Santo knows some guys—I guess the people who help him sell the product." Ben shrugged and dropped his hand down where it smacked against his folded legs. "They straightened out the people I was planting with and that was it."

"What do you mean 'straightened out'?" Cello asked, glancing back and forth from Ben's face to the stained Crown Light sign.

"Talked to them. Settled on some money, I guess, to get them to let me work in peace."

Cello felt a rush of relief. Whoever these people were doing business with Dr. Santo and Ben, they couldn't be anything like the Josephs. A Joseph "straightening out" was very different from what Ben described. "That doesn't sound so bad," Cello said.

"No, of course not." Ben half laughed.

"So, why'd you lie about it?" Cello asked.

"I don't know. I was surprised. You guys literally came out of nowhere. And it's a complicated story."

"It's not that complicated," Cello said, nudging Ben's foot with his own.

"It's less complicated than what you've got going on with your whole not-family and their magic soil operation."

"I told you, I don't want to talk about that," Cello said, leaning back to get a better look at the drop spot behind the convenience store.

Ben stood and stretched, taking a step closer to Cello. "Why not?"

Cello shook his head, trying to keep an eye on what he had come to guard, but watched Ben's approach instead. He put his hands on either side of Cello's face, and again Cello was stunned by how foreign the gentle, affectionate touch was to him.

"Dude, you're so jumpy. Just take a deep breath, and at least tell me what we're doing here."

"We're waiting for someone to stop right there." Cello pointed out the drop spot. "And dig for something."

"Um. Dig for something?"

"Yes." Cello twisted his hands together and looked down at the cracked pavement. "The person is a bad person. A very bad person."

"Should I be scared?" Ben smiled a little.

Cello looked him in the eye as he answered, "Yes."

"Maybe I can help."

"You're helping now," Cello said, ducking his head away, feeling suddenly disloyal to Joanie, to Sil, to Marcela and Sabina and the rest of them.

"What about your parents? Can't they help?"

Cello shook his head, trying to keep an eye on the Crown Light sign, but watching the other boy instead. The dip at Ben's throat, just between the collarbones, was a cool dark shadow. Cello wondered what it would be like to put his mouth on that spot.

"I don't have any parents. I think they're probably dead." It was difficult to speak, flooded by Ben's nearness.

"You don't know?" Ben skimmed a hand across the top of his head and squinted at a rustling from the tangled, dense branches surrounding them.

"I never met them." A familiar current of shame flowed through Cello as he admitted it. He didn't like to think about who his parents had been; he couldn't stop himself from assuming the very worst.

"I'm so sorry."

Cello nodded, grateful for the thin shade of hair over his face. "It must've been hard, growing up not knowing them."

Cello didn't speak at first, feeling the empty places in his mind where the answers to such a question would exist in any other person. Here was Ben, though, so close that Cello could barely move without touching him. He wondered what it would be like to want him all the time, the same way he had wanted Joanie. For so long, Cello thought that he could only love one person, and that his one person was Joanie. Cello could feel the difference between them, between Joanie and Ben. He couldn't understand how he could lean into two such different people, but he knew, now, that he wanted Ben. He wanted his reassurance. Ben, who existed outside of the garden, and the loss within it. Cello craved the calm of that otherness. He felt magnetized to the other boy, wanted in. He watched closely as Ben smoothed a pile of dirt with his foot, and felt himself opening in a way he never could at the garden, telling the truth.

"I don't know," Cello finally said. "I guess it was hard. Actually, a lot of times it was."

Ben looked up. "Oh, no, I'm so sorry. I wasn't trying to upset you. I'm a total asshole." Cello winced away the tears that stubbornly clung to the corners of his eyes. He hadn't really noticed, but as he'd been thinking, Cello drifted closer and closer to Ben, until it was nothing, barely a step, for Ben to close the space between them. Cello felt his arms around the other boy, and felt arms around his own body. He sank into the embrace, rolling into it, like a clean blanket.

Cello felt grateful for this unexpected comfort. He wondered, stunned, if this was what everyone was like outside of the garden. Cello's eyes were closed, his head and cheek against the other boy's pollen-dusted shoulder, letting the soothing feeling wash over him—and he missed it.

Cello rarely missed anything, and had never missed Sil's heavy step through a sheet of drying brush. At least, he'd never missed the sound before. It wasn't the sound of Sil that startled him next; it was another pair of hands on his body. Cello felt his head beat back against the brick wall of the convenience store, the burst of blood from the side of his head and its hot, liquid track down into the collar of his shirt. Ben was gone, and Cello discovered that he was on the ground. That he'd been thrown there. He lifted his head a little and forced his eyes open.

"I told you I saw him," said a voice. But the voice wasn't Sil's.

"Well, Mr. Lees, I sure do appreciate you calling us. These children have been missing for the last few days, and we didn't know what to make of it. But I can take it from here." From Sil, Cello was sure of it.

"It sure don't look that way," said the other voice. "Hey! Where'd that other one go? Y'all got another boy working at your place? Here, hold this one, and I'll track down the other."

Cello shook his head, trying to piece together a complete thought through the throbbing in his head and now his elbow. The man, or men, began to strike out at Cello on the ground. It seemed like some octopus creature with extra bodies affixed to itself kept shoving him.

"Franklin, this isn't your place." Sil's voice was careful, but Cello could tell he was desperate. "It's up to Letta to punish the boy. Or even Mother Joseph, come to that. He's hers to judge."

"If this is how Letta's raising them, this don't bode well for y'all," said the same, slurred voice. Cello caught a flash of orange before he lost consciousness.

25

The space beneath the bridge was damp. Layers of sediment and sludge clung to the old stone struts. Joanie sketched into the muck. She copied one of Helen's simplest patterns for worship—a scrawl of scaly loops—onto the muddy wall. She stepped away, squinting, identifying gaps in the pattern that she could fill, searching out places to embellish. She concentrated on the warmth of her baby in her arms, drawing in the sweet feeling like cold soda through a straw. She pushed into the pattern, and the sensation of having him with her ran through her hands.

She etched the pattern into the sopping riverbank, too, strengthening it with the repetition. Then Joanie emptied the cotton sack of ashes and mixed them into the creek with her own bare feet. She'd mix up the recipe here, in the running stream—the one she'd seen in her vision. With every stamp, she layered on her intentions for the worship, holding on to the image of her son's body glowing like the blinking eye of a lighthouse.

As Joanie worked, a dark figure interrupted her work, cooling her, and slowing her down; it was the looming shadow of her mother-in-law, the woman who had stolen her son. The Vine sang to her from where she had tucked it in her back pocket. It called a promise down through their bond, a promise to eliminate Mother Joseph's sinister presence.

As she drew Helen's patterns under the bridge, Joanie held on to the imaginary swell of the baby, pulling him toward her and away from that shadow of Mother Joseph. She cleaned her palms, smearing the soil residue down the fronts of her thighs, and pulled the last cutting from her pocket. The green coil arched into her touch, like a cat's back. Joanie lifted it to her teeth and broke the skin of the Vine one last time. She drank deeply, draining the entire emerald loop. The cicadas were loud, echoing through the night. She climbed up the slope from beneath the bridge and waited in the grass for her Work to catch.

As Joanie lay in the dark by the old bridge, she wondered whether she would die—if death really was a consequence of pursuing Helen's work to the end. Would the Work destroy her, or would it be turned toward someone else? Had the Vine already turned that force toward Mother Joseph? She felt Helen's blessing as solidly as if the woman's body had been draped over her lap. Joanie listened to the affirmation of the creatures around her, the chorus of frogs and chittering insects. She lay still until she felt like she was part of the ground, another little hill, another corpse abandoned on the field. Bugs marched through her hair where it streamed into and against the dirt. She waited for the night to fully fold over her, until the boundaries of her body disintegrated and whatever was left of her poured out onto the battlefield. She dreamed of the dead men, packed tight as roots in the earth below. She dreamed of them shifting in their graves, of turning over in the ground.

When she sat up, it didn't feel quite like sitting up. When she walked, it didn't feel quite like walking. To Joanie, it seemed like she had been diffused. That she was being misted over and through the space of the battlefield. The thickness of the night pushed down onto some mysterious chord, and suddenly the world was folding back over and onto itself, lapping around decades and roads and telephone lines. The field stretched out before her exactly as it had been after the battle, steaming with fresh death.

Bodies were scattered thickly, decaying on the ground under the stars. The dead men were all so thoroughly clothed. She marveled at the hats still affixed to oozing skulls, and at the socks still pulled up over shins that were nearly just bone. Joanie organized her mist-self into some kind of body, and felt her feet on the ground, submerged in a pile of leaves. It was autumn here, she realized, shuffling around the cluster of corpses. She looked down at the fields, at the places where the most blood had darkened the ground.

It wasn't hard to find the spot, so black with decay it didn't look like soil anymore, but instead some hellish marsh. Clumps of earth and leaves, and the husks of old cornstalks rose from the murk, overlapping with the shapes of the dead men. Joanie walked among the darkened piles, and began to move them exactly as the Vine directed her.

The path she made began as an arithmetically perfect, horizontal line. She pulled and pushed, and bound the shapes together. She was building a border, to keep all of her power in. Joanie added more and more until she had formed the outline of an arched door. A doorway to her son, she knew that. The curved cap of the door was difficult to build. She knew it must be fluid, perfect, and so she cracked and wove the empty, humanlike shapes together until she created a perfect inverted C. Her vision of the battlefield, of all of those lives submerged in this single place, flashed over the doorway she created. Some of their faces were beautifully preserved—unblemished and young. Others were lined and bearded. Some of the faces were destroyed, with dark blurs where their features should have been.

The men stared out at her, as though the bodies themselves had all been transformed into enormous, knowing eyes.

Joanie floated to the center of the space she built and rubbed her palms together until they were glazed with heat. She pressed her hands onto the bodies, and each place she touched, a tiny fire began to burn. Joanie stamped her hands over the landscape she had built until one continuous stream of fire burned atop the ridge of dead men. All of her other worship had been practice for this one, wild accomplishment.

She pressed her hands to her belly, to the place where her baby had grown, and waited for the blaze to take, to scrape her clean and obliterate whatever fault in her that Mother Joseph had exploited, to repair whatever had been broken. She willed the fire far, as far as it could go, to the full extent of its power, to burn clear the Joseph poison in the chromosomes of her baby, to clear an honest path to him.

She stacked her hands, one on top of the other, over her heart. Joanie pushed into her chest, with the same force she'd slammed into Josiah's. A miraculous combusting that illuminated as it destroyed, all plunging through the center of her chest between her breasts, a hole, a cavern, another hot mouth—all just swallowing down, cleaning, burning, lit. She let it burn until she was empty and open, merely the tool of some other power.

Joanie was prepared to wait. Waiting, waiting, waiting, letting it all flicker to quiet. She could feel the Vine twisting out and away, winding toward the target it had promised her. When the fires were satisfied and burned out on their own, Joanie began to move the ashes. She shuffled sheets of ash down the slope of the riverbank to the blue thread of the creek. She used both hands to cast the ash in, stepping into the liquid, mixing more of it into the river. Joanie submerged herself in the water. She swam forward, directing the force of the river toward the heart of one monstrous woman who deserved to die.

26

Cello woke in an old shed choked with dusty sunlight. Something about it was familiar, he thought. It definitely wasn't the kids' trailer, and it definitely wasn't the back of the convenience store. He rolled to his side, and in a tide of pain, he remembered. It was where they'd found Joanie. He wondered where she was, and if she was safe.

His arm throbbed and his chest and stomach burned with bruises. His head ached, and he reached up with his good arm, discovering a palm-size wound at the back of his skull, sticky with blood. Maybe he would bleed out, or the wound now clotted with debris and bacteria from the shed's walls and floor would fester, killing him off miserably, like some medieval combatant.

A word, his name, swirled out from a corner. He put a finger to his ear, gently tapping against it to make sure he could still hear, that he hadn't been knocked deaf. A girl's voice repeated itself. Was it Joanie? Were they back to that night a year ago? No, that couldn't be, because the sun was there, pouring in, drowning him in musty heat. It was so hard to breathe—

Cello tried to respond, but he couldn't quite catch enough air. There wasn't enough air in his lungs, nothing was happening.

Had the Josephs taken Ben, too? Cello hoped the other boy was far from this place, but he had a life outside of this—people at the college at least. He would be looked for; Ben would be alright.

A hand then, no, not a hand, just a few fingers—began to pull on his shoulder. Cello tried to turn, to examine the source of the pulling, but he couldn't move his neck. His name again, and then a shake. Suddenly, a face over his face—Marcela. A filthy, weeping Marcela, but still Marcela.

Then, despite the sun, and Marcela's voice and shaking, Cello dropped away to somewhere else. He heard Marcela screaming, and other voices around her, too. He felt his body being moved and pulled at. A wound at his temple split farther open, and more blood ran down the crusted side of his face.

When Cello managed to open his eyes again, it was still daylight—except now he was outside, on the overwatered front lawn of Mother Joseph's house. Marcela stood nearby, red-eyed and drooping. Letta was there, too. He could hear the lilt of her voice and saw the outline of her figure slightly blurred by his imperfect vision. He blinked hard, trying to establish clarity of sight, trying to decipher this interaction. He could tell that at least—that this was another negotiation between Letta and Mother Joseph.

As his vision began to sharpen, he saw that Letta's attempt at looking put-together that afternoon was thin. Her ankle-length slip dress was unwashed, and her dyed chestnut hair was pulled back in a careless bun. But her nails gleamed, Cello noted. He observed the power in her sharply filed, gold-lacquered fingernails, and felt relieved. It was almost like a hug, or the closest Letta would ever come to hugging him, that she was willing to confront Mother Joseph, to reclaim the children who belonged at the garden. Cello was not so naive, though, to believe that this was all about him—it was about Marcela, too, and a matter of pride for Letta, not to be crushed by Amberly Joseph.

In each of the deliveries to the Josephs', Cello had seen Mother Joseph as an unpredictable, trampling beast, and Letta as her corresponding player, her flashing matador. There was an inherent symbiosis there, a magic in the performance—but never was there a question about who was strongest.

Mother Joseph lurched toward Letta, their bodies only a few inches apart. Letta's face was a cool blank.

"Well, Analetta, care to have a seat? What all can I help you with today?"

"Just a small family matter, nothing that should take up too much of your time."

"What, this matter right here?" Mother Joseph's bushy eyebrows lifted in an arch as she pointed at Marcela, and to where Cello lay on the ground.

"That's right. Here to collect my children, that's all." Letta brushed at the front of her dress, smoothing over the place it puckered in front of her solar plexus.

"Oh, your children? Am I hearing this right, Harlan?" Mother Joseph called toward the house. "Because it sounds like Analetta here is trying to take what doesn't belong to her. Seems to me, Letta, like you forgot how to make a deal."

"We both know that's not fair, Amberly," Letta said, crossing her arms in front of her chest.

"Fair is fair," Mother Joseph fumed, her face flushed and sweating. "You think I like fixing problems you made? Just out of the goodness of my sweet heart?" She beat her chest with the flat of her palm, as though revving the beating muscle there. "These two belong to me now. If you can't control your own, I'm not going to do it for free."

Letta turned her back to Mother Joseph, revealing her face to Cello. He could now see that Sil and Sabina were here, too, hanging back in the shadows of the trees. "Just give me the boy, then. You can have Marcela."

"That's funny! Ain't that funny, Harlan?" Mother Joseph didn't even pretend to engage Harlan this time, only the sky. "Still sounds like you're asking me for a favor."

"What about Joanie?"

"What about her?"

"You don't have her?" Letta was incredulous.

"I haven't seen that trash in weeks. You know, when they accused me of theft!" Mother Joseph spared a contemptuous wave for Sil. "Maybe we ought to go back to how it was before you started your little garden."

"Now, Amberly, that was your idea," Letta said, her hands held in the air like she was pushing some invisible door open.

"And why not? It was a good idea." She turned her head and massive neck toward Marcela and Cello. "Do the right thing, I thought. Thought the children'd be better off away from the house for a time, let them grow up with some freedom, but seems I was wrong. Can you imagine how that makes me feel?" She turned fully this time to stare at where Marcela and Cello had crumpled over onto each other. "I wanted them to stay innocent while they could, but you couldn't manage that. You let the devil in, didn't you? With your lazy, narrow mind. Couldn't help yourself. You just don't have a pure heart. That's your problem." Mother Joseph stabbed a finger out at Letta. "Only a wicked heart could've raised a thief like that." Here she pointed directly at Cello. "And the child who killed my boy."

"I know you're upset, but try to get ahold of yourself and think clearly." Letta straightened and moved toward Mother Joseph. "My Joanie would never do something like that. She's a good girl." Letta pointed a glittering fingernail into the air, perilously close to Mother Joseph's bulging throat.

It was so odd, Cello thought, seeing them speak this way to each other, outside of the forced, prepared speeches they offered up while conducting business. He thought, in a strange, clear flash, that they were speaking like people who loved each other. It was coming out of them so obviously, Mother Joseph leaning out toward, practically into Letta, and Letta pulling her in. He shivered in his sweat-soaked clothes, and Marcela wedged her elbow into his side.

He looked down at her wrists, tied tight with twine. She was trying to pull off the restraints, but it wasn't working. Mother Joseph's angry words wound around all of them, like roads on a map. The Joseph cousins seemed to have shrunk to a harmless toy size. From where he sat, Cello felt in a concrete way that he was no longer in danger from them, despite the pain in his head, the blood on his face and his ruined elbow.

"How dare you, Letta? One of your children *killed my son.* I tried to be reasonable—maybe it was an accident, I told myself."

"Of course it was," Letta said.

"But now this?" Mother Joseph thrust her arm at Cello in a forceful punch at the air. "Disobedient behavior and theft, too?"

"That's right—theft." Harlan strode forward, shoving Cello over and banging into his bad arm. "Don't worry, Amberly. We'll straighten him out." *Straighten him out*, thought Cello. An echo from some other conversation, but who with? He couldn't remember.

"Shut your mouth, Harlan, and don't interrupt me. I'll let you at that boy soon enough," Mother Joseph snapped.

Letta looked undeterred, but softly said, "Nobody's perfect, Amberly." She reached out, trying to grip Mother Joseph's arm with her bony hand in—what Cello thought had to be—some familial embrace. As Cello squinted, trying to magnify their images, to interpret the bizarre display in the yard, something even stranger began.

Mother Joseph's face twisted, the pockets of fat under her eyes bulged out as though inflated by some mysterious minia-ture pump. Her mouth continued to move, but Cello couldn't identify any intelligible words from the sounds she emitted. He wondered if he was fainting again, if the distortion of sound was some other delayed symptom of the wound that throbbed so mercilessly near his left ear.

Cello saw them all—Sil and Letta and Sabina, and the Josephs, too—curling back from the mountainous woman, as though lava were spilling from her mouth, swiftly flowing down to scorch them. Her jaws were stretched wide, frozen in a giant yawn, and then she was falling. Nobody moved to help her, or to break the fall, so she kept falling and then roiled there in the grass at the foot of the porch steps.

It was Letta, and not Harlan, who finally approached Mother Joseph when she stopped moving altogether. She had settled in a painfully contorted position—her pelvis pressed to the earth but the rest of her twisted skyward. The faded yellow sweatshirt she'd been wearing had ridden up over her stomach, revealing a wave of white flesh, nearly the size of a full-term pregnancy. Letta's hand darted to Mother Joseph's throat, looking for a pulse, probably.

"Well, help me turn her, Lord!" Letta called to the cousins flanking Cello and Marcela on the ground. The men moved slowly. They flipped her fully on her back, but with reluctance, as though the unconscious woman would snap awake at any moment and gnash out at them in fury, appalled that they'd dared to touch her.

Mother Joseph's nephews and cousins drew back, and Letta leaned over, examining her for signs of life. It was shocking, Cello thought, the way Letta touched and prodded the other woman's body as though she'd done it before. The more Letta touched, though, the more she seemed to shrink back.

In the commotion, Cello and Marcela were released. Sil sliced apart the restraints around their wrists with the same knife he used to splice shoots and bulbs. Marcela and Cello followed Sil to the main house where Sabina blotted Cello's face with peroxide-soaked toilet paper, and Marcela washed her face and hands. Sil and Harlan stayed huddled together on the porch as it darkened into evening. The little kids, Cello noted, were probably waiting in the truck, hopefully asleep.

The mosquitoes were out and biting viciously. Cello wondered when they would leave, or if Sil and Letta would leave at all. He wondered if he'd be allowed to stay with them and continue to work on the farm. He worried about Joanie, and thought about the Stuckey's on Route 9. His face felt hot and swollen, and when he blinked, he noticed a lingering darkness over his right eye. The elbow still hurt, but the pain hadn't worsened. He stood up from his cross-legged position on the floor, in the same spot where Sabina had treated him, and went out to the truck to check on Miracle and Emil.

Nobody stopped him as he walked toward the vehicle. Cello noticed that Letta had moved closer to the porch, forming a rangy triad with Sil and Harlan. A familiar expression bled across her face, that ravening look that Letta got whenever she had a plan. Cello knew she wanted the house, that she wanted everything that had belonged to Mother Joseph. He knew, maybe even if the other Josephs didn't, that she would get it. Because the Joseph men were fools. Mother Joseph had done everything in her power to keep them foolish and easy to maneuver. Most of them could barely read.

Emil and Miracle were awake when Cello found them. They sat up on their knees, both of their faces side by side staring out the window into the dark. Cello snapped open the door, and in the weak light of the truck's interior bulb, he saw their little bodies slacken with relief and even some joy.

"Cello!" Emil said.

"Letta said we might not see you again," Miracle said. "Never."

"Yeah, well, Letta doesn't know everything." Cello pulled them into a halfway hug. "Hungry?" he asked.

"Yeah," Miracle answered, "but Letta said don't leave the truck no matter what."

"It's safe now," Cello said. "Let's get you something."

He guided them out of the truck and brought them around to the house. Marcela sat in a faded lawn chair, fiddling with a cigarette.

"Mar, you want to get them something to eat?" Cello asked.

Marcela looked up at him, her eyes still wide in shock. "Why don't we all go?" she asked, a panicked lilt running through her voice.

Marcela snatched away Emil's hand and led them up to the house. Most of the first-floor lights were burning, while a few of the Joseph cousins prowled in the yard.

Marcela pulled the screen door open, held it for them and let it slam behind her.

"Marcela, Jesus," whispered Sabina. Her feet shifted and creaked on the ancient, swollen planks of the entry hall.

"The children are hungry," Marcela said.

"They're having a meeting in there," Sabina hissed, waving her hand toward the front room.

"Cello, go feed the kids," Marcela said, shooing them all into the kitchen.

Cello fixed them peanut butter sandwiches while voices—mainly Letta's—echoed through the old, creaky house.

"Harlan," she said, "you can't control those boys, and I sure as hell know Frank can't." A long pause. "Even though Amberly and I didn't always get along, you know it's what she'd want."

So, just like that, Cello thought. Letta didn't care that Mother Joseph's body was still out in the yard, growing cold. She was ready to claim her authority.

"What about the baby?" At first Cello thought it was Sabina asking. When he left the kids on the kitchen floor and moved toward the front room, he saw it was Marcela. "Now you're in charge, Letta, you can make them tell us where he is."

"What baby?" Harlan's cragged face puckered.

"Joanie's baby," Marcela said sharply, edging closer to Harlan as she said it.

"They don't have him, honey," Sil said, his voice low. "I think we'd know by now if they took him."

"Joanie thought he was here," Cello interrupted. "Said she recognized Mother Joseph's handwriting on the note. Seems strange you didn't, Letta."

"Excuse me?" Letta turned all of the force of her newly amassed power on Cello. "I think I know my own cousin's hand, and I can tell you that wasn't it. You think Joanie knows more about Amberly than me? And speaking of Joanie, where is my daughter?" Cello shied away from this new, stronger Letta. He wasn't going to lie to her, because a lie about Joanie wouldn't help anyone. If Joanie wanted to be gone, she would be. Cello was shocked by how quickly the fear of that possibility receded, like touching a hot surface and not feeling the pain you imagined.

"She was at the motel on Route 9. By the freeway," Cello said.

"And how'd you pay for the motel on Route 9, pray tell?" Letta asked, squinting at Cello. "From biting the hand that feeds you? You don't know how lucky you got, son. You really don't."

Cello stayed quiet.

"Joanie have any money now?" Sil asked.

"I don't know."

"Really? Oh, we'll just all have to have a talk about this." Letta clapped her hands together. "Go on and get her, Harlan. You heard him—the place on Route 9," Letta said. "We're going to have a little family chat." She motioned for Sil to stand beside her.

"Now that it's just us, you need to tell me exactly what you and Joanie are up to."

"I can't," Cello said.

"What do you mean you can't?" Letta continued.

"I mean, I don't know." Cello shrugged, and winced as his likely broken elbow protested.

"Well, you're going to find out," Letta said, pinching the bridge of her nose.

A wave of refusal, of distaste, rose in the back of his throat. He was going to resist Letta's commands, and he was going to win. "No," he said quietly.

"Hey," Sil said, standing abruptly. "You better watch yourself."

"Maybe you're the one who should watch yourself," Cello said, suddenly overwhelmed by a desire to act, as he staggered toward Sil. Cello's head throbbed and his sight blurred and cleared in waves. Before Sil understood his intention, Cello lunged at the old man and knocked him to the floor. As he slapped and punched Sil into stillness, Cello was acutely aware of the force he used; not too hard, just enough to explain this new turn to Letta. He didn't know where his strength came from, only that he was grateful for it. Cello hit out at all of the lies he'd been told, striking down for that hard center of truth until he was drawn out of the strange collision of smells and bodies by a voice pealing out: "I did it! I did it, it was me! I did it!"

Sil was quiet beneath him, but his eyes were open. A thin stripe of blood trickled down from his nose. Cello felt the man's labored breaths pulling his ribs wide. The pain from his own injuries hurtled back into him with surprising force once the adrenaline of the fight had dissipated. He brought Sil to his chest and soothed him like he would Emil, patting his back right there on the floor.

"I did it—it was me!"

Sil and Cello watched as the voice elevated and persisted, coming from—of all places—Sabina.

Letta turned from Sabina, to the halted scuffle, then back to Sabina again. Marcela had already approached her sister and looped an arm around her shoulders.

"What did you do, honey?" Marcela asked her sister, so softly Cello wasn't sure if she'd said it, or if he imagined it. He smoothed Sil's shoulder, thin and withered under his faded work shirt.

"I took the baby," Sabina said, pressing her forehead into Marcela's chest. "I took him," she repeated, this time directly to Letta. "I'm so sorry. I shouldn't have." Sabina wasn't crying, but her body shook and twisted in the way of a sheet drying on a clothesline. Nobody moved, only Sabina, her body crumpling under the confession.

"What did you do with him, honey?" Marcela said, turning her sister so that they faced one another, blocking out the others, blocking out the room.

"I took him to the Baptist church on the other side of the creek and I left him there."

"Outside?" Marcela murmured, holding her sister close. "Did you leave him outside?"

"Inside. I broke the glass in the door. I figured someone would find him if I made the alarm go. A police car came, so I left."

Marcela rubbed circles into Sabina's back, and Cello noticed he was doing the same thing to Sil, transfixed by the sisters before them.

"Why'd you do it, Sabina?" Cello's voice sounded strange, distorted by the pain in his head.

"I wanted him to have a chance. To be regular, and have a real life." Sabina's voice was muffled by her sister's shoulder. "I didn't want him to be like us."

Cello felt Sil suck in his breath.

"I shouldn't have done it, Mar." Sabina shuddered against Marcela and repeatedly slammed her fist into the side of her leg.

"No, you should. You did the right thing, honey. No baby should be born like this. No baby should turn into us." Marcela hushed and soothed her.

"What about the notes?" Cello asked, suddenly furiously hot, pushing Sil's shuddering body away from his own. "Was it you leaving the notes?"

Sabina didn't speak, but Cello watched her nod against Marcela's shoulder. Cello heard Letta scramble toward the heap of Sil he'd left on the floor.

"Why would you do that? How could you make us all so scared? You're not like that, Sabina." Cello stood and moved toward the girls, feeling the violence swell up once again. Marcela, though, blocked him. She wouldn't let him near enough to hear what Sabina answered.

"What?" Cello hollered.

"I said, I did it for Mar. So we could save up. To get away like she wanted. I didn't want her to end up married off to some other Joseph, and never see her again." Sabina's speech was more weeping than talking, and Marcela shushed into her ear. "So, we could have a chance, too."

"Where is it? What'd you do with my money?" Cello was astonished by his anger, but he let it come.

"At home. In the kids' trailer under the stove. Cello, I—I'm so sorry," she stammered.

At that, he was out the door. Cello felt for the silver crunch of Sil's keys on top of the front left tire. He moved like a confident stranger, into the truck and behind the wheel. He peeled away from the Joseph place for the last time, and drove back to the garden. Cello's vision still hadn't settled. And the world through the windshield bulged and contracted with every blink. He drove slowly, but arrived at the garden in one piece.

It was quiet, vacant, unfamiliar without the noise and bustle from the other kids. He fiddled with the latch to the kids' trailer, finally shouldering it open the way Letta had done many times before. He tried not to look at their shabby things as he made his way to the stove, crouching low, feeling under the broken appliance where the linoleum was somehow both sticky and dusty. He saw one of Miracle's shoes and closed his eyes tightly, feeling only for the money.

He found it—a packet, paper wrapped around the money he'd earned with Ben and Marcela. Ben, Marcela, Joanie, Sabina, Miracle, Emil and the baby he'd wished belonged to him—they all hemmed in around Cello where he lay, sprawled on the floor, as though they were really there. He didn't understand what he was doing, coiling away from all of them, away from the garden, away from all of it. What would happen to the rest of his family if he went his own way and deserted them all? What would happen to the girls, and the little kids? What would happen to Joanie? Even though Mother Joseph's body was lying out in the grass of her front lawn, it didn't make the rest of them any safer. The Vine still demanded worship, demanded tending. The only truth Cello understood was that he didn't want to be like Letta or even Sil. He didn't want to continue with the Josephs' violent way of doing business, and he didn't want it to corrupt the people he loved.

Cello took the money and crammed it into his back pocket. And then, despite his reason, the voice that screamed at him to escape alone—the part that had fought Sil to the ground, the part that had discovered his love for Joanie wasn't what he thought it was—Cello began to pack.

He took the sheet off Emil's cot and spread it on the floor. He plucked up a few things for each kid, just small things, little, worthless treasures that they would miss: a gold headband, Miracle's blue tin box, a patterned crocheted blanket, a book and a silver whistle. Before he knotted the bundle closed, Cello moved to the empty space in the kitchen where the baby's crate had stayed. He picked up the pacifier on the counter. He hoped with all of the energy he had left that the baby was alright, that he was safe and warm in some new home, with some new family.

Just because he didn't want to leave it there, Cello pocketed the pacifier. He took the bundle out to the pickup, and rested his forehead against the center of the wheel. It was awful, this place of time where the change had to happen. He understood the next part would be difficult, but it would be for the best.

Cello drove to the last place he thought he'd ever think to visit for help. He drove to the neatest, strangest, most beautiful place he'd ever been.

27

Joanie kicked herself afloat in the running water. Even though she was moving forward, and there was no going back, she felt alone in her progress. Emptied. She had given so much—to the Vine and to Helen, both. She hadn't felt so alone and so lost since after her trial in Mother Joseph's front room, since Amberly Joseph made Joanie disappear.

Weeks, Joanie thought. At least ten days. Time spent alone, locked in the shed with Josiah's turtle. Mother Joseph had locked them away together, as though they were both to blame for Josiah's death. All through that time Josiah's decomposing body waited outside, rolled in a blue tarp awaiting burial, because Mother Joseph wasn't sure about what she wanted to do. When the wind turned, she could smell him.

As his father's body became less of a body, the baby's grew silently inside of her. Joanie shivered during the nights, and used a corner of the shed for emptying her bladder. No food, nothing from the Josephs, but her hand dipping into the rain barrel through a splintered opening in one of the slats—handful after handful of musty water, drinking down clots of drowned gnats. It was the only thing she could do to keep from dying. She handed little sluices of rainwater down into the turtle's tank. They were lucky that it rained most nights. Mother Joseph expected her to be dead, from the venom and neglect. Joanie whispered affectionately down to the dull, rough shell. Of course Mother Joseph had forgotten about the green plastic rain barrel. She'd forgotten how thin Joanie's arms had become. She'd forgotten that Frank had kicked into the shed a month ago, nicking an opening into the back wall. It was nothing for Joanie to poke and peel away at the small split in the wood, nothing for her to widen it just enough to reach through.

Drinking the rainwater and scraping Helen's pattern for worship onto the shed's dirt floor was all she could do. She knew better than to try to escape, weak as she was. Even then, through her dulled senses, Joanie knew something else was coming.

Joanie had removed the turtle from his stinking aquarium and set the creature on the floor, thinking maybe it wanted or needed to walk. But it only sat there, sealed inside the graying, cracked shell. Joanie understood that the turtle was going to die. She understood that she was going to die, too. She wondered, if the turtle died first, should she bury it? Would it be cruel, wrong even, to hack into the packed dirt foundation of the shed, and strand him there in the gloomy monument? If she died, she wondered what would happen to her body. Joanie knew Mother Joseph would leave her in the shed forever if she could.

At first, Joanie thought about anything but the Josephs, practically replaying her entire life up to the day before she wed Josiah. She decided she preferred to die before contemplating them. But inevitably, she fell back into thinking about the family, about the cellar. In all of her lonely sickness, she began to beg. Not out loud, but silently to Helen, over her attempts at scratching the worship patterns into the dirt from memory.

She prostrated herself on the ground, and begged and begged and begged.

It wasn't long before Helen answered her, and the shed began to bloom. Verdant sprays of ferns spurted from the slats, and the thick scent of roses settled over their bodies—over Joanie's and the turtle's. A montage of soft mosses grew, plush, out of the hard-packed ground, and soothed the soles of Joanie's chapped feet. Joanie held the turtle up to her chest, close, so the creature could feel the movement of her heart. They were in their graves, she thought, that was why it was suddenly so beautiful. They were lucky, allowed to luxuriate in the fragrant jewel-box of their joint tomb. It was like they were pharaohs, Joanie and Josiah's turtle, peeking their heads into the afterlife. Joanie held the turtle close, drawing patterns onto his shell to protect him, to protect them both.

It was almost a disappointment to be found. When Cello and Sil pulled her from the shed, their hands under her armpits, she felt a thud of annoyance. One of them, Sil probably, pulled the turtle from her hands and threw him away onto the ground like an old stone.

Breaking into the fresh air outside of the shed had been terrible, like a series of slaps. No one could possibly understand what Joanie had become inside of the shed. She was something outside of a person, and putting her back into the world was a terrible idea. It was a return that would break things, that would change things for the worse. Joanie had felt ruin run out of her fingertips, ruin that overwhelmed everything she came near.

Floating in the water she wondered if now, finally, she was fixed. If by her work to restore her son had she restored herself, and all of the things she had lost at the Josephs'? An echo of the Vine's earlier message flickered through the moving water that— by doing the worship and removing Mother Joseph's distorted influence from the earth—she'd done the right thing. Joanie swam and swam, buoyed by the Vine's voice.

28

Dr. Santo opened the door slowly, peeking around his two stacked hands through the gap in the door. "Yes, young man?" he said.

"Maybe you don't remember me, but I came to your house once before. With Ben." Cello passed a hand over his forehead. He winced at the pressure near his eye.

"I see you've run into some trouble since I last saw you." Dr. Santo nodded to the thick smear of blood and bruising on Cello's face. "Why don't you come in and I'll call Benjamin to join us."

"Yeah. Thanks," Cello said, following the man inside. Dr. Santo disappeared into the too-clean kitchen and Cello stood in the hall, wincing as a blast of air-conditioning kicked on.

Dr. Santo returned holding a towel filled with ice. "Why don't you have a seat," he said, gesturing to the tufted-back sofa in the adjoining living room. "I've left a message for our mutual friend. I'm sure he'll be along any minute."

Cello walked ahead of him and sat on the floor, careful to stay away from the spotless cream carpet. Dr. Santo put a hand over his heart. "No, no, young man," he said, stooping to guide Cello by the arm. "Please, sit here." He deposited Cello on the couch and handed him the ice. "I'm sure this will be more comfortable."

They were quiet, letting the air conditioner breathe around them. Dr. Santo stood by the window with his arms crossed, while Cello set the cool towel at his temple.

"If I needed help, where would I go?" Cello asked, the words coming out too quickly, colliding against one another and falling into the room.

Dr. Santo seemed startled. "For medical attention, do you mean?" He took a few steps toward Cello and then stopped, abruptly. "Are you feeling very unwell? Should I call an ambulance?"

"No, no, no, that's not what I mean." Cello shook his head so firmly he felt the blood moving from one ear to another. *Maybe I should just go*, he thought. The room didn't look right—Cello wasn't in the right place. He pressed a finger into the wound near his eye and made a hard sound in the back of his throat when the pain burst back at him.

"If I had a problem, and needed help, who could I ask? Ben said you knew someone who could, I don't know, smooth out a situation."

"I suppose that's true. I do have some, ah, contacts." Dr. Santo ducked down to inspect Cello's head wound more closely. "What situation are you looking to smooth?"

"How would I find these people?" Cello asked, his voice pitched higher than he intended.

"Well, they don't exactly have *business cards*, but if you're in trouble, they might be of some assistance. Let me just check my address book." Dr. Santo stood and rummaged on a bookshelf across the living room. "Just to warn you, these men aren't the most friendly, but I suppose it's part of the job." Cello watched Dr. Santo flip through a tiny leather-bound book. "Aha! Here we are, Harlan Joseph. Shall I write it down for you? The number?"

Cello slumped forward; the sudden rush of blood to his head cast another dark shadow over his vision. *Straightened out*—it was what Ben had said.

"Oh, no, young man, let me help you." Dr. Santo rushed over and propped him up. "What happened?"

"You've been working with Harlan Joseph?" Cello said, wiping a smear of blood from his eye with the cold, folded towel.

"Yes, he's the gentleman I've been collaborating with to sell our local ginseng in specialty Asian markets, where it's so highly coveted."

Cello leaned into the back of the sofa and pulled the towel from his forehead. It had turned mauve from his blood. "Oh, no," he said, holding the dish towel out to Dr. Santo. "I got blood on your words."

"What? Young man, I'm going to get an ambulance." Dr. Santo moved to stand, but Cello gripped his sleeve. "I really don't think you're well," Dr. Santo said. "I'm calling for help right away."

"No, please don't. No. I'm just real tired. I need to get some help for some people. Not from Harlan."

"You need to get help for some people, but not yourself?" Dr. Santo looked skeptically from Cello, to the window, then back to the kitchen where the phone was installed. "Wait a minute, are you also acquainted with Mr. Joseph?"

"I need to get some help for some kids." Cello abruptly closed his mouth. He forgot—he wasn't supposed to tell Dr. Santo anything, really. Just see if he could find Ben. Even Dr. Santo, in this supposedly safe, clean house, had contributed to the Josephs' work. He shook his head again, and pressed his feet into the floor, calculating his chances of standing up alone.

The doorbell rang, a sweet trill disrupting the tension between the man and the boy.

"Ah, that'll be Benjamin," Dr. Santo said, and went to let in Ben. His whole body loosened with relief.

"Oh, my God, Cello," Ben said, not stopping to wipe his feet on the mat. Cello noted that he hadn't thought to do that when he followed Dr. Santo inside, and guiltily looked down at his boots. "Are you alright?" He sat beside Cello on the sofa and rested the palm of his hand between Cello's shoulder blades. He turned toward Ben and gave him a small nod, despite the rising pain in his head.

"What happened?" Ben asked, moving the ice pack away from Cello's face and taking in the full scale of his injury. "Those guys—I should've helped you. I'm so sorry—I don't know why I ran." Ben shook his head. "Jesus, they did this to you?"

"It's not that bad," Cello said, avoiding most of what Ben had said.

"You need a doctor, Cello."

"That's just what I said," Dr. Santo said, nodding. "I mean, the boy knocked at my door, asking for help. I didn't know whether to call an ambulance or take him to the hospital myself…"

"That's okay, Ray," Ben said. "I'll drive him down there. Thanks for calling me."

"Of course. Be careful now," Dr. Santo said, walking them back to the door. "And stay safe yourself, Benjamin." Cello handed the cold, lumpy towel back to Dr. Santo. "No, no," he objected. "Do keep it. You'll have more need of it than I, I think."

At the hospital, Ben helped him. The light was bright and harsh, and had nothing of the gentle warmth of the hospitals Cello had seen on TV. Cello stared while Ben filled out the papers people kept handing them, and sat with him on a thin mattress behind a curtain. Cello felt the coolness at the crook of his arm where clear liquid channeled into his body from a bag through a length of tubing. He wondered whether it was like irrigating a field, or putting the right things back into the soil. For the first time, he wondered if it could be possible to take care of a body the way one could care for a field.

When the social worker came, she stood very close to the bed and put out her hand for both Ben and Cello to shake.

"Alright, gentlemen, I heard you needed some help in here," she began.

"There was a problem. My foster sister's baby," Cello murmured.

"Let's just slow down a minute. Your name please, son?" she asked.

"Cello."

"Yes, I see that here, but your last name?"

Cello shrugged.

"Alright." She made a note on her clipboard. "How about an address?"

"I stayed at a place about ten minutes west off Route 9. I never saw an address. No mail or anything, I don't think. My foster family stayed in trailers."

"I see," she said, scratching the bridge of her nose. "Give me a moment and I'll have this sorted out in no time." She held a clipboard at arm's length, and squinted at what was written there.

A doctor whisked back the curtain separating Cello's bed from the rest of the room, blazing with fluorescence.

"Oh, good," the doctor said. She was a tall, dark-skinned young woman, her hair braided and twisted back with a blue band. "Are you the guardian?"

"No, I'm Doreen, the social worker," she said. "I guess we haven't met yet. You're new?"

Both women stared, shifty-eyed, at one another. "Yes," the doctor said. "I'm Dr. Bartholemew." She made the next announcement to all three of them. "This patient needs a CAT scan. I suppose you can push that through. Since you're the social worker?" She directed this last sentence to Doreen.

"That's right," Doreen said.

"I should also add that this patient appears to have no vaccine history." The cleanliness of the doctor's speech lulled Cello into a different place. A different time, even. "I suspect there's been a brain bleed—not a significant one, but he will need to stay here in the hospital for treatment."

"Will he be okay?" Ben asked.

"He'll be fine. He's in the right place," the doctor said. She turned to Doreen. "The patient informed my colleague that these injuries were inflicted by a group of adults. We need to advise law enforcement to visit the address immediately."

"Of course, I see," Doreen said, scribbling on her clipboard. "I'm going to make a phone call, excuse me."

"What's going to happen to Cello?" Ben asked the doctor.

"He'll go in for some tests, and we'll treat him. He'll stay here until he's well enough to go home. At that point I'm sure this will all be worked out." Dr. Bartholomew plucked Cello's chart from the foot of his bed and attached a few sheets of paper from the sheaf she carried to it.

"Can I stay with him?" Ben asked.

The doctor appraised Ben's appearance in an efficient sweep. "When we move him up to the pediatric floor, see the receptionist for a visitor pass."

Cello drifted through the scan only half-awake. He never truly slept, thanks to all of the machines that beeped in the hallways and over his body.

After the scan, a blonde woman with an unearthly high ponytail efficiently stitched the wound on his face closed, and then he was sent up to a two-bed room where Ben had waited for him.

The room was dark. A thick stand of pines shaded the one window, and the sun was on the wrong side of the building. Cello's roommate was asleep. It was a little girl, no older than Miracle. Her parents sat by the bed and kept their hands on the blanket. Ben pulled the curtain across, obscuring them from view. Cello kept touching the large square of cotton that had been taped down over his wound. He wanted to say something to Ben, to tell him the truth about "the guys" he and Dr. Santo had been working with. The deviants they'd been working with.

A soft knock heralded Doreen's entrance into the room. "I guess we have a couple things to discuss, now that I have a better handle on your situation. Cello, would you like me to ask your friend to leave? I know this is, well, it's sensitive information," she said.

"No, that's okay," said Cello.

"Well, if you're sure." Doreen pulled a pair of reading glasses from a lanyard around her neck and held them to her face as she read from the folder in her hands. "Seems you were placed with the Joseph family sixteen years ago. Is that Miller's Road address correct? It states here that you have five other foster siblings?"

"That sounds right, but that's not who I stayed with," Cello said.

"Alright, then who was it you stayed with? It wasn't the Josephs?" Doreen's brow remained creased as she spoke.

"I don't know their last name. The thing is," Cello said, "Mother Joseph recently passed."

"Oh!" Doreen said, the glasses slipping from her fingers. "Well, my records here didn't show that. I'm so sorry—my deepest, deepest sympathies."

"It only just happened." Cello cast his gaze down, hesitant to look at Doreen or at Ben. He did love Sil and Letta in a way, like you could grow fond of a place. He hated to betray them so thoroughly, but he loved Sabina, Marcela, Miracle and Emil more. Maybe he'd lost too much blood to make sense of it. "I think the kids there aren't safe," Cello said, looking at his hands on the faded, striped blanket.

"I see," Doreen said. "We do have law enforcement scheduled to check in, but I'll call over and see that they hurry on up. I'll call my office, too. All of those children will have to be placed elsewhere immediately. It's going to be a late night. Guess I'll be ordering a pizza," she said with a cheerful wink. Doreen opened the door to leave. "I'll be back as soon as I have any news for you."

Cello looked up as Ben stood from the chair. "Move over a little," Ben said, climbing up next to Cello. He turned on his side and put a hand over Cello's wrist. Part of Cello was pleased, to be so close to Ben, but mostly he felt stiff and weary.

"Why didn't you tell her about the baby?" Ben asked.

"I nearly did. A couple times." Cello forced himself to speak up, loud enough for Ben to hear. "But Sabina said she left him at a church. If he got found, he got a new family. I don't want something bad to happen to Sabina. She doesn't deserve that."

"What about you?" Ben asked.

"What'd you mean?" Cello stared up at him, puzzled.

"I mean, what do you want to happen? To you, after all of this gets worked out."

"I don't know. Maybe I can come live with you?" Cello looked at the other boy's half-turned face.

"I wish you could, man," Ben said with a reassuring squeeze of his hand. "I don't want you to think I don't care about you, or the rest of your family. It's not that at all."

Cello looked at the sheet where their hands lay touching.

"But I'm at school. I'm living in a dorm. People aren't supposed stay with me."

"No, but I could. I don't take up space, and I'm quiet." Cello felt, as he tried to convince Ben, like a man marching up a steep hill. "And it's not like I'd stay with you forever or anything. I can figure out my own way." A spate of coughing from the roommate's side interrupted Cello's speech. "We could be friends. Roommates."

"I already have a roommate, Cello." Ben didn't move from the spot on the bed beside him, but he already seemed very far away.

"What about Dr. Santo?" Cello begged.

"Ray?" Ben gave him a crooked smile. "Look, I know things might be kind of crazy for you while this all gets fixed, and I'll keep checking on you."

"What about the senging? Won't you need help?" Cello said, ashamed of how desperate he sounded.

"I think you're going to have a lot more to deal with than senging." Ben's voice was low, and he settled an arm around Cello's shoulders. "And I'm sorry about that."

"Are you?" Cello asked, stunned by his own bitterness. "What's going to happen to the rest of the kids? Should I not have told her?"

"No, you had to tell her. You absolutely had to. I don't know how this works, but I'll wait with you until we do know. Okay?"

Cello nodded and slumped forward. "You think I could find a job someplace?" Cello asked. "Get myself settled?"

"I know you could. That I can help you with. You did the right thing, Cello," Ben said, his voice lost in the series of beeps and alarms that signaled Cello's next dose of medication.

29

Joanie let the river hold her. She imagined the current twisting into an illustration of a beautiful water creature, with seaweed-green hair. Joanie could feel the sea-woman's arms around her, nestling her close—a sodden cheek resting against the woman's warm breast.

She didn't mind the water carrying her. Joanie knew it was bringing her to her son. Even when she collided with the rocks and was caught upon the riverbank, she felt a measure of correctness in it. The worship demanded balance; she couldn't get something for nothing. One had to be worn down, broken up into small pieces. There would still be someplace for her. She felt a blink, that same bright cry from her infant calling her forward—warm and constant as a heartbeat.

She was outraged when the dulled sensation of the river's waves receded and real pain announced itself. The sea-woman was no sea-woman at all, but a human, middle-aged hiker wearing a soft fleece jacket. Joanie tried to resist the woman's attempts to revive her. She closed her eyes against the woman's attention, trying to sink back into that earlier murkiness. She wanted to plummet back into the worship, and permit it to drag her to its conclusion. Joanie tried, but couldn't resist the shock and lights of the ambulance the hiker had called. The voices washed over her, too loud, jolting her back into her body.

"Temperature's low," one of the voices—a man—said.

"Glucose depleted, hook her up," a woman said. Joanie felt them stabbing and pulling at her.

"Support the airway, Terrance, come on," the woman barked. "I don't see any ID on her. Ma'am, you coming with us?" The woman EMT held the door wide for the hiker. "Hold on, I think we've got consciousness. Can you hear me, sweetheart?" the woman called, too close, practically in her ear. Joanie winced away.

"Ma'am, looks like you saved a life today," Terrance called to the hiker.

Joanie heard as the woman climbed into the vehicle, unable to resist doing more good. Joanie hurt all over. She rolled her throbbing eyes in her throbbing head. In the back of the ambulance more people, just horrible, regular people—not the angels or demons she'd imagined would communicate with her in the early morning of this particular day—spoke to her.

"How'd you come to be in the river?"

"I'm not sure."

"How old are you? What's your name?"

"I don't know."

"Can you tell me what day it is?"

"No."

"What year?"

"No," Joanie said, a mutant sound in her throat—half sob, half laugh. "Where's my baby? Where are you taking me? I won't go without him."

"We'll get you the help you need, sweetheart, and then you'll go home. Don't worry—we found you just in time. Everything's going to be fine."

"Right," Joanie said. She fell away from them all, dreaming of the flowering shed, and the cold turtle clutched in her hands, of her son asleep beside her.

Joanie opened her eyes to a swath of pastel-printed curtains. Her body was bound and bandaged all over, but her mind was clear. The hiker who pulled her from the river sat by the bed. Her hair was dry, and she wore a neat yellow blouse, but Joanie was certain it was the same woman. She held a stack of folders in her lap, and a pair of reading glasses she wasn't using hung on a lanyard around her neck.

"What happened?" Joanie asked. "Do you have my baby? Where am I?" Her voice felt smoother, different.

The woman startled, looking up from the sheaf of papers in her hands. She smiled, pressing her lips together and widening her eyes like an excited child. "Hi there, Joanie. My name's Doreen. I'm the social worker here. Can we talk a second? I think we already found who you're looking for."

WEST VIRGINIA, 1999

Cello spotted the little wooden house in the clearing easily. The flat roof was glazed in a bronze layer of autumn leaves, and every tidy corner glinted in the sunset's filtered blaze. He couldn't help but admire his own work—well, Sil's, and Ben's, and Marcela's, too. They had built such a perfect, habitable secret. Eyes that didn't dwell there, or hadn't contributed to its construction, would skip right over it.

The little house exhaled warmth, like a campfire, drawing him involuntarily nearer, almost like it knew he was supposed to be there.

"Cello!" a voice called from the half-open window. Emil ran out, disrupting the stillness of the forest, and leaped at his foster brother. Out at Joanie's place, Emil had grown sturdy and joyful; he wasn't that scrap of a kid he'd been in their last summer at the garden. Cello suppressed a little swirl of regret over leaving them all and missing out on the ways Joanie, Emil, Miracle and Sabina were connecting as a new family without him.

At first, Cello was worried that the state granted custody of all of the kids to Letta and Sil. He was afraid that they would just go back to the way things had always been. But Joanie said they'd leave them alone, and she had been right. Letta needed Joanie to be happy in order to keep up her side of the bargain with the Vine. Something had changed after Mother Joseph's death; the Vine was no longer satisfied with the planting rituals done by just anyone. All of the Work had to be Joanie's. In return for her cooperation, Sil and Letta let Joanie and Sabina keep the little kids, along with a monthly payment that Joanie and Sabina alone decided how to spend.

"Joanie said you might not come," Emil said, reproachful.

"I had to study for a big test I got coming up. But I still need to eat!" On Ben's suggestion, Cello was studying to take the GRE, but he still wasn't ready. He didn't know if he would ever be. He wiped a smudge of grease from Emil's forehead. "What've you been working on?"

"I'm building a radio." Emil held his hand and led him up toward the house. "With Sabina."

"Wow," Cello said, whistling. He grasped his brother's palm a little more tightly, struck with an unexpected bolt of happiness to know that Emil was not too old to take his hand, to be excited to see him. "How's school?"

Emil looked over with a theatrical grimace. "What do you think?"

"Okay, that's fair," Cello said with a smile. "It's a lot to get used to."

"Miracle loves it, though." Emil shrugged.

"And you've got to keep her company," Cello said.

"I guess. Come on, Marcela brought doughnuts."

"Doughnuts? Aren't we eating dinner?" Emil dragged him up the little rocky slope and shoved the front door, opening into a compact kitchen where Joanie stood chopping basil.

"Oh, hey," she said, turning toward them. "Emil, go set the table in the back. We're going to eat outside—that alright with you?" she asked Cello, leaning over and pulling him toward her with a free arm.

"Sure," he said, hugging her back. "Can I help?"

"Nah, we're almost done. Where's Ben?"

"Working." Cello gave her an apologetic smile.

"Everything okay with you all?" she said, watching him closely even as she chopped.

"Completely fine."

"Maybe it's actually better that he couldn't come—better that it's just the family, I mean."

Cello made a sound in the back of his throat. "Marcela already here?" He pulled off his gloves and stuffed them into his jacket pocket.

"Yeah, she's out back with the girls. She's doing so good," Joanie said with a wide-open smile. Marcela had moved in with some friends of Ben's from Grove, and was already halfway through beauty school.

"I knew she'd be fine there. Where's the little dude?"

"Asleep. He's teething—those molars are coming in," Joanie said, wincing. "So I'm not going to bother him. Can you bring out plates and remind Emil he's supposed to be helping?"

Marcela and Sabina sat at the picnic table outside, their heads pitched toward one another. Miracle sat on the far end of the table, a comic book splayed open beneath her hands. "Cello!" Sabina said, springing up to hug him. "I didn't think you were coming."

"Of course I came," he said, a little too brightly. "I wanted to hear all about Mar's new job." He set the plates down and motioned Emil over to take them. "Hello to you, too," he said pointedly to Marcela and Miracle. "Don't y'all get up at the same time."

"I won't," Marcela said, midyawn. "I'm exhausted. I had to work an extra shift for Carol since one of the girls called in sick."

"Hey, Cello," Miracle said without lifting her eyes from her book.

"Don't take it personally," Sabina said with an eye roll toward Miracle. "She's growing up."

"She's moody, you mean," Marcela corrected, leaning over to pluck the book away.

"Stop it!" Miracle stood and grabbed it back. "I'm going to my room," she said, adjusting her new glasses where they slipped down her nose.

"Nope, you're not—we're eating now." Joanie pushed the screen door open and held a pan of lasagna with a mismatched pair of oven mitts. "Emil," she called, frowning over the table. "What did I say?"

"Sorry, sorry." Emil rushed around her, sloppily throwing down plates and forks.

"Miracle, go get the salad from the kitchen, will you?" Joanie set the pan down and waved away a curious bee. "I'm telling you, they got so spoiled so quick."

"No way." Cello sat down at the picnic table, straightening his place setting, and the others around his. "You and Sabina are doing a great job with them."

"We'll see," Sabina said with an indulgent smile.

"Sit down, everybody," Joanie said, taking the salad from a reemerged Miracle. "Who wants what?"

As Cello watched his family eat together, a feeling of loss bubbled up in his chest. He was missing so much of it. But, he reminded himself, it was by his own choice and his alone. Sabina and Joanie would have been happy to have him back at the garden, but he couldn't deny that it didn't feel quite right. Not just because he had his own place, and a steady job with a land-scaping company. The bargain Joanie made—with Letta and Sil, but mainly the bargain she'd made with the Vine—that compromise would never feel seemly to Cello. The Vine took too much, and what it gave in return was not always a gift.

"Mama? Cela!" Joanie's son toddled out from his little bed in Joanie's room and swayed, still groggy, at the back door.

"Good morning, little dude," Marcela said, suddenly standing and beamy. "Wow, Riv, you got so big! I can't believe how fast he's growing," she said, shaking her head at Joanie.

"It's because he eats so much," Joanie said. "Don't you?" She gathered her son up in her arms and kissed him under his chin until he laughed.

"We should probably get started," Sabina said, apologetic. "Shouldn't we, sugarplum?" She blew a raspberry on River's chubby little leg.

Cello didn't like the way they were all maneuvering around what had to come next.

"Alright, let's go," Cello said, clapping his palms together. "You need me to do anything special?"

"No." Joanie's voice was tight, as it always was when Cello mentioned the worship.

"We just need you to be there," Sabina said, overly cheerful.

"The Vine needs you to be there," Joanie corrected.

"Seems strange the Vine doesn't need Sil and Letta, too. They were part of this garden for a long time. How are they out there at Mother Joseph's?" Cello couldn't resist asking. He cared about them the way you cared about a place you couldn't visit again but that you'd always remember. He'd also meant it to be the smallest dig at Joanie and Sabina, at the way they still took money from Sil and Letta, how they still profited from the commerce both Cello and Marcela had rejected.

Joanie's fingers dug into her skin where she held her crossed arms in place. He could see her struggle to remain neutral, and not to snap back at him. She looked down at her son, who scooped Cheerios from a plastic cup. "They seem old," she said. "Especially Letta. She looks tired."

"I'm not surprised," Marcela cut in. "She took over Mother Joseph's whole operation—what did she expect?"

"She's getting what she wanted, I guess." Joanie lifted the toddler into her lap, and he half leaned into and half squirmed away from her. "At least they're keeping their promise."

"And you're keeping yours," Cello said.

"Yes," Joanie said, curt.

"Actually, that's a good question," Marcela said. "How come Sil and Letta don't need to be here, too? Cello's right—they lived at the garden a long time. A lot longer than us."

"It's not about who was at the garden or when. It's about our family. It's special. The Vine needs our family to be here," Joanie replied, her voice firm. "And this worship is important because we're clearing the last of Mother Joseph's energy out of here and replacing it with all of ours. Let's go and get this done so we don't need to hold up anybody any longer than we need to." She shot a pointed look at Cello.

After dinner they walked down to the garden. The tiny chapel Joanie and Sabina had built had expanded to the size of the old kids' trailer. They added to it week by week, until Joanie said that the Vine was satisfied. All the trailers at the garden had been removed from the property by the state. The garden was only a garden now, and all of the Vine and any of the other plants that grew there belonged to Joanie.

Cello had resisted visiting Joanie's chapel all through the time he and Ben were getting settled into their new life. When Joanie finally convinced him to take a look, he itched to leave, feeling so unsettled inside of that jade green music box of a place. He still didn't fully believe, not like Joanie and Sabina, but he couldn't deny that the Vine held mysteries he would never understand. Why it required his presence for this kind of ritual, he would never know. And whatever way he felt about the worship or the Vine, he couldn't deny that it had transformed Joanie. She was different, patient, *more* somehow. When she led them in worship she seemed larger than a person—he knew it didn't make sense, but it was like she contained more than one type of body, a new energy surrounding her.

Cello stood at the very back of the chapel and gripped Emil's hand while Sabina and Joanie drew swirling, glittery shapes in crystals of salt strewn across the ground. They worked slowly, their attention keen as a blade. Cello didn't know how long they lingered there, but he was sure that the light had changed from late afternoon to evening. No one complained, or grew tired or bored. Even little River stood with them and watched, nearly hypnotized by his mother's movements. Every time Sabina and Joanie neared the end of a pattern, Cello felt the same thrill of fear—like the earth would pull them all apart in some strange, powerful tide. Joanie called the girls forward, and they linked hands, circling the shimmering shapes on the floor. When all of their hands were connected, the salt gleamed. Only when the last pattern was complete, did Cello let go of Emil's hand so they could all go back out into the fresh night air.

"Well?" Marcela asked, the very first stars shining over them. "That's it?"

"That's it," Joanie said, flushed and happy.

"Did it work?" Cello asked.

"I think so," Joanie said. "But I guess we'll see."

★ ★ ★ ★ ★

ACKNOWLEDGMENTS

It is no exaggeration to say that I've been moved to tears on multiple occasions over the course of this book's journey. So many lovely people have been endlessly generous with their kindness and support, and I can't even believe my luck in knowing them.

First—and perpetually—thank you to my patient, smart, and thoughtful agent, Kate Johnson. Thanks to Rach Crawford, world's best maternity cover, and everyone at MacKenzie Wolf for their sustained support over the years. My thanks to Dillon Asher, too, and his exciting future visions for *Daughters of the Wild*.

Thank you to my brilliant editor, Laura Brown, who pushed me to make this book the best it could be. It was an honor to work with someone who cares so deeply. I am immensely grateful to the entire gifted team at Park Row, especially Erika Imranyi, Heather Connor, Randy Chan, Rachel Haller, and Punam Patel. Thank you to super publicist Justine Sha for so much dedication and optimism, and to Gigi Lau for the stunning cover. Without this excellent group of people, this book wouldn't have made it into your hands.

Daughters of the Wild would absolutely have stayed inside my head without the encouragement and guidance of early readers like Tracie Martin, Janet Walden West, Susan Bickford, Kelly Cabrese, Erin Foster Hartley, Ted Thompson, Sofia Groopman, and Emily Clark.

I have been so moved by the generosity of other writers throughout this process, and want to thank anyone and everyone who boosted this book along the way. Thank you to Jessica Valenti, Adam Wilson, Jessie Chaffee, Danielle Lazarin, Julie Buntin, Robin Wasserman, Erin Khar, and Iris Cohen for all of their kind support.

I also want to say thank you to my talented Elsa, Ramona, and Freya Project colleagues; each of them makes my day jobs a source of real joy—Zeb Millett, Keegan Grandbois, Jeremy Wilson, Margaret Fitzjarold, Eleanore Pienta, Marcos Toledo, Kate Ladenheim, Paige Jacobus, Libby Flores, and Nonie Brzyski, you are all treasures.

And of course, maximum thanks to my beautiful and hilarious extended family. I am so blessed to have in-law siblings like Scott Schneider, Lis Schneider, and Eva Hogan, who are the very best. Thank you, too, to Arnie and Nancy Schneider for all of the childcare and kindness over the years. I wouldn't be who or where I am without my own intrepid and loving mother, Irka Zazulak, and my sister, Milya. I drew so much for this book from my isolated childhood summers, and my brother, Olesh Burian, shared these strange, magical, and often unsettling experiences with me.

Anyone familiar with West Virginia geography will know I took some liberties with distance in this book. I hope it doesn't pose any insurmountable distractions while reading. I have so much appreciation for the Antietam Visitor center, where I passed many hours over the course of one muggy summer. Thank you, too, to Tracy Wilson and Holly Frey, the podcast hosts of Stuff You Missed in History Class. Their Voynich Manuscript episode was the seed for the Vine of Heaven and this entire book.

Finally, every last one of my thanks to my husband, Jay Schneider, who I love so much that it's borderline gross. All of my gratitude goes to whatever forces of the universe let me parent my two wacky and wonderful daughters, Viola and Leonora—without them, nothing would be the same.